THE CROWN THAT LOST ITS HEAD

The Agency of the Ancient Lost & Found 2

JANE THORNLEY

PROLOGUE

A *révalo Castle, Spain*
12:45 a.m., July 24, 1568

IT WAS AN UNHOLY NIGHT WHEN THE MAN IN THE BLACK VELVET CLOAK, accompanied by a pair of soldiers and two priests, approached the tower. Despite the warm evening, a gusty wind blew across the plains, forcing the men to duck their heads as they approached the fortress walls.

The gatekeeper recognized the man in black at once and bid the group to enter without a word. This was not the first visit the king's secretary had paid to their special prisoner but he prayed it would be the last. Still, the presence of the two priests puzzled him. Surely it was still too soon to administer the last rites?

The five men trod the torchlit halls without speaking, focused on the task ahead. One priest held a velvet pillow upon which rested a priceless object covered in a silken cloth while the other gripped a Bible as if the holy book was all that kept him on this side of the earth. Meanwhile, the soldiers kept their eyes fixed straight ahead, their faces expressionless as they left the corridor and trudged up the stone stairs to the very topmost floor of the tower. Only one prisoner was held here.

The guard, dozing on his stool by the door, awoke with a start and leaped to his feet. Seeing the king's secretary, he bowed deeply. "My lord, our prisoner d-does not rest this n-night," he stuttered. "He flings himself against the window attempting to take flight and still refuses to eat or drink." Straightening, he shot a nervous glance at the priests and bowed again.

"Have you administered the draught as I have bid?" the man inquired.

"Yes, my lord, though the prisoner drank but a small amount before throwing the goblet at the wall. He will not drink more. Says that he has been abandoned and desires only to die."

At that moment, a wail escaped the room, such a heart-wrenching reverberation of voice on stone that it was as if some poor creature had been dragged to hell while clinging by his nails to the walls. The sound echoed for a second longer before petering to a pitiful whimper.

The king's secretary closed his eyes briefly. When he opened them again, his handsome face was pained. "In the king's name, I demand that you pay no heed to any sound that issues from this room this night. Should you disobey my orders and an alarm be called, you will pay with your life."

"Yes, my lord, of course, my lord. I hear nothing, nothing. The prisoner, he screams and cries most every hour. We hear nothing, nothing."

"Pass the keys and go," the man commanded.

The guard, daring not to raise his gaze another time, took the ring from his belt and made to insert the iron key but one of the soldiers intercepted —a cue for him to make his escape while he still could. The iron bar clanged overhead as he bolted down the steps.

At last the wooden door flew open and the king's secretary stepped into the room accompanied by the priests. He was accosted by a sight pitiful enough to give him pause even for one unused to pity. The well-appointed room, fitting for the status of its charge, lay in shambles. The red brocade bed curtains hung in shreds, the furniture tumbled over, food smeared on the floor. The crucifix that had been bolted to the wall now lay upside down on the floor, and the air reeked with excrement. The secretary forced himself not to visibly recoil. "Your Highness?"

The heap of torn clothes in the middle of the soiled floor twitched and lifted its ravaged head. "Why has he forsaken me?" he whispered.

The secretary fell to one knee. "You are not forsaken, my prince, but soon will be honored in the manner to which you were born. Your veins flow with royal blood and it is time to meet your destiny. Your Highness, your coronation day has arrived."

"My coronation?" The man stirred, for he was a man, after all, though one deformed by nature and left broken by those who knew not how to give him love.

"Your Highness." The secretary rose, bowed again, and smiled. "We have brought your crown." He flicked his fingers and the two priests stepped forward, one unfurling a silk ermine-lined cloak, the other revealing a jeweled crown glimmering in the torchlight as it rested on the velvet pillow.

The man stumbled to his feet. "Mine?"

"Yours," the secretary said with a nod.

"Fine as my father's, yes?"

"More so—more beautiful, more sacred," the secretary assured him.

"Sacred?"

"Sacred, yes. We shall crown you, my prince, and you will become Holy Roman Emperor of all that lies above and all that lies beyond—king of the realms. Your power will extend far beyond your father's as you will be rendered immortal and rule forever more."

"Immortal?" the broken man asked. "But I have wished...only to die. My father has...forsaken me," and he began to cry.

One priest draped the ermine robe over the man's shaking shoulders and stepped quickly away while the other held the crown aloft and began chanting in Latin. The king's secretary retrieved an upended chair and set it in the center of the room. "Sit, my prince. You will live anew and we shall worship you forever more."

"The day has come?" the man asked, gazing at the man with his one good eye, the other now so infected it looked like a bloodied egg.

"It has," the king's secretary stated. "And I have brought you wine to celebrate and to help us anoint you in this holy moment. Drink, Your Highness." He passed the broken man a goblet into which he had poured a liquid from a silver vial. "Drink deeply this night so you will live again."

"Live again?" The man tried to smile as he took the goblet with his filthy hand and began to drink, the red liquid dribbling down his beard and onto the ermine robe.

3

The priest holding the crown stepped before him and bowed. "Your Highness. I crown you King of the Holy Forever."

"Yes, yes, I will be king...king," the broken man said, rocking back and forth as the crown was placed on his deformed head. "King...king...king!"

The men watched in silence until the crowned man began to still, the priests crossing themselves and praying while the draught took hold. Moments later, the broken man's eyes glazed over and his ruined head fell back against the chair. A priest rushed to brace him before he toppled, one hand keeping the crown in place. "Call the soldiers, my lord. It is time," he whispered.

The king's secretary snapped his fingers and the soldiers entered, both holding mallets and fists full of bolts.

"What we do tonight, we do in Your name," one priest whispered, averting his gaze as a soldier took the first blow.

I

One evening early in September, I reluctantly agreed to take my first social foray outside my flat for a private function at the British Museum. The idea was to present my electronic business card for the Agency of the Ancient Lost and Found while pumping up the volume on my previous exploits like some TV host pushing season two—from six feet away.

In case I lost my gumption, I brought along my extroverted friend and colleague Penelope Williams, aka Peaches, for moral support. Peaches didn't do introversion. She just got on with things.

A small cluster of guests and dignitaries had been brought in after hours to commemorate the repatriation of a beautifully preserved Roman slipper that our agency had located many months before. Since the slipper still bore its decorative leather tooling and was perhaps one of the earliest examples of fine Italian shoe design found in Britain, it had attracted lots of interest. I half expected Ferragamo to drop by, as if "dropping by" actually happened anymore.

The museum gave the slipper prominence in Room 49: Roman Britain, where we now stood properly distanced in a semicircle around Dr. Wong. The director of Roman Antiquities was speaking on how the importance of the find helped to understand life in Roman-occupied Britain. The topic would normally interest me but I was edgy and fearing contagion everywhere.

"Is that Sir Rupe I see standing on the other side?" Peaches leaned down to whisper, looking magnificent in a tailored rust Italian pantsuit with a matching patterned face covering. Somehow she even made virus avoidance look fashionable. My mask, on the other hand, was of the surgical variety and probably looked more like a diaper. It was testament to my state of mind that I didn't yet care about the optics.

I couldn't see over the glass display case but Peaches, being taller than most humans, commanded the view. "Probably. He'd finagle a way into an event like this," I said.

"He looks thinner," she whispered.

"Thinner, as in sick?" I asked, stifling my concern. I might be annoyed with him but I'd always cared about the guy.

"Maybe, but I presume he used lockdown to recover."

I nodded. He'd been under a doctor's care for pneumonia the last I'd heard but admittedly we were out of touch. "Is he alone?"

"Evan's not with him, if that's what you're asking."

That's exactly what I was asking. I hadn't seen either Sir Rupert or his supposed right-hand man since our last mission, which was followed by the global quarantine. Actually, I almost relished the distance since I had put my heart into self-isolation. I needed time to adjust to the new reality there, too. "Look, as soon as Dr. Wong stops talking, I'm bolting. I'll leave you to do the promotion, if you don't mind. I still don't feel up to socializing."

"You've got to meet with him sometime, Phoebe. May as well get it over with."

Dr. Collins, the stunningly photogenic professor of British History at Oxford, shot us a visual *hush* from her position across from me. A reporter stood equally spaced on her other side recording on his phone, while six feet to my left a masked Interpol agent was looking pleased with himself. I nodded at the man, who I'd worked with before. Interpol hadn't had much of a role to play in this particular acquisition but somehow managed to take most of the credit. I didn't care about that, either.

At last, a chorus of polite clapping erupted in which I quickly joined while saying to Peaches, "Sorry to leave you holding the virtual cards but

I'm out of here. You stay and do the well-spaced networking thing, if you want. I'll see you back at the fort."

I successfully worked my way through the gathering without breaching the spacing protocols while easing my way toward the gallery door, thinking only of a speedy escape. I'd miscalculated: this was a museum of treasures. There were guards and rules, most taken seriously.

"Sorry, madam," said the uniformed masked man blocking the gallery door. "We ask that all guests remain in the designated area until such time as the event is over and we can escort you to the main entrance—for security reasons, you understand."

"Of course. You can never be too careful." Trapped, then. I smiled as graciously as I could before remembering that I wore a mask. So how was I to communicate acquiescence now? I turned on my heels and walked straight into Rupert.

"Really, Phoebe, you did not think you could avoid me forever, did you?" he asked, lifting his paisley silk mask.

I stepped back. "Rupert. What a surprise. Put your mask back on right now. You of all people need to protect your health."

"I'm very well now, thank you. Actually, I was diagnosed with the dreaded pestilence almost six weeks ago but am recovering, albeit slowly, thank you. I consider myself among the lucky and, furthermore, feel quite secure in present company knowing that you have not left your facility for months."

"I hadn't heard. I'm so sorry."

"Never mind. Let us not dwell. This blasted virus has devoured enough of our energy. My point is that we can now share a bubble together with impunity." Definitely thinner but no less dapper in his Savile Row suit in a fashionably late-summer linen-and-silk weave the color of burnt sugar, he stepped toward me as I took another step back.

"You knew I'd be here, as I did you," he continued. "Indeed, I expressly inquired whether the Agency of the Ancient Lost and Found had received an invitation, seeing as you are responsible for this particular find. Isn't it time that you emerged from the shadows? The Covid restrictions have loosened, which is our signal to rejoin the world, I say. May we speak in private?"

I looked around. "We *are* speaking in private, Rupert. No one is paying us the least bit of attention." In fact, they were still circling Dr. Wong to admire the new acquisition.

He took my arm, leading me back into the gallery toward a far wall where a golden ceremonial helmet held center court in halogen-lit splendor.

"Whatever happened to social distancing?" I muttered.

"Phoebe, this cannot continue. We are colleagues now—not under usual circumstances, I realize, but colleagues nevertheless. Everything I hid from you in the past was absolutely necessary."

"Of course." I moved back until I again stood six feet away. "I understand completely. I can't deny how endlessly useful I've been to all concerned, thief and Interpol alike." The fact that I had been leading my possibly deceased thieving ex-boyfriend to various priceless artifacts for years was beside the point. My only saving grace there was that I had finally nailed the bastard.

"Phoebe, my friendship toward you has never been feigned—well, maybe in the beginning but not afterward. You do understand that, don't you?"

I was staring over his shoulder, straight into the glass case where the glided helmet gleamed coldly in the light. "Of course."

"I have tried to express myself in my letters and emails but I fear my attempts have been clumsy at best," he continued.

I sighed. "Rupert, please just get to the point." He was never known for brevity.

"Very well. Let us forge a new beginning. I have a case for us to crack."

New beginnings were fraught with possible failure, in my view. I found it easier to hide out on the tail end of a minor triumph. "Fine. Of course, we will proceed as colleagues, just not right away. Give it a few more months, maybe until the vaccine has been vetted." I turned, hoping to make another bolt for the exit. "How do I get out of here?"

Rupert snapped his fingers and a guard came dashing over. "Tell Dr. Wong that I must escort our esteemed guest from the gallery immediately as she feels unwell."

"Yes, sir, right away."

Taking my arm again, Rupert steered me into one of the adjoining galleries.

"What, you can just command your way through the British Museum now?"

"I am well known around here, Phoebe. Several pieces on display are here because of my efforts, too, so naturally they know I won't be pilfering anything. If you weren't so modest, they would also recognize you as an asset," Rupert continued.

"I prefer to keep my assets to myself, thank you. Besides, I'm grieving, remember? Lockdown just allowed me to bury myself a little deeper."

"Well, do dig yourself out, Phoebe. If the Agency of the Ancient Lost and Found is to continue its success, you must get back in the game. I know this Noel business has delivered you a terrible blow but we must get on with it and all that."

"Is that the British stiff upper lip thing talking?"

"Even delightful Canadians like yourself know the truth of that old saw. Get back to work, Phoebe, and let the healing begin."

We were now in Room 85, where bust after bust of Roman heads watched us proceed down the aisle.

"Besides, it is not fame I wish for you so much as respect," Rupert continued. "You deserve to be credited for your work in preserving history for posterity, which leads me to the matter at hand. Indeed, I have our first joint assignment, if you'll agree to accept. In fact, it could be a paid assignment, hopefully the first of many to come."

I should have been more enthusiastic regarding the monetary part. Instead, I shook my head at a Roman glowering at me from the shelf. "I'm not ready to go back into the field. Maybe later." I moved on down the row.

"This is a matter of some importance, Phoebe, and time-sensitive. It must be handled speedily and with some delicacy."

"Sounds like a job for Interpol."

"But we are affiliated with Interpol. This is a job for us."

"What could possibly be that important?" I asked, stopping beside a terra-cotta woman from the late Roman Republic missing both hands and not looking too pleased about it.

"A great deal more time is required than we have now to explain the details, but let it suffice to say that it concerns a client who has lost his head, quite literally."

He knew that would get my attention.

"Oh, come on, a headless client?"

"Truly. Please meet me at my gallery tomorrow afternoon at 1:00 p.m. and I will explain further."

He almost had me.

<hr />

"You didn't need to wait," I said to Peaches when I emerged from the museum to find her standing near the wrought-iron gates. "But I'm glad you did. Shall we take the tube?" I adjusted my mask, relieved to be back outside with enough fresh air to oxygenate myself.

"Sure. Anyway, by the time I finished chatting and doing the electronic card transfer thing to every museum bigwig in there, I figured I may as well hang around. I was everybody's token woman of color. They practically fell over themselves to introduce me to doctor this and director that and then waited around for me to spew my qualifications."

"And what did you say?"

"I said I was a Jamaican gunslinging engineer who brings art thieves to their knees."

I laughed. "So modest."

"Modesty doesn't cut it when you want to be remembered. I told them that if they needed an ancient item retrieved, we were the ones to do it."

"And then what?"

"And then I grilled a few board members over what they intended to do about the museum's looting in its colonial past. A significant number of objects in that collection were stolen in the name of imperialism, I said. I named a few from Africa. The Oduduwa helmet mask in particular gets my blood boiling. Did anyone even ask if Nigeria wanted it back? It's not like it was taken with their permission. It belongs there, not in England."

"And you watched them squirm."

"Yeah, with pleasure. They all looked hemorrhoidal but that's not going to stop me. This is a conversation we've got to keep on having. If Black Lives Matter, so does black culture. So what did Rupert say?"

"He offered us a job that involves travel, money, and a headless client," I told her as we strolled down Great Russell Street.

"Headless? Fantastic—much less backtalk. I was wondering how long it was going to take before something interesting happened. When do we start?"

"I said I'd have to think about it."

She stopped dead. "What's there to think about, woman? We've been buried alive for months. Let's do something that doesn't involve a computer."

"There's a pandemic in progress, remember? Do you really want to get on a plane right now? Besides, we have too much work to do," I pointed out. "We're only halfway through cataloging our brothers' hoard." Both of them had been art-heisting drug dealers, which had certainly helped us bond.

"So? You'd choose cataloging over travel, funds, and a headless client—are you crazy? Cataloging can wait, headless clients can't. As for the pandemic, we'll take precautions. We are now free to move around the cabin, remember? I hear that plane travel is perfectly safe with precautions. Besides, you and Max need a break from one another."

Initially I didn't see that last point. I'd become good at avoiding my partner/godfather, Max Baker, since our relationship had grown fraught. Our new facility provided lots of room and I tried to remain well-spaced until matters improved.

"Focus, focus, Peaches. Let's finish what we've started," I said while marching on.

At first Max had handled the fallout of the Morocco and Venice adventure rather well, considering. We continued to emotionally support one another through the weeks that followed. Then came Covid, which provided too much time for each of us to mull. After the third FaceTime session, things began to change.

We both had wounds that needed healing. For me, the man I loved turned out to have been using me as a lost-art sniffer dog for years, but since he also happened to be Max's biological son, matters were complicated. I guess we had both underestimated the toll the event had taken on us. Now we were back to working, socially distanced, side by side.

"I HAVE TO ASK YOU AGAIN, PHOEBE: DID YOU MEAN TO KILL HIM?"

I looked up from where I had been scrolling through my emails. It was the morning after the museum event and we had all been busy at our computers cross-referencing artifacts and emailing experts.

Max stood in the doorway of my temporary office wearing his checkered mask and gazing at me with what had become a familiar pained expression. We were about to have the discussion that had been playing over and over again between us for weeks. None of them had ended any better than I knew this one would.

I lowered my phone. "Max, I know we're both still trying to process what happened so I'm going to try to explain again: I didn't deliberately set out to kill Noel but I wasn't about to let him escape with the treasure, either. What I did, I did out of desperation—"

"And anger."

"And anger, yes, and why not?" I was trying to keep the emotion from my voice. And failing. "Hadn't I just watched him kill one man and attempt to assassinate another, not to mention threaten Peaches and steal a fortune of cultural significance? And that's not even mentioning the way he used me. Yes, I was angry, damn angry, but that doesn't mean I deliberately set out to kill him. That's not who I am. Besides, we don't know I even did kill him, remember? He was unconscious when I left him."

"You tasered him right over the heart and left him by the side of the road for dead!" Max rasped, the pain in his eyes fierce enough to twist my gut. "A man you said you loved, my *son*."

"The taser tool was all I had." Taking a deep breath, I closed my eyes. "I used it to disable him only. The thing was faulty so maybe it zapped too high a charge." It was actually a super-smartphone with a taser app but that was beside the point. This wasn't the first time he'd heard all this.

"He was my *son*."

Here we go again. "And your son, the man we both thought we knew and loved, turned out to be a murderous, thieving, underground vulture. He's not the man you thought he was, Max. He's a man who has been using me for bait for years. Face it: life on the run has turned him into something else."

"He's still my flesh and blood."

I swallowed hard, trying not to cry. I'd done enough crying in the past months to swamp a galleon. "I know, Max, and I'm sorry—sorry that the dream we shared of Noel didn't come true, sorry that he left us both broken. But I absolutely am not sorry I tasered him. I did what I had to do and now all that's left is for us is get past it."

"I just can't, Phoebe, just can't—not yet, anyway." And he turned and walked away. Talk about the walking wounded.

I grabbed a used surgical mask crumpled on the desk and blotted my eyes. Bad idea, I know.

Minutes later, I walked up to Peaches as she stood inspecting the renovated lab and instructing workers to fix some detail. "I'm meeting Rupert this afternoon to discuss our next case. Do you want to come?"

2

I didn't expect this visit to Sir Rupert Fox's gallery to be easy. For one thing, there was Evan, whom I formerly believed to be Rupert's assistant only to discover that both worked undercover for Interpol more or less as equals. That meant that the whole time I thought Rupert an unscrupulous but lovable art dealer accompanied by his bodyguard-cum-driver, he was actually operating undercover with a colleague. My brain needed time to recalibrate.

As we rang the bell to Carpe Diem, Rupert's Knightsbridge by-appointment-only gallery, that afternoon, I was fortifying my backbone with the starch of professionalism. "I'll just remain friendly and courteous and shut down any effort either one of them makes to discuss their duplicity," I said. "To avoid awkwardness, you understand."

"Sure," Peaches remarked. "Why not shake hands while you're at it?"

I was going to say that shaking hands was not recommended given the pandemic but the door flew open before I had a chance. There stood Evan, former MI6 agent, devastatingly handsome man of a million attributes, the least of which was the ability to look at me as if he had more than business on his mind. How a man can look sexy wearing a black face mask was beyond me.

"Phoebe," he said, his eyes alight. "I'm so happy to see you again at last. It's been—"

I extended my hand briefly before pulling it back. How soon we forget. "Too long, I know. Evan, what a pleasure. I trust you've been well?"

I sensed he was smiling behind the mask. "Yes, I've been well. All bullet wounds are healing nicely, thank you."

"Excellent, and you received the Get Well Soon card I sent?"

"A few months back, the one with the red balloons? Yes, duly received." Amusement was definitely twinkling in those fine gray-green eyes. You may find me mentioning those eyes repeatedly.

"The cards were all picked over," I said in my defense.

"Hey, Ev," Peaches said behind me. "Nice to see you again. I read that book you recommended to me, by the way, the one about Renaissance architecture—great read."

She gently moved me aside and enveloped Evan in a big hug, which he returned with gusto. I stood staring, mildly offended by this open display of affection in the age of Covid, yet feeling strangely bereft. But I quickly got over it. Soon we were all strolling into the inner sanctum of the antique haven known as Carpe Diem.

"Excuse me for one minute," Evan said. "Must check on a few details, but Sir Rupert will be along directly." Then he had disappeared.

"'Ev'? And I didn't know you two were in touch," I said.

"So? Every time I brought up his name, you shut me down. By the way, I was only joking about the hand-shaking thing—are you kidding me? That man took a bullet for you."

"What else am I supposed to do—kiss him?"

She would have had a comeback for that but luckily we had arrived at the salon door. Rupert was stepping out to greet us, complete with another interesting face accessory made of pleated silk. "Phoebe and Penelope, I'm so delighted you came. I was momentarily afraid you might decline."

"Thank Peaches," I said. "She convinced me that a headless client was too good an opportunity to miss."

"And a very wise conclusion indeed," he said with a nod. "Please come in. Dr. Collins will explain the details."

"Dr. Collins?" I gazed past him at the illustrious doctor of British

Studies at Oxford waving at me from across the room in a red suit and a lovely patterned mask that could be genuine Jacobean.

Rupert stepped aside to let me walk across the Persian carpet to meet her halfway. "Dr. Collins. Great to see you again even if the last time was only yesterday." Her mask, I noted, was fashioned from a scrap of genuine Jacobean vintage fabric, probably dyed in woad that perfectly matched her blue eyes. This prompted my first serious twinge of mask envy.

"Connie, please. Twice in one week—lucky us." She was about to grasp my hands before pulling away and clapping with a delighted grin. "Oh, Phoebe, I'm such a fan. I'd wanted to tell you that but never had the opportunity. Rupert is always describing your exploits so I live in awe thinking how fabulous it would be to chase art criminals around the world and wrest treasures from their gnarly grasps." She plucked the air as if snagging a bad guy midflight.

I could only gape. The esteemed academic television personality was my fan? "I'm flattered," I said. "Make that stunned." I saw no need to mention that most of the bad guys I'd snagged had been either relatives or my ex. A woman needs to embrace kudos where she can.

"You are such an inspiration. All I get to do is babble on about my passions, but you get to go out there and live them. I'd love it if someday you could make a guest appearance on the show, when things become more normal, of course."

Articulate and academic but never stuffy, Dr. Constance Collins was a media personality for a reason. Her popular British history television series delivered the past with doses of style and wit while she held down an esteemed Oxford seat and looked amazingly fetching while doing it. How she managed, I'll never know, but I was as much a fan of her as she of me. "I can't imagine being on TV but thanks, anyway." I grinned back at her. "So what do you have to do with my headless client?"

She slapped a hand to her blond bobbed head. "Oh, it's such a mess, Phoebe. Come, ladies, and I'll explain." Taking Peaches by one arm and me by the other, she steered us over to one of Rupert's clubby leather couches and bid us to sit.

The spacing protocol had suddenly evaporated and I felt this crazy need for a hug, but of course I restrained myself. "Peaches, I champion you on tackling Dr. Wong and crew with your colonial looting statements yesterday. Time to shake up those stodgy male enclaves, right? Tea, anyone?"

And she poured, leaving Rupert and Evan—esteemed members of the stodgy male enclaves—to twiddle their thumbs once deprived of their hosting roles. Both took seats at the opposite ends of a couch across from ours and looked on while Dr. Connie ran the show. Since we were about to take tea, we removed our masks with relief.

"So, let me begin with my qualifier: nothing I disclose here has anything to do with Oxford University, my area of study, my television show, the museum, or even Britain, perish the thought. By necessity, I'm remaining very much behind the scenes."

"In other words, you're not even here," I said.

Connie smiled and nodded her glossy golden head. "Exactly, but when Rupert suggested that you could help, I leaped at the chance. With you being on the covert side of Interpol, perhaps only you can." She waved her phone, which was opened on our website. "He is truly looking for something ancient and lost here."

"He?"

"Your prospective client."

We had a prospective client already? "We're not actually a part of Interpol, only affiliated." I always felt obliged to stress that point. The Agency of the Ancient Lost and Found was funded totally from my brother's ill-gotten gains: I spent his thieving profits in the name of repatriation while he spent time in prison. Seemed a fair exchange given the damage he'd wreaked. Yes, you can love someone and still watch them suffer punishment, one of the unbearable truths I'd come to learn. Even so, that money couldn't last forever.

Connie slipped her phone back into her pocket. "That's why you're perfect for the mission. You can fly under the proverbial radar, the preferred approach right now."

"Okay, now that you've got our attention," I said, "what's going on?"

"It concerns the client I referred to—my brother, as it happens," Connie said.

"Your brother?" Peaches asked.

"Yes—"she clasped her hands "—my brother is the famed British forensic archaeologist Markus Collins. Perhaps you've heard of him?"

Neither Peaches nor I had.

"Well, famed in other circles, then. In any case, his services were requested by an archaeological team in Lisbon recently to help process multiple remains found in an old crypt flooded by torrential rains. The crypt is part of a small chapel built in 1147 but last used for interments in the late fifteenth century. Still, that's no less hallowed ground, you understand. The original church was destroyed in the Great Lisbon Earthquake of 1755 and rebuilt in 1784, but the crypt remained more or less intact until recent flooding. Even after all this time, it's no small matter to disturb the dead."

I nodded sagely. I tried never to do it myself.

"Considerable controversy surrounds the whole thing—disinterment, a forensic autopsy," Connie continued. "The Catholic church doesn't approve such things lightly. The remains had to be removed to an unused morgue for temporary safekeeping, so why not do a few tests while they were at it? They finally received approval to begin the disinterment. Perhaps you caught some of that on the news?" One look at our faces prompted her to hurry on. "Anyway, DNA samples were to be taken to look for general health of the occupants, prevalent diseases during the years of the European Renaissance, and to trace the whole ancestry tangle."

"There is even DNA left after so long?" Peaches asked.

"Oh, yes, where there are bones there is usually DNA." Connie seemed unable to contain her enthusiasm. Death became her. "In 2012, archaeologists found the remains of an adult male under a car park in Leicester that turned out to be King Richard III. You might say he'd been missing in action for a while, seeing as he met his end at the Battle of Bosworth. His identity was only determined through DNA testing. Seems we've been driving over the poor man's bones for decades."

"And he was just left there by his contemporaries?" I said. "I always wondered about that. I mean, a king is a king, right? Were they getting him back for the whole princes in the tower scandal?"

"Which was never proven," Evan said quietly. "What is ever proven to be true that far back in time? Everything is filtered through a combination of current prejudices combined with a contemporary rival's viewpoint, not to mention hundreds of years of supposition." He didn't quite sound like the Evan I knew but more like a man in a suit with a big degree wearing a mask, all of which looked good on him, by the way.

"Yes, exactly," Connie said, sending a beatific smile in his direction. "But back to Markus and this particular situation. An X-ray revealed two skulls in one coffin and that captured everyone's interest from the beginning." We waited as the television host paused for perfect timing. "He—and it was presumed to be a he, by the way—was missing the rest of his skeleton. The other fellow was intact."

Peaches snapped her fingers. "I knew it! Our headless client reveals himself at last."

"Do we know who he is—was?" I asked, itching for the details.

"Ah, there's the rub," our scholar added. "Markus has not yet had the opportunity to take DNA samples, but he's since done enough research to present a working theory identifying the owner. The skull had certain contusions and abnormalities that made it somewhat easy to identify after a little preliminary research. If his assumption is correct, the bodiless skull may be related to the Spanish royal family at the time."

"And the time was?" Peaches asked.

"We're thinking 1568."

"And who does Markus believe this royal skull belongs to?" I asked.

"I have been instructed not to say. He will give you the rest of the story if you agree to help," Connie said.

"Fine but answer me this if you can: does this skull belong to a king, or a prince, or something?" I was leaning forward at this point.

"Probably the minor prince kind of something since the final resting places of all the Portuguese and Spanish kings of the time have been accounted for—to our knowledge at least," Connie said. "This chapel had never been associated with monarchy. And, to heap mystery on top of mystery, the skull of our possible royal chap was found wedged beside an ordinary citizen's remains in the same coffin, almost as if it had been dropped in or stuffed in, perhaps."

I pulled back. "Someone beheaded a crown prince and dropped his skull into another person's tomb and nobody noticed?"

Connie frowned. "Those were dark times, Phoebe. Recorded history only knows half of what went on and leaves us to guess the rest. Now an anonymous party badly wants to find the missing skeleton and unite the bones so that the remains can be buried where they belong," she added.

"And does this anonymous party know where that location is?" I asked.

Connie spread her hands. "Markus is working on that. He has a lead but would rather discuss the details in person. I don't know the complete information myself. There is a certain sensitivity to the whole matter. This may be a piece of Portuguese and Spanish history, after all."

Peaches shook her head. "I still don't get why Interpol wouldn't get involved in finding the remains of royalty."

"Because, Penelope," Rupert said quietly, "and pardon me for being crass, but unless there is clearly something of monetary value involved, Interpol remains officially uninterested."

"Yes, indeed," Evan added. "Interpol has no time to chase skeletons, so to speak, when they are far too busy tracking down stolen art and antiquities pilfered for drug money and arms deals. No, such a plum job as this has fallen to us."

"And you will receive monetary assistance for your efforts apparently," Connie continued. "Markus is willing to fund your efforts to begin with and presumably the anonymous party will fund the rest."

"And if we don't find the skull?" I asked.

"Then at the very least your expenses will be covered before we decide next steps," she said.

"But why even do this?" I asked. "Granted, retrieving an intact royal personage to place in their final resting place is important, but why fund four people to help do it?"

Connie wrinkled her pert little nose. "Well, because, Phoebe—and this is unknown to all but a few—Markus tells me that the missing skull may have been wearing a crown."

3

Tracking down a crowned skull that had been missing for over five hundred years wasn't exactly in my skill set. I was more of an art historian with a specialty in textiles and trauma, the latter mine. Apparently, I had the uncanny ability to locate lost artifacts while barely escaping with my neck intact, a tendency that kept me too busy to formally diversify. But I am insatiably curious.

This is a long way around saying that we took the job.

"Besides, we need the money," Peaches remarked as she attempted to sip water with her mask half-off while sitting beside me on the plane, the seat empty between us. She had resolved to poke the bottle up under the mask and toss her head back. As a result, water dribbled down her chin.

I watched in fascination. "Try the straw," I suggested.

Flying post-lockdown was even less enjoyable than I imagined. No in-flight service. Masked crew members. No in-flight service. Hand sanitizer coming out of your ears. No in-flight service. Luckily, London to Lisbon was a reasonably short flight and was frequented enough to ensure that we weren't canceled at the last minute.

As we rode a taxi from the airport into the city later, our faces indented from being masked for hours, it suddenly occurred to me that I was finally back in the wide world. It felt good and a little unnerving, too.

Though it was still only 6:45 p.m., dusk fell early in September and all I could see through the cab windows was a surprisingly modern city with plenty of concrete and spacious boulevards. That changed the moment we headed up one of the nearly vertical streets where the buildings became older, more crowded together, and intriguing all at the same time.

The driver pulled into a narrow side street halfway up a hill and assured us that we had arrived. A tall white balconied building stretched far overhead.

"This is it?" I asked.

"Entrance around corner," the driver said, stirring the air with his finger. "One-way street."

I nodded and hastily paid our fare—by credit card only—and the driver helped us haul our two bags onto the sidewalk before dashing back to his seat to dose his hands like we were plague bearers. At first I felt totally disorientated as masked people squeezed past us on the narrow sidewalk.

"This way," Peaches called, heading up an even narrower road leading off the main street. Slinging my backpack over my shoulder, I followed, glad that the two of us had decided to travel lightly.

We were to stay at one of Lisbon's Airbnbs, which Rupert insisted made the perfect cover for our under-the-radar operation. Let me just say that I would never have put the name Sir Rupert Fox and Airbnb in the same sentence otherwise. Rupert owned a house in Belgravia and a country estate. Rupert did not do tourist class. However, given that he had been playing an act for all the years I'd known him, who knew the real Rupert in action?

I had agreed to let the Evan and Rupert duo make the accommodation reservations but insisted on flying by ourselves, as if that small measure of independence meant anything. Whether I liked it or not, our working lives were inextricably connected to Sir Fox and Evan Barrows.

"This is the place, all right," Peaches announced once we crammed ourselves onto a strip of sidewalk outside a large door, "and according to Ev, we have maybe forty-five minutes to check in, change, and get our tails off to supper somewhere up there." She had her phone in one hand while thumbing over her shoulder toward the mostly vertical streets. Meanwhile, I rang the buzzer.

"Are we meeting Dr. Collins there?" I asked.

"I think so—over supper. Ev didn't say who was on the guest list."

After being checked in by an amiable young woman with excellent English who plied us with maps to all of the local sites, we quickly showered and changed inside our spacious two-bedroom apartment.

"Wow, look at this place," Peaches enthused while gazing over the terra-cotta rooftops of our balcony as the last of the sun bled away over the horizon. "You take the bathroom first. I'm just going to stand here and admire the view."

I opened my backpack travel bag and stared down into my clothes. Since I'd exchanged roller bags for an adaptable satchel-cum-backpack that I could run with if necessary, my options had become more limited. My one nod to style was that this backpack was created from an old Turkish carpet—a carpet backpack.

Lifting out a blouse and pair of black corduroy pants to wear with my jacket, I strode to the bathroom. The jacket, a gift from an Italian friend, had multiple pockets, secret receptacles, and a built-in gun holster, currently empty.

Minutes later I emerged, trading places with Peaches, and twenty minutes after that, Peaches left the bathroom smelling like a piña colada. She had changed into a bright pink printed dress under a Chanel-style jacket with her long brown legs ending in a pair of booties. There'd be a mask to match the outfit, I knew. Once she'd traded the island vibe for high street fashion, she embraced style with gusto. On the other hand, I was more of an arty disaster dresser, more Bohemian than anything. However, now that we were on the move, I had managed to pick up a few dozen nice masks at Heathrow.

Turning my gaze away, I scanned the living area, only vaguely taking in the open plan and tastefully neutral decorating scheme. "I thought maybe they'd leave us a message or something."

Peaches stepped back into the room. "Who?"

"Rupert and Evan."

"You set the terms for how we work together, remember?"

"All I did was keep up the courteous and formal thing."

"Maybe warm and friendly would be a good start. Aren't we establishing relationships here? That's what you always tell me when I'm yelling at the contractors."

"Right, so do I look presentable?" I studied my reflection in the mirror, carefully adjusting my knitted pre-Raphaelite-inspired Melancholy wrap, admiring the multiple shades of green and mahogany that played nicely in the lamplight. It went so well with my black jacket and millefleurs shirt, with the black face mask adding to the look.

"You could use some color. How about I lend you a scarf in a lighter shade of gloomy?"

"Thanks but I'm just not into bright."

"Stop thinking depressed is a color group. Besides, you're seeing Evan tonight and Evan is a good-looking male who adores you." She studied me carefully, her hair pulled up in a classy topknot in comparison to my free-form curly mass. "You could do with a dose of good-looking male after the Noel shitstorm."

I shook my head. "No, thanks. I'm on the rebound from a broken heart, remember? The last thing I want is another relationship."

"Oh, stop. You took a hit in the heart like most women do at one time or another. Get over it. Sure, your hit was more like a nuclear explosion but so what? The wrong man sucker-punched you. Now it's time to notice the right man and give him a chance to show you how love is done."

"Are you speaking from experience? From your own admission, you haven't found your 'right man,' either."

"Which doesn't stop me from looking. As soon as I find someone man enough to be with a woman like me, I'll let him in. Until then, I'll keep my door ajar. Besides, your right man is right under your nose. Tall, handsome, makes breakfast, takes bullets for you, adores you—or haven't you noticed?"

Whether I'd noticed or not was irrelevant. Yes, Evan and I had always flirted, but after the Noel fiasco I was done with romance. My fault lines ran too deep. Besides, it was humiliating being played the fool by one man under the knowing scrutiny of another. "I'm not interested."

"Like hell you're not. Do you think those looks you two exchange are fooling anybody? Besides, my mom used to say to always get back on the horse that threw you, and Ev looks like a horse worth riding no matter how hard he bucks. In fact, the harder, the better!" She belted out a dirty howl.

I sighed and tapped my watch. "Let's get going. We only have fifteen minutes to find this place."

Armed with a tourist map, we stepped out the main door of our building and started striding upward, our phones in our hands. *Upward* alternating with *downward* were the operable words for Lisbon, I was to discover. Occasionally we had to weave into the street or against a wall to avoid oncoming foot traffic.

My thighs groaned as we trudged up the steep hill beside tile-walled buildings and narrow streets with treed boulevards opening up at adjacent corners. Everything seemed a jumble of old and new, of intensely vertical with pockets of spaciousness here and there. It was charming. Sometimes I'd pause long enough to stare into a shop window or admire the tile work paving a building, but mostly I kept on climbing.

Twenty minutes later, we paused. "Are we lost?" I panted.

Peaches may have made a face. "Probably." She flagged down a passerby and pointed to the address on her phone. Somehow the man managed to provide directions from six feet away.

"Ever notice how here people don't look at me like I'm black? I'm just a person among many," she said minutes later.

"Didn't notice—sorry." Peaches made a point of teaching me about the black experience, and no matter how difficult it sometimes became from my position of white privilege, I resolved to take it on the chin. That evening she wasn't inclined to be too forceful with her punches.

We crossed the street, ambled through a tiny square, and began climbing again, this time up a narrow cobbled street that curved away from the main artery. The streetlights beamed down on little shops and residences forming a wall of illuminated windows. I was appreciating Lisbon more and more.

"This is the place," Peaches announced as we stood outside a tiny restaurant. "But it looks pretty squeezy in there."

I peered through the window. Several tables had been spaced around the room but many seemed to contain whole extended families. "This is the address. Let's go," I said, stepping to the door.

Inside, privacy was impossible even with the table spacing. I thought that we must have the wrong spot until I glimpsed Evan waving at us from the back of the long narrow space. I interrupted the hostess and pointed. She smiled and waved us through.

Somehow Evan had found us a room tucked way in the back of the eatery. Granted, the space was the size of a walk-in closet with seating for ten now reduced to six, but at least it was private. Besides, the walls were plastered with photos of old Lisbon and the scent of food along the way so tantalizing that I felt immediately happy—correction: *happier*.

Both Rupert and Evan appeared delighted to see us.

"First things first," Evan announced before we took our seats. "We can dispense with the masks as we are now officially in a business bubble."

I didn't know there was such a thing as a business bubble but it made sense. I watched as Evan removed his manly black face covering, prompting Peaches and me to remove ours.

"Please place your phones in the box provided along with any smart devices you may have on your person." He pointed to a long narrow receptacle he must have brought with him. "That container will block your signals and protect our conversations against eavesdroppers. The room has already been scanned."

We dropped our phones into the box.

"I suppose you've brought us new devices to replace these?" I asked. I knew he had.

He smiled, an altogether pleasant gesture, trust me. "I did." He passed Peaches and me each one of his modified smartphones. Evan's technological mastery was only one area of his considerable genius.

"I've been lusting after one of these of my very own since Morocco," Peaches said, waving hers in the air. "What does it do—X-ray scanning, bug removal, zapping murderous thieves with a jolt big enough to leave them toast like Phoebe did Noel?"

An uncomfortable pause followed.

"Sorry," she said, looking at me.

"The last device was faulty, Evan," I said after a moment. "It melted in my hand and may have killed Noel, not that that's necessarily a bad thing." I held up my palm to show the square-shaped scar.

He reached out to take my hand but I snatched it away. "Phoebe, I deeply regret causing you even a moment's harm, but as for Noel Halloran, he got exactly what he deserved. The only thing I regret is not being there to witness it."

"Don't worry about it. I just wanted to mention the defect in the interests of quality control."

He held up one of his modified better-than-smart phones. "I have improved the taser feature considerably, including the addition of a smaller charge designed to merely incapacitate the quarry. I've also added a few new killer apps besides. I do hope they are to your liking. A list of features is waiting in your in-box but allow me to provide a brief overview."

Rupert held up his hand. "Another time, old chap. Come sit, ladies. The food here is excellent so we chose this as our rendezvous of choice. May I say that I am most delighted to see you both. Allow me to treat you to supper in honor of our new endeavors. We all must eat, mustn't we?"

Peaches and I took our seats opposite one another while Rupert carried on talking. "Evan has a way of finding the best locales, don't you, dear man?" He sat down himself, unfurling a napkin over his knife-pressed jeans, and smiled. "Wine, anybody? It is a quite delectable red. I must say that Portuguese wines are the unsung heroes of European vintages and this one is yet another of Evan's discoveries."

I risked glancing at Evan—brown hair curling around the collar of the green shirt straining over his biceps, gray-green eyes on me, the warm smile, the way he remained standing until we were seated in some old-fashion notion of etiquette.

"Still acting as the world's best concierge?" I asked him.

He plucked the wine bottle from the table and readied to pour me a glass. "Research is just something I'm good at," he remarked, holding my gaze. "I have other things I'm good at, too. Perhaps you'll permit me to demonstrate someday?"

"Such as pretending to be the loyal servant, which you're clearly not? Were you and Rupert equal colleagues the whole time?" I held up my glass and watched it fill with red liquid, keeping my eyes on the wine not the man. Actually, both had practically the same effect.

"We were undercover, Phoebe," he said with a note of pique.

Right, so he'd always called me "madam" before and now I had to get used to hearing my name massaged on his lips like some sonata in A minor.

Meanwhile Peaches was asking Rupert where Markus Collins was.

"He will be along directly," Rupert said, checking his no-doubt-über smartwatch. "I have yet to meet the gent but spoke to him earlier and found him sounding most distressed. I am certain he will disclose all upon arrival. I trust you found the accommodation suitable?"

Rupert was wearing a yellow polo shirt underneath a tweed sports jacket with a lime-green silk ascot tied at his neck. This had to be his Englishman Does Tourist look circa 1970, but his unusual pallor dampened the effect. I was used to seeing him ruddy and brimming with health the way a man in his fifties should look.

"Fine, thanks," I responded, taking a deep gulp of wine. "Which floor are you two on?"

"Top-floor penthouse." Rupert smiled. "My apologies for commandeering the best view."

I laughed. "I'd expect nothing less. Were all the Airbnb castles taken?"

Evan chuckled. "They were. I couldn't find him a room with a pool, either, so we had to make do. Try the pastries," he urged, offering me a plate of delicious-looking appetizers. Typically, I was ravenous and wondered if it would be rude to take one of each. As if sensing my thoughts, Evan forked over a selection and passed me a plate.

After more bantering, more wine, and enough pleasantries for me to believe this arrangement might actually work, the door flew open and a man slipped inside. In his thirties, bearded, with longish blond hair and spectacles, wearing a mask like a sagging diaper, he looked like he could have been chased by a rabid dog. Closing the door behind him, he tore off the mask and stared at us while trying to catch his breath.

We froze, staring.

"Dr. Markus Collins, I presume?" Evan asked after a few seconds.

"Yes, I am Markus Collins," the man said between gasps. "I recognize all of you...from Connie's descriptions and...thank you for agreeing to help me. I do hope I haven't...dragged you into the maelstrom. Mind if I sit?"

Evan slid out a chair into which the bearded archaeologist collapsed, shooting us all a brief smile before propping his elbows on the table and burying his head in his hands.

"Pass over your phone, please," Evan requested.

Markus looked surprised but plucked the mobile from his pocket without comment.

"Dear man, are you all right?" Rupert asked, leaning forward.

Markus studied us, one by one. The blue eyes magnified behind the wire-rimmed glasses seemed so deeply barricaded into their sockets they could be in hiding. I could see the resemblance in the siblings in the coloring if nothing else.

"I'm still alive, which is saying something." He sat back and dabbed his forehead with a napkin. "How long I can stay that way is left to be seen. I'm sure I was followed here. Mind if I have a glass of wine?"

Peaches leaped into action to fill the man's glass. "Drink up. You look like you need it."

"Let's order our dinners and get down to business," Evan suggested before retrieving menus along with our server and providing translations where needed. Of course Evan spoke some version of Portuguese. Minutes later, we placed our orders, each choosing a dish for sharing before settling in to listen.

"Now tell us what happened, dear man," Rupert began. "I understand that you and your team have come across a rather notable skull."

Markus sighed and shook his head. He was still perspiring heavily but appeared to be trying to pull himself together. After taking several sips of wine, he began. "If only it was that simple, but on the surface, yes, we found a skull missing its skeleton."

"So, only the skull?" I asked.

"Yes. There were two skulls in the coffin that belongs to the original occupant, a Pedro Alavares Fidalgo, who was complete. Initial X-rays indicate that this second skull has strange cranial markings and growth abnormalities."

Markus set down his glass. I had many questions but he quickly continued. "We—we being my colleague, Jose, another archaeologist, and I—needed to remove the coffin lid to investigate further, of course, but as scientists we follow a rigorous methodical system to ensure the contents were not contaminated."

"What about these cranial markings?" I interrupted.

He swallowed and gripped his glass. "The skull had cranial abnormalities indicating that the man must have suffered a severe head injury during his lifetime. However, the most alarming feature was the regular holes encircling the top part of the skull as though something was bolted onto the bone. That it was a crown is only conjecture. From what we could determine, whatever that object was, it was removed some time ago."

"As a result of some long-ago tomb robber?" Rupert said, dabbing his lips.

"Or maybe someone removed the object and hid it for safekeeping," Markus said.

We all looked at Markus dumbfounded. "Seriously?" I said.

"Perhaps. Consider this: presume that initially the skeleton was buried with a possible crown. Later, for reasons we have yet to determine, the skeleton was removed and buried elsewhere, and whether the crown was removed at that time or not, we don't know. All we know for certain is that a skull with cranial deformities and holes indicating the application of a possible permanent headpiece was buried with Senhor Fidalgo minus his skeleton. Otherwise, we have no way of knowing when the headpiece was removed or why or even where the rest of the skeleton lies."

"And you haven't opened the coffin to take DNA samples or whatever you guys do?" I asked.

He turned to me. "No, of course not. We might damage or possibly destroy the contents. There are protocols in any forensic investigation. We are scientists first and always," he said testily. "Oh, Lord, that sounded pompous—apologies. Anyway, we were waiting for more sensitive and modern equipment to arrive from another facility and only used the lab's ancient X-ray in the interim."

"Okay..." I said. Like that would have stopped me.

"Nevertheless, that inferior machine still revealed this extraordinary find," Markus continued. "There were ten coffins in total, all found within Capela de Soa Maria Baptista's tiny crypt, untouched since they were first laid to rest, or so we believed. Once we saw one coffin with two skulls, one with severe skull contusions, we knew special precautions were in order. We knew that we may have found the remains of some minor royal or, at the very least, somebody with some incredible mystery surrounding his remains."

"Indeed," Rupert remarked, looking as if he had just swallowed a bug. "And what precautions did you take exactly?"

Markus sighed. "For one thing, we agreed not to breathe a word to anyone until after we had alerted the proper authorities—standard procedure, you understand—and secondly, we knew we must guard the find until said authorities arrived. Jose and I agreed to spell one another off in shifts. Is there more wine?"

Evan topped up his glass before Markus continued. "Try the appetizers," Evan suggested, passing him a plate.

Markus took the plate but ignored the food. "We had only two nights until the authorities were due to arrive to assess our find—things are still very slow with Covid and we were a skeleton team to begin with, no pun intended. We were taking turns watching the facility overnight while the other slept. All very straightforward, really. Though we had thought about hiring a security watch, that would be like signaling that something interesting was on-site so decided against it."

"Sounds reasonable," I said. "And?"

"And the skull went missing on the second night." Markus took another swig and coughed before gazing at me in abject misery.

"The skull is gone?" Rupert asked, sounding affronted.

"Yes, I have made a terrible mistake," Markus said miserably. "I broke my own cardinal rule and unleashed a Pandora's box."

Rupert leaned forward. "Dear man, will you please fill in the details? How did the skull disappear on your watch? Where were you when it happened? What horrendous crime could you have possibly committed?"

Markus gazed down at the pastries with unseeing eyes. When he lifted his head again, his expression had changed from distraught to bleak. "On that last night, as we were approaching the graveyard shift—no pun intended—Jose received a phone call from his wife saying there was an emergency at home and that he had to leave."

"Leave the mortuary?" Evan asked.

"Yes. We had been doing shifts in pairs with one of us sleeping and the other watching, as I said, but on that last night, he left at 12:15 a.m. Where was the harm in that? we thought. The lab was mostly unused and we had only commandeered it for our purposes under special arrangement with the morgue. Staying with the coffins was only a precaution. No one but a handful of people knew we were there and the facility is well off the beaten track. Who'd be interested in bunch of long-dead remains but a pair of forensic archaeologists?"

"So what happened?" Peaches asked.

"That's just it, I don't know, at least not for certain." His brief attempt at self-control was cracking. "It's not like we had working security cameras in the facility, but I'm assuming it had something to do with my actions between the hours of midnight and 2:00 a.m. While I was sitting around trying to stay awake, I took photographs on my phone of the X-rays for my own use and risked a little online research using the antiquated printer to make copies. In retrospect, I can't believe I did that."

I stared at him blankly. Online research had always been my go-to activity for off-hour pleasure—that and knitting, of course. Nothing he had confessed so far seemed like the crime of the century.

"In other words, I *Googled*." Markus spoke the word as if it was synonymous with "machine-gunned innocent bystanders."

"Googled?" Rupert said, as if that confession was the last thing he expected.

"Yes, but in my defense," Markus went on, "it was rather a boring stint and, thanks to Jose, I already had a few clues as to the identity of the possible interloper. I wanted to learn more. It had to do with the elongated jaw and the other cranial contusions that sent me off on the research trail."

Evan was several strides ahead. "You Googled what, exactly?"

"I Googled search terms associated with royal personages during the relevant years, along with the Capela de Soa Maria Baptista crypt and, on Jose's suggestion, the crown princes of Spain and Portugal in those same years, notably those with possible spinal or cranial deformities."

"In other words, you left a search trail for any hacker prowling the Internet," Evan said, making a steeple with his long fingers. "Either that or someone may have been electronically stalking you the whole time."

"Yes, something I now realize is ridiculously easy if one is technologically astute, which I'm not particularly," Markus said with a groan.

"And the server was not secure," Evan added, as if he saw how it all unfolded.

"I'd been using the Wi-Fi at the old morgue because I didn't want to overtax my data plan. Now that I think about it, I doubt it was secure at all since nobody used it much anymore. I didn't bother to check. Why would I? Would you?" he asked Evan directly, as if trying to shore up his self-defense.

"Always," Evan said. "Internet security is one of the first things I check anywhere I go, especially when dealing with sensitive material. It's also critical that you always tape over the webcam on your computer. The web provides the easiest way to glean every one of your personal secrets these days, almost including your very thoughts."

"So, someone was tracking Markus online?" I asked, finally cluing in, at least partly.

"Apparently," Evan said.

Markus turned to me. "Somebody must have been, right? Thus, I inadvertently revealed our exact interest in the remains, including where we found them and what the coffin contained, and even went so far as to input a few clues as to the possible royal interloper's identity. This included details as to his deformed skull, indicating that the person must have suffered a head injury even before the possible application of the crown." He turned to Evan. "But surely all that couldn't have transpired from a mere hour of searching?"

"More likely that you and your find have been the subject of somebody's interest for some time, old chap," Rupert replied. "Your sister informed us that the supposed violation of those tombs hit the media here in Lisbon a while ago."

"Well, yes. There was controversy but we thought it had died down. Certainly we didn't disclose where we were taking the coffins."

"Wait, who is the suspected interloper missing his skull?" I asked.

But Evan had the deeper, more commanding voice. "What happened next?" he demanded.

"So at 1:25, I took a sleeping bag into one of the adjacent offices and caught a bit of sleep, something I would usually do only if Jose stayed on guard. But this time I couldn't stay awake a moment longer and thought to catch a few minutes rest, only I slept for hours while leaving the lab unprotected."

"Maybe you were drugged?" I suggested.

He looked at me. "I thought of that but that would mean Jose had drugged me, which I seriously doubt."

"Not necessarily. Was the office soundproof?" I asked.

"No. It was just a regular office down the hall from the lab, but I had left the door open and, when I came to, it had been closed."

"So somebody broke in?" Peaches asked.

"It wasn't hard—the outside lock had been jimmied apparently. Sometime between the hours of three and four—my best guess—someone entered the lab and stole the skull from that coffin. Not anything else, you understand, just the skull, and no other coffins were touched. It was a very specific theft, as if the thieves knew exactly what they were looking for. The coffin had been tipped onto the floor and left in shambles. Pedro Fidalgo still had his gold rings but was left in a pile of bones."

"My word, man," Rupert erupted, "but what about this Jose fellow? Could he be a suspect?"

"Definitely not," Markus said as he buried his head in his hands. "Jose was already dead."

4

It took several minutes and more wine to get Markus to stop trembling and keep talking.

"It seemed like an accident," he said. "The police will probably think it *was* an accident but I know it was murder. Jose rushed home, taking what I understand to be his usual route—he only lived a few blocks away from the morgue—and he tripped over a curb and hit his head on the sidewalk hard enough to break his neck? What are the chances of that happening? But I'm afraid that's what the police will deduce."

"Initially, perhaps, but they'll figure it out eventually," Evan said, patting the man on the shoulder.

"Yeah," Peaches piped in. "The police are not nearly as dense as people give them credit for."

"I agree that it was too much of a coincidence," I said. "What was the emergency that sent him home?"

"Fire. His wife, Ana, called to say that she smelled smoke in the flat."

"And was the flat on fire?" I asked.

"Apparently," Markus said miserably, reaching for more wine. I stilled his hand, pouring him a glass of water instead. "I spoke to her days ago just after it all happened. She was distraught, of course, but there had been a fire in the basement, quickly put out but real nevertheless. That, too, could have been deliberately set to draw Jose away." He clutched my arm. "Don't you see? Somebody was already on our tail. They wanted me alone, and had I been awake when they entered the premises, I'd probably be dead, too."

At that moment there was a knock on the door. Our food had arrived, delivered by three servers, all of whom shot concerned glances at the man blotting his forehead with a napkin. Conversation stopped as the plates were delivered and the water refreshed, and Evan drew the servers away with some explanation that set them nodding with sympathy before quietly shutting the door.

"I said that your girlfriend broke off your engagement," Evan said when he took his seat again.

Markus managed a wry smile. "She did, in fact, only months ago."

"Here, eat something. It will fortify you," I suggested. "Did you say anything to the police about the robbery?" I began passing around platters of chicken, fish and baked beans.

"Yes and no." Markus sniffed, staring down at the platters without interest. "I told them there had been a robbery, of course, but didn't disclose the exact nature. They believe that somebody had broken in and tried to plunder the coffins, thinking to steal jewelry and such. Old tombs are always susceptible to looting. The police believe I interrupted the robbery and that the thieves got away with nothing."

"My word, man," Rupert exclaimed while slipping a few sardines onto his plate. These were huge sardines, by the way, and by no means the minuscule canned variety. "What about the skull?"

"I didn't mention it."

Rupert paused. "Why the devil not?"

"Because," Markus said, struggling to control himself. "Because before the police arrived that night, I received a threatening phone call."

My first forkful of chicken and mushrooms paused halfway to my mouth. "From whom?"

Markus shook his head. "It was anonymous—a man with a deep voice, Spanish accent. He said that if I was to utter one word about the skull or disclose those X-rays to anyone, I'd be dead. I didn't know that Jose was dead already but I believed him nonetheless. It's not like I'm used to being threatened. My kind of archaeology is hardly of the Indiana Jones variety. Until now." He stifled a nervous laugh.

"And?" Rupert prompted.

"And I was instructed to destroy any evidence I had, including deleting my search strings—which he named, by the way, so he definitely was hacking me—and he said not to tell a soul about what I found. Or else," he added.

For a moment we were all silent.

"And did you do that?" I asked.

Markus nodded and then shook his head. "Yes and no. I deleted the photos from my phone and cleared the cookies on my laptop but didn't destroy the actual printouts or the two X-rays. How would he even know about those? I had printed out my search results on the cruddy old printer earlier and stuffed them inside my jacket along with the X-rays. I thought, how would this person know if I did or didn't obey all his instructions, and really, why should I? Wasn't it bad enough that he plundered our forensic investigation and possibly the biggest discovery of my career? There were no cameras for the bastard to spy on me. By that time, the shock was wearing off and I was furious." Something hard and resolute burned in his eyes.

"But surely this man knew that *you knew* what you had discovered, meaning..." I trailed away when I realized where that was going.

"Meaning that he actually needs to get rid of me if he wants to erase all the pertinent evidence—I reached that same conclusion. It's either that or he needs me alive for some reason."

"Which means that we're also on the hit list because we now know what you know—cool," Peaches said with a grin. We didn't share the same views on risk management.

"But what about the police?" Rupert asked.

"I saw no one, I assured them, which I didn't. The X-ray machine was never mentioned and the plundered casket spoke for itself." Markus poked a fork at his food but made no move to eat. "I suspect that will be the end of the investigation, which, under the circumstances, is probably for the best."

"My word!" Rupert exclaimed while delicately decapitating a sardine.

"I agreed to have Connie contact you because I don't know how long I can keep this up," Markus continued. "I need your help. I need you to catch these bastards, retrieve that skull, and keep me alive in the process.

I have a little money to pay you but I believe I can access more, if needed."

"How did you communicate with Connie?" I asked.

"By the hotel phone." Markus shook his head. "Another blunder, I know."

"Had we that skull, we could use DNA testing to determine if it belonged to a royal personage, I take it?" Evan inquired.

"Yes." Staring at his food, Markus nodded. "The phenotype aspects like the color of the eyes plus geographical origin and the presence of certain mutations would have confirmed what we suspected all along: that the crowned individual was a Hapsburg."

"Hapsburg?" Rupert gasped.

"Wow, a Hapsburg," Peaches exclaimed. "Those are the royals with the mega-jaw, right?"

"Among other abnormalities. This skull had a Hapsburg jaw as well as certain bone markings that indicated the subject had had primitive brain surgery," Markus commented.

"Brain surgery in those days?" Peaches asked.

"It was a rare event, but presumably a royal who could afford the best surgeons in the land might be in enough of a crisis to warrant such extreme measures."

I badly needed to brush up on my European royalty but at the moment I was fixed on separating our allies from our enemies. "Connie said something about somebody offering to help? Is this the source of the money you mentioned?" I asked.

Markus sighed. "Another anonymous contact. That particular message came to me by way of a note shoved under the door of my room. It's in my package."

"Package?" Even asked.

"I brought it with me."

Evan and Rupert exchanged glances. Peaches and I did the same because we caught them doing it.

"Right," Evan said, standing. "We're here to help protect you and track down that missing skull."

"But you must tell us everything. Who do you believe is this hapless headless Hapsburg interloper? Where are these X-rays and printouts?" Rupert asked.

Markus tossed down his napkin and stood. "Right here. This contains everything I know. You take it. It feels radioactive to me." He reached inside his jacket and brought out a plump manilla envelope, which he held over the table. Both Evan and Peaches reached for it at the same time but Peaches, being closer, won.

"*Perfecto!*" she said, waving the envelope in triumph at Evan. "We'll start here."

Markus took his seat and picked up his fork. "I suggest you study the contents someplace else. You'll need plenty of table space. Maybe we should go back to your accommodations after dinner?"

"Excellent idea," Rupert said, "but can you tell us anything about this anonymous employer in the meantime?"

"He's Jose's friend," Markus commented between bites. "You'll have to read the note."

5

It was close to ten o'clock before we finished supper, ending our meals with a plate of the delectable custard pastries the Portuguese call *pasteis de nata* for which I was to develop an addiction. I even took a box back to the Airbnb.

Stuffed and a little buzzed after the wine, we left the restaurant with Markus beside Rupert walking in the middle of the sidewalk and Peaches and Evan taking positions front and back. We were in guard dog mode.

I was left to scan the perimeters for possible stalkers from the rear, something for which I'd had plenty of practice. But the leafy streets and roads were quiet except for the occasional car or tramway slipping by, and the shadowy doorways and narrow alleys guarded their secrets. If anyone was ghosting our heals that night, we saw no sign, making it a quick and uneventful downhill trek to our accommodations.

Less than twenty minutes later, we were settled around the table of Rupert and Evan's penthouse suite beside a pair of double doors open to the cool evening air. The only thing in our line of sight were the tops of the tile-roofed buildings.

Peaches handed me the envelope while Evan made the coffee. Everyone looked on while I placed the pages of Markus's package on the table in some kind of linear fashion. Four poor-quality black-and-white printouts taken from Wikipedia were laid out along with two prints of portraits from the same source. Two brackish, nearly indecipherable X-rays crowned the top, and I placed the plain white envelope from the anonymous contact at the very bottom.

"You can see that my research was very preliminary. I only began to Google after Jose left so I could gain a basic understanding of what our find involved."

The portraits caught my eye immediately.

"Who's this?" I asked, picking up the print of a boy standing in a doublet with an ermine cloak over his shoulders and a castle in the background. Though the copy was muddy, it was clearly of some wealthy offspring in the 1500s, ermine being reserved for only the richest and the royal-est, and doublets a gent's fashion statement of the day. Of course, the castle's curb appeal brought its own cachet.

"Crown Prince Don Carlos of Spain, who died in 1568."

"So you think he's the owner of the missing skull?" I asked, staring at the youth.

"Almost 99.9 percent certain based on the skull alone. Don Carlos had noted spinal deformities plus a serious head injury in his early twenties that resulted in an extraordinary surgery that ultimately saved his life," Markus said. "Verdi made him into the hero of an opera but the truth indicates he was anything but heroic."

"Actually, Schiller was the author of that play and Verdi put it to music," Rupert said, "and it truly was a work of fiction with little relation to the truth therein but the personages themselves."

Evan strode to the table with a tray of mugs and a coffeepot. "That's Don Carlos? By all accounts he was a mentally disturbed young man even before the fall that severely damaged his skull. He wreaked such havoc in his short lifetime that his father was forced to lock him away until his death."

"Ah, yes, Don Carlos," Rupert mused, taking the picture from my hand. "That fine opera based totally on fictional elements was the only known benefit of the poor boy's existence. By all accounts, he was a nasty piece of work who liked to whip girls and torture small animals. I deduced that it might be him. Though inbreeding of European royal families at the time—both Don Carlos's mother and grandmother were Portuguese princesses and his parents were double first cousins—caused numerous genetic issues, I cannot see why a lad such as this would end up in a Portuguese tomb. His parents were buried in Spain."

"There lies the mystery," Evan remarked as he poured a round of coffee for all.

I pointed to one of the articles. "And this Don Carlos had a deformed spine as well as the Hapsburg jaw?"

"He was described as 'hunchbacked and pigeon-breasted' with one leg considerably shorter than the other, but without the skeleton to examine we can't attest to those deformities," Markus said, accepting a mug. Much calmer now, the man simply looked haggard. "Nevertheless, from the skull alone I believe he's our boy, the heir-apparent to King Philip II of Spain."

"*That* Philip II of Spain?" I asked, picking up another portrait of a man wearing an intricately embossed suit of dark armor over white silk breeches and hose. Men knew how to dress in those days. "One of the kings of the Spanish Inquisition, the one who sent the Armada after Queen Elizabeth I?"

Peaches leaned over my shoulder. "He was big on making a statement with his clothes, I see."

"Royalty knew that clothes speak," I said. "This outfit says, 'I am mighty in battle, a born conqueror, and my daddy can beat your daddy any day.' That daddy would be the Holy Roman Emperor King Charles V. Watch out, mere mortals."

"And Protestants," Evan remarked. "King Philip would come to see himself as the defender of the Catholic church and owned lands on every continent of the then known world. He sought Catholic world domination."

"And this is one of the Titian portraits," I marveled. "For ten years Titian worked for the Spanish court, transcribing parts of Ovid's *Metamorphoses* into paintings. At one time he even served as the royal portraitist."

"Bet King Bling couldn't have been too happy at having a less than perfect eldest son," Peaches commented. "Those dudes preferred perfect progeny, didn't they?"

"Most parents prefer it, I suppose, but kings demanded it. What about his queen, the royal mother?" I asked.

Evan stroked his chin. "If I recall correctly, King Philip had four queens in total with all but one predeceasing him, including Carlos's mother, his first wife."

"Maria Manuela of Portugal." Rupert was reading from one of the Wiki printouts. "She gave birth to the prince in 1545 and died four days later, poor lady." He pointed to the portrait of a woman, her expressionless face gazing away into space as if anticipating her fate.

"It was not a good time to be a woman," I whispered, gazing down at the portrait, "or a physically and mentally challenged prince, for that matter."

My eyes slipped up to the X-rays. Both were as hard to distinguish as a puddle of shadows, but one was more promising than the other. Here, a ghostly image of a skull rose from the background with evenly spaced holes visible around the upper circumference and an alarming fissure that appeared to have fused together. "Is that where the supposed crown sat? It does look like it had been..."

"Bolted to the bone? Precisely. You can just see what looks to be holes," Markus said, following my gaze. "That's what started this mess—a skull that once had something appended to the bone, something that could have been a crown."

"Somebody actually banged a crown on this poor guy's head while he was still alive?" Peaches asked.

Markus sipped his coffee. "Possibly. Hard to tell whether the man was alive or dead at the time without the skull to investigate and even that might not reveal much after all this time. However, I think it's safe to say that whoever did this had a bone to pick with the prince—pun intended. First the deed was done—probably close to the time of the prince's death—and then, presumably sometime later, the skull was moved to the crypt of Capela de Soa Maria Baptista, perhaps with the crown intact."

"Possibly for safekeeping," Evan mused.

"Possibly," Markus agreed, "only someone either stole the crown at the time of the decapitation or at a later date. And then, for whatever reason, someone stole the skull earlier this week."

"But why?" I asked.

"That is the question." Markus nodded, looking away. "It seems as though somebody long ago believed the prince and his ill-gotten crown required protection."

"But what value is the skull without the crown?" Evan asked. "Crowns are precious commodities in themselves but skulls are not, unless…"

"Unless the skull had some reliquary-like value," I added.

"But why was he permanently wearing a crown in the first place?" Peaches asked.

"Yes, why? No royal personage that I am aware of was ever buried wearing a crown, let alone one pounded into their skull," I said.

"Because the crown belonged to the monarchy, not the monarch," Rupert pointed out.

"This one couldn't have belonged to the monarchy, at least not officially," I said. "Someone would have noticed it missing."

"Making *this* one a special crown," Evan remarked. "Special enough for the monarchies involved—Spain and Portugal, to begin with—not to miss it when the crown disappeared, presuming it did disappear and wasn't of some secret nature from the start."

"But lots of people must have known about its existence initially," I said. "I mean, if Prince Carlos was crowned under unusual circumstances, as in at the time of his death, and his crowned skull later moved for safekeeping, what does that say? Nothing about this is a one-person job."

"Indeed, it has all the making of a secret society," Rupert said, rubbing his hands together.

"Do we know if the prince's intact remains are at his place of burial in Spain?" Evan asked.

"We have yet to make those inquiries," Markus said. "Officially he was buried near Madrid at his father's El Escorial palace and monastery complex, which is where most of the kings and queens of Spain were interred after the mid-1500s."

"Those tombs are closely guarded and everyone will assume that they have remained undisturbed," Evan said.

"In any event, he was first and foremost a prince of Spain, regardless of his various royal affiliations," Rupert remarked. "Though no one has had reason to exhume the remains, at least not officially, I can't imagine his skull being shuffled off to Portugal with his father's knowledge."

Markus cradled his mug in his hands, as if he found the warmth comforting. "I can only say that there would have been no room for two intact bodies in the casket of Senhor Pedro Alavares Fidalgo. According to his stone effigy, Fidalgo was a portly man and would have filled the coffin with his own girth. From the best we can tell, the prince's skull was added later, with or without the crown."

"Skulls are easier to transport than full skeletons," Evan remarked.

That grim fact settled in around us as we stood sipping our coffees and considering the implications.

"And then last week, someone picked up the trail and stole the skull. How weird is that?" Peaches said, setting her mug down on the kitchen counter. "All righty, so who else knows about the true nature of the theft besides you, Markus, this poor Jose dude, the tomb robbers, and now all of us?"

I stared at the white envelope on the table. Rupert picked it up, unfolded the thick bond contents, and began to read aloud.

"*Dear Mr. Collins,*

"*Jose Balboa contacted me with details of your extraordinary find, knowing as he did that it would be of great interest to me. Now I have learned through my sources that he has been murdered and your discovery stolen. You are in extreme danger but know that you are not alone.*

"*My resources are at your disposal. Please meet me in the gardens of the Museu Nacional de Arte Antiga at 5:00 p.m. on Friday, September 12. I can be recognized as a white-haired gentleman with a cane carrying a Hieronymus Bosch carrier bag. Please make every effort to come as to do otherwise may have dire consequences.*

"*Arrive alone and, at all costs, exercise the greatest caution.*

"*A Concerned Friend*"

. . .

"A CONCERNED FRIEND?" Rupert turned to Markus. "How extraordinary."

"He knew Jose. What do you think your dead colleague may have told him?" I asked, turning to Markus.

Markus frowned and put down his mug. "I'm guessing everything, at least everything we knew up to that point. We had only taken the X-rays that afternoon and Jose must have called the man shortly after that. He was always dashing off to pick up lunch or buy us coffee so he had plenty of opportunity. It wasn't until later that evening when we were keeping watch that Jose confessed that he'd told an interested party about our discovery. Naturally, I exploded. We had agreed to keep the lid on this find and there he was disclosing the details to this friend."

"What was his defense?' Evan asked.

"He explained that this was a very powerful person who could intervene if necessary in case the skull was hijacked by another interested party. By the time the call came from his wife to return home, I was almost relieved to have him go."

"And then this supposed powerful friend slips this note under your door," Evan said.

Markus rubbed a hand over his eyes. "So bloody cloak-and-dagger."

"Do you plan on keeping the appointment tomorrow?" Rupert asked, turning to him. "Because, I must say, it seems most unwise to do so given that you are clearly in some danger."

"I don't know what to do," Markus moaned. "On one hand, I want to get to the bottom of this and, naturally, I want that skull back and to continue our work—if the authorities will permit it. But I'd rather stay alive as long as possible, thank you very much, and with the thieves threatening me, I figure I'm already as good as dead. All the interested parties must know that I've told the four of you but what alternative did I have—say nothing and go this whole thing alone? I doubt I'd even be safe back in England right now."

"Fear not, my good chap, we are on your side now and will get to the bottom of this while keeping you safe. You must stay here tonight—we have a perfectly serviceable pull-out couch—and Evan will go with you to fetch your things from your hotel in the morning," Rupert said while patting Markus on the arm. "But, indeed, you should not meet this mysterious emissary tomorrow as that would be far too risky. One of us will go in your stead."

"I will," I said with all the authority I could muster. Both Rupert and Evan looked ready to protest as Peaches gave me a thumbs-up. "As a woman, I may be less threatening considering that it's Markus that Mr. Anonymous is expecting. Peaches will be my backup."

6

Convincing the team of my suitability was not easy. It was a tiresome argument that I'd had many times with Rupert and Evan but wasn't in the mood for that night. I pointed out that brawn, height, and even MI6 training were probably not needed when meeting a "white-haired gentleman with a cane." I didn't even mention my own martial arts capabilities, of course—that would have been overkill. In all respects, I was perfect for the job.

Admittedly, I've been known to be wrong.

"Look, guys. Mr. Anonymous probably does his homework. He'll know that Markus called in assistance when things turned dicey. He'll do background checks on everyone involved. That's what I'd do, anyway," I said. "How do you think he'll react when an ex-MI6 guy shows up instead of the scientist he expects? Wouldn't that ring alarm bells? However, a female art historian is considerably less threatening."

"Unless it's you," Evan said under his breath.

"You'll be watched, Phoebe, doubtlessly followed," Rupert grumbled. "A gray-haired man carrying a Hieronymus Bosch bag does not mean that he can't be dangerous or accompanied by a posse of hidden thugs," he said sternly.

"I know that," I said.

"Who's Hieronymus Bosch?" Peaches asked. "Sounds like a rock band —Hieronymus Bosch and the Bastardly Beaters."

"I'll introduce you to him tomorrow," I replied, "just before we head for the rendezvous because," I added, turning to Rupert, "Peaches will accompany me, of course, and Evan will no doubt be close by."

That probably clinched the deal or at the very least saved me a few minutes of argument.

⁂

"There's no way I'd let you leave me behind," Peaches said later as we readied for bed in our apartment. "As your bodyguard, I intend to follow you everywhere."

She had decided to be my bodyguard some time ago and took it very seriously. "I didn't plan on leaving you behind, but we need to keep you hidden since he's expecting Markus. Besides, he said to come alone."

"How will you approach him?"

"I'll probably walk up to him and say that Markus couldn't make it."

Peaches pondered this for a moment. "That might work but you'll have to be careful. This guy probably will have people watching him, too."

"So you'll be nearby but staying out of sight."

"No worries. We'll go separately and I'll attempt to look inconspicuous."

Making a six-foot Amazon inconspicuous is not easy but there was time to worry about the details later.

Just before heading to the bedroom, Peaches paused. "Do you seriously wear that thing to sleep?"

I gazed down at my oversize van Gogh T-shirt with the self-portrait of the artist with a bandaged ear. "I picked it up in Amsterdam a million years ago and it's comfy. I wore it all through lockdown. I consider it my Covid Couture."

"Are you kidding me? I wouldn't let the tooth fairy see me in that. What happens if you have a romantic encounter? That getup will scare even the bravest of dudes away."

"Peaches, we're in a pandemic, remember? Comfort rules, not romance, even if I wasn't on a chastity diet."

She shook her head and sashayed into her bedroom. "You have to shake that attitude, girl, if you are ever going to mend that broken heart." The door clicked shut behind her.

Meanwhile, the coffee had left me wired, and while Peaches could sleep with jet fuel in her veins, I wasn't so lucky. I spent the hours between twelve and two trawling the web on my laptop. Evan had provided me with a plug-in device that shielded my search from prying eyes, and I had no doubt that prying eyes were everywhere by now.

First up, I scrutinized the available online portraits of Prince Carlos, knowing as I did that the royal painters were not likely to reveal the man's deformities and, of course, none did. Presumably, neither king nor prince wanted anything to taint the image of the crown prince of Spain and Portugal. Portraits were the visible legacy of crown and country for all the centuries to come, the ultimate selfie. However, most portraitists had caught the sulky cruelty of the boy's demeanor right down to the willful glint in the eyes.

Prince Carlos hailed from the House of Hapsburg, notorious for the inbreeding in the royal lineage. Besides the complications Rupert had noted, his maternal grandmother and paternal grandfather were siblings, as were his maternal grandfather and paternal grandfather. The boy's gene pool was an incestuous swamp all in the name of linking Europe's ruling houses. These were marriages of alliances, a crucial component of royal marriages throughout history.

One portrait by Jooris van der Straeten revealed Carlos in his early twenties wearing rich armor over a silken doublet and white hose. The stockings were designed to display a well-turned leg and artfully hid that one shortened limb. Here the artist had captured a sense of the boy's desired potential and anticipated military prowess, which was only fitting as son to a mighty king. Entitlement nearly leaped off the page in every detail, from the extravagant ceremonial armor to the rich background. Portraiture as propaganda had always been a thing.

Still, nothing I'd read or seen so far explained why someone would crown this prince, possibly posthumously, let alone steal that crown after the fact. It was all a curious boggle. Crowns were generally costly things and belonged to the monarchy, so why bury a prince with one in the first place? Furthermore, why this prince? He was so unhinged that his father finally locked him away and metaphorically threw away the key.

Next, I moved on to a summary of the five-act play by Schiller upon which the Verdi opera was based. The plot was supposedly based on Carlos's life but bore little resemblance to the boy's real existence. The essence of the tale focused on the prince's brief betrothal to Elizabeth of Valois, a beautiful young woman who his father, King Philip, ultimately decided to marry himself. That sort of thing could make any family dysfunctional.

The play had the young betrotheds shattered over the broken engagement and mostly focused on the two thrashing around being miserable. I noted the play's plot points, paying most attention to the list of characters, all of whom must have been based on real people in the court of King Philip of Spain. It was interesting to note that one other woman played a leading role: the Princess of Eboli, Ana de Mendoza, the princess with an eye patch. I vowed to check her out at some point.

When my eyes wearied of screen time, I pulled my knitting from my satchel and cast on a row. At one level, I was brewing over the missing skull, and on another, I was trying to design something for Peaches. Knitting often helped me to work out issues while calming another part of my brain, a curious paradox that knitters understand. I'd even been known to unscramble tangled thinking with only two sticks and a ball of yarn.

That night, however, that part of me trying to design something to capture my friend's Jamaican spirit hit a wall. In order to catch the complexities of her personality, I needed her power color of choice—pink. I stared at my assembled colors—black, mahogany, chartreuse, and various shades of green. No pink. I had always considered the absence of pink to be a good thing but now reconsidered. If I was to continue this project, I needed a yarn store, which wasn't on the immediate agenda.

Leaving my needles on the table, I strolled to the window and peered out across the darkened roofs of Lisbon. Grand old buildings, winking lights across the broad sinuous river, and, below, the portico of a spot-lit church with a coat of arms above the arched central window. My gaze drew down to where a figure stood on the church steps staring up at our building. I backed away to turn off the light. Seconds later, I returned, keeping well behind the curtain. The figure had gone.

Late the next morning, I returned to the research trail on my laptop, leaving Peaches to assess the neighborhood on her own after I told her about our night visitor.

"Sure you don't want to come out with me and get some air?"

"No, because I have too much research to do. I've downloaded material that I need to cram-read," I commented, my eyes not leaving the screen. "But if you need help or see anything interesting, text me."

"Sure, and I'll also let you know if I see any interesting shops open. A little wardrobe renovation wouldn't hurt you one bit," she said on her way to the door.

"I already brought one couture outfit with me, compliments of Nicolina a couple of years ago."

For some reason, my fashionable friends always wanted to give me a makeover or at least a seasonal reboot, especially my wealthy Italian one. On the other hand, I figured that if a piece cost a few thousand dollars to begin with, it should probably last longer than a couple of years. That morning I dressed in jeans and a black turtleneck, thinking to remain as inconspicuous for the day's rendezvous. "I'm good, thanks."

Peaches may or may not have rolled her eyes. "Suit yourself. When are we leaving to meet Mr. Anonymous?"

"Let's go separately and meet at 2:00 p.m. in front of the painting entitled *The Temptation of Saint Anthony*. You're going to love Hermy. Anyway, that should give us plenty of time to scope out the museum separately afterward."

"Right. I'll be back before then, anyway. I'm heading down to the church steps to see if your guy last night left any evidence." Besides reading a diet of bare-chested romance books, Peaches had taken a liking to police procedurals.

I returned to work as she exited the apartment and a few solitary hours passed with me taking notes. By noon I had breakfasted on six Portuguese custard pastries and three mugs of coffee, scanned an ebook on Emperor Charles V of Spain and his wife, Queen Isabella, plus another on his son, Philip II, as well as brushed up on my Titian. I was revisiting online portraits of Crown Prince Carlos when a text came in from Evan on my secure phone.

Have just delivered our package and am back at our lodging. Could we meet briefly to discuss our sightseeing plans?

Secure phone or not, the man wasn't taking any chances. In moments, I was knocking on the penthouse door. Evan stepped aside to let me in.

"Phoebe, I trust you slept well?" Dressed in jeans and a T-shirt in his own version of tourist attire, he looked better than breakfast, better than coffee, just plain delicious. Sometimes it was all I could do to remind myself that men were not in my viewfinder at the moment.

"I didn't actually." My gaze landed on Markus sitting on the couch staring at the floor. "Good morning, Markus."

He lifted his puffy-eyed gaze. "It's afternoon, Phoebe."

"So soon? Are you all right?" I asked.

"Not dead yet, despite appearances," he replied.

"Death by hangover is not a thing," Evan told him sternly as he locked the door behind us.

"I'm not referring to the hangover. Since you have just dosed me with some kind of concoction that might be embalming fluid, I'm hoping the cure isn't worse than the affliction."

I caught Evan's gaze and smiled. "In that case, you'll either be back to normal within the hour or preserved for antiquity. Since you're into forensics, you should appreciate that. Did you two see anything suspicious when you went out?"

"Three men are watching our building 24/7 and one tracked us all the way to Markus's hotel and back," Evan replied. "You'll be followed to your appointment this afternoon, too, so be careful. We can't even begin to determine who's working for the anonymous friend and who is part of the thief's gang."

"Do you think it is a gang?" I asked him.

"I think it must be something of that ilk," he remarked. "How extensive the group is left to be seen. Our thieves may simply have hired mercenaries to watch us every moment."

"Good afternoon, Phoebe," Rupert greeted as he shuffled out of his room in his paisley silk dressing gown. "Has Evan offered you tea?"

"No, actually, but I'm a bit overcaffeinated at the moment. I will take a tracking device if you have any lying around."

"Ah," Evan said with a nod. "I always keep an assortment of tracking devices to serve with coffee. I have some ready for your perusal right here on the table. Come, I'll show you."

The table we had used last night was now covered with various technical bits including electronic circuitry and chips plus a selection of small disc-like tracking devices. Three laptops were set up around the room and most every other available surface was covered in books or printouts. So they brought their own printer and possibly half a library plus a workshop, too? These men never traveled light.

"Impressive as usual." I turned to Evan. "Do you intend to track me while I track Mr. Anonymous?"

"Of course. Your phone will keep me apprised of your movements. I won't be far away and Rupert will be with you virtually at the apartment."

Rupert pointed to the laptop propped on the coffee table while Evan placed a tiny wafer into my palm. "Drop this into the gentleman's pocket or even into his carrier bag so you can track his movements on your phone." He paused, studying me. "You have read the itemized list of phone features I provided, I presume?"

"Yes, I skimmed them this morning. Impressive." Evan's itemized cheat sheets were so detailed they required a good hour to peruse properly, preferably with a dictionary. I had only taken a fleeting glimpse that morning.

Evan had more preparations to share including a map of the museum grounds and possible locations in the garden where he would wait. "I will never be far away," he assured me.

By the time Peaches arrived minutes later, I was in the process of refusing the gun Evan had manifested from somewhere. "Take it, please, Phoebe. You have no idea where this day will end and it's best to be prepared," he said.

"Not yet." I hated guns on principle. Even though my principles had taken a bit of a hit lately, I still wanted to avoid the inevitable. Besides, this appointment was in broad daylight and on the museum grounds. What could go wrong?

"If she won't take it, I will," Peaches said, stepping forward with her hand extended.

Lisbon's famed museum of ancient art sits on top of a hill overlooking the Rio Tejo with views across the long wide river and beyond. It was another breathtaking vista in a city so full of them that visitors rarely get to put away their phones. Though I yearned to linger under the trees and take pictures with the handful of tourists, the museum was the bigger draw. Besides, I would be meeting Mr. Anonymous in a couple of hours in that very garden, but first I needed to connect with Peaches.

But by 2:35 I was still standing transfixed before *The Temptation of Saint Anthony* by Hieronymus Bosch. It was a triptych I'd longed to view in person since my student days, but even so I didn't expect the impact of those bizarre, almost whimsical figures dancing about a phantasmagorical world to be so intense. Bosch's perverse imagery always made me smile. Every detail, from the cross-beaked bird with the funnel hat to the snout-nosed demons riding fish in the smoky air, struck me like a drug-induced dream. A horrible dreamscape of sin and temptation, yes, but wickedly humorous, too.

I checked my watch. Peaches should have been there at 2:00 p.m. but was unusually late. An art historian in a museum of ancient art is worse than a starving kid in a candy store and I was itching to see more of the museum. Where was she? We had agreed to enter the museum separately and then go our own ways. I heard a rustle behind me and swung around.

"This is..." My words died on my lips. A masked elderly man in a gray suit holding a cane in one hand and a Hieronymus Bosch shopping bag in the other had shuffled up behind me in the otherwise empty gallery.

"Good afternoon, Ms. McCabe. My apologies for startling you but I thought it best that we meet in private." Possibly in his early eighties with longish silver hair and deep blue eyes, his voice was surprisingly energetic considering the stooped frame that contained it.

"You know who I am, sir?"

"I make it a point of researching the identity of my appointments in advance, especially if they are otherwise uninvited. I am Senhor Silvio de Carvalho," he said in well-modulated English touched faintly by a Portuguese accent. "A lawyer by profession but now semiretired with perhaps too much emphasis on the 'semi' part. You may address me as Senhor Carvalho for expediency sake."

"Well, Senhor Carvalho, you are early," I said, pointing out the obvious.

"Indeed I am, but it appears that my proposed meeting in the gardens has been garnering too much attention to be safe." He waved one hand toward the door. "I have secured a more private location for our conversation. There are many spies about and I would rather not be overheard. Please be so kind as to follow me." He began shuffling toward the door.

I hesitated. This was not going the way I had planned. Maybe I should make an excuse to use the toilet in order to shoot a quick text to Peaches and Evan.

Senhor Carvalho turned as if sensing my thoughts. "It is best that you come along immediately, Ms. McCabe. Your friend will not be able to meet you as arranged."

I stared hard. "Senhor, if you've harmed Peaches—"

"Ms. Williams is currently being detained by museum security for entering the premises carrying a firearm, but I assure you that no harm will befall her as long as you cooperate. That is not a threat but a statement of fact. She will be released as soon as it is safe to do so."

"Safe for whom? I don't understand, senhor." I pulled the phone from my pocket thinking to send Evan a quick SOS.

"And I have taken the added precaution of having your devices jammed —I do hope that is the correct term—to prevent any further communication or tracking."

I stared. No signal on my phone. That anything could disable one of Evan's super-phones was shocking in itself. I narrowed my eyes at the man leaning on his cane. "What is going on here?"

"I intend to explain all but only when it's safe. Please do try to cooperate, Ms. McCabe. Given that it isn't you that I invited to meet with me today and that your companion arrived armed, I have been very obliging."

He had a point—sort of. "Dr. Collins didn't feel safe enough to come in person," I said.

"Understandable, but the more people involved in this situation, the more perilous it becomes. Already matters are spinning out of control. We are all in great danger and I urge you to cooperate. I may be in the only position to protect you for the moment."

"Protect me how?" I asked.

"Later, Ms. McCabe. Trust me when I say that we must get away from here."

What choice did I have? I pocketed my phone. "Lead the way, senhor."

I half considered alerting security but the noticeable lack of people, let alone guards, in the hallway nixed that idea. "Where is everybody? I entered a busy gallery and now the place is deserted."

"Not deserted exactly," the man said as we approached an elevator. "The museum is under emergency closure. It happens whenever suspicious activity is detected." Was he referring to Peaches...or Evan, who must be somewhere on the grounds by now?

"And yet you are permitted to walk around freely, sir?"

"As a museum patron, I am afforded that privilege, yes."

"Where are you taking me?"

"Someplace safe," he replied.

Safe was the last thing I felt at that moment. On the other hand, I found myself believing the man. Stepping into the elevator beside him, I watched as he swiped a keycard and pushed the bottommost button.

"Did you know that this museum was once a grand residence?" he asked. "The Palácio de Alvor-Pombal was built in the seventeenth century by the first Earl of Alvor and most of the museum has been constructed around the original building."

"I didn't know that," I said, watching the buttons light up at every floor. "As a patron, do the staff here work for you?"

"We cooperate, as only proper, under the circumstances. Indeed, I do wish I could take you on a special tour, but some other time, perhaps. We would need far more than a few hours to properly experience one of the foremost museums of ancient art in the world, as I am certain you are aware." I sensed he could be smiling behind his surgical mask. "Still, I am very happy that you managed to see my old friend Hieronymus."

I was too agitated for conversation. We seemed to keep going down and down. Though I counted three floors from our original level to the supposed bottom button, we were dropping even farther. Just before my anxiety bubbled to the surface, the elevator doors flew open.

"Ah, here we are. To the right and to the very end, please."

From a long hallway I could see glass rooms stretching away in both directions. Our progress was slow due to my companion's halting gait, so I could observe the lab-coated workers in the sections in passing. Paintings propped on easels, ceramics being carefully restored, and at least one large

Byzantine mosaic bathed in halogen caused me to pause. "Is that what I think it is?"

"From the reign of Justinian I—a relatively new acquisition. Pity that I cannot take you in for a closer look but we must hurry." He had pulled a phone from his pocket and was peering down at the screen. "Matters have grown more alarming by the moment."

"More alarming how?"

"Hurry, please."

At the end of the hall we were buzzed into an empty room, a combination storage room/garage with crates lining two walls and three white vans parked on the other side of a large plate-glass window. A round table sat in the center, bare except for a laptop. A flat-screen monitor with loud speakers on either side was angled toward the table from the wall ahead. Various live camera views were visible on the screen but only one interested me: the one showing Peaches pacing a small room.

"Where have you taken her?" I asked, turning to Senhor Carvalho.

"I have taken her nowhere, but museum security object to guns being brought into their facility. She is in a room down the hall where she will stay until the area has been secured and it is safe for her to leave. I have instructed the guards not to have her arrested but to contain her for now."

"Let me see her," I asked, making for the door.

"If you choose to see her now, I will be unable to share the full story of the missing skull. After today, I must stay away from Lisbon and it would be wise if you and your friends followed my example."

I swung back to him. "What's going on?" Evan must be alarmed now that my devices were dark. He'd know that something was up. "Senhor, I am just about jumping out of my skin here. You know my friends will come after me and then where will that get us?"

"Exactly, Ms. McCabe, and what will that do—get somebody harmed unnecessarily? Your man has been seen on the museum grounds and will be arrested as soon as the police arrive, providing he should live that long. Arrest by the police is perhaps the best scenario given the situation, but I am certain he would prefer neither."

"What do you mean by that?"

"I will show you. Patience, Ms. McCabe." He sat down before the laptop and removed his mask. "I cannot breathe in these blasted things."

He began tapping on the keyboard several times. Apparently frustrated that he couldn't get it to do what he wanted, he barked something in Portuguese. There had to be a microphone somewhere.

"Keep doing that and the computer may seize up in a sulk," I said.

He nodded at that. "Indeed, but I am no more patient than you are, it seems. Oh, here comes Manuel. He will wrest this beast into submission."

A masked young man dressed in a white shirt with a red insignia on the left pocket had dashed into the room, greeting me with a nod before taking over the laptop while the senhor looked on.

"Regard the screen above, Ms. McCabe," my host said. "Do you see those three men and the one over there? Manuel, are you able to zoom in on that fellow by the statue?"

The screen had switched to show eight exterior views. We were staring at the garden from cameras fixed around the museum premises. Amid the swaths of flowers and the statuary, several men appeared to be lounging on the benches or snapping photos. There was nothing casually relaxed about any of them. Tourists don't furtively study everyone around them while pretending to gaze at their phones. "Who are they?"

"Our enemies—and make no mistake, they are armed and dangerous. Explosives have been detected on one and firearms on the other three. There are several such men around the grounds."

I looked at him in alarm. "Surely they wouldn't attempt to blow up the museum?"

"Not the museum, perhaps, but certainly you and your companions, and me, of course. They will stop at nothing to keep their secret safe and have little concern for who may get hurt in the process. One man has been seen waiting in a cab near the museum. I suspect he hopes to kidnap you should you hail a cab. These men are ruthless. They have killed already and will target everyone who knows about the skull, which now includes you and your companions. We are all in great danger." He turned to Manuel and spoke in Portuguese. The man nodded and left the room.

"Ms. McCabe, the police are on their way, and your Mr. Barrows, who is currently keeping out of sight, will be arrested if our enemies do not locate him first. You must tell him to leave the premises immediately. You and I will proceed to a safe location and Ms. Williams will be escorted back to your apartment once it is safe to do so. You in particular cannot risk being seen leaving the building. I have your phone unblocked long enough for you to text your friend. Do be quick about it and do not attempt anything foolish."

I didn't hesitate. In seconds, I had the phone out of my pocket and typed out my text.

Evan, leave the grounds immediately. Place is infested with men armed with explosives and the police are on their way. Peaches and I are fine. Will contact you later.

I showed the screen to Senhor Carvalho, who nodded before I hit send.

"Now we must leave," he said, adding something in Portuguese as he pushed himself to his feet and grabbed his cane.

"But to where?"

He hobbled to the door to the garage. "I will explain on the way. Hurry, please."

Ask me if I thought that jumping into a vehicle with a strange man to drive to some undisclosed location was a good idea. On the other hand, leaving with no further information about this confounding situation seemed a worse one. Besides, I trusted Senhor Carvalho for reasons I couldn't explain and could see no good reason why he would be making this stuff up.

So I climbed into the back of a white panel van marked by the museum's red MNAA insignia with Carvalho. Manuel helped the older man up until the two of us squeezed together on flip-down seats facing the van's back door. The vehicle still bore the remains of packing-tape bits and straw so was clearly designed for transporting cargo not people. Manuel took the driver's seat and soon we were winding through the cars and empty parking spaces on an upward curve.

"Manuel says we must keep our heads down the moment...we reach street level," Carvalho said a little breathlessly. "It is doubtful that we can be seen back here but just in case."

"Tell me where we are going now, senhor. No more excuses," I said.

"I am taking you to my quinta where I hope we will be safer than here in the city, at least for a time. Your friends will be given instructions to follow us when the confusion dies down. I simply cannot risk transporting more than one of you at this time. Let us hope that the police can restore order quickly." He stared straight ahead as he spoke, both hands grasping the cane he clutched between his legs. I had the sense that the unfolding events were taking a toll on his health.

The van began zooming through the underground garage, picking up speed as the tires peeled around the corners. Senhor Carvalho and I continually slid into one another, each one trying to brace against the centrifugal force.

Manuel, clearly not trained in speeding through enclosed spaces in a panel van, muttered to himself and occasionally swore in two languages. Twice the van scraped against the wall in a screech of metal against concrete and once I feared we might smash into a parked car.

Senhor Carvalho gripped the handhold, his gaze fixed ahead, while I tried to brace myself against sliding into him every two seconds. The lack of seat belts didn't help.

I turned and saw a garage door opening ahead at last—the proverbial light at the end of the tunnel—but before I could exclaim my relief, the van shook as if the ground beneath our wheels was shattering into a thousand pieces and then something heavy struck the roof. Both of us tumbled to the floor.

7

Earthquake, it had to be an earthquake! Lisbon had suffered many catastrophic shake-ups. Was this the next big one? I imagined crumbled buildings, devastating fires, massive tsunamis...

"Stay down!" Senhor Carvalho cried as the two of us tumbled around against the back of the van. Manuel was shouting; we kept moving; and I could see sunshine blazing through the windshield.

Manuel was talking to somebody on his car phone.

"Manuel...says part of the garage was...blown up. He says stay...out of sight," the senhor said.

"The garage?" I asked, raising my head an inch off the floor. "Not an earthquake?"

"*Explosão! Explosão!*" Manuel cried.

Got it. I raised my head. Between the two front seats, I could see that we were now beetling down a busy street. I ducked back down. Several minutes of bumping along followed before I realized that my companion lay on his back breathing heavily.

"Are you hurt, senhor?" I crawled over to him. Even in the shadowy light, I could see his pallor.

"Do not worry," he panted. "Just my...old bones. I will just lie here for a...few moments to catch my breath."

Without thinking, I squeezed his hand as if he were my father since he reminded me of my own dad long passed. "Is there something I can do? Here." I took my jacket off and folded it under his head. "Manuel," I cried. "Senhor Carvalho is injured!"

Manuel called back. "Must stay down. Call for help!"

The senhor spoke to him in Portuguese, something that sounded like instructions.

"What did you just tell him to do?"

"To keep on driving...not to stop...until we reach our destination."

"But, senhor..."

He patted my arm. "No, Ms. McCabe, we are in...too much danger... but thank you for caring. My assumptions...as to your character...were correct."

And mine about him apparently. I settled my back against the wall, remaining near him while the van rolled on. "Senhor, what if my friends were hurt in the explosion? I must use my phone."

"Your phone is...free...now that we are away from the building. I confess...I tricked you. No service...on that floor. But—" he paused to catch his breath "—using it...is still...not wise."

Of course, he was afraid that we'd be tracked through my phone's GPS. Could I be absolutely certain we wouldn't once I switched it on? Evan's antitracking devices had always worked but this enemy was clearly more technologically advanced than previous versions.

"Please keep it...turned off just in case. Manuel says that...it appears Mr. Barrows escaped...safely but so...did most of the...Divinios."

"The Divinios?"

"This group of hoodlums that insist...upon wreaking such havoc...on the modern...and ancient world." He was practically gasping now. "Help me sit up, Ms. McCabe, please."

I helped him lean back against the wall, the two of us wedged side by side as the van continued rumbling along. After a few minutes, he appeared to have recovered somewhat, though his breathing remained ragged. "Emphysema," he panted. "Neglected to bring...my puffer."

Several minutes passed before I asked the questions crowding onto my tongue. "Could you explain these Divinios?"

"They call themselves...*Los Divinios* after...*derecho divino de los reyes*."

I recognized enough root syllables to figure that one out. "Oh, my God—the Divine Right of Kings? Surely that concept is dead?"

"It should be. Indeed, few royal houses...would ever abide by such a thing today...and yet a small group of men—a brotherhood, if you will—have borne...its standard for centuries. It's actually...a religious sect."

Manuel shouted something and I could feel the van slowing down. We were now bumping along what felt like a dirt road. "But these men can't seriously intend to restore a monarchy?"

"They seriously intend to restore their own power. It's always about power. We must stop now...and change vehicles," my companion said.

The door slid back. Two men in green uniforms with matching masks stood outside with Manuel behind them, his ear pressed to his phone. One man helped me and the senhor out, giving me mere seconds to squint around at the surroundings. Nothing but bare rock and rough scrabble with Lisbon just visible over a bend far below. A narrow road wound through a hilly forest ahead. I turned back to see Senhor Carvalho shaking Manuel's hand beside the battered museum van while the other men waited by the glossy truck.

"Good luck, senhorita." Manuel waved to me.

"Thanks, Manuel. If you see my friends, please tell them I'm all right."

"Yes, I will."

Moments later, we were helped up a loading platform and into the back of a waiting truck, this one a deep forest green with flourishing gold signage to match the men's uniforms.

Now Senhor Carvalho and I sat opposite one another on the truck floor amid packaged laundry with racks of clear-plastic-covered clothes dangling from overhead. Between the cab and cargo area, a row of suits hung from a rack, letting in very little light and no opportunity for me to talk to the men even if I wanted to. Getaway by laundry truck.

"Our enemies will...soon pick up our trail." My companion sighed and rested his head against the wall as the vehicle rumbled forward. "They know where I live—have always known. The explosion caused more disruption...than they must have anticipated...but I have no doubt they will...come for us."

"And then?" I asked.

"And then we will have to...work out another plan, Ms. McCabe," he said grimly, closing his eyes.

"Please call me Phoebe. After all, we are sharing the back of a laundry truck."

He smiled at that. "Phoebe, then." He did not offer to have me call him by his first name and doing so would have seemed all wrong to me somehow.

But he was fading fast. Rather than press him further about the Divinios, I swallowed my questions and focused on the clothes swaying above me on padded hangers.

Even in the half-light I could see deep jewel-toned velvets, shimmering silks in every hue, and gentlemen's suits in various textures and fibers. I longed to run my hand over those naps and silken folds, me being a shameless textile hedonist. In times of anxiety, I took comfort in soft wear. I snaked a hand up inside the plastic wrap and flipped a jacket label—Armani. All righty, then.

We bumped along for several minutes before the wheels hit smooth pavement. Now I found myself sliding inches toward the rear door. Senhor Carvalho with his head lolling to one side was listing, too. I braced myself against the door to prevent him toppling over. I desperately hoped that he was only dozing and hadn't lost consciousness.

I so wanted to use my phone to ensure that everyone was all right back in Lisbon, but the phone remained shoved deep into my pocket. It felt like treason not to trust Evan's technical prowess enough to fear tracking.

I wasn't certain how long we traveled but it seemed far too long on a road too steep, especially with Senhor Carvalho's alarming pallor and shallow breathing. Finally the truck lurched to a halt. I heard shouting and the back doors flew open followed by a blast of crisp cool air. I squinted against the shards of sudden light. "Help me, please. Senhor Carvalho is not well," I cried.

Two men and one woman appeared from somewhere, calling in Portuguese, and soon I was standing in a tiny graveled courtyard watching as the men helped Senhor Carvalho toward an arched doorway, the woman dashing beside them murmuring something.

We had arrived in a deep forested area with a grand turreted structure rising overhead, a mini yellow castle with balconies hanging over arched windows and an abundance of ornate rococo details. I gaped. This was the quinta—with turrets?

The doors of the laundry truck slammed shut. Soon the vehicle's tires spat up the gravel as it zoomed down the drive. Out of sight, a gate clanged shut, leaving me alone.

It felt as though I'd just been dropped into the midst of a Walt Disney special minus the remote control. Nothing about this mini castle looked old or worn or otherwise real. The whole experience struck me as more akin to somebody's idea of a fairy tale.

A brilliant sunset blazed over top of the trees, gilding the surrounding gardens as my feet crunched across the gravel toward the doorway. I tried the brass knob—locked. I knocked. No answer. Probably in the trauma of the ailing senhor, I had simply been forgotten. Visions of Alice in Wonderland crowded into my head.

Fine, so I'd just try the front door. So says a woman completely unaware of how large a country estate can be, let alone exactly which end was which.

I trod along what I took to be a side path beside a wall-like hedge heading in the direction from which we had arrived. At least, I could just see the lane the truck had taken before disappearing into the woods and that had to mean something. Besides, I caught glimpses of lights through the trees. Was that toward the front?

Obviously not, because soon I was surrounded by foliage so thick I could hardly make out anything in the fading light. Totally turned around, I found myself wandering into the garden, or one of them. Banks of flowers swayed in the golden light and a fountain tinkled somewhere out of sight.

I needed to stick to a path because paths are supposed to lead somewhere good, or that was the theory. But there were paths branching in every direction. Do I choose the one going down or the one heading up, to the left or to the right?

Choosing left for no other reason than I liked the look of the marble bench marking the fork, I ended descending into a wooded grove where mist snaked low against the ground. A moss-covered well tangled in ivy added to the atmospheric interlude, perfect for something out of the

Brothers Grimm. Backtracking, I arrived more or less where I started, only nothing looked the same.

Alarmed, I wandered into a circular rose garden and inhaled the fragrant blooms as a kind of consolation prize for the hopelessly lost. Seconds later, I emerged beside a huge stepped fountain with a bronze dragon spewing water into a bowl big enough for a small swimming party. In desperation, I climbed the fountain steps to get a lay of the land. There, several feet aboveground, I could finally see the house glowing in a mass of lights to my right—not too far away actually, if I could only figure out how to get there.

But I wasn't expecting the fountain behind me to burst into a sudden foam-spitting light show. I may have yelped as the dragon above turned from green to orange while spewing colored water from his jaws, splashing into the pool and onto me. The entire garden blazed with artful light shows like Vegas crossed with the Tivoli fountain. Okay, so maybe I was getting cranky. The hell with dragons, anyway.

Moving away from the spray, I pulled out my phone, thinking to activate my geo-positioning device, but gazing at the blank screen sobered me. Did I really want these Divinios or whoever the hell they were to track me into fairyland? I shoved the phone back into my pocket just as I heard shouting coming beyond the botanical maze.

"Over here!" I called. "By the dragon!"

The dragon kept me company in its fashion as I leaned against the marble pool watching the flashlights bob through the dusk toward me. Occasionally, I'd gaze up at a particularly spectacular sparkly spew as the giant reptile spat colored water into the pool.

A few minutes later, two masked men and a little girl wearing a glittery pink kitten face mask arrived.

"We are most sorry, Ms. McCabe," an older man said in thickly accented English from the bottom of the steps. "We lost you. We look everywhere but gone!"

"But do not worry because we have found you now!" the little girl called up.

"It's all right," I said, stepping down. "I should have stayed where I was put."

But then one of the men pulled a gun.

"Whoa!" I said, putting up my hands.

"My apologies, senhorita," the man said. "This for temperature. Not a gun. Sorry to alarm. Please step down."

"Oh, right." I climbed down the rest of the stairs and leaned forward while he aimed the laser thermometer at my forehead. It was one of those weird Covid moments worth tucking away along with all the others. By now I had quite a collection.

"You are cleared to come into the house," he said. My welcoming party removed their masks except for the child, who still wore her kitten variety.

"Oh, good." Because I had no idea what I would do if they refused.

"Hello." A little dark-haired girl grinned up at me, her heart-shaped face and wide brown eyes beaming with delight. "I am Ana Marie Carvalho."

No older than seven or eight and dressed in perfect girlie clothes—a lovely pink crinoline skirt and matching velvet jacket—she looked ready for a birthday party. "This is Senhor Abreu and Senhor Afonso. They work for my grandpapa, and behind you is Draggy, my dragon. Grandpapa gave him to me for my seventh birthday. Mama allowed me to come welcome you."

The short-haired older fellow who had taken my temperature and his young black companion both wore identical navy shirts and trousers and seemed otherwise delighted to see me, too. Each shook my hand in turn, smiling all the while. It seemed that, in their minds at least, once my temperature had been determined as normal, so did everything else.

"Very pleased to meet you, Ms. McCabe. I hope Draggy did not wet you," Senhor Afonso, the younger man, said.

"Only a little. Hi, Ana Marie, Senhors Abreu and Afonso," I greeted. "I'm very relieved that you found me since I was completely lost. Sorry for causing you any trouble. Why don't you call me Phoebe?"

The child tugged my jacket. "I am not sure my mama will let us call you Phoebe but please come now. We will be late for dinner. We are dining early tonight because I am allowed to join you. My bedtime is usually at eight o'clock, which is too early."

"Hush, Ana Marie—do not pester the poor lady," Senhor Alfonso scolded in a tone that implied that nothing this child did could ever shake his patience.

I grinned. "I am not pestered, believe me. In fact, I am totally charmed."

The child took my hand and tugged me down the walk toward the house, or in the opposite direction of the house actually. "But this place is so confusing."

"My grandpapa says it is supposed to confuse. It is a maze. He calls it a big adventure but I know the way. My grandpapa and all the grandpapas before him designed the grounds like a fairyland. I love it best at night because it is magical. Sometimes Mama will let me go out to see all the fountains but not so much anymore, not since... Here, we will take a shortcut."

"The grounds were once open to the public," Senhor Afonso said, trudging behind, "but now we keep the gates locked."

I assumed that was related to Covid but had no opportunity to ask because Ana Marie ran on. Soon I was being led through spotlit hedgy tunnels, beside reflecting pools that captured the twilight glow, past a topiary pruned like a rearing unicorn, and finally through another arched door that led into a flagstone patio by the house. A flashing light panel on the wall indicated a security system, which one of the men tapped in passing. The door clanged shut behind us.

"Is this the front?" I asked.

"No, the front is waaaay over there." Ana Marie pointed roughly to the left. "Mama says I am to take you straight to your room so you can change for dinner and have a bath." She giggled. "I should have said to have a bath and then change for dinner. Do you think my English good?"

"I think your English is amazing," I told her as she took me down back hallways leading to kitchens and laundry rooms and maybe a larder. The place was a warren of rooms. "But I don't have a change of clothes."

"Mama or Auntie Leonor will find you something. She leaves tomorrow but has lots of pretty dresses. I was allowed to choose one of my own so I could wear it to dinner tonight—see?"

"It's beautiful!"

"Thank you. It is one of my favorites but I never wear it because we never have fancy dinners anymore. You will love the dresses my mama picked out for you."

If Mama had been the woman running behind Senhor Carvalho when we arrived, I doubted she'd have anything to fit. I was of the curvy persuasion whereas that woman was model lean. Still, here I was in a fairy-tale castle about to dress for a formal dinner. After months of takeout and frozen dinners in my flat, I may as well have fallen into a magic kingdom.

A woman in a navy maid's uniform smiled shyly and stepped aside as we passed. No masks worn here, I noted. This must be a house bubble.

"Mama would not be pleased that I take you this way but it is much faster!"

Ana Marie let go of my hand and bolted up a curving staircase that obviously curled up inside one of the towers. I hurried after her as we climbed around and around the stone column.

"Ana Marie, is your grandfather all right?" I puffed. "I meant to ask you sooner but I became distracted."

I heard the footsteps falter. "Mama says he needs to rest more. Hurry, three more floors!"

By the time I reached the top, I was secretly cursing every exercise video I skipped during lockdown, and there'd been plenty.

"Here we are!" Ana Marie squealed in delight. "Mama has given you a turret room just like I asked because it is designed for princesses! This room will be mine someday but for now Mama wants to keep me close to her." She spun around on her patent-leather shoes, a butterfly taking flight.

I gazed around the half-circular room with three arched windows, a grand four-poster bed, and a fire burning in the grate. Lamps glowed on the side tables and a light had been left on in the small adjoining bathroom. Had I been Ana Marie's age, I would have leapt on top of that blue velvet counterpane and spread myself out like a snow angel.

Instead, I pulled away the window curtains. As expected, the room had a commanding view, with the garden light fantasy spreading out in all directions below. Fountains, circular shapes marked out in colored spotlights, huge topiaries casting strange shadows on the lawns, and something that looked like a miniature castle outlined in flashing pink were alight. From above it looked like a cross between a wonderland and a miniature golf park.

"I used to go out and play for a half hour every night in the lighted garden but not now," a small voice said behind me. "Now I am only allowed to look through the window but it is not the same. None of the grown-ups will take me, but I miss seeing Draggy with all his sparking water breath and my own little castle playroom. I miss my daddy more. I know he is hiding out there somewhere and I would go find him, only Mama will not permit me."

My heart caught in my throat. I turned to the child. "Why do you think that your daddy is hiding?"

Big tear-filled eyes looked up at me. "Grandpapa says he disappeared. I heard the adults talking. He went into the gardens but did not return. They told me that he never would come back and that I must wait for him in heaven. That was six months and two days ago and I think heaven is too long a wait."

I knelt down before the child and brought her closer. "I'm so sorry to hear about your daddy, Ana Marie. That must make you very sad."

And then she hugged me, sobbing into my shoulder while I hugged her back, feeling all the profound sadness that comes with trying to console a child facing infinite loss.

"I know all the secret paths to everywhere..." she said through her tears. "I could find him, I could! He's hiding from the bad ones. Nobody believes me."

What do you say to a grieving child? Do you distract her? I stood up and tried to smile. "Maybe you could show me around the gardens tomorrow. Are you allowed to go out in the daytime?"

She nodded. "As long as I am with a trusted adult. You could go with me, I think, but I want to go now."

"Maybe not now." I turned back to the window. "Come, point out where all your favorite places are."

"The lights will turn off in one minute." She held up her sparkly pink phone. "Grandpapa makes them to go off at 7:30." And before my eyes the garden was doused in absolute darkness. When I turned back to Ana Marie, the child was gazing up at me with the kind of haunted expression no child should wear.

"There are evil creatures in the garden now," she whispered. "They will snatch you away, but I am not afraid." And then her phone beeped as a text lit the screen. "Mama wants to know if you like the dresses. Come, they are on your bed."

Taking my hand, she led me to a carved four-poster bed where a selection of gowns had been laid out on the deep ultramarine velvet bedspread.

"Mama says I am to leave you now but that someone will come for you in an hour for dinner—probably Suzanna or Alma." Ana Marie was reading a text on her phone. "She says that she is sorry not to greet you in person but she was with Grandpapa. Oh, here, she will tell you herself." She passed me her phone.

I gazed down at the screen at a woman of about my age. Dark hair formed a glossy bob around a long angular face graced by magnificent cheekbones, all the elements creating a singularly beautiful woman.

"Hello, Ms. McCabe. Welcome to Sintra." The accent was barely noticeable. "I am Adriana Carvalho and I apologize for leaving you wandering in the dark only to then place you in the care of my chatty daughter. My lack of hospitality was due to my concern over Papa Carvalho. He does not follow his doctor's instructions, let alone mine."

"I totally understand. Is he all right?"

"Much improved, thank you. It is his emphysema. He is not to get excited or to overexert himself but he does too much of both. For now he is resting but will see you later."

"Please don't feel the need to apologize for leaving me with this charming little princess here."

Adriana smiled. "Princess Whirling Dervish?"

Ana Marie was now investigating the clothing options on the bed but paused long enough to shoot me a grin. "Mama was going to send you up with Auntie Leonor but she cannot move as fast as me."

"Ana Marie, hush! Do not be rude. My daughter is half princess, half indomitable spirit," Adriana laughed. "We will talk more over supper soon. Goodbye for now. And, Ana Marie, leave our guest in peace. She has had a difficult day."

I returned the phone to the child.

"Did you have a difficult day?" the girl asked, looking up at me with those enormous eyes. "I am very sorry to hear that. Mama says I should never forget that others hurt, too. Today I studied history, maths, and geography and it was hard. Mama says that I am a good student but too easily distracted. Will you go into the gardens with me?"

"Of course I will. Maybe tomorrow during the day."

She nodded. "I had better go now but I will see you at supper. We eat tonight at the big table." And with that the little whirlwind ran to the door, pausing to add, "I like the maroon one best. It is the color of the chocolate cosmos in the garden—my favorite flowers because they smell so chocolatey and my daddy planted them. My tutor says I am very good with English but must improve my maths. Bye for now." The door shut, leaving me alone in fairyland once again.

◈

My heart ached for that child. I swallowed hard and strode to the window again to pull back the curtains. So this was Sintra. We were high up in a wooded mountain with lights in the hollows along with what looked to be other grand residences and maybe even a real castle in the distance. Really, a fairyland by any other name, despite the dark ominous garden brooding below or the missing father or the Divine Right of Kings...

Turning away, I stroked the clothes on the bed, three outfits still bearing forest-green-and-gold dry-cleaning tags dangling from the labels. Would I or would I not fit into the long burgundy silk gown with the coordinating velvet jacket, Ana Marie's favorite, or the deep gold satin gown with the elaborate neckline beading, or—heaven forbid—the turquoise silk muumuu? They all looked to be roughly a size fourteen bordering on twelve, providing one is minus hips or a bodacious bust. The muumuu was more like a satin tent.

I took a pile of fluffy towels into the blue-and-white tiled bathroom and poured a tub of scented bubbles. Once soaking, I studied the intricate harbor panel of tiles above my head, entranced by the ships laced with fanciful seashells and ornate motifs that proved why Portugal was famous for its tile work.

At the same time, I wondered what I had fallen into besides hot water, and how Evan, Peaches, Rupert, and Markus were faring. It seemed so wrong that I was steeping in luxury while they were, what—fretting over me? Escaping an explosion with their necks barely kept intact? At least I had been assured that they were all fine, but they still deserved to hear from me, no matter what. For that, I'd request the use of a landline.

And the Divine Right of Kings in the twenty-first century? Most monarchies were no more than figureheads and many more had been replaced by dictators and republics of all stripes. Still, I was always struck by how little I knew about the world and how the knots I stumbled across in history and art always dumbfounded me as I tried to pick them free.

When I emerged minutes later and tried on all my clothing options, the burgundy ensemble won. Yes, it was too tight across the bust and sitting would likely provoke extreme seam stress but the kimono-style jacket hid the result of too many Covid cookies. Besides, the silk and velvet apparently matched a chocolate cosmos somewhere in the garden, which was good enough for me. Should I or should I not wear a mask? I decided to bring it just in case.

I was still scrunching my curls dry as I walked behind the young uniformed woman who had arrived to accompany me to the dining room. We descended a stairway hung with large portraits, some modern, some possibly ancestral, on a carpet runner I recognized as late-nineteenth-century Persian of at least fifty knots per inch. My fingers itched to check but that would be rude.

The house opened up around me in marble, paintings and sculptures, more lush carpets, and potted plants. An orange tree grew in a conservatory glimpsed in passing and everywhere dark carved wood furniture lined the eggshell-white walls. I could happily linger over every detail, study the art, the carpets, even the chairs, but I was led into a large domed dining room tiled in more intricate scenes that teased my eyes all over again.

Two women rose from the small sitting area next to the fire as Ana Marie ran toward me clapping her hands. "Oh, Mama, look at Phoebe! Doesn't she look like the queen of the cosmos? And, Auntie Leonor, your dress looks so beautiful with her red hair, just as you said it would!"

Oh, yes, I did adore that child.

Soon I was flanked by the women, thanking each for their hospitality while learning that they were sisters staying at the quinta off and on since the beginning of the quarantine but that Leonor was leaving early the next morning. Adriana was a teacher and Leonor a lawyer, both relieved to realize that, thanks to the pandemic, working from home was possible with today's technology.

"However, I must return to my own home in Lisbon tomorrow," Leonor said.

"Oh, please stay with us, Auntie Leonor, please, please!" Ana Marie begged. "Uncle Gaspar can come here, too."

Leonor placed her hand on the child's head. "No, my princess, I must return to my own life as I have explained many times, but I will visit again soon and we can always Skype."

"It is not the same," the child said, lowering her head.

"Nevertheless, it is how things must be." She returned her gaze to mine and smiled. "In law it is mostly research and documentation unless there is a trial," she explained. "Now that lockdown lifts, the courts have much catching up to do and I am needed in Lisbon."

Eventually they commented on their gowns, each beautifully made custom silk and velvets designed by a seamstress in Lisbon, they said. Isabella wore a column of beaded navy satin and her sister a lovely velvet skirt and tunic the color of fine claret. They didn't always dine so formally, they assured me. "This is the first time we've been out of our leggings for weeks," Adriana said. "We decided to put on the dog, as you say in English, because at last we have a guest."

"And guests are always a gift, my grandpapa says," Ana Marie piped up.

Their English was excellent, probably better than mine because they spoke with the precision often gained among those for whom English is a second language. They ran an English household in order to help Ana Marie's education now that she was being homeschooled, but Adriana assured me that this in no way undermined their passion for Portuguese. "It is a fascinating and dynamic language," Leonor agreed, "with a story behind every consonant."

"I believe it," I said. "After all, Portugal is the nation of explorers and mariners. How can your language be anything but dynamic?"

"The Portuguese are not a boastful people," Adriana said, "but we are no less proud of our heritage."

By the time we took our seats at the long polished dinner table ladened with bowls of early autumn flowers, we were on a first-name basis except for Ana Marie, whose mother insisted she address me as Ms. McCabe.

I fell into the rhythm of the conversation, chatting about the impact the virus had on our lives and what silver linings lay behind this particular toxic cloud. I forgot how much energy comes from socializing with new friends and how badly I had missed it.

"When quarantine first began, everyone withdrew to their country houses, if they were lucky to have them. We consider ourselves blessed that Papa Carvalho kindly wished that my sister and our extended families join him here. It is not as if he was crushed for space," Adriana remarked, waving a hand around at the huge room.

"We had cousins staying with us, too, but they have returned to Lisbon now," Ana Marie offered.

"Yes, your uncle and cousins have returned to the city and we miss them all, don't we, Ana Marie?" Adriana said, smiling at her daughter.

"My husband is back to traveling for business," Leonor said, "and we thought it would be lonely for Ana Marie, Adriana, and Senhor Carvalho to be rattling around this huge house by themselves so I remained here a bit longer. Now it is time I left."

An exchange of glances passed between the sisters. Still there had been no mention of Ana Marie's father and I decided not to ask questions for the moment.

Sipping a delicious pureed vegetable soup, I smiled. "And suddenly a stranger falls into your lap from the back of a laundry truck."

Lenore laughed. "Yes, exactly. You cannot trust deliveries these days."

"And then Alice stepped into a fairyland filled with dragons and mazes," I added.

"*Alice in Wonderland* is one of my favorites!" Ana Marie giggled. "I have a Mad Hatter tea party at the end of the south lawn!"

"All designed by indulgent parents based on their children's favorite stories over the generations," Leonor added. "It was Senhor Carvalho who added the lights five years ago."

"A bit over the top, as they say, but children adore it. The garden used to be called the Story Garden in English and it had been open to the public for a few weeks each year. Now we keep the gates closed always," Adriana said, eyes fixed on her plate.

"Because the evil ones came and took Daddy away. Draggy tried to protect him," Ana Marie whispered, suddenly serious. "Maybe he is keeping him safe underneath his wing?"

Adriana leaned over and patted her daughter's knee. "Hush, darling, and please take the bread to our guest."

The child complied, holding the basket in both hands as she made her way carefully to me, eyes welling.

"Thank you, Ana Marie. You are a very gracious host," I told her, taking a roll.

The child's gaze met mine. "Can you help us, Phoebe—sorry, Ms. McCabe? Will you help us?"

"Of course!" It was an automatic response but no less heartfelt.

"Ana Marie, sit back down, please," Adriana said. "Know that you are welcome here, Phoebe, but it may be best that you leave with Leonor tomorrow morning."

"Mama, no!"

"Hush, Ana Marie, and you may return to your seat and finish your supper."

The child complied and picked up her spoon.

"I'll stay, if you don't mind," I said. "My friends and I came to Portugal to help." Once I found out exactly what matter I was helping, that is. What did this family have to do with the Divine Right of Kings? What happened to Ana Marie's father?

"You will be relieved to know that plans are in place to bring your friends here tonight," Leonor told me. "They arrive and I leave but that is how it goes. There you have it."

I almost sputtered into my soup. "Really? Oh, that's wonderful—I mean about them coming! I have been so worried and was going to request the use of your landline so I could contact them."

"Which friends?" Ana Marie asked, pausing from her careful soup-sipping. "I hardly ever see my friends now."

"Ms. McCabe's friends, and you will be able to see yours soon enough, I hope. We will have more company briefly in the meantime. Won't that be fun? They will be leaving shortly, too. Now eat your supper," her mother told her. "Your bedtime is coming soon." She turned to me. "As your friends are currently on their way, perhaps it's best to wait."

"Senhor Carvalho keeps their passage secret," Leonor remarked. "There are so many secrets here."

"Secret from who?" Ana Marie asked.

"It is from *whom*, darling, not *who*, and you are slurping again. Please concentrate on eating and not on the adults' conversation for now," her mother scolded.

Ana Marie frowned and returned to her dinner but I sensed her ears were practically vibrating.

It was difficult to know how much to say in front of the child so I decided to stick to something safe. "Is Senhor Carvalho your father, Adriana?"

"No," she said with a small smile, "but we are all family just the same."

Now I was totally confused. Adriana called Senhor Carvalho "papa" and Ana Marie referred to him as "grandpapa" but Leonor had used the formal signatory at least once. That could mean that Ana Marie's missing father was Senhor Carvalho's son.

The main dish of spicy roast chicken and vegetables arrived, after which followed a scrumptious rice pudding so creamy I felt I could sail away on a cloud of vanilla. Conversation remained on neutral ground but I was still eager to get answers, though it seemed that nobody there was prepared to give them.

"Forgive me, Phoebe," Adriana said at last, "but it is time I took Princess Dervish to bed and read her a story. Please excuse me. I will leave you in the excellent care of my sister and hope to see you later tonight or tomorrow."

I said my good-nights and watched as the mother strode hand-in-hand with her daughter toward the door, Ana Marie waving at me as they went.

"Leonor, what happened to Ana Marie's father?" I asked as soon as we were alone.

The woman set her glass down and turned to me with her large dark eyes luminous in the candlelight. "I'll put it simply: they killed him, right here on the grounds—threw him to his death at the bottom of an ancient well. We have yet to find his body as the ground is too unstable to continue the search. Still, we know he is gone. The Divinios, or whatever those monsters call themselves, may kill every last one of us before they are done. That is one of the reasons why my husband refuses to return here and why I have been called home."

8

When Leonor escorted me to Senhor Carvalho's quarters later, I had learned little more except that the Divinios had somehow caused her brother-in-law's death. That was only the beginning, she assured me. The rest of their diabolical affinities were far worse but she claimed that was not her story to tell.

"If I could take my sister and Ana Marie away from this accursed place, I would, but that's not to be. Adriana refuses to leave and there's some question whether they would even let her go."

"They let her? What do you mean by that?"

She shook her head. "I will leave Senhor Carvalho to give you the full history. Adriana and I must ensure that your friends' rooms are ready for their arrival and I wish to spend time with them while I can. I will say goodbye here and wish you all the best of luck. Just knock and enter. He is waiting." With that she left me standing in front of a thick rosewood-and-ivory inlaid door.

I knocked and stepped into a marble vestibule large enough to serve as a foyer of a separate residence. In fact, it was so large that I thought at first that this had to be the library only minus the books.

"Phoebe, please keep walking," I heard the senhor call.

So I continued on into a huge semicircular room hung with thick gold velvet curtains on tall windows and walled with books. For a moment all I could do was stare. It was as if I had been dropped into the library of an ancient mariner with antique maps framed about the walls, a magnificent floor-mounted celestial globe dating from at least the 1500s, various brass navigational instruments in glass cases, and even a glinting sword suspended on one wood-paneled wall. But then my gaze swerved to the right and stopped.

Maybe I even gasped. A large portrait of a magnificent woman in a red velvet gown hung on the wall to my right. I recognized it as the famous painting of Isabella of Portugal painted by Tiziano Vecellio—Titian, in other words—that supposedly hung in the Prado Museum in Madrid. So, why was it here?

I stepped closer. Though I certainly didn't have that portrait memorized in such detail that I could recognize every aspect, something about this one seemed off. The Venetian red in the gown seemed too bright, for one thing. The background's ruby velvet curtains almost competed for attention with the subject herself, and yet how many portraits of Isabella of Portugal could there be?

"I thought you would be interested," Senhor Carvalho said, gazing at me from a leather chair by the fire, "but if that one strikes you so deeply, consider the other."

He was indicating the full-length painting of the empress holding court over the fireplace. Here the queen was portrayed standing, her gaze half-turned toward the viewer. Though she wore the same deep Venetian red gold-threaded velvet gown as seen in the first, a shade that perfectly picked up the henna tones of her hair, this fabric seemed real enough to touch.

Fine washes of paint had been layered on to create the richness of the fabric and to enhance depth. Creamy satin poured down under the sleeves in a glossy ivory color with such clarity I could almost feel the fabric gliding through my fingers. In one hand she held a rosary with her index finger pointing to the floor on her right and in the other a small book, probably a Bible.

Masterfully painted not only in terms of detail but of lighting, the subject emerged from the background in a halo of magnificence as befitting her station. After all, she had been the most powerful woman of the then known world—Holy Roman Empress, Queen Consort of Spain and

Portugal, Germany, and Italy, plus Duchess of Burgundy—all through her marriage to Emperor Charles V. She was known as just, wise, and hardworking as well as beautiful. She also happened to be Prince Carlos's grandmother, though she had died many years before he was born.

"But this one is by Titian," I said, unable to contain myself, "and the other one should be by Titian but isn't!"

My host chuckled. "Ah, yes. I forgot that you were an art historian, and one with an expert eye, it seems. You are correct, at least in part. The one on the left that should have been a Titian was first painted by Seisenegger in 1531, but Isabella's husband, Emperor Charles, was not happy with the results. He commissioned Titian to redo the painting in 1534, the one which hangs in the Prado today. This is the cast-off, so to speak, but nevertheless an original, though not by the master himself."

"So Titian copied and improved upon the first?"

He stifled a cough and continued. "Yes, indeed. One wouldn't think the master a copyist but a commission is a commission. The one you stand before now is by Titian, you are quite right there, and painted after her death. Very few people know of its existence as it has been in my family for centuries, hidden away here as it were. There is an old tale that to release it to the world would bring destruction onto the family. Old lineages are filled with such stories."

I turned to my host so excited that I forgot my manners. "But how did your ancestors manage to secure two royal portraits, one of them by Titian?" I asked.

"The story goes that the empress herself requested that her likeness be sent back to her family in Portugal after her death as she knew that she would never return in person. These two paintings were to be her visitation by proxy, you might say. The Seisenegger arrived in 1535 and the Titian many years after her death in 1568."

"The same year Don Carlos died," I whispered, leaning closer to the masterpiece. Because it hung too far over my head with my nose ending more or less at the queen's feet, I could see very little close-up. Still, it seemed that a small corner of the work appeared more vibrant than the rest, as if centuries of varnish and candle smoke had been carefully wiped away.

"You've recently begun restoration but stopped," I remarked, peering closer at the original depth and beauty of the master's brushstrokes hidden beneath.

A painting of this age would be nearly buried alive under grime unless properly restored. If it was this beautiful under that sludge, I could only imagine how it would glow once fully revealed.

"True. I had a conservator in residence before the pandemic but she had only just begun to work before quarantine forced her to stop. She later caught the virus and has now passed, I am sorry to say. A tragedy as she was very gifted. Perhaps I am guilty of saving the best until last but dear Senhora Belo was quite close to tears when she began to work on what she claimed was her first master artist. I am only sorry she was unable to finish it. She had a little workshop set up by the elevator."

The painting hung over the fireplace stretched a good five feet above me, a life-size portrait. I stepped back, pulling out my iPhone to magnify the surface while roaming the camera from left to right over my head. Evan's super-magnification feature was impressive but not perfect considering that I longed to investigate with intense scrutiny. No time for that now.

"Do you mind if I take pictures?"

"Not at all."

Once that was done, I turned to my host. "Senhor Carvalho, please put me out of my misery. Is your relation to this Divine Right of Kings because Isabella of Portugal is your ancestor? Is that what's going on here?"

He leaned forward on his cane, eyes twinkling. "Dear Phoebe, you remind me of my granddaughter—quick to reach conclusions, eager to find answers, and brimming with passionate interest. Unfortunately, my answer to your question is both yes and no. Yes, my family can trace our lineage back to the House of Aviz, but no, that is not why I am involved in the Divinios matter, or at least not directly."

I shook my head. "I don't understand."

He got slowly to his feet, gripped his cane, and joined me before the empress. "She is indeed my hallowed ancestor but I have no direct claim to the Portuguese throne even if such a thing still existed. We are, after all, a republic, and rightly so. No, my involvement stems from the property this quinta is built upon, the very earth under my feet, as it were."

"But this house doesn't look old," I said.

"And it isn't, having been built in the early 1800s. After the big earthquake of 1755, most of the castles and quintas in the area were left in shambles and the residences seen around here were built upon the ruins. However, the land predates all of that. Sintra has been held in reverence by the Romans, the Templars, the Moors... It was known to be the site of many religious orders as well as renowned as a mythical and mysterious area with its own unique power. Though little aboveground remains standing, it is what lies below that drew me into the crosshairs of the Divinios brotherhood."

"But..." Really, at that point I was so lost I didn't know what to say. "Please just give me the short version, senhor."

He chuckled. "Let me try. Come, Ms. McCabe, I will show you something."

I followed him over to a bookstand where he tapped his finger on a large dictionary-size book that lay open to photographic plates of King Philip of Spain opposite his firstborn son, Don Carlos. "The Divine Right of Kings is a concept as old as time itself. Emperor Charles believed in it, as did his son, King Philip, seen here, and all the rulers going back far through recorded time, including the ancient Egyptians. Believing that the king was a manifestation of God on earth is not new."

"Pardon me for interrupting but the short version, please," I urged. "I understand all that. Who are the Divinios and what do they have to do with the stolen skull that may have once worn a crown?"

"Very well, then, the story in a nutshell: the Divinios believe that a king will lead the world back to a holier earth free of dissidents and dangerous individualism unified under one God and one religion. They believe that such a king will herald the Second Coming, Christ's corporal chief-in-arms to His spiritual being, as it were, and that all sacrifices made in his name are justified."

A chill ran down my spine. "Are you saying that these Divinios hope to start another 'holy war'?" I put the term in air quotes.

"They believe they already have. The proof to them is in all the catastrophes occurring on earth at this very moment, some of which they believe themselves directly responsible for, though I suspect they are taking credit for much of what has occurred naturally."

"But that's crazy!"

"Is it? Does what we consider to be reality make more sense?" My host was studying me; grooves of fatigue dug deeply around his face, yet the eyes remained vividly alive.

"Okay," I whispered. "I get your point: one person's crazy is another person's ideology."

"Precisely so. Bred deep into the psyche by centuries of ritual, patterns of belief become accepted truth and are potent enough to drive seemingly sane individuals to do what might be otherwise considered bizarre. Religion is the proof. Catholicism, my religion, believes that a saint's bones hold powerful magic while another religion believes it sacrilege to kill a cow. Religion and ritual have nothing to do with rational thought."

"And these Divinios believe in what rituals exactly?"

"We don't know the details. They certainly consider themselves Catholic Christians. We know that the brotherhood began during the rule of Emperor Charles and continued forming during the reign of his son, Philip. The Spanish Inquisition played a part. Whether Philip knew of the cult's existence is not known but I hardly think he could remain unaware. Unfortunately, he was never at court for very long at one time. Furthermore, it seems that the cult has been holding secret ceremonies in Sintra and in other locations in Spain ever since. We also know that a crown was created for the sole purpose of anointing their chosen king, a secret crown."

"The stolen crown?"

"Yes, the stolen crown, reportedly an object of great beauty containing ancient talismanic stones and probably commissioned by King Philip's adviser, Antonio Pérez."

"And this Pérez was the original Divinio?"

"He worked to build power within Philip's court and by all accounts was most successful, so yes, I would say so. Closely tied to power and monarchy in Spain at the time was religion itself. Much as in Britain today where Queen Elizabeth is also head of the Church of England, in Spain the kings were also deeply connected to church politics."

"And Pérez was involved in crowning Don Carlos?"

"That is our belief. He had access, being King Philip's close friend and right-hand man, and would have been involved on the perimeters of the

Inquisition. Much evidence exists that indicates that he both did King Philip's bidding and worked against him for his own ends."

"So he arranged to crown poor Prince Carlos."

"While presumably acting on the king's request to put an end to the unfortunate prince's life. By then Prince Carlos was locked away at Arévalo Castle, attempting to throw himself out of windows and otherwise end his own miserable life. There was ample evidence that he had attempted to commit treason against his father, though in all probability that was at Pérez's instigation. Whatever the case, he died under mysterious circumstances in 1568."

"But what good is a crown for the Divinios if the king wearing it is dead?" I was only taking a stab in the dark.

"A living king is not necessary. They only need his skull and the crown to make their king live again, symbolically speaking. It all harkens back to the intense belief in the relics of faith."

Suddenly I felt ill. "So the crowned skull becomes the symbol—the saint's bones, as it were—for the rituals this brotherhood performs. If they have the complete set, so to speak, they believe they have everything they need."

"Now you are grasping the seriousness of the situation. Yes, the Divinios believe they need both skull and crown. They have been seeking those two components for centuries. Once those elements are again united, presumably they will feel empowered to enact their final deed."

"Which is?"

"We don't know what is planned, but since they apparently claim responsibility for everything from Chernobyl to Covid, we must assume it will be something catastrophic."

"Catastrophic how?"

"We can only guess. To their way of thinking the world needs what my son, Ricardo, used to call a 'major reset.' It was he who convinced me of the gravity of this situation. Before then, it was too easy for me to believe that the brotherhood was merely an archaic and tiresome cult. His research proved otherwise." He paused for a moment. "And they killed him for it."

I swallowed hard. "I'm so very sorry. How exactly?"

"They threw him down an ancient subterranean well on this property.

His body was never recovered. His lamp was located nearby along with footprints we have been unable to identify. We tried for weeks to retrieve his body but the earth is too unstable, quarantine was in full affect, and I could not risk more lives."

I swallowed. "Are you sure that this wasn't a tragic accident?"

"Positive. It was no accident, it was murder." His eyes misted but he soldiered on. "My son was a professional archaeologist and amateur historian, all studies he undertook in his drive to...learn more about Portugal and Sintra's history. Excuse me, but I must sit." He lowered himself heavily into a nearby chair.

"Senhor, if you need to rest—"

"There is no time to rest. As I was saying, it was Ricardo who uncovered an ancient site he believed still in use for ritualistic purposes on this very property—an inverted tower or a well. The two terms are used interchangeably. There are other sites, too, many as yet uncovered. Sintra is riddled with them. Some are Templar remains, others older still. It seems the Divinios will borrow anything they believe hold ancient power."

By now I had my fist pressed to my mouth and my eyes were moist—from fear or sorrow, I didn't know which.

"Ricardo would take too many chances—roaming the land around here until well into the evening, excavating, always excavating. And I would beg him to stop but he was like a dog with a bone, my boy. He had a friend, Jose Balboa, who would help, plus he trained many men on the estate."

"Markus's colleague, the one that was killed the night the skull as stolen?"

"Yes. When the Divinios killed Ricardo, Jose vowed to help bring these beasts to justice, at his peril obviously. That was a little over a year ago and Jose worked with me to trace the existence of the skull and the crown ever since...until they murdered him, too, that is."

"But they used him to track the skull, which he did. That's why he told you about the X-rays. He was working to find the skull and crown all along?"

"Correct, but we had no idea that Prince Carlos was in any way connected to the Divinios before that find, and Jose was following a hunch. Once he told me what those X-rays revealed, I knew we had found our king."

"And after he'd served his purpose, they killed him for it."

"As they will kill us all once we serve ours. We know too much but the crown has yet to be retrieved. I'd wanted only to warn Senhor Collins away from further investigation when I asked him to meet me today, but instead he has dragged you all into the fray."

"For the record, I don't feel dragged anywhere. We must stop these crazies but are you safe here?"

"They need us for cover. As long as the Carvalhos remain here, a mantle of normalcy shields their actions. You must leave. I would have had you escape Lisbon today but had no way of doing so and was forced to use my own escape hatch already arranged."

"I'm not leaving, I said. We're going to find that crown and stop the madness."

"At first that is what I wanted, too. Now I desire only to protect my family. Ms. McCabe, you are all in grave danger. I will attempt to help you and your friends escape the country as soon as possible."

"No. This madness affects us all worldwide, which makes it my battle, too. I don't want to escape, I want to win," I said, pulling myself straight. "As soon as my team arrives, we'll formulate a plan."

It is always a question whether one is brave or simply mad. In my case, it was probably more the latter.

"You might want to ask them first," he said wearily. "My resources are at your disposal, whatever you decide, but first understand what you are getting into."

"I am beginning to."

"I strongly advise you to leave now while you still have the opportunity, but if you refuse, let me say that I am both heartened and dismayed. I want no more deaths on my hands. The Divinios will soon regroup and strike again. I have long suspected that many are among my staff."

"Do you know who exactly?"

"Unfortunately, no. I wait and watch. For now we are safe because they need us, but finding the skull has emboldened them. I have security guards patrolling the grounds day and night and we use state-of-the-art electronic security, all of which is no help if the enemy lies within."

I shook my head as if that might dislodge what I couldn't immediately absorb. Taking a deep breath, I stared down at the portrait of Prince

Carlos. "But tell me, why this poor physically and mentally challenged young man?"

"According to Ricardo's research, the brotherhood had recruited Prince Carlos under Pérez when he was in his early twenties and secretly groomed him for the role he was to play."

"Under his father's nose?"

"Philip II was never around. When you rule multiple lands on multiple continents while waging war on one nation after another, you are always in the saddle or aboard a ship."

"Okay, so Carlos was more or less alone with his entourage."

"Yes, there were those who attempted to shield him—Queen Elizabeth of Valois and her mostly female entourage, but the power circle were mostly men, many of whom worked with his father in the name of the Inquisition. Pérez and his men were a powerful group...continually strategizing for more...in a court run by a deep current of religious fanaticism. They were the...core of the Divinios' brotherhood and they included a band of renegade monks. Excuse me, it is time for my puffer." He pulled out an air chamber and inhalant from his pocket and took two deep puffs.

"Maybe you should rest, senhor?"

"Now, don't you start. One women admonishing me constantly is quite enough. As I was saying, Philip II and his father, Charles, before him believed that Catholicism was the one true religion and that all others were heretical."

"Yes, and bloodshed, martyrdom, the Inquisition, the Spanish Armada, and general persecution followed—all in the name of Jesus. Where's the irony in that? But why would this Pérez take a mentally ill young royal and crown him as this particular holy warrior?"

"Because," Senhor Carvalho said, sighing heavily, "his mental instability made him ripe for the picking, as you say in English."

"They used him, in other words."

"Just so. All they needed was a man of royal blood who would submit to their rituals and embrace the fervent belief that he would be made God on earth. Neither Charles nor his son, Philip, took that bait for they already considered themselves agents of God. Prince Carlos, on the other hand, was always being sidestepped by his father, who recognized the boy's instability at an early age. Pérez had only to wait in the wings playing the treason game."

"So it really was all about power."

"It is always all about power, Phoebe. The brotherhood formed by Pérez wanted it all. Though they believed in the Divine Right of Kings, in their view neither Charles nor Philip carried persecution far enough. For example, they wanted women even more subjugated than they historically were and would never have tolerated a queen like Isabella being made regent in her husband's absence. Philip's queen, Elizabeth of Valois, on the other hand, knew her place."

My gaze swerved to the Titian portrait. "How the beginnings of this brotherhood must have rankled during the years of Isabella's regencies."

"How they must have, that fury continuing as the group further strengthened during Philip's reign. All they needed was an agent at court like Pérez to spur it on and then Don Carlos develops into a very disturbed young man. They sought a male of royal blood to be their chosen king and there he was."

"But then Carlos died or they killed him. How could a dead prince serve them?"

"Because, Phoebe, it does not matter whether the king is alive or dead as long as he has been anointed during his lifetime. Prince Carlos was crowned while he was still alive and it is only his skull and crown that matters now."

I thought of the X-rayed skull with the rivets in the cranium and sat beside him in a nearby chair, my stomach churning. "The brutal bastards. And now they have located the skull."

"Yes, but presumably not the crown. That went missing centuries before and we must locate it before the brotherhood."

A phone jingled from my host's pocket. He pulled it out and peered at the screen. "Your friends have arrived.

9

Seeing Peaches, Rupert, and Evan trudging up the tower stairs at that moment rated right up there as the best thing that had happened to me all year. Senhors Abreu and Afonso and another employee I didn't recognize arrived behind them carrying some of our luggage. I waited until Peaches reached the landing before I lunged at her in a hug.

"Whoa, Phoebe! Glad to see you, too, girl! What's with the dress?"

The fact that hugging Peaches always placed my face more or less at her chest was another matter. I pulled away. "It's borrowed. Are you okay?"

"Yeah, sure, I'm okay, though I just had the most interesting transportation experience in ages—beats the jeep-with-snorkel-and-crate-of-chickens thing I had going in Jamaica."

The three employees arrived on the landing with Markus, Rupert, and Evan. Markus greeted me at the top of the stairs with a weary wave. "Nice dress," he commented as he followed the men down the hall.

Rupert arrived at the top of the stairs, puffing, and demanded: "Do I receive a hug also? I daresay I'm overdue."

I waited until he reached the hallway before I heartily embraced him. "There, there, Phoebe," he said, patting me on the back. "Not so tightly, if you don't mind. I have no breath left after that interesting train ride we just took...in a cargo carriage keeping company with canned goods and crates, if you don't mind. Nevertheless, I am very happy to see you, too."

I stepped away, practically ramming into Evan. He set down the bags he had been lugging and readied himself for his hug. Never did a man with a mask dangling from one ear and day-old stubble look so attractive. "Where's mine?" he asked.

"I'm guessing your room is that way. Follow those guys." I indicated the three employees leading Rupert down the hall.

"I wasn't referring to the room, Phoebe."

"No? But you'd better hurry before Rupert claims the only other turret."

Senhor Afonso called: "This way."

Evan cocked an eyebrow at me, quirked a smile, picked up the luggage, and followed after.

Peaches leaned down and hissed: "Coward."

But I had already launched into tour guide mode and beckoned her into the room next to mine. "Look, luxury accommodations after your harrowing day." And it was amazingly luxurious with a fire in the grate and supper awaiting on a table by the window.

She dropped her bags onto the bed and checked under the chafing dishes. "Ah, soup and a sandwich, wine and bread. You have no idea how starved I am."

Dashing into the adjoining bathroom, she washed her face and hands and emerged to nab the sandwich. "Okay, start talking while I eat. Tell me everything that happened from the time you left for the museum until now and don't leave out a thing. Security locked me up, by the way. I totally forgot about not taking a gun into a museum but they gave it back. No hard feelings. Is Covid not a thing around here? Nobody is wearing masks."

"Did you have your temperature taken?"

"Yeah, sure."

"Well, I guess we've all been cleared, then. All I can say is that it's alarming how easily I've slipped back into my pre-Covid ease. Anyway, let me fill you in." I perched on one of the chairs and recounted the day sequentially, right down to Senhor Carvalho's startling admission about the Divinios.

She paused halfway through spooning up the last of the rice pudding. "You mean we're dealing with some kind of nutsy religious sect?"

"Something like that. This has been going on for centuries with the Divinios waiting for their moment to achieve world dominion—a brotherhood of sorts."

"They are always brotherhoods. Sisterhoods have better things to do."

"And like most brotherhoods, this one is misogynistic, secretive, and fueled by fanaticism made even more dangerous now that they've found their anointed king's skull. All they need is the lost crown," I continued.

"Holy shit."

"Aptly put."

"Christians?"

"Hard to grasp but yes."

"If you had told me this a few years ago, I would have thought you had a screw loose."

"I do rattle sometimes."

"My mama is a staunch Baptist and nothing gets her goat more than people using Christianity as an excuse for violence and murder. Actually, any religion, for that matter, and most of them have."

"And it's been going on for thousands of years, as you know. This particular sect is similar to all the other fanatical groups who believe everything they do is justified in the name of their beliefs. My brain catches me thinking that surely all that's in the past but then I see the news and realize it continues on and on."

"And men keep clawing their way to power. Reality keeps playing the same old tune."

"Exactly."

"Well, shit and damn." She wiped her mouth with the napkin. "Let's get the bastards. Wait, I'm vibrating." She pulled out her phone. "Ev just texted to say that the guys are getting cleaned up, will quickly eat, and are then requested to meet Senhor Anonymous—"

"Senhor Carvalho."

"Him—in a library somewhere."

"I know where that is. I'll just change out of this gown into my own clothes before I rip something."

"And I need a shower and a change. I had to pack for you and just let me say that now I'm convinced more than ever that you need a makeover. Loved some of those rags that Nicolina gave you but the rest is just sad, Phoebe, sad."

"You just like sparkly things more than I do. Come by my room when you're ready."

Peaches got to her feet. "Hmm," she said, still studying her phone. "Doesn't look like the sisterhood is officially invited. The message reads: *Rupert, Markus, and I have been invited to take a glass of port with our host in his library.*"

I laughed. "Is this like one of those nineteenth-century gender divisions where the women retire to discuss pretty dresses while the gents retire to the boys' club to smoke cigars?"

"And chew away on meatier topics like politics and world order."

"Like they didn't make a mess of that over the centuries," I said. "I'm sure that's not the intention here but let's go bust a party."

"Right on."

With that, I went to my own room. It only took a few minutes to remove Leonor's lovely gown—luckily without rips or stress tears—and climb into my own comfortable clean pair of corduroys with a deep green vine-printed long-sleeved shirt. For a moment, I eyed the velvet spread on the bed longingly. Swanning around in velvet had always been one of my childhood fantasies, but I discovered early on that I wasn't right for the job—too many spillages. At the last minute, I added a pair of green-leaf dangle earrings and swept my unruly locks into a top knot to dial up my elegance factor.

While Peaches showered, I slipped down the hall toward the men's rooms. If I wasn't mistaken, Rupert would have claimed the turret at the end of the corridor, meaning that Evan probably took the room next to his. That left three bedrooms in between. Since two of the unoccupied bedrooms had their doors flung open, it was easy to tell that Markus had been allocated the room next to Evan's. From some quaint notion of propriety, the women were at one end of the hall, the men at the other. Otherwise, we were kept together on the same floor despite the building's multiple wings.

I knocked on the door, hoping that he wasn't indisposed. It opened immediately on Markus holding his cell phone in one hand and his shirt half-buttoned. A suitcase lay open on the bed behind him and the largest table held the remains of his meal.

A bread crumb had snagged in his beard like a shell nesting in a bed of seaweed. "Phoebe, hi. I was just about to take a shower." His round glasses magnified those pale blue eyes under that mop of lank blond hair.

"May I come in? This won't take long."

He blinked but backed away. "Sure. To what do I owe the pleasure?"

I walked into his room, noting the open laptop on the table near the window. "How long did you know about Jose's connection with Senhor Carvalho and the truth about the Divinios and when did you plan on telling us?"

He looked like I'd just smacked him. "What do you mean?"

"Oh, come on, Markus. Nothing irks me more than having my intelligence underestimated. Don't give me any more reason to distrust you than I already have. I figured out that you knew exactly what you were looking for when you and Jose began investigating that flooded crypt. The only thing you didn't know in advance was the connection to Prince Carlos, right? That part and the fact that you were being spied on is the only aspect of your story that rings true."

He swore, and turned away. "You figured it out sooner than I'd hoped."

"Once Senhor Carvalho mentioned that his son was friends with Jose and that the two of them had been helping with the excavations here in Sintra, I got the picture. He also mentioned your name, by the way. Were you involved in that, too?"

"No, Phoebe. This is my first visit to Sintra, believe me."

"And yet I have trouble believing anything you say now. I researched yesterday and discovered your name associated with Doctors Jose Balboa and Ricardo Carvalho a little over a year ago on another forensic investigation in Spain. You've been looking for the lost skull and crown for a while, haven't you?"

He turned to face me. "All right, yes, but what of it? We didn't know that Prince Carlos was the Divinios' supposed king until we found that coffin, but okay, so Jose, Ricardo, and I have been seeking the missing crown and skull for about a year. Now they are both dead. I presume you know that part, too."

"Yet you neglected to mention such critical details."

"I needed time to grasp the entire background before letting you in on the facts, didn't I? Besides, what would you have thought if I'd told you that we were really on the trail of a fanatical sect who believed that a crown and a skull held magical powers?"

"How about *informed?*"

"Yes, well, I regret not telling you sooner, all right? I was only interested in locating that skeleton with Jose and Ricardo. Besides, I was sworn to secrecy. Everything that happened this week feels like a tsunami of catastrophes. Once I discovered that I was responsible for alerting the Divinios to the connection with Prince Carlos—that I may even be inadvertently responsible for Jose's death—I panicked. Besides, I couldn't risk you refusing to help, could I? Getting involved in this is like signing your own death warrant."

"Is that supposed to pacify me? How much does Connie know?"

His hand chopped the air. "She just thinks I'm off on some kind of Indiana Jones caper. She hopes to do an episode on me when I return."

I narrowed my eyes. "And how well do you know Senhor Carvalho?"

"I don't. I know of him and he of me, that's all. I knew the note shoved under my door was from him because references to Bosch became some kind of code between him and Jose. All this was going to come out tonight, anyway. I've considered hiding up here in my room in case Evan throttles me."

"Maybe I should save him the trouble."

He shot me a startled look. "Look, I'm sorry to have kept this from you. It won't happen again. I was confused, frightened, and didn't think straight. Let's just put this behind us and move forward, shall we? God knows we're going to need to work together if we're going to find these bastards before they try to vivisect us or whatever these nutcases do."

Charming thought. "Don't give me any more reason to distrust you going forward."

"I assure you I won't."

Turning on my heels, I left the room. From the very beginning, everything about Markus's behavior had set my teeth on edge. Now more than ever I didn't trust the man.

I marched down the hall and knocked on Rupert's turret door next. The sound of running water told me that he was in the shower, so without giving it a second thought I rapped on the next door over. It swung open immediately on a freshly steamed Evan wrapped in nothing but a towel. Bare muscular chest. Damp hair combed straight back from his forehead. A little scar on the right temple. I stared.

"Phoebe. Are you all right?"

I kept my gaze fixed on his eyes—green like sun on agate. I felt my face flush, no doubt wine-induced. "I'm fine," I blurted. "I just need a minute of your time."

"Come in. You can have all the time you need."

Maybe it was telling that he said "need" instead of "want" but admittedly *want* was on my mind. While keeping my eyes averted from any part of the man below the neck, I filled him in on Markus's duplicity. He swore softly and strolled away toward the bed, which was the only time I allowed myself a moment to appreciate those long muscular legs and the way the damp towel adhered to his body. Yes, I am that weak.

I tore my gaze away. Books and papers sat stacked by his bed and a laptop was propped on the desk with the remains of his supper neatly piled on a tray by the door. He'd been deep into researching something while multitasking his way through a mental checklist was my guess.

The scent of Portuguese lemon olive soap suffused the air above a faint layer of the man's subtle spicy cologne. "I never trusted him from day one," I said, leaning over to read the top of a stack of photocopies neatly fanned on the bed. "Don't ask me why. Maybe it's because he seems so weaselly and sweats too much. Or then again, maybe I've just gone off archaeologists as a breed."

When I turned around, he was standing there wearing a little smile. And just that towel. "Perspiring—that's as good an indicator of lying or withholding information as any but it could also be caused by fear. He did have killers chasing him at the time." The man was ex-MI6, remember. "Still, the weaselly part is pure—"

"Instinct?"

"Instinct and astute observation. Nevertheless, you know I've always appreciated your instincts, Phoebe, as well as just about everything else about you. As for the archaeologist part, I presume you're referring to Noel. I—"

"Probably shouldn't go there," I finished for him. "Sorry I brought it up. What are all these?" I indicated the printouts on the bed in an effort to change the topic.

"I had them emailed to me from a librarian friend in Barcelona and printed them up before we left Lisbon. They comprise a fascinating collection of research on Don Carlos. For instance, this one—" he leaned past me and picked up a folder "—describes the early years of the young crown prince."

"Written in Spanish?"

"I can read Spanish, Phoebe," he remarked, "though reading Portuguese still eludes me."

"Give it time."

"In any event, these letters and accounts were originally written in archaic Spanish with a smattering of Latin here and there but later translated into modern Spanish by scholars across the centuries."

"Do you mind summarizing?"

"Certainly. This particular paper elaborates upon the young prince's tendencies. Apparently, he was notoriously self-willed and obstinate, which led to outbursts of bad-tempered violence. For example, following his father's extended absence in the 1550s, Carlos went into the stable and maimed twenty of the steeds to the point where they had to be put down. One of the letters from the household advisers at the time claimed that Carlos liked to roast small animals alive."

I held up my hand. "I get the picture: Don Carlos was a dangerous and sadistic little horror. What else does the research say?"

Evan stood there with his glasses on the bridge of his nose reading from his sheaf of papers as he'd totally forgotten that he was practically nude. You've got to love a man that entranced by his interests and a woman who can appreciate it, aesthetically speaking. "Here's something else illuminating: the reports indicate that the boy was only interested in food, wine, and women. Apparently, he developed a passion for one of the servants—'passion' in this context meaning that he chased the poor maid around the castle in order to force himself upon her—which resulted in him stumbling down a dark stairwell and suffering a massive head injury. That must be the skull contusion Markus referred to that we saw in the X-rays. In any case, the injury was so severe that his brain began to swell, causing him to lose his sight in both eyes."

"Any mention of his briefly betrothed Elizabeth of Valois or any other women in his life?"

"Valois is mentioned only as being his fiancée before his father the king decided to marry her himself. There is some rumbling that the king feared his son was not suitable for marriage."

"Which he wasn't, and seemed truly unable to form bonds with any person."

He looked up. "Shall I continue?"

"Aren't you cold?"

He grinned and pushed his glasses farther up his nose. "Not in the least." I was certainly warm enough.

"Then carry on."

"Right." He returned to translating the document while passing me a sketch of three men standing around a prone man who appeared to be having his head drilled. "This is the treatment for the prince's head injury."

"Trepanning."

"Yes, you know of it. This is a medieval illustration of the procedure showing a surgeon boring a hole into the skull to relieve pressure on the cranium wall."

"It's actually the forbearer of a similar procedure still in use today." I remarked.

"Yes, indeed. This account states that the royal surgeon attempted this on Don Carlos without success and by all accounts the court believed the prince was ultimately on death's door. King Philip rushed home to the castle." He paused to gaze at me over the top of his glasses. "Here's where it gets interesting."

"It's all interesting."

"It is, isn't it?" He flashed me a grin and continued. "So, Carlos's father, the king, spent his days and nights in prayer for his poor son while calling in all the healers across the land. Nothing worked. The king grew desperate and in a last attempt to save his son allowed the Franciscan fathers to bring in the remains of the holy Fray Diego, who had died a century before. His bones reportedly bore healing properties."

"A skeleton?" I asked.

"A holy mummy that was placed in bed beside the prince, who was raging in delirium by then."

"If he wasn't before, he soon would be after. Sleeping with a corpse would do it for me."

"The account reads that Don Carlos dreamed of the blessed Diego that very night and woke the next morning cured. Remember what I've said many times about the devout Catholic's belief in the power of bones and the holy dead?"

"I remember very well. And the mummy thing really happened?"

"It's all in these accounts mentioned multiple times by various courtiers and by the king himself. This is a faith that believes in miracles, Phoebe."

"All faithful believe in miracles. I know that you were raised Catholic but I really don't get the holy bones concept."

"And yet you believe in faith in general?"

"Of course—in deep spiritual conviction, just not on bones infused with magical properties."

"Magic and faith brew from a similar fount, Phoebe," he said softly.

I was leaning over his bicep, staring down at the printouts of cursive script and typed translation. That scent of lemon and soap was so heady my head spun.

"I'd better let you finish getting dressed," I said, pulling away.

"But there's more."

"Another time." I backed away toward the door.

"In the meantime, I'll pay a quick visit to Markus on my way to the library."

"And do what?" I asked.

"I'll put him through my own internal lie detector test," he said with a smile.

"Good." I took a deep breath. "One more thing and speaking of holy bones: we are on the trail of a group called the Divinios. Have you heard of them?"

A tremor of shock crossed those chiseled features. "The Divinios? Yes, of course I've heard of them. The brotherhood has worked to undermine the European governments for centuries."

"They reportedly began in the court of Emperor Charles and grew in strength during the years of his son, Philip."

"So that's what's behind all this."

It was growing increasingly warm in there. "I have never bought into any of those conspiracy theories but I may just have to change my mind. It makes sense that events like this holy cure of Prince Carlos by this dead saint's bones further fueled the Divinios."

He was staring into space, deep in thought.

"Anyway," I said, "I'm sure we'll have lots to talk about when we get together in Senhor Carvalho's library later so I'll leave you to finish getting dressed. Bye." I practically launched myself through the door, my face flaming, my head crammed with images of holy bones, damaged princes, and a half-naked man.

I returned to my quarters just minutes before Peaches swept in wearing one of her long purple wrinkle-proof stretch numbers with the matching spandex and sequined bolero jacket.

"What's wrong with you?" she asked.

"Nothing, why?"

"Your face is red."

"It's the wine."

"Yeah, well, you'd better lay off that stuff. You know you're a lightweight in the drinks department. Okay, so how'd you get a turret room?" she exclaimed, looking around.

"I'm a princess obviously." I shrugged.

"Well, I'm a queen," she said, thumbing her ample chest. "I can trace my heritage so far back it'll make your head spin. My aunt Rosemary was the pineapple queen in Kingston for decades and my uncle Jack was king of the Port Douglas Couch Festival for five years running. Can you beat that in the royalty stakes?"

I snorted. "No way. Your lineage beats mine hands down. My dad didn't even win the Lunenburg herring festival when he tried twenty years ago. His haul was a good ten pounds too short. You absolutely deserve the turret room, not I."

"Damn right I do!"

We burst into laughter. And quickly sobered.

"With all this talk about the Divine Right of Kings, what the hell happened to the divine right of queens?" I asked.

"I wondered the same thing."

"History will say that the concept applied to both genders but unless you had steel and fire behind you, women had to fight ten times harder to keep their power. Most queens of the day remained in the background but there were famous exceptions. There are two portraits of Queen Isabella of Portugal here—that's the later queen not the medieval edition who married Ferdinand—and one of them's by Titian. How does she play into all this, or does she?"

Peaches shrugged. "Sorry, not my field."

"No matter, let's get down to the library in case the men try to solve the world's problems without us."

"And we know how well that's worked out in the past."

I stepped into the corridor. "But seriously, here we just joked about monarchy being won according to merit, but in the Divine Right of Kings mythos it's bestowed by right of birth." I shrugged. "That never made sense to me."

"And it's not going to make sense to you now that the supposed divine king is no more than a bag of bones and a crown."

"True."

On our way downstairs—and admittedly I got lost once or twice and needed reorientation from one of the staff—I explained my suspicions about Markus.

"I thought there was something fishy with that one," Peaches remarked while studying a vaulted ceiling in one of the halls. "We'll keep an eye on him. Did you say he was just wearing a towel?"

"I said that Evan was wearing a towel. Focus on the important bits, Peach."

She grinned. "I was. Maybe it's time you did. Speaking of bits, that good-looking black guy, Lino Abreu, told me there's a child in the household who sometimes tries to go out at night when she shouldn't. He said the house locks up with a security system like you wouldn't believe but I talked him into letting me have the code. I've been locked up once today and I don't need it a second time. Here, take a picture of the numbers with your phone."

I pulled out my phone and quickly snapped a photo of the numbers she had typed out on hers. "Done. By the way, that child is Ana Marie," I whispered back. "She's our host's granddaughter and believes her daddy is still out there. He's been missing for months."

"Poor little darling. Did you ever want kids?"

"Not at the moment."

"Of course not at the moment. You haven't even set yourself up with a man yet."

"I mean, let's not talk about this now."

"Sure. Where is this place, anyway?"

A man approached us wearing what I recognized to be the house uniform and escorted us to the library. Minutes later we were comfortably ensconced with the gents, each having graciously welcomed Peaches and me into the inner sanctum as if we'd been invited all along. Based on the "pick your battles" concept, neither of us mentioned our uninvited status.

Senhor offered us a glass of port from the decanter on the other side of the room and we helped ourselves before settling down in the capacious main seating area. Across the semicircle from me, Evan sat looking somber (and clothed) while Rupert sat next to Peaches, frowning into his glass. Markus had yet to arrive.

"I was just bringing your companions up to speed on the Divinios," Senhor Carvalho said, "and requesting that they leave Portugal before this goes further." He sounded bone-weary and I couldn't help but worry about him.

"Which we absolutely refused to do," Evan remarked, glancing at me.

"We are in complete agreement there," I said, meeting his eyes, which looked nearly hazel in that light.

"Indeed, we came here to find a headless client and to return him to his rightful resting place, which is exactly what we'll do, regardless of the grandiose notions of a band of holy thugs," Rupert added, looking resplendent in his paisley silk smoking jacket. Despite his usual blue-blood attire, he was still looking unusually weary and pale. I stifled a pang of worry there, too. "Where is his final resting place?"

"In the El Escorial Royal Monastery of San Lorenzo in Madrid," Evan replied. "I checked. As far as anyone knows, he's still there—complete."

"But now we know otherwise," I said.

"Yes," Rupert agreed. "And we must endeavor to bring together the chap's missing parts."

"But the risks, Senhor Fox," our host reminded him while rubbing his temples, "are not small and affect more than just you. I admit that stopping the Divinios is no longer my focus. Now I wish only to protect my family.

Those 'holy thugs' have established a considerable network, some of whom are no doubt powerful in their own right, and they will kill anyone who gets in their way."

"And yet now that we know what they intend we can't let them get away with it," Evan said.

"And yet we are hardly in the position to stop them. We don't know the half of it. I have a friend in Spain who has a vested interest in our efforts, too, and is mustering additional resources as we speak, but it may all be for nothing. Let us never underestimate the power of the Divinios. They have killed two already and God knows how many in the past. Should they find the crown before we do, we may all be doomed."

"Do you have any idea of where the crown could be located?" Evan asked.

"No," Senhor Carvalho said. "We have been searching for years but for an intact skull and crown. At times we believed it must have been hidden on Spanish soil, but then a new clue would be found that sent us back here to Portugal. Then Jose and Markus located the skull without the crown in Lisbon—that was a shock, I can tell you. The fact that the two elements must have been buried separately or separated in later years complicates things immensely. Ricardo was convinced that something was buried here on this property and focused his search here until...the end. Many archaeologists and historians have been helping him."

"Like Markus Collins?" I asked.

"Yes, including Dr. Collins. Where is he, may I ask?"

"Taking a shower, I believe," Evan responded. "I dropped by to chat with him, which no doubt caused a delay." He glanced at me. "I am certain he will be along directly."

"He didn't tell us that he knew Jose Balboa or your son, your identity, or even anything about the Divinios," I said.

"Totally unacceptable," Rupert grumbled. "To think that the man had asked us to assist without providing the full background detail is a breach of good faith, at the very least."

"I had no idea," Senhor Carvalho said. "In Collins's defense, however, I had cautioned Jose to involve as few people as possible. I would not have agreed to your involvement had I known in advance that Markus planned to engage your services."

And then as if on cue, Markus knocked and entered the room. "I apologize for being late." Crossing the space, he briefly scanned the two royal portraits without meeting anyone's eyes before proceeding directly to our host and extending his hand. "Senhor Carvalho, please don't get up. It is a pleasure to meet you at last."

"And I you, Senhor Collins," the gentleman said, grasping his hand in two of his. "We were just discussing your involvement."

"Call me Markus, please. Yes," he said, turning around slowly, "and I apologize again to my companions for not telling you about the Divinios. I was terribly conflicted—too many deaths, the threats. I didn't know what to do. I hope we can get past this."

"That will be left to be seen," Evan stated mildly while pinioning the man with an icy stare. That warm green could chill in an instant apparently. Markus abruptly looked away.

"Help yourself to a glass of port, Markus," Senhor Carvalho said, "and I shall proceed with my story. I was just about to tell your colleagues about my son, Ricardo, whom you knew, too."

"Um, yes...Ricardo..." Markus turned as if looking for an escape route and aimed for the decanter, where he proceeded to pour himself a glass with trembling hands. "Fine fellow. Sorry for your loss, Senhor Carvalho. Yes, Ricardo and I worked on a dig together in Spain." He took a swig.

"And you were hunting for the Divinios' king even then," I remarked after taking a sip from my own glass. Rich and delicious with a robust red color that was akin to the queen's red dress, the liquid slid down as smoothly as silk-lined velvet. And zapped my brain. I was struck by the sudden effect it had on me. An intense warmth reached my toes immediately, accompanied by a wave of sudden sleepiness. Good but not good. I set the crystal glass on a nearby table and kept my attention focused on the archaeologist.

Markus had begun speaking quickly. "I didn't know him well but I admit to being fired up about his quest for a crowned skeleton when he first told me. At the time we had been investigating crypts in Valencia and I thought that this sounded like a jolly good adventure—hunting for a crowned skull...why not? My work up until then had been dead boring—"

"Pun intended?" Peaches interrupted.

He stared at her uncomprehending. "Pardon? Oh, yes, pun intended."

Markus coughed and carried on. "Of course, I didn't realize the extent of it—had no idea, really. Had I known, I might not have accepted the challenge. All this Divinio business was new to me, though my sister, who has more background on European history, gave me a quick education. In any case, we stopped investigating for a while due to Covid and there you have it." He shrugged and took another sip.

I leaned forward. "It seems to me that you're left out plenty, Markus, especially since a forensic archaeologist like yourself must be so methodical."

He glanced at me before focusing on his glass. "Methodical, me? On the job, yes, but otherwise no, not really."

"Let us move along, shall we?" Rupert urged. "About the Divinios, of course most of the modern world have always believed that this sect died out long ago."

Senhor Carvalho nodded. "And for a while we had hoped so, too, but there were too many signs that they may have been operating for centuries. We should have heeded our instincts then and stopped the hunt long ago, but my son could not let go. To his mind, we had come too far to stop, but if we had, he might still be alive today."

"And the Divinios knew you were on their tail?" Evan asked.

Senhor Carvalho wiped a hand over his eyes. "Not at first. To this day I have no idea how they discovered that we were researching their history. Perhaps we were more careless than we thought or there were spies, always spies. We had even engaged trusted help from the museum to shield our efforts. Regardless, Ricardo's death was a warning, one which the Divinios believed I had heeded until I intervened following Jose Balboa's murder."

"Perhaps Jose tipped them off when Markus called you, Senhor Carvalho?" Markus said. "They must have been hacking him, too."

"Possibly," Peaches agreed, glancing at Markus, "but that doesn't make you any less of a slimeball." She stared at the archaeologist as if she wanted to slap him silly, prompting the man to take another gulp.

"Whatever the case, they now realize that everyone in this room knows that Prince Carlos is the Divinios' crowned king. You all have been identified and will be targeted," our host stated.

"And who knows how long they have been stalking me—us. Poor

Ricardo, poor Jose," Markus said, still standing. He took another swig of port and looked around for a seat. "We are all in this together."

Evan pulled a chair out from against a wall of books and set it down beside him, patting the seat as if inviting a small dog. "The question remains why did they not kill you, too? They had the opportunity the night they stole the skull," he remarked.

Markus half perched at the edge of the seat as if readying to bolt. "I wondered the same thing. Maybe they think I know something and will lead them to the crown."

"And do you?" Evan asked, his tone mild but the tensile strength of his warning unmistakable.

A flash of panic crossed Markus's face. "Me? No, or at least not that I know of. I keep reviewing everything Ricardo and Jose discussed, everything we researched as a team in Spain, but nothing comes to mind. In fact, I often thought they were keeping things from me. I'd overhear them speaking in Portuguese, of which I know only a little. In any case, we all must keep up the search."

"I suggest that you all reconsider. I cannot bear to see more people harmed." Senhor Carvalho turned to Peaches. "And do you feel the same as your fellows, senhorita?"

"'Senhorita'—I like that—but I'm with the others. We're the Agency of the Ancient Lost and Found and we've come to get a head."

"And I've already told you my position," I said, turning to our host. "Do you believe this brotherhood will really come for you here?"

"They already have," Senhor Carvalho said, setting his glass down on a side table. "The security around the property was strengthened long before Ricardo's death and we put patrols in place even then, but it was still not enough. We believe they have found one of the ancient tunnels snaking under this land and have access to the property beyond my property lines."

"And your staff?" Peaches asked.

"Most are like part of the family but I feel as though we are constantly watched," Senhor Carvalho replied.

"Nevertheless, any security can weaken over time and every detail requires constant evaluation. I saw the fence when we entered—impressive but not foolproof," Evan remarked.

"There lies the dilemma, Senhor Barrows. It is almost impossible to secure fifteen acres of property given the present circumstances, especially since the greatest security risk lies underground."

"You say that there's a network of tunnels below the property?" Peaches asked.

"An extensive one and that system extends all through Sintra. Many are impenetrable, others have been secured with gates and blockades, and many still remain undiscovered. Ricardo had been excavating one in particular that led him eventually to an underground tower—more of dry inverted well—where he met his death. It was quite a find archaeologically but we begged him not to continue, to leave it alone, to stop inviting this madness into our lives, but he could not let go."

"A dry inverted well?" Rupert asked. "That would be a find indeed."

"It is really more of a subterranean inverted tower used for long-ago ritualistic purposes. Ricardo used to tell us about it," Markus remarked. "It is a fascinating find actually, one of great historical import, but would require a huge investment to excavate properly."

"And Ricardo believed it has been in use by the Divinios for centuries and possibly even recently," Senhor Carvalho continued. "The widest part lies on top with a circular stairway leading around and down to a narrow bottom platform that was most likely an altar of some kind. One access can be gained from under the site of my granddaughter's dragon fountain, which leads to a network of tunnels, and the other entry point, which is far more direct, lies in the forest. That one we've gated."

So that's where Draggy fit in. "Where did Ricardo go missing exactly?" I asked.

Senhor Carvalho heaved himself to his feet and shuffled over to a large map cabinet, indicating for us to join him. "I will show you."

Soon we all were gazing down on a large diagram of something that almost looked like a funnel-shaped tower with an open staircase twisting around and around and ending at a dizzying drop to the platform below. Worked in pen and ink, each aspect of the drawing was rendered with precision and labeled in Portuguese.

"This is Ricardo's drawing and is, I believe, an accurate depiction of the site he was excavating at the time of his death. Most of the initial structure was intact and appears to have been repaired multiple times across the centuries by various civilizations and interests," our host explained.

"Ricardo showed me a photo he had taken of the diagram back in Spain just before he returned here to begin his own excavations." Markus leaned over and took a photo with his phone. "It will be thrilling to see it in person."

"We will arrange for a tour tomorrow," Senhor Carvalho said, "but I warn you, the area is treacherous and you cannot go in there without a guide."

Peaches whistled between her teeth. "A disaster waiting to happen, no matter how you look at it."

"And a disaster did. My son disappeared near this subterranean tower in April. There are deep fissures left over from the earthquakes all through that area and it appears as though he was thrown down one of them. Our staff searched everywhere but found no trace. A full rescue operation was not possible with lockdown in effect, but that may have made little difference. Even now the authorities believe the area too dangerous to risk a more invasive search."

"Is there a possibility that he may have fallen by accident?" Evan asked.

"Absolutely none, in my opinion. He had roped or barricaded off every exposed treacherous crevasse. Besides, he was last seen by his workmen standing by the gate about to lock up for the night."

"And were the workmen trustworthy?" Rupert asked.

"They have been in our employ for years. No, the Divinios tackled him when he was alone, dragged him back into the tunnels, and pushed him to his death. The fissures are so deep we may never retrieve his body, and with the area's instability, the authorities will not even try. I have considered launching an excavation with my own resources now that lockdown has lifted, but the risk of the whole garden collapsing is too great."

"How heartbreaking," Rupert commented. "I am so very sorry. To lose a son...well, it is must be excruciating."

"Thank you," Senhor Carvalho acknowledged. Though his voice trembled, it refused to crack. "Where heartbreak is concerned, what may be the most difficult for my family is the lack of closure. My dear granddaughter still believes her daddy is alive...somewhere...and how can I convince her otherwise?"

"But are you certain he isn't still alive?" I asked.

"To be alive and not return to his family? That makes no sense at all," the gentleman insisted, "and it has been far too long to think that he may have survived...down there." As his gaze turned to me, it's as though I felt the burden of his grief.

"Do the authorities believe the Divinios were involved?" Evan inquired.

"Very few know the Divinios even still exist. One doesn't mention their name without fear of censure. It would be like saying that my granddaughter's dragon comes alive at night, so no, they have no idea. I certainly would not introduce the subject. Instead, they believe Ricardo must have fallen down one of the fissures by accident, as if Ricardo would ever be so careless. No, the Divinios killed him, pushed him down one of those shafts, killed my son as if his life was of no consequence, and now they will come after the rest of my family."

"My deepest sympathies, Senhor Carvalho," Peaches said, "but why do you think they'll come after your family?"

"Because shortly after Ricardo's death I received an anonymous phone call threatening just that if I didn't stop searching. I planned to stop—did stop for a time. How could I not when my son had gone missing and they threatened my family? Then Jose Balboa contacted me, followed by his recent murder, and here you are. Now it starts again."

We fell silent for a few seconds. I glanced at Markus and found his gaze so fixed on that diagram that it was as if he hadn't heard.

"Your condolences are appreciated. Now you must excuse me but I will retire for the night," our host said with a sigh.

"Of course, you must be exhausted, sir," Rupert said.

"It has been a longer day piled onto an even longer few months and I am too weary—weary in body, weary in soul. Besides, I must go to bed before my daughter-in-law scolds me."

Leaning heavily on his cane, Senhor Carvalho stepped away from the cabinet, paused, and turned back to us. "Please consider this library your own. It will always remain open for your use. All of the material my son gathered on the Divinios is here, plus more besides. Do not worry about awaking me because I sleep far overhead in the main tower." He pointed above, causing us all to look up at the ceiling. "Good night for now, my friends."

We watched him shuffle toward a carved wooden door at the far end of the room and said our good-nights as the door clicked shut behind him.

"I believe I will retire for the evening, as well," Rupert said wearily. "It has been a long day for all."

I checked my watch, amazed to discover it was already 11:32. I had been stifling yawns for the past hour. "Yes, it's definitely past my bedtime, too."

We all agreed that we'd had enough for one day and made our way for the door. Just before exiting, I cast one look over my shoulder at Titian's Queen Isabella. It was all I could do not to bow.

Rupert sidled up to me. "Magnificent, isn't she? But I was dumbfounded to find two such royal portraits here, one being by Titian, since so few remain in private collections."

"Apparently, both paintings have been in the family for centuries and the Aviz family will not let them go."

"I cannot blame them, in truth. Had I a queen in my family lineage, you can be certain that I would want her likeness reigning over my household for eons."

"Don't you have an earl or two in the family tree?" I asked.

"Low-hanging fruit in comparison, Phoebe. Not the same at all," he sighed.

Rupert's late wife had been the daughter of a British earl, so his affinity to royalty was much stronger than mine. Nevertheless, since his own father had been an antiques dealer, he was much closer to the common man—and me—than he preferred to acknowledge.

We continued on our way, the five of us wending toward our quarters through the hushed house. This time we took an elegant main staircase that led three floors up to our wing.

By now, I was realizing the extent of my exhaustion, and the others must have been feeling the same since we barely spoke. All the other family portraits hanging on the staircase walls passed without comment.

The stairs ended at the top landing next to Rupert's turret.

"I'm surprised there's no elevator here," Rupert huffed as he opened his door. "There is one, but it heads up the main tower from whence we came, a private one for Senhor Carvalho's convenience, but I daresay another is required."

I hid a yawn.

"Maybe we can ask for a tour of the house tomorrow?" Peaches suggested.

"As much as I'd enjoy seeing the entire castle," Evan said, opening his door, "the subterranean chambers and the inverted tower interest me more."

"You are such an on-task dude, Ev." Peaches grinned at him.

He grinned back. "I try. Don't forget to scan your rooms, friends," he reminded us. "You never know who's watching. There's a scan app on your phones."

"Oh, you mean for bugs. Right. Night, gentlemen," Peaches said. "I suppose that's his version of 'sleep tight,'" she whispered as we strode down the hall. She pulled out her phone. "I've never used the bug app before. I presume it's the feature with the green beetle icon?"

"Yes. Just tap the icon, hold down the volume button, and run your phone over every lamp and crevice. If the light remains green, you're good. If it turns red, let me know and we'll do the removal bit together. I doubt we'll find anything but it's best to be sure."

"Cool."

We passed a table with a bowl of flowers and a three-tiered painted lamp, also some small landscape paintings, and continued on to our respective rooms. I gave Peaches a little good-night wave and entered my turret.

Stepping inside, I paused. No matter how tired I was, I had an unwavering prebed ritual: first secure the door, then scan the room for surveillance bugs, next prepare a getaway outfit in case I needed to bolt. Yes, that had become my traveling life in a nutshell. All other basic nighty-night things like brushing teeth and washing my face had to wait.

Step one: I threw the antique brass bolt—rudimentary but presumably sufficient in a castle surrounded by guards, or so I hoped. Step two: I powered up my phone, skimmed the earlier text messages, and tapped the green bug app icon. In seconds, I was scanning every likely spot to plant a bug while awaiting a flashing red light alert on my phone. None came. All systems go in the surveillance department.

That done, I peeled off my clothes and pulled on my van Gogh sleep shirt, put my shoes next to the bed, and flung my jacket over the closest chair. There. My final task was to lay my phone faceup beside my bed with the detector app activated. This handy feature would alert me should it detect an intruder's body heat. That done, I brushed my teeth, washed my face, and collapsed. Once my head hit the pillow, I was out.

But I never sleep well the first night in a new bed no matter how exhausted. The first few hours are deep and restful but then something inevitably wakes me up. Sometimes it's an unfamiliar sound but mostly I end up blaming my internal anxiety meter.

That night I sprung to sitting, glanced at my phone, which detected no sign of intrusion, and sat there with my heart thumping at 3:25 a.m. Since I had turned out all the lights, the room was dark except for a thin bar of light under the door to the hall.

I flopped back against the pillows and lay with my eyes fixed on the darkness above. And tried to sleep. Twenty minutes later, I was still wide awake and feeling thirsty. I dragged myself from the bed and scouted my room for a water bottle, using my phone for a light. My own empty water thermos had been stuffed in my backpack and I wasn't sure that taking water from the taps was a good idea. Too much lead in these old pipes. Maybe I'd have to stay parched until dawn or find the kitchen.

Perching on the side of the bed, I skimmed my texts and messages again. Most were a flurry of questions about how I was getting along from Max and assorted friends, a request for a review from the Airbnb in Lisbon, plus confirmations of this and that. It was the message from Connie Collins that made me pause:

Phoebe, how goes the adventure? Be very careful over there, won't you, and let me know if you need help from this end? And don't permit my esteemed brother to drive you to distraction. He can be such a pain sometimes but his heart is always in the right place. Put me on speed dial using this number so we can stay in touch.
—Connie

Connie wanted me to put her on speed dial? She knew about the Divinios, too, since Markus implied as much.

I responded with: *All fine here so far but it seems that there may have been a few critical things you neglected to mention when you hired us.*

I was just about to pocket my phone when an answer came back pronto: *Mea culpa, Phoebe. Trust that I could not share the details. Surely now you understand why given the gravity of the situation? BTW, is your phone secure?*

I trust this phone more than either of you, I answered before pocketing my phone and striding to the window.

Now I was not only wide awake but irritable as hell. Pulling back the curtains, I gazed out into the night.

A beautiful still early morning stretched before me and for a moment I savored the Moorish castle far on a hill to the right with its illuminated crenellated parapets before skimming over the village below. A quick glance and it could be an Alpine village with all those ornate roofs bathed in up-lit grander. Taking a deep breath, I attempted to still my twitching self.

I was about to raise the window to get some air when I caught a flash in the garden below. I stared. There it was again, just a burst of light quickly extinguished. Somebody in the garden with a flashlight?

Backing away, I pulled my jeans on under van Gogh, snatched my jacket and phone, shoved my feet into my sneakers, and tiptoed to the door. I simply intended a reconnaissance to see who might be up and about that early.

The lamp was on, the hall hushed and still, as I padded along heading toward the main staircase. At first I assumed that my companions were all asleep until I saw a light beaming from one door—Markus. Without hesitating, I knocked softly, expecting a moment of commiseration between the sleepless. When no one answered, I nudged the door open far enough to find the room empty.

Backing away, I picked up my pace and marched off down the hall. Could Markus be the one wandering the grounds by himself? Not likely since he hardly seemed the courageous sort, but maybe he'd seen somebody awake about the house.

In seconds, I had dashed down the four levels where the kitchen lay, where I paused. Everything was dark, not even a night-light. To my knowledge, nothing lay to the right except laundry and storage with a corridor leading to the main wing, while to my left lay the kitchens and back entrances. If Markus was in the kitchen, surely he'd turn on a light?

I was just about to head back upstairs when I heard whispering. Or at least I thought that dry scratchy hissing sound coming way back in the darkness was whispering. I listened, a chill running up my spine. Why would anyone be down in the dark whispering unless they were up to something?

I padded down the hall in the direction of the sound, using nothing to guide my steps but the memory of a wide straight corridor where I'd entered the day before. After five yards, the sound abruptly stopped. Now

I couldn't tell which way to turn, left or right? Then came a shuffling sound, followed by a click, followed by silence.

Turning on my phone light, I padded in that direction but there was no way I could tell exactly from which of the warren of rooms the sounds came. I spun around, hoping for something to go on, but nothing lay ahead except a long hall of endless rooms combined with mute silence. Turning, I headed back for the stairs.

I badly wanted to track down Markus. What were the chances that that was his light I'd seen outside or that he'd been one of the night prowlers on the bottom level?

When I reached the second floor, I paused, noticing a light about midway down the hall. Had I missed that on my way down? I'm certain I hadn't. That would be the library. Taking a deep breath, I strode forward and burst through the door. There at one of the room's numerous work tables sat a bedraggled Markus, head down over a spread of documents and printouts.

"Markus?" In the lamplight he looked as though he'd been dragged headfirst through a thorn bush.

He glanced up, shoving a strand of hair from his forehead. "Phoebe? Couldn't sleep, either, I take it?"

I stepped forward, noting the half-empty teacup with the damp squeezed bag on the saucer rim, the crumpled biscuit wrapper, the little pocket flashlight on the side of the table. "Have you been to the kitchen?"

"Not necessary. Our hosts have kindly set up a carafe of hot water and snacks on the buffet against the wall." He thumbed in that direction and, sure enough, an ewer of water and an electric kettle sat on the counter.

My gaze returned to the archaeologist. "I must have missed that announcement."

"One of the employees set it all up earlier last night."

"And you're sure you haven't been outside tonight?"

He laughed. "Are you serious? Do you really think I'd just walk out one of those doors and trot around that garden of earthly frights by myself?"

"Well, you *are* a forensic archaeologist, so if anyone has the stomach for 'earthly frights' it would be you."

"Let me guess: you saw a light?" Something flickered behind his eyes.

"A light in the garden moving around."

"Probably one of the night watchmen. Apparently, there are guard teams prowling the grounds. Wouldn't that make more sense than accusing me of some pointless nocturnal ramble?" He sat back and crossed his arms. "You really don't like me much, do you?"

"You haven't given me much reason to."

"I admit that I deceived you and accept all the blame and recriminations that I deserve, but I am not your enemy, Phoebe. I am not working with the Divinios to overturn life as we know it, but remain firmly on the side of the good guys attempting to prevent destruction. Look—" and he shoved a drawing toward me "—this is my latest theory."

I picked it up and studied the notations printed out by hand on a photocopy of Ricardo's tower diagram. "What's this?"

"My assessment of where the crown may lie based on what we know now."

"And what do we know now?"

"That the Divinios are likely here on this property and therefore so must be the crown. I theorize that it may be hidden below the altar at the bottom of this well that we will finally visit tomorrow."

"But wouldn't Ricardo have found it before now?" I was peering at the arrows pointing to the rectangular shape at the base of this unusual construction. Strange etchings appeared to be chiseled into the rock. "Are those hieroglyphs?"

"Roman numerals and a cross. Ricardo discovered the remains of at least two forms of ancient writing on the slab including what he hypothesized to be the Roman numeral I. The point is that multiple groups spanning many centuries have been using that altar for their purposes."

"Making it the perfect place to bury a crown?"

"Exactly."

"A bit obvious, isn't it?"

The blue eyes magnified behind those glasses held a twinge of annoyance. "That was the area he was working on before he died and possibly the reason they killed him, Phoebe. Think."

"I *am* thinking."

"It's the only thing we have to go on and the evidence speaks for itself."

I made an effort to rein in my pique. "Depends on what language you use." I cast a quick glance toward Queen Isabella standing in the shadows. I turned back to the archaeologist. "Well, thanks for sharing, Markus."

I couldn't help but reach out and pluck a leaf tangled in his hair. "Been sleeping in the woods tonight, have you?"

And with that, I poured myself a glass of water and returned to my room, more convinced than ever that Markus was up to something.

10

The next day after lunch we assembled in the garden under the watchful gaze of Senhors Abreu and Afonso plus two other men to whom we were not introduced. Both of the new guys kept their heads down and made no eye contact.

"Please do not stray from the path," Afonso said. "We take you by safest route. There must be no changes."

Abreu nodded. "We take you to the well, down the stairs to see altar, then quickly back. No lingering."

"Very dangerous," Afonso added. "Stay behind me. Stay on path. Senhor Abreu, he follows last. Our men help you if needed."

And so we set off through the garden, heading for the forest, traveling in single file like young children with their daycare teachers. Markus remained directly behind Afonso while Rupert, decked out in his safari jacket with a wide-brimmed hat and looking more prepared for a wildlife trek, followed behind him. Somehow I ended up dead center between Evan and Peaches with Abreu and the two men bringing up the rear.

For some reason I had pictured the entrance to the mysterious well to be closer to the castle but we left the gardens and headed for the forest instead.

It was, I realized as I gazed around, the epitome of the fairy-tale woodland. Tall trees shielded the forest floor from sunlight while a rich threading of white woodland flowers bloomed amid the ferns. The paths were wide and in places even manicured, with small pools opening up here and there to reveal swans floating in pale splendor on the calm surfaces. One such pond even had a little castle-shaped duck house on the center island.

"Even the ducks live well here," Peaches remarked. "Many of these are specimen trees."

"Pardon?"

"See that fig tree up there?" She pointed overhead.

"Yes," I said.

"Those are indigenous to South America. Somebody a long time ago introduced specimen trees here."

We continued for almost twenty minutes further until Rupert requested a rest.

"We are almost here," Afonso called. "Few steps more."

By now we had left the path and had begun climbing a steep incline. Rupert trudged valiantly upward and plopped himself down on the first mossy rock he found at the top. Behind him stood a chain-link fence so overgrown with vines and foliage that unless you knew it existed it would be nearly impossible to see.

"Rupe, are you all right?" Peaches asked while patting his shoulder.

"Fine, Penelope, fine. I just need a brief respite before we continue."

So rest we did, giving Abreu the opportunity to dispense water into paper cups as if we were on a picnic.

"Do you guys drop bread crumbs, too?" Peaches whispered to Afonso as he stood nearby.

He grinned. "If you need. Are you hungry?"

"Depends on what's on offer." She smiled back. I figured that probably got lost in translation, which was no doubt a good thing.

Ten minutes later, the men unlocked the chain-link gate and we proceeded through a narrow path to stand by a large circular opening approximately thirty feet across strung with draping fines.

"This is opening to well. Best now when sunshine beams overhead. Stairs very steep and slippery. Be very careful. Remain on left-hand side on way down. Do not go near open part," Afonso instructed.

From this vantage all I could see was moss-skimmed marble and strands of ivy hanging down. Minutes later we were carefully negotiating the stairs, bracing ourselves against the left wall as we descended around and around a circular staircase that opened on one side to a straight drop.

At one point, I leaned over and clung to one of the pillars long enough to risk glancing down. It was a dizzying view made more vertiginous because the staircase narrowed as it wound its way down. It felt like gazing at an upside-down Escher drawing from the top of the Leaning Tower of Pisa. I estimated the drop to be around 150 feet.

Finally we arrived at the bottom, which measured a considerably smaller circumference than the top—maybe twelve feet across at most. A raised table-size marble platform dominated the center and for a moment all we could do was stare at it as we shuffled around in a circle to find standing room. At our backs six doors in various states of decay, each either blocked off with stone or gated, led away into the dark earth—the tunnel system. The dark scent of earth permeated everything.

"Where do you believe Ricardo Carvalho fell?" Peaches asked.

"We think here or in one of the tunnels. Very deep holes there, the earth unstable. Senhor Carvalho Senior ordered all tunnels blocked after the search. Too dangerous," Afonso replied. He was gazing around at the doors that encircled up, seeming edgy and uncomfortable. "We not stay long."

A brief silence descended on the party, broken by Evan. "That is most certainly an altar," he said. "Possibly Roman in origin judging from those stones at its base."

It appeared as though a two-foot hunk of once-smooth marble had been placed on top of the huge hunks of carved squared stone. He crouched down to run his phone along the numerals carved into the surface. "And these are definitely Roman—MC and the other letters have been worn away. Possibly the altar was originally used for a suovitaurilia sacrifice."

"True that the ancient Romans had sacrificed pigs, sheep, or bulls to Mars as a gift to the Gods," Markus remarked.

"But it looks like a Templar cross over here," Peaches said. We followed her around to stare at the distinctive four-armed cross with the flared ends carved into the stone.

"Yes, and I'm guessing that Senhor Carvalho was correct in his belief that this altar has seen many uses over the centuries," Evan remarked.

"Including human sacrifice?" Peaches asked.

Markus leaned over to inspect the carved image more closely. "Possibly. We don't know which of the Roman mystery cults may have worshipped here or the nature of their practices. There have been indications but nothing definitive."

"The sun shining through the oculus-like opening may be significant," I said, gazing upward.

"Maybe Mithras," Markus commented as he circled the altar, taking photographs. "Mithras was a solar deity, so perhaps rites were performed when the sun was directly overhead, and the Romans would worship Mithras in caves or underground places like this."

"But that upside-down tower overhead is much later," Peaches mused, looking up. "The foundations are Roman, maybe, but those columns are medieval through and through."

"And other pagan religions may have used this site," Rupert added. "Indeed, with a full moon overhead shining directly upon the platform, what a prime time it would be to mutter incantations to conjure up the earth gods." He raised his hands and murmured something incomprehensible.

"But if that cross is Templar, which I agree it must be, then Christians had taken over this spot for their own uses." I stared at the platform. "Maybe the Divinios. Any signs of recent use?"

"Footprints would have been brushed away," Peaches said, studying the stony ground beneath her feet. "Or packed down."

"It's been an excavation site up until a few months ago and I would think it easy to eradicate all signs of recent use," Rupert remarked as he leaned against the altar.

I was gazing around at the six evenly spaced doors exiting to tunnels. "What's through there?" I asked Abreu, pointing to one at random.

"That way to dragon fountain," he said, indicating the gated opening behind Peaches. "This one to house." He pointed to another door that had been walled over with stone. "And that one Senhor Ricardo ordered closed when one man almost fell through. No idea where it goes. Very dangerous, all very dangerous. Possible to go through only if you know way."

I nodded. Turning away, I noticed that Markus had stepped back to speak to one of the two guys that had accompanied us. They stood together in the shadows making hand signals. I shuffled toward them, but by the time I'd gone counterclockwise, Markus was back taking photos of the altar.

Rupert was still leaning against the altar, fanning himself with his hat by then. "Blasted warm in here, isn't it?"

One of the men caught sight of him and barked something in Portuguese, pushing Peaches aside to advance on Rupert with his fists clenched. Peaches caught the man by his collar and pinned him to the spot while Abreu stepped in front of him, muttering something in angry tones. An argument quickly erupted, which Abreu silenced with a chop of his hand. He sent the man away before Abreu returned to apologize to Rupert.

"I am most sorry, Sir Rupert," he said. "Some employees new and not well-behaved."

"Indeed," Rupert remarked. I may have been the only one who caught the instant that Rupert had reached for the gun he always carried inside his jackets.

"No leaning on the displays," Peaches said to Rupert. "Bad boy."

"Perhaps not," he said, straightening. "Still, how excessively rude."

When Abreu announced that it was time for us to leave, nobody protested except Markus, who was on his hands and knees studying the altar's base. A few minutes later we were all trudging up the stairs.

"Stress fractures everywhere around here," Peaches said, pointing to a lightning-bolt-shaped crack nearly severing one of the marble pillars in two. "Another shake-up and this place goes."

"Yes, I can see that," I said, touching the wall. If possible, looking up is even more dizzying than looking down.

When we had stopped by the pool to let Rupert rest on the return trip, I sidled up to Markus. "So what were you saying to that guy there?"

"Senhor Craca?" he asked, turning his magnified blue eyes to me.

"You know his name?"

"I asked his name, Phoebe—not so difficult, is it? Anyway, I was just asking if I could be allowed to take a brief look down one of those tunnels."

"And?"

"And the answer was a very decisive no." He illustrated with a mini air chop. "Satisfied?"

I wasn't actually.

The remainder of the day passed with the team cloistered in the library combing Ricardo's research material. While the men focused on the court of King Philip of Spain and his son, Don Carlos, I took a slightly different tact. I studied the queens, specifically Queen Elizabeth of Valois, Philip's French queen, and Queen Isabella of Spain, his mother in the portrait.

There were two queens in Spanish history who had stood out across the ages, both named Isabella. Isabella I, known as Isabella the Catholic or Isabella of Castille, ruled jointly with her husband, King Ferdinand, until her death in 1504. She was undeniably a force to be reckoned with, a queen of the Inquisition who also held the banner for Spain's dominion over land and sea, heaven and earth.

On the other hand, the Portuguese-born queen, her namesake, Isabella of Portugal, was born the year before the other queen died and came to the Spanish throne through her marriage to the Holy Roman Emperor Charles V of Spain.

Queen Isabella, Empress of the Carnation as she was named, emerged as an able consort for the powerful ruler and the union appeared a love match, strangely enough for the times. This was the queen in the portrait I couldn't take my eyes from, a queen among queens. She assumed regency roles in her husband's absence and proved a strong and able leader.

She must have seemed the gold standard of queens of the day: pious, strong, adored by her husband, and powerful in her own right. Philip's queen during the Don Carlos years, on the other hand, may have felt overshadowed by her late mother-in-law. Elizabeth of Valois was the daughter of Henry II of France and Catherine de' Medici, so no slouch in the lineage department. By all accounts she kept a low profile and thrived on personal pursuits surrounded by female friends rather than on politics.

The female painter Sofonisba Anguissola and Princess Ana de Mendoza became her friends shortly after Elizabeth's wedding and remained in her company for the rest of her days. I could only imagine how those women relied on one another in the politically fraught male domain of the court. Elizabeth even picked up the brush herself under Sofonisba's tutelage and pursued a creative and nurturing role in the court. By all accounts, she remained fond of the disruptive Prince Carlos and was a mother to Philip's other children, illegitimate and legitimate alike. Not all queens yearned for power but saw their duty in other roles.

I lifted my eyes to the portrait of Queen Isabella. In many ways, Elizabeth of Valois was the polar opposite of her mother-in-law. One queen held the country together through politics and might while the other worked a different kind of feminine power.

※

EXHAUSTED AFTER SUCH A LONG DAY, I MUST HAVE SLEPT FOR SEVERAL hours that night dreaming of queens lost in dark tunnels. And suddenly I was shaking. I bolted upright thinking, *Earthquake!* I was going to fall into a dark hole and never be seen again! And there was that alarm! Then I noticed my phone flashing red.

"Phoebe?" a small voice whispered in the dark.

I blinked down, trying to still my thumping heart. A short shadowy figure stood beside my bed, one hand on my arm. A pink light illuminated her face.

"Ana Marie?" I snatched up my phone, disengaged the app. "How did you get in?"

She pointed toward the table. I stared, not understanding. "There are double walls. I can go anywhere."

I got up and checked, flashing my phone light under the table at the small hatch-like door that hung open. Pushing it shut, I realized that it was virtually undetectable. "So you came to visit me in the middle of the night?"

She nodded. "Do not tell Mama but please help me find my daddy now."

"Now?" I straightened. "I mean, why now, honey?"

Taking my hand, she tugged me over to one of the windows and pulled back the curtains. "Look!"

I gazed far across the darkened gardens at what appeared to be three flashlights weaving in and out of the hedges.

"It's Daddy," the child whispered. "I watch for him every night. Tonight he signals me to come. He wants me to find him. Please come with me, please." She tried to tug me toward the door.

"Wait, Ana Marie," I said, holding her back. "Those are probably the guards patrolling the grounds. It's not safe to go out there at night, which is why your mommy won't let you go."

"They are not the guards! On Saturday nights, Senhors Pao and Rios patrol and they always take the same route. Senhor Pao is on the other side of the garden near my pond and Senhor Rios is near the woods. And there were *three* lights tonight. Sometimes I see even more."

I shivered. "All the more reason not to go out there."

"But I have to!" she sobbed. "I miss my daddy and I promised never to go alone!"

My heart breaking into a thousand pieces, I fell to my knees before the girl and gripped her little shoulders. "Ana Marie, your daddy wouldn't want you to go anywhere dangerous. He would want you to stay inside where it's safe."

"No! I thought you would help." She pulled away. "Daddy needs me!" And she unfastened my lock and dashed out the door.

11

I ran after her. "Ana Marie, I'm coming with you," I called. I didn't care if I woke everyone—that was the idea. "Wait for me!"

I could see her phone light against the walls as she ran down the corridor. In seconds, she had darted down the turret stairs as I bolted after.

Dashing down the steps in my bare feet, all I could think of was stopping that child. I had broken every cardinal rule of emergency exits and didn't care. Around and around the curved staircase I went, hearing her footsteps pattering below. Her phone cast long shadows on the tower walls, but the moment I reached the last step everything plunged into darkness.

"Ana Marie?" I paused, flicking on my phone light. No more footsteps, no more telltale glow, and not a single sound but for the mechanical whir of a refrigerator somewhere. Then something banged at the end of a dark hall to my left that sent me scrambling after.

A speck of light followed by a clang. She had to be heading out a back exit. My bare feet padded on the tile floor until I reached a steel door, which I flung open onto a blast of chill air. One step farther and gravel was biting into my feet as the door slammed shut behind me. An alarm began screeching from the house above.

"Ana Marie!" I cried. Now I could see her light bobbing through the hedges somewhere ahead. I took after her, only I couldn't figure out exactly which way she'd gone. Every direction ended in a wall of boxwood, and backtracking just brought more of the same. I was in a damn maze!

Guessing that this smartphone might connect to Evan instantly, I hit the speed dial and blurted into the phone as I ran: "It's Ana Marie! She's run into the garden searching for her daddy! I'm outside looking for her."

"Phoebe! Where are you exactly?"

"Damned if I know." Then I glimpsed a light weaving somewhere to my right. I switched back to the light app and bolted after.

The house alarms were pealing so loudly I doubted she could hear me over the ruckus now but that didn't stop me from trying. "Ana Marie, wait up!"

Maybe I'd hit it right with the direction gods for once because a path opened up and soon I was bounding across an open lawn slick with dew. With her light still bouncing ahead, I thought I was finally catching up. But suddenly the light stopped. Just stopped. Maybe she was waiting?

Then something dark reared up before me and flung me facedown to the ground, phone flying from my hands. Briefly winded, I rolled onto my back and kicked out but whatever it was had gone. *Disappeared!* How did a mass big enough to throw me to the ground simply disappear?

I stumbled to my feet, snatched up my phone, and ran toward the fallen light, maybe a hundred yards away. It was her phone, all right, the sparkly case lying on the path still beaming pink light into the night. But Ana Marie was nowhere to be seen.

Picking up her phone, I called her name until my throat grew raw. Spinning both lights around 360 degrees, I saw nothing but dark topiaries with tendrils of mist snaking close to the ground. Where did she go?

"If you hurt her, I swear I'll make you pay!" I croaked. He had to have kidnapped her, whoever that thing was that attacked me, and if he harmed that child... It didn't bear thinking about.

I started running, my lights beaming straight ahead, trying to catch movement or something, but all I caught were shadows smudged by that shifting mist.

And then my feet left the grass and I was plunging through ferns and bracken in a downward hurl. Ana Marie's phone slipped from my grip but I managed to hang on to mine until a branch snagged my ankle and pitched me facedown into a bed of wet ferns.

I slid on my stomach for several feet before coming to a stop, my shirt soaked, everything dark. Pushing onto my hands and knees, I felt around for my phone. The light had gone off, leaving me blind. Damn, damn, damn. Like I had time for this.

Here, the mist was thicker, the shadows darker. Somehow, I wound up in the woods with no idea how or where—one minute I was on grass and the next not. I stood listening, sensing the shapes of trunks, ferns, and mossy rocks all around me, my heart thumping hard. Every childhood fairy tale I had ever read had dropped me right in the center of the deep dark forest and left me alone with the big bad wolf.

Grow up, Phoebe. Little Red Riding Hood has martial arts training now. But there was still something uncanny about those woods. Maybe it was only my imagination, maybe it was only that shifting mist, but the atmosphere prickled my skin. I couldn't bear to think of Ana Marie lost out there even though she must know this area better than anyone. I was the lost one.

I felt for the phone with my feet. No luck. "Come here, phone," I called in a moment of folly. Amazingly, a light began pulsing, reminding me that this was a brighter-than-average smartphone.

I waded through the ferns to where an alien emerald-green glow beamed into the night. The moment I picked up the phone, it started talking in a computer-generated version of Evan's voice: "GPS activated. Proceed to left. Follow route outlined on the screen."

"Where am I going?" I asked.

"Return to house," it said.

"I'm not returning to the house without that child," I said.

"Return to house," it repeated.

Damn.

Stepping forward, I brushed through the undergrowth following the red directional arrows on the screen until I realized that there was a path there all along, overgrown, perhaps, but there. After climbing up a set of stone steps, I was back on the lawn, delirious with relief.

A light beaming far ahead sent me running. A black shape loomed against a starry sky as my light picked up gleaming scales—the dragon fountain. *Draggy!*

In seconds, I was dashing around the base, beaming my phone on the marble foundation. An entrance to the tunnels lay below this fountain so maybe they—surely that dark shadow thing was part of a *they*—had taken her that way, deep underground where her father had died months before.

And then I saw it: an opening under the fountain, just a dark rectangular door with a light glowing deep inside the tunnel's throat. Someone was definitely in there. I scrambled down the narrow steps and froze. It was could be a trap. And if I did encounter the kidnappers, what was I going to fight them with—my bare hands, feet, what? Here I was barefoot, wearing nothing but a ragged sleep shirt. Even with martial arts, I needed help.

I pressed the speed dial again but the phone kept pulsing red with the mechanical Evan repeating, "Return to the house, return to house."

I held it up. "Shut up," I whispered.

The phone shut up.

"Engage taser app," I ordered.

"Taser app engaged."

"Keep flashlight on."

"Flashlight on."

"Send message to Evan that I am under the dragon fountain."

"Message sent."

Now we're talking. I took a step down, looking around for another weapon that didn't require me getting too close to the monsters. I didn't have time to scan the app menu.

A bare earthen floor and a pile of loose rocks on one side offered the only options. I picked up a stone, holding it high in my other hand. There was some kind of stationary light straight ahead, a lantern, maybe. That's what I'd follow, not that there was any place to hide, not that they wouldn't see me coming, but a child could be trapped down there.

Several yards farther and the ground dipped. The corridor widened and there was a bright yellow reflective barrier to my right, broken as if by an ax. There'd be a fissure behind that. I didn't need to see it to feel it yawning. Electric lanterns lit the way as far as I could see.

And then it was if a hunk of clotted shadow detached from the wall and came toward me in a football tackle. I brought the rock smashing down onto his back while my other hand tried to zap him with the taser but missed. He knocked my phone from my hand and spun away long enough for me to see a black-robed man in a black ski mask and hood coming back at me.

I kicked out, catching him in the gut and moving in for a second hit, when something caught me from behind. It was as if I'd been snarled in a huge net that covered my head to my shoulders and pinned my arms to my sides. Swinging around, I tried to kick out but the man at my back only laughed while the other stepped up and punched me in the stomach. I bent over gasping while the other began pushing me down a sloping tunnel, my feet scrabbling to break my pace.

The ground declined sharply. I was stumbling so quickly I couldn't brake and, with the man pushing me along, I was in a helpless trajectory. Then I saw the crevasse ahead. Or at least I assumed that's what it was—a dark cold drop to somewhere—and at that instant I feared that this might be the end game.

I fell to my knees trying to stop my fall, but with my arms useless it was easy for the men to kick me over as if I were a Russian doll. I tried to kick out again but one took me by the shoulders and dragged me to the fissure.

"Adeus," one snarled as he kicked me down into the depths. Bizarrely, I thought he murmured something else in Latin before a shower of small stones rained down on my head and the lights extinguished.

Meanwhile, my legs shot out to slow my descent and, after several scraping seconds, the netting over my head snagged on a piece of rock and held. There I dangled literally by a thread supported by my aching legs hanging in the dark. I barely dared to breathe. I wondered if this was how I was going to die—alone in the dark.

But I couldn't have fallen more than six feet. Should I risk trying to climb back up? One sliding inch convinced me of the wisdom of holding still, excruciatingly still. Even the slightest movement threatened to send me skidding down. After minutes—seconds?—of wondering how long I could hang on like this, I remembered my phone. If they'd left it where it had fallen, I had a chance.

"Phone," I cried. "Start alarm!"

I waited, wondering if the thing could even hear me this far down. Seconds later, the Evan robot voice said, "Alarm set."

"Add pulsing lights!"

"Pulsing lights added."

The noise was deafening but I was too relieved to care. Minutes later a posse of men plus Phoebe and Evan were calling down to me overhead. "Hang on!"

"Trying not to go anywhere," I called.

Peaches called. "We're coming to get you."

As the aching minutes passed, I could hear men shouting somewhere, heard footsteps, felt my legs splitting in two and my feet scraped raw. Someone was lowered down in a sling to fasten a harness around my waist —Peaches.

"Good timing, Peach," I whispered. "Don't know how long this butterfly net would last."

"Some butterfly net. Nylon fishing net, more like it. Hold on while I get this thing between your legs."

Once I was securely harnessed, the men above lifted me to the surface with Evan waiting to take me into his arms.

For a shocked moment, I stood trembling as his arms wrapped tightly around my shoulders. Gazing straight into his eyes, my face only inches away, I managed to say, "Thank you, thank you to everyone, and your new phone is... great..."

"You're welcome," he whispered, holding me like he had no intention of ever letting me go. "I'll take you back to the house now."

I stiffened. "No!" I pushed him gently away. "I haven't found Ana Marie yet. No child goes missing on my watch."

He pushed a lock of hair from his eyes with a muddy hand. "She's home safe, Phoebe. She arrived back under an hour ago."

⁂

I SAT IN THE LIBRARY WITH MY FEET BATHING IN A BASIN OF WARM water and floating flora. Every inch of me ached, stung, or burned, my stomach and feet especially, but Ana Marie was safe and that was all that mattered.

Those dark monks had terrified the child so badly that she had bolted back home like a frightened rabbit, her knowledge of the secret routes probably all that had saved her. As much as I wanted to talk to her then, she was cloistered with the family, so that would have to wait.

"Those bastards tried to kidnap her," I said again to no one in particular. I sat wrapped in a blanket across from Rupert, who had fixed me a soothing pot of tea and added one of his own special digestive biscuits to the saucer. Peaches was crouching at my feet, fussing with my cuts while applying Band-Aids where necessary. The Carvalho family remained upstairs and Evan and Markus were with the security team combing the grounds.

"It can only be those unholy thugs attempting to use that poor child for their devious purposes," Rupert said. "That any group could be so disconnected from their callous hearts to use a child for such a purpose is unforgivable. They must have been plotting a blackmail scheme."

"They're fanatical," I said. My voice was slowly improving thanks to Rupert's medicinal tea. "They killed Jose and Ana Marie's father, too, remember?"

"Do you really think they'd sink so low as to harm a child?" Peaches asked, looking up from dabbing my knee. "Wait—forget I said that. Of course they would. Anything to further their depraved agenda, right? The monsters. I swear I'll throttle them to within an inch of their lives for this."

"Only if I don't get there first," I said. "They must have been trying to lure Ana Marie outside all along. She thought her daddy had been signaling her and I saw the lights myself. Imagine luring a grieving child that way? Those were the same dark monks who attacked me. They were after Ana Marie all along."

Rupert leaned forward. "At least we know them to be vaguely human. Had you said that you'd been accosted by something supernatural it wouldn't have surprised me considering this extraordinary location."

I shook my head. "They were definitely part of the material world—men in a black-hooded robes. Monks in ski masks who blend into the shadows."

"So, these Divinio chaps are running around in monks' robes?" Rupert asked, widening his eyes above his bristled brows. I appreciated how he reduced these creatures with words like "chap" and "thugs," as if refusing to grant them more power than they deserved. In fact, at that moment, I appreciated that so much that I beamed at him in gratitude.

My sudden blaze of warmth must have taken him aback. He stared at me for a moment before saying, "The tea *is* rather fortifying, isn't it? It is the honey, I believe. Would you like a little top-up, Phoebe?"

"No, I'm fine, thank you. I'm just really thankful for my friends tonight—both of you, all of you," I whispered. And let's face it, tea and sugar can be very fortifying.

Rupert met my eyes and smiled. "As we are you, Phoebe." He cleared his throat.

"Yeah," Peaches added. "I don't fall at the feet of just anyone."

I smiled. "And stick just anyone's feet into a basin of watery twigs."

"Herbs," she countered. "Comfrey, bay leaves, sage, plus a dash of oregano. If that doesn't soothe your feet, at least we can make a pizza out of you."

I glanced down at the muddy water in which I steeped. She and one of Ana Marie's nannies had gone into the gardens to gather herbs under her instruction. Apparently, her Jamaican granny had taught her all there was to know about medicinal herbs.

Rupert emitted a little cough. "Meanwhile, it would appear that as Senhor Carvalho surmised, these *thugs* must be using those tunnels for their own foul purposes, possibly entering the tower chambers from multiple avenues."

Peaches remarked without looking up: "We have to block those suckers off."

"If we can determine their entry and exit points, we will have something to go on indeed," Rupert agreed. "It is quite probable that they believe the crown is buried down there in the depths, which is as good a theory as any, I surmise. Apparently, the dragon entrance had not been used since before Ricardo's death, to anyone's knowledge."

I nodded. "That's what I was thinking. This time they used it to lure a child."

Rupert paused to read his phone. "Evan informs me that they have found nothing further but have located the child's phone. Currently they are securing the area for the evening."

He leaned forward. "Phoebe, pardon the sudden change of topic, but I am alarmed to see the outfit in which you have chosen to wear in this establishment. Am I truly seeing correctly and you have donned a ragged shirt emblazoned with van Gogh's unfortunate bandaged ear?"

"Fitting under the circumstances, don't you think?" I pointed to my wounded knee before pulling back the blanket far enough to reveal the artist's bandaged head, which actually was so plastered with mud it was hardly recognizable. I pulled the blanket tight. "Well, you get the picture."

"To the detriment of my sensibilities, indeed I do. Surely you sleep in something more proper?"

Peaches raised her head. "Yeah, Rupe, you tell her. Phoebe does the comfort-over-style thing."

He paused as if considering whether to protest the amputation of his name and, deciding against it, continued. "Indeed, one does not exclude the other," he said, warming to the topic. "I always assure my well-being by packing five pairs of the finest silk pajamas so that my comfort does not preclude style for a single moment. One never knows where one might spend the night, such as in a majestic Portuguese family home owned by ancestral nobility, for example."

Peaches glanced up. "I'm with you there. I bring a selection of slinky nightgowns just in case. You never know. 'Be prepared' is my motto."

"Girl Guides?" I asked.

"Girl *Scouts*, badass division," Peaches countered. "Guides do brownies and chocolate chip cookies. As I was saying, I always sleep with a pair of leggings on under my nightie for just such emergencies as these. You should try it sometime."

I stared at her. "Seriously? Look, I usually take my nighttime excursions fully dressed but I didn't want to lose sight of that child for a minute. Good thing, too."

"Still, van Gogh T-shirts just don't cut it in our business, Phoebe. What did I tell you?"

"If I recall, you suggested I wear something slinky and weren't referring to danger management."

Any fondness I felt for my friends bristled. I adored them but I wanted to throttle them sometimes, too. Thus is the contradiction of human relations. My sharp comment died on my lips when Evan strode into the room.

"It's done," he said, his voice heavy with fatigue. If possible, he looked worse than I did in the scratched and worn department. That made him no less attractive, by the way. "We searched every inch of the gardens, secured as much as we could, and the rest will have to wait until morning. The house is finally returning to bed."

"I'm not surprised that you didn't find anything. Those brutes have some hidden route where they can leave us all in the dust," Peaches remarked while I quickly began wiping down my legs and feet with the towel she'd brought.

"How are you doing, Phoebe?" Evan asked softly.

"Much better, thanks." Without looking at him, I was now attempting to squeeze my feet into my sandals, Peaches helping by holding them still. I imagined how bad I looked. "In fact, I'm ready for bed, so whoever wants to come with me. I mean, accompany me." *Just shut up, Phoebe.*

"I'd be happy to accompany you to bed, Phoebe, but hopefully you don't expect to just walk unassisted?" Evan said.

"Of course I—"

But he strode over to me and simply picked me up as if I were two years old and proceeded toward the door before I could protest. "You're in no condition to be walking anywhere more tonight."

"This is ridiculous," I protested.

"Just stop talking, Phoebe. Your throat is sounding raw," he said with the smallest of smiles.

"I'll be up in a minute," Peaches called behind us.

"And I will be along also," Rupert added, "as soon as I gather my tea stocks."

I was gazing at Evan. "As much as I appreciate your manly manner, please don't think that helplessness is going on my résumé anytime soon."

"I wouldn't dare make such assumptions. I'm merely taking advantage of the situation while I can," he said with a grin. "By the way, I'm leaving you with a pistol to keep with you at all times."

He got no argument from me this time. And I didn't half mind throwing my arm over his neck, either, if I was being honest, though that did dredge up memories of another man at another time.

As we passed through the door, I caught Queen Isabella's eye in a moment of female understanding: the age-old conundrum of female sovereignty under the power of the male will.

12

I had a delayed start the next morning, sleeping late and rousing slowly, but after showering and attending to my scrapes, I managed to don a pair of jeans and a fresh long-sleeved shirt. My mangled van Gogh sleepwear ended in a waste bin on my way down to breakfast, deposited with regret.

"Can you walk?" Peaches asked, meeting me in the hall.

"Of course I can walk—just not comfortably."

Peaches nodded. "All righty, then."

We had received a text from Adriana saying that breakfast would be served in the library, and by the time we arrived, Rupert, Evan, and Markus were already sitting at a circular table set up in the spacious tiled foyer. It's as if the library was to be our communal sitting, dining, and convening room, removing us from the family, whether by accident or design I didn't yet know.

Everybody appeared to be reviving themselves with copious amounts of coffee poured from a silver urn. The buffet table also held a selection of bread, cheese, and fruit. Once I answered the inevitable questions about my well-being, I loaded up a plate and sat down beside Markus, noting that he at least seemed unruffled after the night's events. In fact, freshly showered with his hair combed straight back from his forehead, he looked relatively pulled together for once.

"Were you part of the scouting party last night?" I asked him.

Without looking up, he replied, "I was. I managed to find the child's phone."

"Big win," Peaches remarked. "Phoebe tackled rabid monks and was tossed down a hole."

"Is this a competition?" Markus asked.

Evan looked up from his fruit and caught my eye while Rupert cleared his throat. "After last night's events," he said, "it appears that we will not be permitted to study the inverted well and the altar a second time. I took the liberty of requesting another opportunity to survey the site again today and was flatly refused."

I looked up from buttering my roll. "By whom—Senhor Carvalho?"

"Not directly, no. It would seem that following the events of last night, Senhor Carvalho has retreated to his chambers and the chatelaine of the castle has taken over. She does not wish us to further our efforts," Rupert said.

"Not at all?" I asked.

"I spoke with the gentleman's daughter-in-law at some length—"

"Adriana?" I asked.

"Adriana Carvalho, yes—Phoebe, do stop interrupting me. We are all just as alarmed as you obviously are. Allow me to continue."

"Sorry."

"So, it seems that Senhora Carvalho has quite made up her mind on the point and insists that her father-in-law feels the same. Regardless, the family went so far as to block off the forest access following last night's unfortunate events and barricaded the dragon entrance once and for all," Rupert explained. "Though I do rather understand the impetus, I admit that the news is most distressing."

I could barely swallow. "But the Divinios were down that tunnel last night," I croaked. "Now that we know they're here, we need to scour every inch."

"Regrettably that's not possible now, Phoebe," Evan said, stirring his coffee. "The work is already done. I checked earlier this morning. Between the hours of 6:00 and 9:00 a.m., a concrete barrier was erected as per Senhor Carvalho's instructions."

"Without telling us?"

"It is his property," Markus reminded me as he focused on spearing a slab of cheese. "He is under no obligation to tell us anything, let alone ask our permission."

Rupert glanced at him. "Indeed. Apparently, he claimed that he could not risk another accident such as the one that befell Phoebe and almost took his granddaughter."

"Senhora Carvalho proceeded to stress that her father-in-law refuses to offer the Divinios one more opportunity to harm yet another person in this house," Evan clarified.

"You cannot blame the poor chap. My attempt to convince the senhora otherwise fell on deaf ears, I'm afraid. We are to remain here as invited guests only." Rupert gazed down at his plate soberly.

I sat back in my seat. "But we're hardly invited guests. We're on the heels of mass murderers. Somebody attacked me and tried to kidnap a child. Are we supposed to ignore that?"

Evan nudged me under the table, startling me so much that all I could do was gape. "Yes, we must," he said solemnly. "As guests we must obey house rules."

I was about to say, *Since when?* but restrained myself. Even without my first cup of coffee, I knew something was up.

"Besides," Evan continued, "we scoured every inch of tunnel right up to the trench where you were attacked and whatever footsteps may have been evident have been packed down or deliberately eradicated. What remains is indistinguishable."

"Who's 'we'?" I asked.

"The five men who Ricardo trained as his assistants. They live here on the property and helped with the search last night," he said.

"And are they trustworthy?" Peaches asked. "I mean, they seemed like straight-up guys but that doesn't mean anything."

Rupert's gaze fixed on hers. "It matters not that they are 'straight-up guys' as you say, since they have won the family's complete trust, Penelope."

Okay, so I was cluing in by now. Either we were under surveillance or somebody in our group couldn't be trusted. "So we're unable to return to the well site from any direction?" I asked carefully.

"No," Evan insisted.

I paused, studying his eyes—green, steady, and worried as hell.

"So we just stop?" Peaches inquired.

"Yes." Evan was watching Markus, who remained engaged in making himself a kind of cheese baguette by piling several slices of cheese on a hunk of bread. His appetite had obviously improved.

"However," Markus said as if sensing Evan's eyes on him, "presumably we can continue our documentary research."

Peaches turned to him. "Have you discovered anything new, Markus, maybe something you have yet to mention?"

The man paused from his slicing and dicing. "Peaches, are you implying that I am working from my own agenda here? Perish the thought. It's true that Ricardo shared specific details of his findings with Jose and me while we were in Spain but nothing that you don't already know—that everybody doesn't already know."

"What exactly were those findings again?" Peaches asked.

"I presume you're not interested in the technical minutiae of our forensic findings," Markus said mildly. "Ricardo had already shown us that photo of the tower diagram, which was startling enough, and I have since shared with each of you my thinking as to a possible location for the crown. The nature of the altar is telling in itself. I believe that the brotherhood has reached the same conclusion."

"Brotherhood?" I asked.

"Yes, brotherhood. That's what they are, right?" He stared at me.

"That the crown must lie under the altar?" Peaches inquired at the same time.

"Where else?" he asked.

"Where indeed," Rupert remarked, brushing crumbs from the table onto a plate. "But unfortunately we are now unable to investigate further."

"All the evidence, including everything we discovered in Spain, leads back to this property and to Portugal itself." Markus waved his knife in the air. "Prince Carlos was half-Portuguese; his mother's family lived here on this land. What better place to hide the crown of her prince but in the land of his mother, especially since Spain was rife with intrigue and therefore hardly safe?"

"You believe that the crown was stolen by the prince's maternal line?" Rupert asked. "I must say, that does seem the likeliest scenario, given what we know. Certainly there must have been a group working counter to the Divinios here if the skull and crown were moved for safekeeping."

"But we don't know the identity of that counteroperative, which is surely key to the crown's location?" I said. I remained fixed on Markus. "What did you discover in Spain, Markus—specifically? And don't worry about it being too advanced for present company." I figured that whatever ruse we were playing, we needed to sound convincing. Anything less than an open discussion of possibilities wouldn't do.

Markus stopped his super-sandwich construction to reply. "Ricardo had launched a research trail using tertiary documents from King Philip's court including the somewhat rambling letters of Prince Carlos himself, but found no mention of a missing crown or a breakaway sect. I believe copies of all those documents are here in this library, by the way. Evan, Rupert, and I have been raking through some of them but doubtless there's more. The point is, Ricardo found nothing significant in the written documents and, so far, neither have we."

"Maybe because secret societies and countersocieties might consider the wisdom of not putting anything down in print?" I suggested.

"Whoever was working against the Divinios did everything in their power to remain covert obviously. A secret society requires a secret counteroperation," Evan said.

"Yes," Markus continued, "but the point is that the only thing Ricardo came away with after years of research was the certainty that both the crown and the skull are buried on Portuguese soil, which is why he returned home to dig. Unfortunately, our physical digging must now stop." That statement was so out of character that I knew Markus was also part of the smokescreen.

Peaches was tearing up a plump roll and dabbing it with marmalade. "That still doesn't mean that the missing crown is here. Wouldn't it have been located some time ago if it was?"

"Not after numerous earthquakes," Evan remarked. "Finding anything in those mangled tunnels must be extremely difficult."

"I guess," she said grudgingly.

But surely in order to understand where that crown was buried, we needed to understand the thinking of whoever hid it? It was a conviction that had slowly been growing in me but one which had to remain off the collective table until we could speak freely.

"Phoebe," Evan said suddenly. "Are you still having trouble with your phone?"

I paused my thoughts. "Oh, yes," I pulled it from my pocket. "The reception has been spotty. I thought it might have to do with the altitude. Will you take a look at it for me?"

"My pleasure." He held out his hand. "Are you having the same issues, Peaches?"

She glanced at both of us. "Yeah, sure. The thing craps out and drives me nuts. Here, see if you can make it better."

In seconds, Evan had both our phones pocketed, leaving us to eat our breakfasts in silence while Markus proceeded to sail his enormous sandwich toward his mouth like a submarine heading into port. I watched in amazement as he opened his jaws wide enough to gnaw a big chunk of bread and cheese. Rupert, who had been carefully bisecting a pear, paused to observe the spectacle before averting his gaze.

"Nice going, Markus," Peaches commented. "You have the bite of a stealth shark."

Markus chewed in apparent enjoyment, making no further comment. That left the rest of us to sip our coffees, eat our bread, cheese, and fruit, lost in our own thoughts. After a few minutes, I took my mug and limped into the main library area, making a slow steady progress toward Queen Isabella.

There I stood before the standing queen, my attention fixed on the piece of canvas that had been uncovered by the conservator, a small dark square in the lower left-hand corner that blended all the shadows together seamlessly. Yet, here the paint seemed unusually thick in that area, as if smeared with solidified grime. Too bad that the conservator hadn't tackled that part. She must have been very methodical since she worked in a kind of grid formation, uncovering the original glory inch by inch but stopping just millimeters before tackling that particularly grimy bit.

Other than that, something about the portrait niggled at me. In all obvious ways, the queen stood in the same fashion as many royal portraits of the time—beautiful, richly adorned, and surveying her domain from afar. Her aloofness was part of the symbolism of royalty perched high above the common man, gaze fixed on her duty to God and King, which were considered one and the same. That, at least, was the accepted royal PR of the time.

Behind her, an open window revealed a deeply wooded mountain that could be anywhere. Turning toward the other portrait, I studied the background there, too—another mountainous scene differing only slightly from the other. Both windows looked similar but not identical—arched stone, as if part of a castle.

"Are you thinking that perhaps those paintings might hold the clue?" Evan whispered.

I looked up at him standing beside me, coffee mug in hand. "Is it safe to talk here?" I asked, keeping my voice low.

"No place is ever safe from surveillance in our business, as you know, but for now, just stay as far away from walls and furniture as you can get and trust no one. I'm doing constant sweeps in the meantime and will recheck our phones' security."

I nodded. "We may have to resort to passing notes. As for your question, surely this family must have considered that possibility of the paintings holding clues over the years. Has anyone identified the landscape behind either painting?"

"I asked Senhor Carvalho the night we arrived and he assured me that all aspects of the paintings have been thoroughly investigated. It is his belief that the geography was designed to appear more or less like any mountainous region in the monarch's dominion, whether it be in Spain, Portugal, or beyond."

"But both portraits were probably painted in Spain."

"Or in Italy and transported."

"I'm thinking Spain and what does that tell you?" I asked, looking up at him.

His gaze met mine. "I hesitate to say."

"Because you know what I'm thinking."

"But, Phoebe—"

Before he could finish, the door flew open and in strode Adriana

Carvalho. Markus and Rupert rose from their seats but she waved them down.

"No, please sit and finish your breakfast. I have come to say only that first thing tomorrow morning a van has been arranged to take you back to Lisbon. It is not possible for you to stay here one more night after this. I apologize for the inconvenience but that is the way it must be."

And then she turned and left.

"No, let me," I told my colleagues as they rushed to the door.

She was almost halfway down the hall before I caught up with her. "Adriana, wait."

"No, Phoebe. It has been decided: you must leave. I would have you go immediately but I am unable to arrange transportation sooner."

She didn't look at me and nothing broke her stride. I had to half run to keep up. "But why?" I asked. "What have we done?"

She looked at me then, her expression fierce and pained. "How can you ask that? The moment you arrived, it signaled to the Divinios that our family was against them."

"But you *are* against them!"

"Everything quieted down after Ricardo died because my father-in-law stopped searching, but then you came and it started all over again. They tried to kidnap Ana Marie!"

"I know, I'm sorry, but that didn't happen because of our arrival. The discovery of the skull has ramped up their efforts."

"Because you are here!"

"No, because now that they have the skull, they need to find the crown and will let nothing or no one stand in the way! Whether we are here or not, nothing will stop them."

"They will leave us alone once you are gone. Besides, your presence is having a bad effect on Ana Marie. She thinks that you will take her to her daddy—you! Her daddy is dead and no one or nothing can bring him back! Now leave us alone!"

Her pace quickened as she strode down the hall. She flung open a door and entered a room, me following after.

"Leave me alone, I said!" she cried, swinging around, her cheeks wet. "You will not change my mind."

We were in an elegant sitting room with brocade couches and a scattering of Persian rugs. A large arched window looked out across the forest. "I'm sorry for Ricardo, Adriana, sorry that Ana Marie thought that I would somehow help her find her daddy, and yes, they tried to lure her away last night and they will try again whether we leave or not. They are still here!"

"I know they are still here. That's why you must leave."

I threw up my hands. "That makes no sense! You banishing us will not stop the Divinios from targeting your family again and again, don't you see? It's too late for that. Your property is positioned over their sacred ground; your family is related to their supposed prince. What's more, the enemy of the Divinios probably operated here all along. How can you escape that? The only option you have is to stand and fight."

"What do you know about fighting?" she snarled, turning on me, fists bunched at her hips. I took a step back. "Do you have a daughter to protect? Have you lost the man you love and stood by while your world literally crumbles beneath your feet? Last night, those bastards tried to take my daughter, *my daughter*. They've already taken my husband. I'll do exactly what he says from now on."

I paused. "Do exactly what he says? What do you mean by you'll 'do exactly what he says'? Did someone give you instructions?"

Her back was to me again and at first she wouldn't answer. Then, without a word, she strode to a wireless phone on a small table, tapped something, and passed the phone to me.

With the receiver pressed to my ear, I listened to the deep voice speaking in Portuguese on playback. "But I don't understand a word," I said.

"Allow me to translate since I know the words by heart: *'The next time we will succeed and Ana Marie will go the way of Ricardo, deep down the earth's black jaws. You cannot escape us, Carvalho. We are everywhere. Your guests must leave or we strike again and then your Ana Marie dies and our holy king will be born.'*"

A chill hit. I pressed the replay icon and played the call again, this time listening for background sounds or some telltale signs that would identify the caller. Nothing. "It must be the same man who threatened Markus. I'd like him to validate that, if you don't mind."

"Yes, of course. As long as you leave tomorrow morning, you can validate anything you like. Be ready to leave at 5:00 a.m. Now go." She sniffed.

Still holding the phone, I tried to dial down the emotion streaming in my veins. "Yes, if that's what you want, of course," I said softly, "but that won't make this end, Adriana. Blackmailers and extortionists don't work that way, especially not cults as vicious as the Divinios. If you give them what they want, they'll still keep coming. You're standing in the way."

She swung back to me. "Go!"

I held up a hand. "Okay, okay, but please think over what I said." Turning, I froze when the door opened and there stood Ana Marie with her nanny, Alma.

"Phoebe! I mean, Ms. McCabe!" She dropped Alma's hand and ran for me, throwing her arms around my waist and burying her face in my shirt. "I am so sorry! Please forgive me for getting you into trouble! I know you tried to stop me but I am a naughty girl who will not listen to reason," she sobbed.

I dropped to my knees and held her. "You are not a naughty girl, Ana Marie. You are a brave whirling dervish princess trying to fight the monsters out there, but you must listen to your mama." I caught Adriana's eye over the child's head.

"Come, Ana Marie," Adriana said. "Say goodbye to Ms. McCabe. She will leave us tomorrow."

"But I don't want her to go," the girl murmured, holding me closer.

I got to my feet and gently unfolded the child's arms. "Go to your mama," I whispered.

"But I don't want you to leave!"

"Ana Marie, come here at once," her mother commanded.

The girl stepped back to take her mother's hand, her eyes never leaving my face.

"I'd like to say goodbye to your father-in-law, if I may," I told Adriana. "May I visit him?"

"You may not," Adriana told me. "He is resting. Last night's events have left him very fragile. Now please leave us."

I passed Alma on my way out the door, surprised that the woman appeared to be trying to catch my eye.

The whole episode had left me reeling. I had failed to convince anyone of anything and now we were being forced to leave just when the stakes had never been higher.

13

I strode down the hall thinking only that I could not let that child or her family come to harm. Yet everything was lining up for exactly that. Our exit would signal to the Divinios that they were winning, opening the way for them to charge through the doors and perhaps raze this castle to the ground, metaphorically speaking.

Hell, I may as well have fallen into a medieval historical drama, yet this was real, hideously real, with that same sense of the surreal that blew in on the winds of 2020.

Bursting into the library, I announced: "The Carvalhos received another call late last night." I held up the house phone. "A man with a deep voice threatened to kidnap Ana Marie and swore that next time he would succeed. He said he would send her down the hole where they buried her father. Who would threaten a child like that?"

Evan swore under his breath. "Bloody terrorists," he muttered.

"Here, Markus, tell me whether this is the same voice you heard the night the skull was stolen. I've brought the house phone so you can listen to the replay," I said, holding out the phone.

My colleagues had been standing around the map cabinet. Suddenly Rupert sat down on the nearest chair, his face pale, while Peaches stood nearby looking ready to throttle somebody. Markus stepped forward while

I hit the replay button. For a few breathless moments we all watched while he listened.

"Yes," he whispered, his arm dropping to his side. "That's him, that's the one who threatened me. What a damn creepy voice, right? Makes me positively ill. I can't believe it belongs to a real human. He must be altering it somehow."

Evan took the phone and listened intently before passing it on to each the others. "He's using a voice camouflage."

Peaches had a theory: "Maybe that call was placed from inside the house?"

"Were you successful in convincing the castle's chatelaine to permit us to stay?" Rupert asked from his seat.

"No," I said. "Adriana wants us gone. She believes those threats absolutely." I gazed toward the door through which our host had exited that first evening. "I have to talk to Senhor Carvalho. Maybe he'd understand that forcing us to leave is the last thing this family needs." I moved toward the back door.

"We tried that," Markus said behind me. "It leads to a locked elevator operated by a keycard. No amount of button-pushing activates the thing."

I continued, anyway, while Peaches quickly caught up. "Adriana's become like the ultimate gatekeeper but I totally get where's she's coming from. She's not thinking straight."

"I don't care if she's not thinking straight. She's risking everyone." We had entered a small marble-tiled alcove no bigger than a coat closet with a single-wide elevator door directly ahead and a smaller door to the left. I pushed the button directly beside the elevator doors, only half listening. "She's clinging to what she has left—her only child—but capitulating to blackmailers never works."

"Still, fear of losing a child can drive a woman mad," Peaches said behind me. "I mean as in grip-your-gut-and-twist-until-you-break mad. You think your whole being is collapsing from the inside out. Losing a child has got to be the most heart-wrenching thing there is and it can leave you so broken you can't hardly think straight."

I swung around to face her, surprised to find her eyes moist. "Peaches?"

"Yeah, okay? So I lost my baby when I was eighteen. I was young and stupid and her father was just as young and ten times stupider. Kenyatta died while RayBoy was taking his baby daughter on a joyride through Kingston. Can you believe the idiocy? You protect your kids, not zoom around showing them off to your buds. Drug wars. Bastards shot up the car with my baby and then-boyfriend inside it. He survived, she didn't. The drug-dealing bastard ended up in prison and good thing, too, or I would have killed him myself."

For an instant, it all played before my eyes in a surge of pain and violence that my teenage self never had to experience in rural Nova Scotia. My friend's grief felt so raw that it emanated from her in waves. "God, Peach, I'm so sorry," I mumbled. "I always thought you grew up in the tropical paradise image I have of Jamaica and your parents—father a doctor, mother a teacher, life sunny and blissful."

She laughed. "It was blissful until my teenage self grew bored and decided to strike out for the big city alone. Anyway, I'm just saying this so you'll understand Adriana. She sees how it could all end up for her when she's probably already hanging by a thread. A parent will do anything to protect her baby even if it makes no sense to anybody else. I didn't do enough to protect mine and I'll never forgive myself." She leaned past me and pushed the elevator button again.

"You were just a kid," I whispered.

"Just stop. I don't want forgiveness. I want to make every bastard that hurts or threatens a child pay."

I had the overwhelming urge to hug her but one look at her face told me this wasn't the time. Turning back to the elevator, I stared at the elevator button, my heart reeling. How little we know about even the people closest to us, when it all comes down to it. I was so stunned by Peaches's admission that I temporarily forgot what I was about to do.

"It's not going to work, Phoebe. We tried multiple times," I heard Evan say from the doorway.

I turned to walk toward him, squeezing Peaches's hand in passing and poking my head in the closet for just a second. The art conservationist supply room. Shutting the door, I made my way back to the library, Evan stepping aside to let me pass.

"We have to do something," I whispered.

"I absolutely agree," he said softly. He took my arm to stop me in my tracks. I gazed up at him, seeing something in his tone, in his eyes. "We have the beginnings of a plan," he said, leaning toward me. Then he abruptly straightened and said aloud, "But if our hosts insist we leave, then we must go."

Had he discovered a new bug and wasn't certain he had caught all the possible surveillance devices?

"Yes, of course," I said cautiously. "But we don't have to like it."

"Certainly not." He glanced back at Peaches, who still stood where I'd left her. "Is she all right?" he whispered.

"She just needs a moment." I took his arm and led him over to one of the floor-to-ceiling windows that looked out over the garden. A gray day had descended on the mountains bringing down a heavy blanket of fog and mist. "So, as you were saying, the Divinio crown is hidden on this property?" They must all be in on the ruse, including Markus, though in his case I was convinced he might actually believe the crown was here."

"The best possible location given what we know to date, don't you agree?"

"Probably, but we can't continue Ricardo's work if we're being forced to leave." My voice sounded plaintive even to myself.

"Sadly, no."

Hopefully that little show would convince somebody, even though anyone who truly knew us would reach another conclusion.

After several minutes of flipping through the papers with Evan, I left him to study further while I excused myself and wandered back to stand by Titian's Isabella portrait. Soon Peaches was beside me.

"She looks so thin and pale in her magnificent duds," she remarked.

"Pallor was the preferred look of the day," I said. "She may have even used powdered lead to whiten her skin, though in her case, I doubt that was necessary," I replied. "According to the accounts, she worked herself to death traveling the land while her husband was away, keeping order and the economy healthy. Her pallor probably came naturally. By thirty-five when Prince Philip was still a boy, she was dead."

Peaches appraised the portrait anew. "So being a queen in those days wasn't all about wearing magnificent clothes and looking out of a turret?"

"Hardly. Being a queen in Spain was all about duty and obedience to God and King. She wouldn't have had much of a life by today's standards

THE CROWN THAT LOST ITS HEAD

but she worked hard as her king's regent and was credited with keeping the land in order while he was off waging war."

"Cool lady."

"And those magnificent clothes you see were extraordinarily uncomfortable, more symbolic of her station than anything else. Her chest was constrained by a bodice designed to flatten her breasts as if negating her femininity. The men, on the other hand, got to prance around with their codpieces prominently displayed and their shapely legs revealed in silk hose. Being overtly male was celebrated, being overtly female never."

"Peacocks," she remarked. "Matron, virgin, or whore?"

"Something like that. Femininity, even of the queenly sort, was all about holding it in and stifling your true self. You never shook your tail feathers if you were a queen."

"Hell," she said, gazing up with a regal bearing all her own. "I can't imagine stifling my tail feathers for a moment."

Since her tail feathers at that moment were encased in violet stretch leggings, I laughed. I took a quick scan around us—no chairs, tables, or lamps nearby to house surveillance items and the fireplace still crackled loudly enough to mask conversation. I whispered: "How are you doing?"

"Fine. I just had a bit of a meltdown. Little Ana Marie is dredging stuff up."

"Sorry."

"Don't be. We all have our wounds. The key is to go through life without bleeding all over the place. I just dribbled a bit back there."

I gave her a quick sideways hug.

"So tell me more about this painting," she asked.

"Something's up," I whispered. "See that blob of sfumato?"

"That blob of what-o?"

"Sfumato. It means to blend like smoke, a technique the masters used to blend tones and colors together to create a realistic shading that recedes seamlessly into the background. It made their subjects shine."

Peaches leaned closer to the painting. "I thought that might be dirt, old varnish or something."

"Maybe it is."

"Excuse me for interrupting," a voice said at our backs. "Penelope, but

149

would you mind terribly if Phoebe and I were to stroll the garden to take a spot of air?"

We turned to see Rupert looking as though he needed something—either coffee or a nap but probably not air.

"Does air even come in spots?" Peaches asked.

Rupert smiled wanly. "A figure of speech, Penelope, my dear, as well you know."

She pursed her lips, then laughed. "Just funning with you, Rupe, honey. So will taking this spot of air involve just the two of you?"

"Yes, if you don't mind terribly. We have had so little time to speak alone for many, many months."

"Sure," she said with a shrug.

"Excellent. We won't go far," Rupert assured her.

14

Moments later, Rupert and I strode into the hall. The quickest route outside would have been one floor down and out one of the many side entrances leading to the gardens.

We were just turning right toward the main stairs when a man stepped out in front of us. I recognized him from the day before—one of the men who had accompanied us to the well, the same man who'd threatened Rupert. Short, muscular with a bony forehead lunging over deep-set eyes, he flashed us an unconvincing smile. "I am Senhor Craca and I will be your escort. Where you go?"

"We were only planning to take a little stroll in the garden, if you don't mind," Rupert huffed.

Craca peeled his lips back from his teeth. "Where you go, I follow," he said. "For your safety."

"Our safety?" Rupert countered. "But we are only taking a brief walk in the garden in broad daylight, I said. Surely that won't require an escort?"

"Very dangerous now. You need escort."

I nudged Rupert, who sighed and stifled his complaints. Together we followed the man without further protest down the central staircase toward the main hall. Once on that broad tiled boulevard, Craca turned right, as if heading for the formal entrance. A maid heading toward us suddenly ducked inside a room while another ladened with a tray of tea things stopped short at the sight of us and retreated quickly down an adjacent hall. Rupert and I exchanged glances.

And so we walked the entire grand central hall and for once none of the treasures on either side caught my attention. We were just approaching the main doors when I glimpsed something small and pink flash out of the corner of my eye. I blinked. It was Ana Marie crouched in a corner behind a potted palm. She was inching forward as if planning to dash out. Rupert motioned her back. She glanced toward Craca before shrinking into the shadows and disappearing.

I paused, trying to see where she had gone, but saw nothing but the wall and a cluster of greenery. Craca ordered to us to hurry, so we quickened our pace.

"There is barely a veil of civility," Rupert muttered as we struggled to catch up. "It is most alarming."

The front garden's formal sweep of boulevards and fountains were shrouded in heavy mist when we descended the outer stairs, the damp pressing against our faces like a wet cloth. Still, I breathed in the moisture-ladened air with a strange sense of relief. It only then occurred to me how claustrophobic the interior had become.

"I fear that I may not have dressed appropriately for the day," Rupert remarked, gazing ahead. His dapper linen jacket did seem a little thin for the day. "Best we keep our walk brief."

"My feet are still a bit sore so that's fine with me. Besides, we may have little choice. The Doberman seems restless," I remarked.

As if he'd overheard, Craca stopped in his tracks and turned to wait for us to catch up. "You stay close. Easy to get lost in mist," he said.

Rupert led me toward the edge of the path. "Surely we're in no risk of becoming lost while on the main thoroughfare," he protested. "If you don't mind, senhor, I would rather not have you walking so close." He flapped his hand at the man as if shooing flies. "Do step back." The man stepped back. "More, more. There. At least three meters distance will suffice."

Craca glowered but remained a distance behind us.

"A most unpleasant guard dog," Rupert whispered as we strolled on ahead.

"Since when did we even have guard dogs?" I asked. "And the fact that he went through the main doors is meant to be a show of power—somebody's, anyway."

"As you've no doubt deduced, the Divinios have infiltrated the castle," he whispered. "That one is proof. Evan is attempting to secure our communication channels just in case we are under surveillance. Since many have no doubt been on staff all along, they have doubtless won the family's trust." He brought his lips so close to my ear I could feel his breath. "We have devised a plan."

"You have?"

"Thank you for accompanying me, Phoebe," Rupert said loudly as we continued down the path. "I merely craved some air. In truth, I have not been feeling quite up to snuff."

"No problem, Rupert," I assured him, patting his arm. We were halfway down the first broad manicured path and Craca was walking only a few feet at our heels.

Rupert spoke more loudly. "What we saw yesterday must be one of the best preserved underground archaeological sites in existence. I have never seen such a thing. I am very glad to have had the opportunity to view it before we leave tomorrow."

"Subtle," I whispered.

He paused to dab his forehead with a hanky, one of the old-fashioned accessories he refused to relinquish. "Oh, my, but all this walking is quite laborious, isn't it? I was feeling unwell in there and hoped fresh air would help."

"Rupert, stop trying to fool me or yourself," I said. "This entire trip has been too much for you given that you are still recovering."

"Nonsense. You do know that the word 'invalid' can also be pronounced with the emphasis on the middle syllable as in *in-VA-lid*. I refuse to be rendered *in-va-lid* by a microorganism. There is only so much insult a man can bear. Besides, I live for adventures such as this." Then he dropped his voice again. "We must talk. No place is safe but this is the best opportunity we have."

"Let's rest," I said loudly as I steered him over to one of the marble benches positioned between a troll-like topiary and a small leaping dolphin statue. "Senhor Craca," I called. "My friend is exhausted. We'll be along momentarily. Don't feel the need to wait."

The man's blunted features seemed even more blurred in the mist as he gave us a curt nod. For a few aching seconds I feared that he'd come stand over us and nix any chances for privacy. Instead, he abruptly turned to talk into his phone, strolling far enough away to put us out of earshot.

"He will not be leaving us unaccompanied for long, believe me," Rupert whispered. "That cur is one of them."

I stared at the man's back. "Okay, tell me what you need to say and please keep it brief."

"Yes, indeed. Senhora Carvalho is merely playing into their hands but leaving the family alone with these monsters is most unadvisable, no matter where that blasted crown may lay."

I leaned forward and lowered my voice further. "I agree that we can't leave tomorrow. And?"

"We have formulated a plan. Truly I am not feeling up to snuff, which can be used to our advantage. Wait for the sign."

"Who's 'we'? And the plan is?"

"Careful, here comes our pit bull."

Senhor Craca was marching forward, his feet crunching on the gravel. "We go now," he ordered. "Move, please."

"Tell me your plan before it's too late," I whispered.

But it was already too late. Craca arrived to stand over us, glowering. Rupert heaved an exaggerated sigh and stood, the two of us making a slow measured progress behind the guard toward the house.

Rupert was perspiring so heavily that I knew his weariness wasn't feigned. Without knowing the details of the plan, I had no idea how to play the situation from here on. Best to just follow his lead. "Rupert, you need to rest. You're in no shape to go anywhere tomorrow," I whispered.

"I don't plan to," he murmured. "We must communicate by note from here on," he whispered. "We have been attempting to line up transportation but it fell through. The coronavirus—"

"What is problem?" Craca barked.

"He can't move as quickly as we can," I snapped.

Craca turned on his heels and marched into the house.

The moment that we stepped into the castle behind him through yet another side entrance, I caught that flash of pink again, this time in the shadows to my right. Now Ana Marie was beckoning us to follow her around a dark corner. Putting a finger to my lips, I pointed ahead to Craca and shook my head. She peered around the corner and pulled quickly back while mouthing something and pointing overhead.

Rupert, leaning heavily on me, watched the exchange. "Senhor Craca, hold on, please," he called.

The man turned and waited, a flash of irritation visible on his broad features.

"I don't feel quite well enough to brave those steps to the bedrooms at the moment—quite out of the question. I would prefer to retire to the library for a spot of tea and recuperation; it's more manageable given my present state."

"I take you to room as instructed," Craca said.

"Instructed by whom?" I asked. "Senhora Carvalho? I am certain she would not want one of her guests to pass out on the stairs. Let me speak to the lady." I held out my hand for his phone.

Craca hesitated. I knew damn well that Adriana wasn't at the end of that phone.

Rupert pressed our advantage. "Do tell her that Sir Rupert Fox is not well and requests a brief respite in the room to which has been afforded for our leisure. Tell her," Rupert said more loudly, turning up the garrulous quotient like a pro, "that I really must insist unless you plan to carry me up those stairs single-handedly. I simply cannot ...manage them...at the moment." Still leaning against me, he mopped his brow. "Shall I call her myself?" He removed his own phone.

Craca stepped forward as if to intervene and for a second I was afraid he might try to wrench the phone away.

"Do you want your guest to pass out on your watch, senhor? Do as he asks and take us to the library, which is much closer at hand," I insisted, though nothing was really close in that place.

Craca began talking hurriedly into his phone. After a second he jerked his head at us and led us down the long hall. His heavy footsteps masking our whispers.

"Adriana is not at the end of that phone," I said.

"I agree," Rupert said between huffs. If he was feigning his breathlessness, he was doing a damn good job.

Climbing even one set of stairs seemed truly challenging for Rupert and by now I realized his condition was more serious than I thought. Craca made no offer to assist, leaving everything up to me. After many long laborious minutes, we finally arrived at the deserted library.

Rupert stumbled to one of the velvet couches and collapsed. "Tea!" he croaked.

Craca muttered something before retreating. We heard him shouting to some hapless servant. I felt Rupert's forehead, relieved to find no signs of a fever.

"It's all right, Phoebe," he whispered. "I am merely exhausted from all this excitement and not on the brink of some nasty virus apocalypse, if that is what you are surmising."

I smiled and held his hand, my eyes swerving to Queen Isabella. "Where are the others?"

"Evan will be in his room…working on the technology. I have no idea about the others."

Minutes later, a maid entered with a tray of tea things. She set it down on the table, cast us a quick smile, and quickly left. I followed her to the door long enough to see Craca standing on guard outside.

That's it, it was official: we were prisoners. When I turned around, something pink was waving from the elevator alcove. Rupert, now propped on his elbows, waved back before sinking back against the pillows.

"I'm just going to sit by the window while you rest," I told Rupert loudly. "Whenever you're ready to go to your room, let me know."

"I shall," he murmured, closing his eyes. "No doubt the tea will fortify me sufficiently to make it up…the next flight…"

I slipped around the perimeter to the elevator alcove.

Ana Marie was waiting, finger on her lips. "Phoebe, I will take you to my grandpapa now," she whispered. She tugged me into the conservationist's closet. "I do not know why Mama will not let you see him but he wishes to see you."

She dropped my hand long enough to dart under a table packed with boxes, shove away one of the containers, and beckon me under. In seconds, her little pink leggings were disappearing as she crawled out of sight. I bent down to look at the two-foot-square opening hidden behind a flap of false wall.

"Come, Phoebe, hurry!"

I had no idea if I could even fit in there, let alone hurry doing it. But soon I was on my hands and knees squeezing through the hatch, fearing that my bottom end would wedge in the opening leaving all of us in an untenable position and me in a humiliating one. But by pushing my elbows against the floorboards, I managed to drag myself forward until I had just enough room to unfold myself into a kind of crouching stand.

The area was dark, dusty, and stuffy. I sneezed.

"Shhh!" the girl warned. Already far above me in the cramped stairwell she was out of sight. I scrambled after her in a narrow twisting stairway that appeared to curve all the way up beside the elevator shaft. Muttering to myself, I used my phone to light the way while stifling sneezes.

At last we arrived inside another closet, this one much larger and filled with gentlemen's clothing, cubicles of footwear, and the scent of cloves.

"Come. No one knows that I am gone but we must be very quick," Ana Marie told me.

"Quick," I said, brushing dust off my sweater.

"Yes, not slow."

"Ana Marie, I'm sorry about last night. I couldn't catch the bad men who tried to hurt you."

She gazed up at me in the half-light, her heart-shaped face solemn. "The monsters tried to steal me away but I escaped them. All things are dangerous now, Phoebe. Grandpapa said that we must be brave."

That shut me up. She took my hand and led me through the hanging suits, past the shelves of shirts and sweaters, and into a spacious round room where the floor-to-ceiling drapes had been drawn against the light. I blinked, trying to adjust my eyes. Around me I glimpsed a bureau, a dresser, dark wallpaper...

"Grandpapa, I have brought her!" Ana Marie dropped my hand and ran across the room toward a bed plumped high with brocade cushions where Senhor Carvalho sat, book in hand.

"Ana Marie! So you have successfully escaped poor Alma again! In truth, I believe she only pretends to sleep so you can get away," he said, setting aside his iPad and awaiting his granddaughter's landing.

The child practically flung herself at her grandfather, tumbling in among the pillows with a giggle. "And I have brought Phoebe as you requested, I mean Senhora McCabe."

"Phoebe, I am so relieved to see you. I did not know how we could manage it at first but this little girl is a brilliant strategist." Senhor Carvalho caught my gaze over top of the girl's head in the midst of giving her a hearty hug.

Ana Marie lifted her head. "What is 'strategist'?"

"It means one who is very clever like you are. Now, my dear, you must leave us and return back to poor Alma so she does not get into trouble once again."

Ana Marie sighed. "Yes, poor Alma. I will come back to see you as soon as I can, but first I must distract Senhor Craca. I like that word—distract."

"Distract? Ana Marie, what are you planning now?"

"I will go out through another way and make him follow me. He runs, I hide. It will make him very cross. Senhor Craca does not like me." She grinned.

"Be very careful, child. That man is not our friend."

"I know, so I annoy him more. Bye, Grandpapa."

Senhor Carvalho shook his head. "Be careful. Remember what I told you: this is not a game."

"Not a game," the child agreed, "but a battle between good and evil. I won't forget. Goodbye for now, Grandpapa, and goodbye, Phoebe. I hope Grandpapa helps you stay." Ana Marie blew him a kiss, tossed me a little wave, and darted back inside the closet.

Only once the child disappeared did Senhor Carvalho speak. "I apologize on behalf of my family for the manner in which you and your friends have been treated. My daughter-in-law is terrified and refuses to listen to reason. She hears only threats and gives too much credence to certain staff. We are now infiltrated by our enemies, who grow bolder by the day."

I stepped forward. "So you do know?"

"How could I not? It is as if we are surrounded by strangers wearing the masks of our friends," he continued. "Some are loyal, others do the brotherhood's bidding either from bribery, cohesion, or conviction, we know not which. Ours has become a tenuous existence."

"But they are forcing us to leave tomorrow."

"Yes, that is why I asked Ana Marie to bring you to me. Their plan is not to send you to the airport but to ensure that you come to a horrible end along the way. That's the Divinios' pattern: accidents, unfortunate events, seemingly random twists of fate. Believe me, Adriana has no idea."

"We can't let that happen and we certainly can't just leave you alone with the Divinios."

"I have been in touch with a Spanish friend to arrange your escape, but with Covid, transportation has become more difficult. He can only guarantee safe passage for three. In the meantime, Sir Rupert and I have devised a plan that keeps him here."

"You and Sir Rupert?"

"Dear Phoebe, do not look so shocked. It is the mistake of the young to believe that those older are unable to plot. Ana Marie has passed several notes between your friend and me, which has assisted us to formulate a strategy."

I laughed, sobering quickly. "I know Sir Rupert's ability to plot. I've been on the receiving end of that enough times. Rupert implied that he was up to something a few minutes ago but didn't get into the details. What exactly are you brewing?"

"The gist of it is this: tomorrow, Sir Rupert will appear too ill to travel. Let them think what they will regarding the cause but it will be necessary for him to stay behind in isolation for which he will require support. He and one other will stay while you, Senhor Collins, and Senhor Barrows are transported elsewhere. It's you the Divinios wish to destroy most. Senhor Fox and Senhora Williams will be safe enough for now."

"But for how long?"

"The Divinios will not harm them or our family as long as we appear to remain compliant. They need to retain an appearance of normality to carry out their diabolical plans. A sick man and his nurse will be of no concern. It's you three they fear the most. You they know by reputation."

"Then we will be the ones to escape to Spain. That's where we'll hunt for the crown."

He studied my face. "That was one of the theories Ricardo was chasing for years but he found nothing to confirm that theory. He returned to Portugal to continue the hunt. I hold little hope that you'll find something there."

"Sometimes we can't see what lies right under our nose."

His eyebrows rose. "Dear Phoebe, what are you thinking?"

"Just that I must get to Spain."

"But you know that Spain is at least as dangerous as remaining here, maybe more so, even with my friend's considerable assistance. There are hundreds of the Divinio brotherhood active there."

"But once that crown is safely beyond their reach, that monster loses its teeth, right?"

"So we hope."

"Then we have to try. It's the only chance we have. Please tell me more about your Spanish friend. You've been so scant on details up until now."

Senhor Carvalho closed his eyes for an instant. "And reticent I must remain at his request. He—they, actually, for there is more than one, though I know the elder best—will remain anonymous." When he opened his eyes again, his gaze held mine in a strong grip. "What assistance he'll offer will be at arm's length but he does have better access to historic places than I. I will contact him again."

"Thank you. My hunch is the best chance we have."

"And what can you tell me about your hunch?"

I smiled. "I prefer to keep my hunches under wraps. Call it superstition but if I expose them to air too early they tend to shrivel."

He smiled slightly. "And who am I to threaten something so fragile? In the meantime, you and your friends must pack for exit. It's imperative that you follow the preliminary plan that Adriana established even if it is only to deviate at the first opportunity. Leave that part to me. Once everything is arranged, I will dispatch a note tonight."

"Through one of the myriad secret passageways that snake through this house?"

He smiled. "Hidden passageways abound in large houses like this. We keep them secret so they can serve us when we need them."

"One more thing, senhor: do you have documentation regarding the exact time the Titian Isabella portrait arrived in Portugal?"

"The Aviz ledgers were destroyed in the fires. So you believe the answer lies somewhere there?"

"Maybe."

"Then good luck, my friend. God knows you'll need it." Studying me from over top of his glasses, his gaze struck me as alert and calculating. "I will communicate with you by note regarding tomorrow. In the meantime, please be safe and keep this with you at all times."

I took the object from his fingers, smiling as I tucked the little metal button down into my jacket pocket. "A tracking device."

"My Spanish friend will need it to locate you."

"I'm sure he will."

"One other thing, Phoebe."

I waited.

"You will need a password. Choose your own and I will ensure that he receives that, too."

"You are a strategist, too, I see." I thought for a moment. "Isabella."

He nodded and smiled. "Godspeed in the name of Isabella."

"You, too," I said, backing away, "and forgive me for what I am about to do."

"Pardon me?"

I grinned. "Desperate times require desperate measures, senhor."

Soon I was carefully negotiating the stairway downward, which had been bad enough going up. When I finally hauled myself out of the crawlspace, I was suppressing sneezes and covered in dust. I took a moment to beat the dirt off my clothes, replace the boxes, and study the bottles, jars, and boxes crammed into the small space. The room smelled faintly of solvents.

I then proceeded to slip into the library and inch toward the seat closest to the garden window, thinking only to pretend to study long enough for Craca to check in. Who knew how long Ana Marie could distract the bastard.

Taking a seat, I stared across the room. "Rupert?" I called. "Are you feeling any better?"

No answer. That sent me to the couch, heart in my throat. There my friend lay stretched out against the cushions, eyes closed, his face pale and shiny, the tea untouched…

"Help!" I cried, running for the door.

15

Supper that evening was a solemn affair. Rupert remained in his room complaining of illness, leaving the rest of us to hurry through our fish and soup, too anxious to enjoy the meal.

Adriana had arrived in the library earlier to deliver instructions for the morning, careful not to meet our eyes before sweeping out. If she knew that the Divinios intended to ambush us somewhere between Sintra and the airport, would she have aborted her plan? I guessed that she was simply in emotional lockdown, trying to keep the pieces together any way she could.

"We're acting like this is our last supper," Markus complained, ladling himself another serving of vegetable soup. The food had become much less bountiful in the past day but no less delicious. It was as if the entire household was operating under occupation.

"It sure feels that way," Peaches mumbled, gazing sourly at her plate.

At 5:00 a.m. a van was to arrive from Lisbon to take us to the airport where we would remain at a hotel until we could negotiate our various flights back to Britain. Or that was the official script.

"I have checked the flights leaving Lisbon for London and have only managed to secure two seats on the Porto flight at 6:00 p.m. so far," Evan remarked. "I will keep trying, of course."

In the meantime, we needed a way to pass a hardcopy of a running dialogue among us, a problem that had been preoccupying me along with everything else. Any obvious transfer of notes might be seen by the spies infiltrating the place. Subterfuge was needed.

An idea came while nibbling on a pastry. "Hey, is anybody having trouble with the mineral content in the water? At first I couldn't find a shampoo that foamed sufficiently," I said, conscious of how ludicrous the topic sounded but determined to see it through. "Nothing seems to suds up the way it should, which left my hair feeling not quite clean."

Everyone stopped eating to stare. I touched my mass of shoulder-length curls and grinned like someone out of a TV commercial. "But I just happened to find a bottle of a hotel shampoo stuffed in my bag that works like a dream. I'd be happy to share when we get back to our rooms."

Evan shot me a heart-stopping smile. "Your hair certainly looks beautiful just as it is, Phoebe, but if you think it would help my locks..." He leaned forward so I could touch his hair. I couldn't resist, tangling my fingers for mere seconds in the stray curls at his neck.

"Oh, just stop," Markus muttered, tossing his napkin down. "I'm trying to eat here."

I pulled back. Still grinning like an idiot, I added: "Oh, come on, Markus. You look like you could use something to strengthen your lank strands—maybe a fortifier? I have one of those, too." In truth, I always lugged a collection of trial-size hair products everywhere since nothing ever worked consistently on my unruly tangle.

"My hair's fine, thank you," he grumbled. Suddenly he jerked forward, his face registering shock. I'd guessed he'd been kicked under the table, possibly by Peaches's long legs. "But of course I'll try whatever you have to offer."

"Good idea," Peaches remarked. "But I don't expect it'll do much for me. Still, if it suds up in the shower, it'll get my vote."

"Luckily I have enough for everyone." I smiled, satisfied that we'd found our communication ruse. "Conditioner, too."

With all our dependence on modern communications, here we were back to operating in longhand like captives from another century. The irony wasn't lost on me. I'd already passed one note around under the table with a brief warning that we were to await further instructions from Senhor Carvalho. I'd save the more important communication for later.

Our phones had already been passed back to us with a sticky note from Evan warning that though he believed them safe enough for normal use, we were still to exercise extreme caution. I had no idea what that meant since we couldn't risk a conversation long enough to find out. Even standing in the middle of the library to whisper as we had done earlier had become too risky apparently. It was to be pen-and-paper notes read and hastily burned in the nearest fire.

By 8:45 we were back in our respective quarters packing while waiting for details we didn't have. I planned to pass a note up and down the hall explaining who would be leaving tomorrow and who would be staying behind. Because I figured there'd be some arguments, I was waiting until we had the partial privacy of our rooms to communicate the details.

After a few minutes, I resolved to explain which three would be actually leaving for Spain in the morning and why. Using the paper found in the desk drawer, I first passed a note to Peaches taped to the travel-size shampoo bottle, saying at the door that after she took some maybe she could give the bottle to Evan next? It was such a limp ruse but the only one I could come up with at short notice. Pathetic how shackled I felt without text and email, let alone conversation.

After that, I returned to my room to sit at the little desk, waiting. It would only take one lucky glance from an enemy spy or a moment of carelessness to bring the whole thing crashing down. On the other hand, few servants came to our floor lately. Bed-making and the other niceties had been abandoned. We even made our own fires, borrowing wood from the library hearth, which was always well-stocked. It occurred to me that I'd better light mine with the one piece of wood remaining.

While I was coaxing the log to burn, Peaches knocked on my door and stepped in. "The guys say thanks for the shampoo. They've all taken a bit to use later. Not much left. I thought for a minute that Evan and Markus might squabble over the last drop."

I stood to take back the bottle, feeling the note taped to the bottom, out of sight in my palm.

"It smells good," she said while striding out the door, "but the truth will lay with the foam, won't it?"

"Isn't that always the way?"

Taking the now-empty bottle into the bathroom, I switched off the lights and peeled off the note to read by the light of my phone.

Peaches in a penciled scrawl: *As her bodyguard, I must go with Phoebe to Spain. I can speak the language, sí? Peach*

Markus using a felt-tipped-pen printed: *I must stay here. The crown is not in Spain, IMO. M*

Evan in his classical cursive hand wrote in ink: *I am the only one who is fluent in Spanish AND Latin so must go to Spain with Phoebe. Markus, you come with us. No arguments. My apologies, Peach. Evan*

And Rupert in his gorgeous almost calligraphic script wrote: *As previously decided, I will remain. The English Patient, Sir Rupert Fox*

I READ THE NOTE OVER AND OVER AGAIN. DAMN. COULDN'T SOMETHING just be simple for once? Of course Peaches would expect to go with me as my supposed bodyguard, and I had forgotten that Evan was the only one of us fluent in Spanish *and* Latin, but why was Markus so intent on remaining? He knew damn well that the place was crawling with murderers who would slit his throat in a millisecond. Unless—I stared into the half-light—unless they wouldn't for some reason. He must know something he'd been keeping from us, which I suspected all along. Shit.

Dropping the empty shampoo bottle in the trash, I returned to my room, tossed the note into the fire, took a fresh sheet of the house stationery, and returned to the bathroom. This time I penned a message solely for Peaches:

Peach, I need you here. Evan's mastery of Latin is critical for going through church documents and other accounts often written at the time of our hunt. Besides, the enemy knows his reputation but they have no idea just how dangerous you are. Plus, you're the only one I can trust to protect Rupert and the Carvalhos, especially our little princess, Ana Marie. And something's up with Markus—I just don't know what exactly. Please say you understand. Also, please be ready to watch my back at 2:00 a.m. I'll explain later.

What was I asking her to do: stay here virtually defenseless in this nest of fiends? And, more immediately, help me to commit a criminal offense against art and man? But Senhor Carvalho believed those left behind would probably be the safest and at least she had a gun and could handle a knife like nobody's business. As for Rupert: "never underestimate Rupert" was my motto. As long as he breathed, he could plot, and I had no doubt that he and Senhor Carvalho were cooking up something.

Taping the note to a tube of smoothing lotion, I knocked on her door. It flew open in an instant, the full six feet of grandeur draped in a Moroccan kaftan.

"Smoothing lotion." I waved the bottle before her eyes. "Hope it works."

She whipped it from my fingers and peered at the label, which was plastered over by the note. "Depends on the contents, doesn't it? The last shampoo had sulfates. You know I detest sulfates. Leaves the cuticles sticking straight up—like I need that."

"I didn't know that you hated sulfates."

"Now you do, and if this one has chemicals I'm not going to like it any better." She peered at the label as if reading it. "Lots of big words here: glycol distearate, isopropyl alcohol, Behentrimonium chloride—are you kidding me?"

She actually remembered that stuff? "Shea butter," I said quickly. "I'm sure I read it contains that, too."

"Fine. Just remember that black hair requires special care just like the women who grow it." The door slammed in my face.

Got it: she wasn't happy about being left behind. I waited several seconds before striding down the hall to visit Rupert.

The English patient was tucked into bed emitting occasional moans, laying it on a little too thickly, in my opinion. When I had approached his bed earlier that evening, he only winked and shooed me away with a convincing cough.

"Rupert, I'm not happy about dragging you out of here tomorrow morning. In fact, given the current restrictions, I doubt they'd even allow you on a plane," I said.

"Then I shall just have to recoup at an airport hotel, perish the thought," he said, coughing. "I trust we can locate one with room service. Where are the private jets when we need them?"

Where indeed. Our Rome branch did have access to a private jet that we'd used in the past, but when I'd texted Nicolina from London, she had informed me that the pilot, Otty, had been struck by Covid. *Things are not good in Italy*, she wrote, *but everyone strolls around as if we were back to normal. We are not in normal, Phoebe. Stay safe. Nicolina*

"Never mind, Phoebe," Rupert said, interrupting my thoughts, "I'm sure I shall be much improved tomorrow."

As if. That's when the show would really begin. "Right. I'll leave you to rest, then."

He'd managed to eat all of his soup, I noticed. Stacking his supper dishes onto a tray, I carried them from his room and left them on the hall table along with a mounting assortment of dirty dishes. I saw that Evan's door was open as he sat at his desk with his back turned, working away at some gizmo.

Edgier than ever, I headed for my room, stopping by Markus's open door along the way. "All ready to leave tomorrow?" I asked.

His head lifted from the diagram spread across the bed but he hesitated before answering. "If I must."

"You must," I said pointedly.

"Are you ready, then?"

"Ready," I said. I had the Glock Evan gave me stuffed into the hidden holster of my jacket, my phone alarm set, and my clothes ready to climb into at 4:30 sharp—actually before. What else was left to do besides wait for Senhor Carvalho's instructions?

I continued to Peaches's room but the sound of the shower running left me to wander back my turret quarters, transfer my collection of notes from my pocket into the embers, and head for the window.

The garden lights were off; in fact, they had never been switched back on following the attempted kidnapping. The house now slumbered in that tense, watchful stillness that I imagined descends upon houses during a siege. Whether that threat be in the form of a sickness or something physical, it must feel the same. I turned away into the darkened room.

The dying fire cast a low glow. For the past day, I'd only left the bathroom light on in case the room was under surveillance, doing every task in the shadows with the lights off, including packing.

I'd take a bath and pretend to get ready for bed, which would kill at least an hour. I shut my door and was heading toward the bathroom when my gaze caught something white under the desk. I would never have noticed if I didn't automatically check Ana Marie's secret hatch since discovering it existed. I swept up the paper and strode into the bathroom with my clothes in my arms.

Once inside with the lights off and using my phone, I read the note, which was scrawled in an ornate loopy hand on monogrammed stationery:

Proceed as planned. All secured for three.

The monogram above read: *Senhor Silvio de Carvalho*

While my bath ran, I slipped back into the room and burned the message in the last of the embers.

16

I didn't expect to get much sleep that night. The fact that I managed to squeeze even three hours before 2:00 a.m. was a bonus. My alarm pitched me out of bed at the appointed time, heart pounding like I'd been dragged from bed by my feet. Fully dressed, I only had to grab my jacket and my phone to feel ready for anything.

When I crept into the hall, Peaches was leaning against the wall, arms crossed.

"What are we doing?" she whispered.

I waited until we were farther down the corridor before answering. "Committing a crime against art."

"What the hell does that mean?"

"Shhh!"

We padded past all the bedrooms, every light off, every door closed. At the bottom of the stairs, I hesitated. The house's deep watchful silence didn't fool me. Somewhere in this acreage of a house, some faction was busy plotting, and they weren't the only ones.

Finger to my lips, I led us down the hall toward the library, keeping against the walls and checking every passageway crossing. Once we reached the library, I tried the door, startled when the brass handle didn't budge. "Locked—seriously?"

"Did you bring your pickers?" Peaches whispered.

"In my room," I said.

She nudged me aside and took out a foldout packet from her pocket, selected a pick, and got to work. "Hold the light," she ordered. I aimed my phone at the ornate lock while she expertly fiddled until it clicked. In minutes we were inside, shutting the door behind us and shoving the brass bolt home.

Why had we been locked out? Probably another sign that we were persona non grata in this occupied regime.

"Watch my back," I whispered, leading Peaches before Titian's Isabella portrait. "Wait here."

She stood stone-still, a gun in one hand, while I slipped around the perimeter of the room to the conservator's closet. What I was about to do was the single most audacious act in my art career and I didn't do it lightly.

I swept my phone light around the six-by-six-foot closet, crammed as it was by easels, jars, a standing light, what looked to be a mobile air purifier, a box of plastic gloves, goggles, and a broom and dustpan. It must have originally served as a storage area for cleaning supplies, fitting enough since its most recent use concerned cleaning of another kind. I studied the bottles and jars neatly lined on the shelf, searching for the necessary solvent.

Art conservation was a painstakingly exacting science that involved removing centuries of woodsmoke, varnish, and grime from priceless artworks without damaging the original. One mistake, one wrong stroke, and the masterpiece was ruined, sometimes irrevocably. As I learned in my student days, it was as much an art as a science and took years of specialized study.

I had but one course taken nearly a decade ago.

Using my phone light, I scanned the labels on every box. Next I pulled on a pair of vinyl gloves, took a pair of goggles, a brush, a tiny palette knife, and a pocketful of cotton swabs and peered again at the solvents.

They marched in a row on the top shelf, all carefully labeled with many jars near-empty. I selected the last one in the row, a distilled turpentine labeled in English pushed into the very corner. It had never been opened. Perhaps the strongest and the riskiest were relegated to the end of the line? I doubted a conservationist would ever want to use something so potent if it could be avoided. A conservator with time on her hands would use a gentler option but I didn't have that luxury. I took the turps.

Back in the library, Peaches watched me approach, her eyes wide.

"Solvents," I whispered, lifting the bottle.

I signaled for her to help me drag over a chair and in seconds I was standing face-to-face with Queen Isabella, my phone light roaming over the background with no time to pay proper homage to either masterpiece or queen. This close I could scrutinize every inch, yet I aimed straight for the square in the lower left-hand corner just above where the conservator's efforts had stopped.

The sfumato here was so leadened and heavy that even considering the application of varnish applied over the centuries, it looked wrong, all wrong. No master of blending would create something that muddy even after years of grime. My guess is that it had been overpainted, maybe multiple times.

Peaches beamed her phone light on the area as I dabbed the cotton tip into the turpentine and proceeded to gently stroke the wad across the canvas.

It was sacrilege. It was a wanton act of desperation prompting me to send silent apologies to Tiziano Vecellio for the crimes I was committing against him that night. If I wasn't so convinced that others had gone before me in this travesty, I would never have continued. There was evidence that the painting had already been tampered with at least once.

As it was, I swabbed the surface; it felt as though every movement raked my gut. The cotton began removing layers of smoky resin, the varnish being the revered preservation medium of almost every age.

Dropping the used swab to the hearth, I pulled out another and this time soaked up more solvent and applied it even more aggressively. My goal was to wipe off layers of actual paint, knowing as I did that I might penetrate down to the original brushwork and possibly ruin a piece of priceless art. This swab came away a sooty black. Dropping that cotton tip, I took another.

"Someone's in the hall!" Peaches hissed.

We switched off our phones and I froze, me standing still in the dark as she padded across to the door to listen, her gun cocked. Fumes from the turps were so strong I wouldn't have been surprised if it rode the air beyond that door.

Nerves strung tight, we listened to voices low and urgent outside, followed by a patter of footsteps and then total silence. I allowed myself to exhale the moment Peaches flicked on her phone light.

I got back to work, removing swab after swab of thick dark paint. Finally something began to emerge from the background: a bit of green followed by a touch of red. Moments later, a leaf came into view followed by a fallen flower, exquisitely portrayed as if someone had plucked the bloom from the queen's fingers to lay it dying at her feet. Peaches stretched up for a closer look. "It's a carnation. Why's that important enough to hide?"

"Don't know but it's symbolic of something. Isabella was known as the Empress of the Carnation but why hide it?" I whispered, staring at the flower. It had been masterfully painted but not in the style of Titian. The artist didn't even try to emulate his brushstrokes.

I dropped that used cotton tip and took another, this time aiming my efforts on the rocky outcrop to the right of the queen's head. Here it wasn't the shadows that bothered me but the brushstrokes themselves. With Titian you barely saw signs of a brush anywhere; the artist so masterfully blended his elements that they seemed to emerge lifelike from the canvas. This paint had been applied heavily, using a technique out of sync with the rest of the work, even with the carnation. In fact, it appeared to have no technique at all.

I applied the solvent thickly, allowing it to soften the paint before scraping the green off with the knife. Layers of green sludge came off like solidified butter, revealing a slightly different shape to the mountainous terrain beneath and a peaked hexagonal watchtower.

I glanced at Peaches, who stood with her mouth open. "Where's that?"

"Dunno," I said.

"Weird," Peaches whispered.

"Isn't it?" Though I'd like nothing better than to dig deeper, those were the two main abnormalities.

"It's almost 3:30," Peaches said.

"Right." I took pictures of the two revealed areas with my phone and one of the entire painting before climbing down. While Peaches gathered the discarded swabs, I returned the tools to the closet and picked up a brush and two tubes of paint, one dark green and one smoky brown, both tubes of Winsor & Newton. I squeezed a small amount onto a palette and diluted it massively with thinner.

A conservator often repaired damaged pieces by replicating the same paints used in the original but exceptions were sometimes necessary. Necessity drove me to great depths that night.

Peaches watched aghast as I returned to my perch and blotted the areas I'd been working on before brushing paint over the cleared patches, covering the delicate plaintive carnation with a brown blemish, smudging the trees around the watchtower with a thick swirl of paint, and burying everything under an appallingly shoddy patch job. Anyone taking a closer look would see the outrage in an instant but I was betting that no one would be looking that closely short-term, especially since the painting hung far from eye level.

That done, I returned to the conservator's closet, packed away the painting supplies, and wiped the brushes on a cloth, but carried the turpentine bottle over to one of the desks, cover off. Placing it on a wad of paper, I arranged papers to look as though some careless twerp had been rubbing solvent on wads of tissue.

"What?" Peaches whispered.

"Decoy," I replied, "to explain the fumes." It might work for a moment, which could be all we needed. Besides, it was the best idea I had.

That done, we cleared up what evidence we could, and just before exiting, I led Peaches to the closet and pointed out the secret passageway. "It leads directly to Senhor Carvalho," I said.

"Fat lot of good that will do me. I'd never get my booty through there."

"It's not as tight as it looks. Besides flesh has give," I said.

"Yours might. Mine's all muscle."

Like I had time to argue that.

After checking the corridor, we exited the library, practically bolting down that hall, up the stairs, and back to our rooms, arriving in breathless triumph until we saw Markus's door wide open.

"Shit!" Peaches exclaimed.

We stepped inside and gaped. The archaeologist had vanished, taking his bags with him.

17

At 4:45 Evan was downstairs spreading the alarm about Rupert's supposed worsening condition to any person he could find. Three staff members trudged to our floor in their nightclothes, all masked and talking excitedly. None would go near Rupert's room. Minutes later, Adriana arrived with a man and woman we didn't recognize and, once we explained the situation, demanded that the wing be sectioned off.

"But you must still leave," she ordered.

"Sir Fox is not going anywhere," Evan said, standing in the center of the corridor, arms crossed, doing his most manly command pose. "He is not well and must stay put until he recovers."

"What is wrong with him?" Her eyes widened with fear.

"I don't know," he said. "Perhaps you can have a doctor visit to determine that point. I can only tell you that he has a fever and a dry cough."

"A fever! This can't be happening! We haven't had a doctor here since—well, for a while. There is one in the village that attends Papa Carvalho occasionally. Maybe he will come."

"I suggest you arrange for testing," he said.

"Testing for...?" Her look of shock made me feel as guilty as hell. This seemed so cruel. "Sir Rupert must go into quarantine," she said after a moment. "The rest of you leave as planned." She looked as though she might burst into tears.

"You can't expect us to just leave him. Somebody must stay and nurse him," I said.

"Unless one of your staff will take on the task," Evan added, "none of us will be leaving this morning." He stood tall, imposing and resolute.

Adriana's eyes looked around her above the white mask, almost as if she was seeking a place to hide. "Fine." She turned to speak urgently to the man beside her and moments later faced us again. "Choose one person to stay with him, then, but it cannot be you, Senhor Barrows, or you Senhorita McCabe. You can stay." She indicated Peaches leaning against a wall behind me.

"'You' has a name," Peaches said, straightening. "I'm Peaches Williams but you can call me Senhorita Williams, if you must. I'll stay with Rupert, under certain conditions."

I glanced at her in surprise. She was setting terms?

Adriana dropped her gaze. "Forgive me if I am rude." Her hands flew into the air. "But I am so alarmed! To have this happen to our household along with everything else."

"No problem. I'll make a list of things needed to keep Sir Rupert and me comfortable. In the meantime, if you don't mind, take your staff away and leave us to it. And we want coffee and breakfast. Eggs would be nice—boiled, not too hard."

"Yes, we will go. The rest of you come downstairs in ten minutes." Adriana turned to Evan. "Where is Senhor Collins?"

"Unfortunately, we can't answer that," Evan replied. "I had hoped you knew."

"Why would I know?" she said, glaring at him. "I want you out of here." She swung around and dashed downstairs with her staff.

"I feel sorry for them," I whispered as their footsteps died away. "To know what she's fearing..."

"Let the virus work to our benefit for once," Evan remarked, returning to his room.

By 5:00 a.m., my backpack and his were at the bottom of the stairs with the two of us standing tense and silent in the hall, waiting.

We had made no effort to find Markus, not just because we were sure that he had left on his own accord but because we didn't have time to search. Our biggest worry, mostly left unsaid but for a hastily scribbled note, was that he had been working for the Divinios all along. On the other hand, I suspected he believed he knew the location of that crown on the property and may have gone off to search on his own—unlikely considering his temperament but not impossible. God knows what archaeologists burning with a quest will try to do, at least in their minds.

But if he did work for the Divinios, it meant that every bit of our plan had been exposed—what little we knew of it, that is. Senhor Carvalho may have been short on details for a reason. The uncertainty, heaped on all the rest, made Evan and me unusually tense.

Evan passed me a piece of paper that I hastily read and shoved into my pocket. *Where in Spain are we going?*

I'm not sure, I mouthed. He lifted his brows at me, maybe not as amused as I had hoped.

Minutes later, we heard footsteps marching down the long hall as two men wearing masks appeared, only one of whom I knew—Senhor Abreu. I stifled my relief at seeing someone assumed to be an ally but nothing in the man's eyes gave any indication that he felt the same.

Abreu introduced the driver, a Senhor Magro, who was to take us to the airport. We hastily applied our face masks, picked up our bags, and followed the men outside. I turned long enough to catch Peaches waving at me from the stairs. I hated to leave her behind and yet was so grateful that she and Rupert would pull together to do whatever was needed back at the quinta.

The dawn hung damp and cool with a band of luminous ultramarine bleeding into the sky beyond the treetops and mist snaking through the grass. We piled into a long gray unmarked six-seater van, our bags at our feet, nobody saying a word. Evan and I sat stiff and watchful.

When the car pulled away down the long drive, I turned back to gaze at the castle, noting lights on at the very topmost tower but the castle otherwise dark. Turning away, I stared ahead, my arm pressing against the gun in my jacket, ready for anything. Gun, phone, and Evan—what more did I need to plunge into the unknown? Actually, I could think of plenty. Would I ever see my friends again?

The van wound down the drive, through the gates, which opened as we approached, and onto a deeply wooded road, but instead of going down toward the village we headed up.

I shot a look at Evan but he kept his gaze fixed ahead, which prompted me to do the same. I watched as the silhouette of the Moorish castle bit into the sky over our heads. We were heading up to the ancient castle? I had seen the illuminated walls from my window and knew that the Castelo dos Mouros had been built in Portugal's medieval Moorish era and destroyed by the Christian crusaders, but what did it have to do with our escape or was it part of the Divinios' murderous plan?

Floodlights beamed up at the gray stone walls when the van lurched to a stop at the foot of the rocky outcrop leading up to the ruins.

"You two go!" Abreu called. "Now. Up the stairs! He waits!"

Who waits? Why up the stairs? Heart galloping, I sprung into action, grabbing my bag and jumping out the door at the same time that Evan exited from the other side.

My heart shattered at the thought of all the things that could go wrong but I couldn't dwell on that now. The van was already zooming back down the way it had come and was soon swallowed by the mist.

"Phoebe, hurry!" Evan beckoned me up a path leading toward a set of rough-hewn stairs. Spotlights illuminating the ruin's exterior walls did nothing to light the stairs between the low parapets. Here the shadows clotted like glue and Evan turned on his phone light to guide our way raggedly upward.

We were climbing up the old castle's battlements with nothing between us and the drop but the remains of the ancient walls, the exterior versions waist-high, the interior ones knee-level. On the right, the mountain opened around us in dizzying glimpses of mist and rocky outcrops, the lights of the village dropping far away to our left, the forest to our right.

Up here the wind cut into my face and the steepness of the climb nearly took my breath away. Soon I was stuffing my mask into my pocket and transferring my bag into backpack mode as I forced my legs to keep pushing.

We climbed and climbed as the dawn bloomed pink all around. Evan was too far ahead for conversation and I didn't have the breath left to try. I knew he had to be feeling as ripped in two as I but his training kept him focused and powering on. But why anyone would wait for us here? It was all rock and bramble with a watchtower ahead and walls curving into the distance. Unless the idea was to ambush us and throw us off the wall, in which case I had to admit the location was perfect.

I paused long enough to gaze through the wind-roughened parapets to catch my breath. Then I heard a faint beating far to the right at the same time as I caught sight of lights weaving through the trees below, approaching from two directions.

Picking up my pace, I launched up the next length of dizzying stairs until I stood beside Evan on the windy battlement watching a silver speck come into view.

"We have more company!" I cried, pointing behind us.

He swore and gazed ahead. In front lay the watchtower, to the left the rocky remains of the keep edged in dawn and rimmed by thick shadow, and beyond that the battlements continued curving like a snake up the crest of the mountain.

It was at that moment that we heard the explosion. Something far down to the left burst into flames and burned in a dark smoky plume. We watched in horror as the object tumbled over and over in flames and smoke, finally dropping straight out of view.

"It's the van!" I called.

"That was supposed to be us," Evan said, voice tight. He grabbed my hand. "Keep moving."

"But—" There was no time for fear or to cry, let alone talk. We began climbing downward now just as we saw the helicopter growing closer by the moment.

We watched as the small silver helicopter came into view overhead, hovering over the ruined keep. Now we saw how the rocks on the inner side of the ruins fell away to a flat gravel space directly below. It didn't look wide enough to land a chopper but that's exactly what the pilot seemed to be doing. He began lowering the machine straight down toward the only flat area on the rock.

Evan and I pressed ourselves against the outer parapet as the blades beat overhead. I turned to avoid the spin of dust and glimpsed the lights bobbing below the lower walls. "They're on the walls!" I called.

The helicopter dropped into the narrow space with amazing finesse and in seconds we were dashing down the remaining stairs and ducking under the vortex toward the open door just as two men appeared on the battlements and started shooting.

"Get up fast!" Evan called to the pilot, repeating himself in Spanish and urging us into the seats. He swung open the door and shouted something. We climbed into the seats behind him as he slammed the door shut, giving us only seconds to strap ourselves in before the machine lurched upward.

My first time in a helicopter and here I was rising in the air from atop a mountain promontory being chased by religious fanatics while heading to parts unknown. Sometimes I'd rather be knitting.

A bullet pinged against the blades.

As I soon discovered as the machine zipped away, helicopters offer the best flight view of any aircraft thanks to that wraparound windshield. This gave me an uninterrupted view of the men scrambling over the rocks below, the sparks of their guns firing, and, as an added bonus, the flashing emergency lights far down in the valley.

Evan passed me a pair of ear protectors from the console between us. I was grateful for the instant quiet but kept my gaze fixed on the shrinking ground, my heart in my throat. He squeezed my hand as we zipped off into the dawn, me squeezing back in silent fear for those we left behind.

We were now flying over land, forests, villages, and towns visible far below. Though my knowledge of helicopters was scant, I knew enough to know that they can't travel as far or as quickly as planes. How far this one would take us was left to be seen and I could only hope that our pilot had a plan.

But despite the adrenaline, my heart began to settle and I must have dozed. It seemed like several hours had passed when a sharp sound lurched me awake. I looked out and saw us going down—quickly—and to someplace in the middle of nowhere. Nothing but sandy hills and a rocky grassland baking in the bright sun, a scruff of forest off to the left, a vineyard to the right.

I turned to Evan with a question but the sound of gunfire answered me before he could. The pilot was shouting.

"The gas tank's been hit," Evan called. "He's got to land before we lose power!"

"Where are we?" I called.

"Somewhere in Spain!"

So we landed somewhere in Spain with a bouncing crash followed by the the crunch of landing gear and the screech of something major breaking off—the tail, we discovered, as we leaped out of the helicopter.

Now we were on the run, heading toward the copse of trees, the pilot in the opposite direction. He called something back to us, Evan translating: "We're to hide. Keep away from him."

No time to ask why. Two white helicopters flew low across the field peppering the ground with machine gunfire. We were almost to the trees when I turned and saw the pilot hit. He spun in a full circle before falling to his knees. I took off after him until Evan grabbed my arm and wrenched me back. One of the helicopters was landing. We had to keep on running.

We bolted into the trees. In a few minutes, they'd be on foot coming after us. An orchard, I guessed. Here the sun filtered down in long motes, beautiful had we time to enjoy. But the cover was scant and we could hear the roar of the second helicopter overhead along with men shouting.

"They're gaining!"

And suddenly we burst out of the trees to teeter on the brink of a steep scrubby mountainside with no option but to scramble down over loose stones. Below we saw a cluster of white buildings, a little village beyond that. Yet we hesitated. Hardly any cover. Parts of the drop too steep.

Across the sky from the opposite direction, another helicopter was speeding toward us—longer, painted in camouflage, two roof propellers. When a bullet pinged against the rocks at our feet, we lunged down the hill, caught in a wild sliding scramble heading roughly for a boulder outcrop. Two men were firing at our backs now.

We leaped behind a pile of boulders as Evan pulled out his gun and fired back. I had my gun in hand as the new helicopter flew overhead.

Evan paused to study the underbelly. "They saw us. Camouflaged AS532 Cougar. Looks like it belongs to the Spanish army. Who did you say Senhor Carvalho's friend is?"

"Another Señor Anonymous. Are they on our side?"

"We can't wait around to find out."

We watched the army helicopter drop low over the gunmen, a soldier leaning out the door firing at our pursuers while the second enemy helicopter was speeding off into the distance. It certainly seemed that they were on our side and they gave us the break we needed.

Instantly we were scudding downward, grabbing on to bushes to brace ourselves as we slid. Our backpacks knocked off our balance so we sent them sliding down ahead. It was all I could do to keep my feet under me and at one point I stumbled, nearly tumbling downward face-first, but I managed to steady myself against a rock. Evan remained ahead, turning occasionally to point out obstacles or to offer me a hand.

"Just go!" I cried. Men.

By the time we reached the bottom and retrieved our bags, the sun hung low in the sky, the gunfire had stopped, and the helicopters had disappeared. We were trudging around a white-walled farm compound. A corral of white ponies whinnied away to the right. Somewhere a dog barked and barked.

"We'll hide in a barn somewhere until dark," Evan said.

We had seen a village farther down the road but who knew what the response would be if two strangers suddenly appeared in the streets? We obviously weren't tourists. We couldn't even claim that our car had broken down on some nearby highway—was there even a nearby highway? Hiding until nightfall seemed the best option.

A man raking a small field in the distance didn't catch sight of us as we scuttled into the walled enclosure. Inside, a small house lay at one end with a cluster of stucco outbuildings forming a rambling rectangle. A fountain looking as though it hadn't spewed water for years sat in the center of a cracked cement drive with a clump of yellow weeds blooming around the base.

We slipped inside a large storage building that smelled of motor oil overriding something musty and hid in a corner behind an old tractor. Sacks of veggies and an upended wheelbarrow kept us company along with a mewing cat that skittered away. Tools hung on the walls, most of them rusted and bearing signs that they'd been repaired multiple times. The last rays of sun were cutting through a high cracked window in long motes as we settled down in the shadows on mounds of sacking.

My heart only then began to settle. I leaned back and closed my eyes.

"Are you all right?" Evan asked, passing me a water bottle.

I sat up to wave away the offer and retrieve my own bottle from my backpack. "Fine, thanks. Just a bit winded. That was close."

"Too close." He rubbed his forehead on his sleeve. "This is a good time for you to tell me where we're heading. We haven't had time to talk."

"I don't know where we're heading exactly," I admitted before taking a long drink.

"Right then, we need to comb the archives in Madrid and search through all the court documents from the reign of Emperor Charles to Philip II. Maybe Ricardo overlooked something. It's a long shot, as is everything else. There's still a chance the crown lies buried beneath the altar just as Markus believes, but in the meantime, Madrid is a logical next step."

He was being so decisive, so take-charge male—endearing. "No, it isn't." That came out more absolute than I intended. "I mean, when I said I didn't know where we were headed, it wasn't because I didn't know what to look for. It's nothing related to King Philip or even Prince Carlos, at least not directly. It's subtler than that. Maybe this will lead us to Madrid or maybe not." I pulled out my phone and opened up the pictures I had taken of the overpainting.

He gazed down at the screen. "You tampered with a Titian?" There was surprise in his tone along with more than a little amusement.

"I wasn't the first, possibly not even the second. Somebody buried clues in that portrait long ago and sent it to the House of Aviz for safekeeping."

"I'm not judging."

"Don't you see? The carnation, which was not painted by Titian but by someone almost as masterful, was covered over with a layer of paint. The same thing with the tower behind the queen's head. They're messages. Whoever did this was counting on no one daring to touch a painting by the royal portraitist since Titian had reached acclaim in his own lifetime and had King Philip's protection. It was a brilliant strategy considering that it kept the clues safe for over five hundred years."

"Until you came along."

"Until I came along, but listen, Evan, that flower means something. I just don't know what. Carnations were Isabella's symbol but why hide that? If we discover who that painter was, we'll come that much closer to understanding. There's a whole language threaded through here, the language of visual imagery and symbolism. The anti-Divinios didn't use words, they used art."

"You amaze me," he said softly.

"Is that a good thing?"

"You know it is." He was gazing at me in that intense way he had that always made me feel like I was only one in the universe for those fleeting seconds.

"Are you with me or not?" I asked softly.

"I've always been with you."

I took the phone from his fingers, which held on maybe seconds too long. "Good. Thank you. I'm thinking no Emperor Charles or even King Philip. Even Queen Isabella was a smokescreen. That they used her portrait to hide clues is significant."

"How?"

"Maybe the anti-Divinios supported the monarchy but not the sect? Maybe they were implying a connection with queens and women somehow? It was a wickedly sexist and often misogynistic age. It's bad enough today but this is nothing compared to what women endured in the fifteenth century, even those of noble blood, maybe *especially* those of noble blood. My point is, in this hunt, think like a woman."

"But I'm a man." Now he was teasing.

"And that's one of the things I love about you, Evan, but I sense a female presence working as our allies across time. For once being a man may not be the usual advantage." I paused and smiled. "But don't feel the need to change on my account."

"That's a relief. Seriously, though, we need to track down the women who surrounded Prince Carlos in those dark days before his death."

"Yes, let's start there. I've done some preliminary research but I need so much more."

"But we'll need our latest Señor Anonymous's help to get there, wherever 'there' might be. If our Spanish benefactor is in any way connected to the Spanish military, he's one powerful ally, and by now should know where we are."

"Because I'm wearing a tracking device?"

"You're wearing a tracking device?"

"Senhor Carvalho gave it to me yesterday."

"I was actually thinking that they would determine our position based on where our helicopter went down, which is a fairly definite clue. Also, the army helicopter saw us."

"Oh, yes, there's that." It was growing so dark now that I could barely see his face.

"But the Divinios have the same information and I expect they'll be on our heels soon enough." He had his phone in his hand. "Sir Rupert texted that all is well back at the castle. They're under quarantine. He says that the 'plague doctor' has been called in from Sintra and would arrive tomorrow. As soon as he tests negative for Covid, the game will be up."

I sighed. "We don't have much time. Where are we, anyway?"

"About fifty kilometers outside of Córdoba."

I skimmed the texts on my own phone—one from Peaches saying that the smoothing lotion had worked; another from Max back in London saying that he was worried about me. *Why no phone call?* he asked. Connie texted to say that she apologized for her brother's behavior but that his heart was in the right place. What did that mean? His heart might be in the right place but the rest of him wasn't. Did she know where he was?

I was about to show Evan the messages when he put a hand on his arm and indicated his own screen. Two red dots could be seen approaching the drive leading to the farm on one of his radar apps—cars, I guessed.

We turned off our phones and ducked down behind the tractor, squeezing deeper into the shadows as car doors slammed and footsteps pounded on the cement outside.

Barely breathing, we listened. Men entering the compound—three, maybe four. One speaking softly but no less definitively, and footsteps spreading out across the farm. We were being hunted. Another set of footsteps ran past from the other direction, a person shouting a question—the farmer?

An argument erupted between the farmer and someone else followed by a third man interrupting in a voice as soothing as liquid honey.

Evan left my side to climb onto the sacking and peered out the high window. In seconds, he was back, whispering: "Three men, one priest."

"A priest?" I hissed.

"It's them. We have to get out of here. They'll find us."

We waited only long enough for the footsteps to spread around the outbuildings before bolting from our cover and risking a dash for the gate. It was a long shot.

We could see the farmer speaking quietly to a man in a dark robe whose back was turned. As long as he didn't catch sight of us and raise the alarm, we could make it.

Only it didn't work out that way.

18

We hadn't counted on guards watching the compound. And now we were surrounded by four armed men wearing stark, grim expressions with matching clothes, their guns pointing at our chests. When two others joined them, we were hemmed in like stray cattle. And that's how I felt—cornered and terrified.

To my left, Evan stood tense, his hand hovering over his hidden holster, and I was afraid he might do something reckless. But we were outnumbered and surrounded. All we could do was wait for a chance to escape. I caught his eye and shook my head.

The priest strode toward us, a little smile on this plump lips. In his early fifties with short graying hair, heavy build, and an expression on his round cherubic face that was unsettlingly mild, he lifted his hands. "Welcome to Spain," he said in well-modulated English. "I am Father Don Santos and you are now in my care."

So this was a Divinio. What was I expecting? Not this. "Some care," I mumbled. "Didn't you just try to kill us and probably intend to do the same again?"

"Do not be an alarmist, Señorita McCabe. For now, we talk only. Empty your pockets of all devices and weapons, and pass them to my men with your bags. Señor Barrows, do not try one of your notorious tricks or your lady here will suffer."

He thought I was a lady and that only the ex-MI6 guy knew tricks? Already he'd given me hope.

We emptied our pockets—phones, guns—as two men stepped up to claim them along with our backpacks. I was beginning to feel ill and more than a little angry. Evan had gone into full alert mode, all senses probably scanning for an escape plan.

"Señorita, you and I will travel together in the first car, and, señor, you will follow with your guards to the second. They have been instructed to secure you by any means necessary so let us avoid further violence, if possible. We have had enough excitement for today."

"Excitement? Is that what you call shooting our helicopter down from the sky?" I asked.

It was as if he hadn't heard me. "Please be so kind as to wear your masks and we will do the same." He lifted one hand as if summoning the wind and bid *adiós* to the farmer watching by the entrance.

"It's a trick!" I bellowed to the farmer, "Call the police!" I should have taken my cue from Evan and saved my breath.

Don Santos sighed and shook his head. "Señorita, señorita…my friend does not speak English, and even if he did he would not believe you. I am a sacerdote—the bond between these people and the church is too deep for you to comprehend."

No doubt the man had also been fed a pack of lies by his dear sacerdote.

Don Santos's black-clad men ushered us toward two white cars parked in the drive—Evan into one, me into the other, accompanied by our guards as though we were off to some unholy communion.

"Where are you taking us?" I asked when I was wedged in the plush leather back seat between the two men, Don Santos sitting up front with the driver.

"Someplace safe. The two of you have given us quite a difficult time and it is necessary for this to cease. Now do sit back and enjoy the ride. This is a beautiful part of Spain."

As if sunsets over mountains and narrow winding roads through gilded orchards would soothe my heart. Trapped and helpless, I sat with my eyes fixed out the window. Evan was in the car behind but my guards refused to allow me to look out the rear window. Any time a car passed, Don Carlos would lift his hand as if bestowing a benediction on the passengers, who would wave in return. There's no way the locals would believe any story we told.

After about twenty minutes, Don Santos's phone rang a few bars of some Gregorian chant. Did the devil have a sense of humor? He answered in Spanish, speaking in that measured way of his, and when the call ended, a conversation ensued between him and his driver that seemed so relaxed and conversational they could be discussing the weather. Meanwhile, my guards—a young man and an older one both clad in black shirts and pants —sat grim and silent.

Finally, we turned off the main road onto a lane that wound farther down the valley into a little village. Glimpses of narrow cobbled streets with strings of flowers strung between the white-tile-roofed buildings rushed by as we turned a corner and drove straight up a long drive toward a church on the hill.

I stared. A church—not surprising considering our host, but this structure was unusually magnificent for the size of the village and commanded its position with absolute authority. A huge painted statue of the Virgin Mary stood in the spotlight, a garland of wilted flowers adorning her head.

The cars parked around the back where it was dark and shielded from the village by the bell tower and a tiny orchard. We were ushered in through the basement stairs, entering a corridor with a series of three little rooms off to one side that opened to a larger function hall.

I caught Evan's eye only briefly before he was shoved into one room while I was marched through the hall flanked by my two guards. Don Santos remained behind.

Glimpses of children's drawings of angels lined the stairs as the guards nudged me upward with their pistols. The sight of those sweet little crayon angels almost brought me to tears. I thought of Ana Marie, of Peaches's dead baby daughter.

The moment we had left the sacerdote's presence, it's as if my two guards eased into minor acts of cruelty. Maybe I could launch a surprise attack—kick out the way I'd been trained, use the element of shock to disarm them. With only two, it might even work, but what about Evan now bound in some tiny room with his captors? I couldn't risk it, not now, anyway.

Instead, I was shoved down the center aisle of the large, beautiful candle-lit church decorated with occasional frescoes, painted statues, and gilded carvings—not rich but still impressive—and was slammed into a wooden chair facing the altar. Before me a gilded carving of the crucified Christ gazed down at me in loving sorrow. At least He had to be on my side.

One guy bound my hands and feet with cruel efficiency while the older one stood over me murmuring what I could only guess were sexual insults. I kept my gaze fixed on the floor, doubting that they would try anything in a church, but what did I know?

A young short-haired woman in a printed skirt and top dashed in with a handful of fresh candles, caught sight of us, and gasped. The older man men yelled at her and she turned and dashed away. He ran after her. I heard a stifled scream, then silence. I pulled against my ropes until the other guard kicked me in the shins. I stopped.

He was standing over me now, holding Evan's and my phones, one in each hand. Turning them over and over, it was as if he expected them to speak. He must have heard that they were special somehow and wanted desperately to crack their secrets.

"Password," he barked. It was hard to see his features in the candlelight especially with that black mask covering his lower face, but he seemed like he'd be a good-looking kid no older than twenty-something.

"No!" I said.

He kicked me again, this time harder. Damn him. My device was voice activated but whether it could identify me through a mask was another matter. Worth a try. "Intruder alert!" I cried. "Burn!"

And just like magic, the phone screen flashed orange, turned smoking hot, and seared the kid's palm. I could smell singed skin through the mask.

He dropped the phone like the burning thing it was and kicked it under the pews. I turned to see it slide three rows down, still pulsing orange before going dark. Evan was a genius.

"There," I said, turning to the kid. "My phone says go to hell."

He might have grasped the gist of that if he hadn't been so busy nursing his hand. He plunged the wounded member into a flask of what might be holy water—no, wine, I realized as the red liquid dripped over the yellow embroidered altar cloth. Shame—it looked to be late-eighteenth-century silk.

When another guard stomped in to find his young comrade still going on about his singed palm, he exploded.

"*¡Me duele, me duele!*" the younger one wailed.

"*¡Callate!*" the man barked, slapping the kid across the side of the head.

"*¿Que esta pasando?*" Don Santos demanded, now striding down the aisle. A flurry of excuses followed that the priest cut off with a chop of his hand. Whatever he said next caused the men to scurry toward the basement door.

"You just can't get good choirboys these days," I whispered, but the priest wasn't paying attention. Glancing from the ewer to the stained altar cloth, he wrinkled his nose and attempted to blot the stains with the edge of his robe.

"You need to soak that in cold water," I said, "Soon, before the stain sets."

He turned to me. "Señorita McCabe, I regret to say that your man has not told me the information I require, which is very unfortunate. This is becoming tedious. Know that we haven't time for games. Now I must ask these same questions of you, and should I not learn the truth, I will be forced to add some painful incentive. Do not force my hand. Answer me this: what is your business in Spain?"

What painful incentive? What had they done to Evan? "We're here because we were forced to leave Portugal and abandon our ailing friend." I was guessing that he knew all this, which meant that I had to keep to the script. "There's a chance that he may be infected with Covid."

"Yet you come to Spain and not London?"

"All flights to London were either booked or canceled so we managed to secure a helicopter—at great expense, I might add. But as you know, small helicopters can't travel as far as jets and our only chance to make it home was to reach an airport in Spain and fly from there. That is before you shot us down. Was that pilot killed, by the way? Is your brotherhood satisfied with the blood they shed across the ages?"

"I will not defend my organization to you, señorita. It is well beyond your comprehension. Are you here to locate the crown?"

He considered his brotherhood an organization, not a holy order? "Hardly. I presume the thing lies in Portugal and is currently beyond our reach. Senhor Carvalho has forbidden us to look further, anyway. Now we just want to escape in one piece, deliver our friends safely back to London, and collect our fee."

He was studying me carefully, the way a man might who had served a congregation as chief confessor long enough to know when someone was lying. He knew I was lying. "What do you know of this crown?" he asked softly.

What did I have to lose? "Only that a pack of religious fanatics have kept alive a cult for five hundred years based on the belief that religious persecution is grounds for a holy war. Like thousands of years of human history has taught us nothing." Go for broke was my next strategy. "These nuts hope to force the globe under one God, one belief system. Like that's worked in the past."

He pursed his lips together, causing his round face to look disconcertingly baby-like and his marble-like eyes anything but. "The faithless do the world a great disfavor. You have so little respect for your betters, or understanding. You are like a dog that sniffs at a wall and believes you know how to design a building. Yet you believe you have the right to this, the right to say that. Your opinions do not matter, señorita. It is time that you learned to bow to a higher authority, woman, and not presume to speak of which you know nothing."

"Then teach me." I was counting on a priest's longing to convert a lost ewe to the flock. "Tell me how the skull of some poor dead prince from five hundred years ago can impart something holy on today's messed-up world."

His dark brows furrowed. "It is because this world is so 'messed up,' as you say, that our crowned king must act quickly to save us all by clearing the way for the world to be born anew. Just as Christ rose from the dead, so must humanity."

"Through a skull and a crown?"

"Dare not speak of what you fail to understand!" he roared. "Our crown contains a fragment of bone from the King of Kings—" he paused long enough to genuflect and raise a hand to the crucifix "—and the skull is merely His corporal representative on earth. Once they are united, we will hear His call and the faithful will be saved."

Oh, good: I was making him angry. "You want to resurrect an archaic notion that the world can fit into some simplistic one-size-fits-all belief system where we all must look, live, and behave the same? Are we going to pretend that the past never happened?" I'd found his button and kept pushing.

"You do not know what you say!"

But I was on a roll. "Would you burn people at the stake, and inflict even more suffering in the world in the name of Jesus, is that what you're saying? Do you really think He would want that?" My eyes had turned to the crucifix. I didn't need to be religious to be incensed. In fact, I imagined Jesus was fully on my side. I could almost hear the angels singing. "The Inquisition is dead for a reason; the world changes for a reason; and this is only one more power play in the name of your patriarchal doctrine! Don't talk to me about entitlement! Men have always demanded entitlement and hidden it under one guise or another!"

He looked as if I had struck him. God, I realized that no one had probably ever spoken to him like that for a long time, maybe never, let alone a woman.

"You dare speak to me that way," he sputtered, adding something in Spanish—either a prayer or a curse.

"If a mortal stands before me and spews nonsense about destroying the earth in the name of religion, I dare speak to you that way." In for a penny...

"The earth is already destroyed," he roared in his pulpit voice. "Look around. The seas are rising, nature is dying, men are still fighting among one another in the name of their false gods and misguided beliefs. Technology is the god of the young. The only way to save humanity is to burn it to the ground so we may be born anew in the name of Jesus Christ!"

His hands rose in the air and he waved them around, as if evoking the gilded angels on the walls to fly. For the first time I gazed into the face of madness and was terrified.

"Enough! I have wasted too much precious time on you two." Suddenly he was sweeping back down the aisle while speaking urgently into his phone, calling for reinforcements from the god of technology.

In seconds, he disappeared, leaving me alone before the altar with the bindings biting into my wrists and my heart galloping. I looked up at Jesus. "So did I mess that up?" But I had maybe seconds until they returned. How could I break free?

I strained against my bindings, kicking my bound feet over and over again trying to loosen the ropes. And then I heard a faint noise behind me. "¡Deja de retorcerse!" a female voice whispered.

Something sawed into my bindings as I stilled. After my wrists sprung free, a young woman ducked in front of me and began cutting the bindings at my feet with a penknife, the same woman who had brought the candles earlier. Now a vicious bruise blackened her cheek. In her twenties with straight dark hair styled in an almost boyish fashion, she caught my eye, beckoned, and slipped back through the altar door.

But I wasn't leaving without my phone. Instantly I was on my stomach reaching under the pew and froze in that position when two men ran down the aisle shouting. The phone just inches out of reach...unless I risked ducking between the pews and kicking it out with my feet. Damn.

The men fanned out all over the church. They'd find me for sure. Suddenly the woman's voice burst in, speaking excitedly, and the men began firing questions at her. Now the guards were dashing back toward the front of the church, the large wooden doors creaking open before slamming shut.

I sagged in relief before standing up and waving at my ally. She waved back from across the aisle. I snatched up my phone along with Evan's and followed her to the vestibule behind the altar.

※

IT WAS A SMALL ROOM WITH A LIBRARY OF BOOKS ON ONE SIDE AND racks of church vestments on another crowded around. Hooks held various church headgear including long white pointed hoods encased in plastic wrap that sent shivers down my spine. What, like the Ku Klux Klan or something? I remembered seeing those hats in a Goya painting without understanding its meaning.

The woman beckoned me on through a back door past two offices, down a short hall, and to a set of back stairs leading both up and down.

One presumably led to the bell tower, the other to the basement and outside. I pointed down. She held up three fingers. Three men downstairs—got it.

Opening up my phone, I was relieved to find it still operable and scanned for a weapon app, something that might disarm someone from a distance. Evan's phones would never shoot bullets but a laser bolt might be a good substitute. I popped open the red bolt icon and crept down the stairs with the phone raised, indicating that the woman remain upstairs.

The steps ended at the back door. To the right lay the hall we'd entered earlier and the room where they held Evan. I heard voices in the corridor, one being Don Santos, who strode from the room talking hurriedly into a cell phone. When he was far enough away and his back turned, I crept to the door and stepped in. Two men with rolled-up sleeves were working over a bloodied Evan.

"Hello, boys."

The moment they swung around, I beamed a bolt of laser light straight into both their eyes, one after the other, blinding them on the spot. As the men screamed and spun away, I rushed up to use the same burning light to sear the ropes off Evan's hands and feet. He sagged forward into my arms just as Don Santos rushed in.

"Stop in the name of our King!" he cried.

I lifted the phone, ready to launch another bolt, when the priest collapsed to the floor. The candle woman stood over his crumpled form, a silver candlestick raised in both hands, a hard look in her eyes. She was one of us.

"Help us!" I cried.

She dropped the candlestick and was at my side in an instant, both of us lifting Evan from the chair. "What's your name? I'm Phoebe," I said, thumbing my chest.

"Phoebe. Me Ilda."

"*Gracias*, Ilda."

She nodded and shot me a brief smile.

"Not...unconscious," Evan whispered through swollen lips. "Can stand. Get the guns...on table."

Leaving him supported by my ally, I snatched up both guns and stuffed them into my pockets. Our bags were on the floor and obviously had been rummaged through. I hastily stuffed everything back into the backpacks, threw one over my shoulder, and grabbed the other.

The two guards were flailing around, screaming about the room with one stumbling into the hall. And yes, I felt pity for them but not enough to let them kill us instead. One was lurching around, arms outstretched, trying to grab somebody. He came too close to Evan, who let go of Ilda long enough to slug the guy in the jaw. The guard crumpled to his knees and stilled.

Two down, four to go. Where were the others? And then as if in answer, we heard voices upstairs. I passed Evan a gun and I cocked the other, shoving my phone into my pocket.

Two men where pounding down the stairs crying out, no doubt seeing the priest's prone form in the hall. Evan leaned out and fired, winging one guy in the arm while the other kept shooting.

"Where are the other two?" I asked.

"Santos sent...them out to pick up...supper," Evan mumbled.

I ducked out from the other side and aimed for the second guy's legs, hitting him in the kneecap. He screamed, dropping his gun and leaving the three of us to climb over the unconscious Don Santos and bolt out the door in the opposite direction.

Outside, darkness had fallen hard as we dashed toward one of two parked cars. The keys were in the ignition, typical rural-style, so we tossed in our bags and folded Evan into the back seat. I took the driver's side and beckoned Ilda to join me in the front.

She shook her head. "No."

"What do you mean 'no'? They know you helped us. They'll kill you."

"No," she repeated.

Evan leaned forward and spoke in Spanish and whatever he said convinced her to climb in. Seconds later I was easing the car down the hill with no idea where to head next except away.

"Give me my phone," Evan mumbled. I dug in my pocket and Ilda passed it back.

"Head for the village—right," he said, trying to read his phone through swollen eyes. "Head for Córdoba. Use your translation app...the one with the...lip icon."

Lip icon? Like I had time to fiddle with a lip icon and where the hell was Córdoba? We were way up in the mountains with nothing like a main highway in sight. We were on a road so narrow a car could barely turn around. Ilda was tapping something into the dashboard's GPS and up popped a map. She pointed to the screen. "Córdoba." Yes, Córdoba, which looked many miles away.

"Evan, can you translate for me?" Silence. I shot a look at Ilda, who slumped in her seat to pantomime that he'd passed out. Right.

"¡Mira!" Ilda cried, straightening.

In the rearview mirror I could see another car gaining fast. "The other two guards." With Evan out cold and Ilda and I officially incommunicado, I had no choice but to keep on driving—only faster.

Ilda was pointing at a signpost, I was putting my foot down on the gas pedal, and all of a sudden a police car was zooming toward us from the opposite direction with another car not far behind that.

"¡Gendarmería!" Ilda cried.

Right, but were they on our side or the Divinios'?

When the car behind us slammed on its brakes and began to reverse, we had our answer. I slowed down and the police car drove right past us, roof lights pulsing, sirens blaring.

A long black limousine pulled to a stop before us. A tall dark-haired man in a suit got out and sauntered up to our car as I lowered the window.

"Buenas noches, señorita. ¿Eres Isabella?"

19

"Isabella?" Evan mumbled as we sped along.

"My password. Are you badly hurt besides what I can see? A concussion, internal bleeding, maybe?" I longed to open his shirt to see if he had open wounds but thought it best to wait.

Instead, I began dabbing his cuts from a bottle of water found in the well-appointed back seat, using a cloth one of the suited men had passed back along with a first aid kit. Ilda had the kit open on her lap and was handing me bandages, antiseptic, gauze...

"I'll be fine," he mumbled through those swollen lips, his head resting against the seat. "They didn't want to knock me out in case...I couldn't talk but I refused to talk...regardless. How did you...escape?" he asked, fixing one half-swollen eye at me.

"I riled Don Santos up so badly by daring to challenge his beliefs—me, a mere substandard human of the weaker sex—that he stomped off in fury. Probably thought that a woman couldn't possibly slip from his grip, but two women bested him in the end. Ilda here saved my life and probably yours, too."

He turned to Ilda and flashed her one of his beautiful, currently distorted smiles. She beamed back. *"Gracias,"* he said, adding something in

Spanish before turning back to me. "First time I've seen that laser bolt...in action." He sounded like a boy with a new toy. "Works...perfectly."

"It's deadly effective, if that's what you mean. I blinded those men, Evan."

"You had no choice. I would have killed them given the chance."

Noel had said something similar to me once: never let your enemies live to come after you a second time. Kill them on the spot. But I could never do it. Besides, those two men would live a long dark life as a result of my actions and that was bad enough.

"Probably...drained the battery," Evan mumbled. "Haven't found a... solution...yet."

I sat up to check my phone for messages, distressed to find that the laser feature had, in fact, completely drained the battery. A charger was handily available on the back of the front seat so I dug out my cord and began recharging. After that, I drifted off to sleep in the midst of worrying about Peaches, Rupert, and the Carvalhos. Oh, and us...

We dozed off and on as the limousine zoomed through the evening. Ilda and I sat on either side of Evan, his head occasionally lolling on either my shoulder or hers. Our rescuers up front spoke little English and either could not or would not tell us who they worked for, but we did learn their names—Salvi and Luis, first names only. Both were in their thirties, both tall and well-built, as if they had been hired based on their physique. Ilda and Luis kept exchanging shy glances in the rearview mirror.

I awoke with Ilda saying, "Córdoba!"

Sitting up, I watched as the car drove over a long lovely bridge, the lights of a cathedral, towers, and arched-windowed buildings reflected on a calm water's surface—a river.

We gazed in hushed wonder as the car navigated wide boulevards and narrow streets, winding its way under up-lit palms toward a sprawling crenellated walled structure. I recognized medieval when I saw it and this fortress with its mellowed gold stone towers had to be at least that old.

"Alcázar de los Reyes Cristianos!" Ilda exclaimed.

Alcázar de los Reyes Cristianos? What did I know about the Palace of the Christian Kings other than to translate the rudimentary Spanish? Nothing. My one trip to Madrid when on a youthful backpacking trip would not help me here.

Evan, stirring beside me, winced and sat up. "The Castle of the Christian Kings? It was actually built from Roman remains on the bones of a Visigothic fortress...before succumbing to the Umayyad Caliphate, so the origins are hardly Christian...though Alfonso of Castille began rebuilding it in the 1200s." Various pronunciations were somewhat butchered due his lip swellings but I caught his meaning.

"Glad you're feeling better," I whispered, "and obviously haven't suffered brain damage."

He mustered a kind of lopsided smile as the car stopped by a guard post and the driver spoke into an intercom. "But why are we here? It's now a national historic site."

"I have no idea," I said.

Ilda spoke beside him.

"She says it has been closed periodically...since the pandemic, and wonders what we are doing here...too," he translated.

Our drivers were the silent types, so all we could do was wait as the car slid in through the gates and wove between imposing stone walls and under arches, hoping that somebody would eventually provide an explanation. When we stopped in a small parking area, a man and a woman were awaiting us, both dressed in dark clothing.

Luis, our driver, opened the door and helped us out while Salvi tried to assist Evan. I'm assuming Evan's Spanish response said that he could walk unassisted since the man stepped aside.

The woman, her hair pulled back into a sleek chignon, wearing a white blouse, a crisp navy jacket with a matching pencil skit, and vertiginous high heels, stepped forward. The only ornamentation she wore were a pair of gold hoop earrings and a large marquee-cut diamond on her wedding finger that flashed the light. Her white mask completed the severe ensemble. "Señorita McCabe, Señor Barrows, and..." She hesitated before Ilda.

"Señorita Ilda Garcia," Ilda said, adding something in Spanish.

"Welcome to Córdoba and the Alcázar, Señorita McCabe, Señorita Garcia, and Señor Barrows. Consider yourselves our special guests. You are most welcome. I am Dr. Sofia Morales and this is my assistant, Señor Barco. We will be your contacts while you are in Spain. Please follow me."

Señor Barco nodded and smiled behind his mask, pointing to the face covering. "If you please."

We hastily applied ours while I gave Ilda one of the surgical variety I'd packed. Señor Barco offered to relieve us of our bags and reluctantly we agreed. We strode down a long white arched corridor that seemed to open up onto a garden on one side, up several flights of stairs, on through connecting hallways, and along a grand hallway paneled with red striped silk with a high ornate gilded ceiling. I couldn't stop trying to absorb every detail from the tapestries to the paintings lining the space.

"Didn't Isabella of Castile and Ferdinand of Aragon live here?" I asked as I dredged my information databanks.

Dr. Morales turned, and then stopped while the men proceeded ahead with our bags. "You are correct. The alcázar, which means 'palace' in Arabic, was home to Queen Isabella and her husband, King Ferdinand, for eight years and also became the headquarters for the Spanish Inquisition for nearly three centuries. It is indeed a fortress with a long, often bloody history."

"And why are we here?" Evan asked, determined to stand on his own two feet as if he hadn't been battered for part of the afternoon.

Dr. Morales studied him. "Señor, may we call a doctor to tend your wounds?"

"I will be fine after a good rest but thank you for the concern."

She nodded. "It is perhaps best that I take you to your quarters to rest before we talk further. Forgive us for being unable to put you up properly, but for as long as you are with us in Spain, you will be our guests inside one of our historic sites."

"We're going to sleep in palaces and castles?" I asked.

I thought I caught a slight smile behind the mask. I estimated her to be in her early fifties but she seemed almost ageless. "Perhaps this sounds more romantic than it is," she said. "They are not designed as hotels but as museums. The facilities you might come to expect are unavailable." She spread her hands, sending her mega-diamond sparkling. "However, these buildings are very secure with guards and the necessary technology to ensure your safety. This makes them our best option to protect you. I will take you to your rooms first and then you must eat."

Which reminded me that I hadn't eaten since the morning. We left the ornate palatial area and crossed a porticoed walkway into a long buff-colored stucco building that appeared almost regimental next to the royal residence.

"These were once were the soldiers slept. Today they are offices but we have set up temporary beds here. There are no furnished bedrooms at the museum sites. We have washrooms available down the hall and have brought in temporary beds. Please let me know if you need anything else. We have set up dinner five doors down and I will wait for you there."

We were shown to three rooms side by side, all furnished alike. Seeing my backpack there, I stepped into the first, a plain butter-yellow room with a crucifix on one wall and a small bookcase against the other. A foldout bed had been made up with a pile of towels stacked next to extra blankets on a chair. Our hosts had thought of everything, right down to a new toothbrush and other toiletries.

Evan arrived at my door minutes later holding an icepack to his mouth and clutching something green in his other hand. "Phoebe?" My name now came out as "Fweebe."

"Evan." I turned.

"Yours, I presume?" He held out a pair of my silk undies that I must have stuffed into his bag by mistake.

"I was in a hurry," I said, taking them from fingers that held on seconds too long.

"I don't mind." He was trying to smile.

"You're in no condition to tease." I whipped them out of his hand, trying not to notice the twinkle in his swollen eyes.

"Always in condition...to tease."

"Wait until the swelling goes down first. Are you hurt anywhere else?"

His shirt was torn and now that he'd removed his jacket I could see the beginnings of a livid bruise forming across his chest. Without thinking, I peeled back his shirt and gasped. The bastards must have punched him repeatedly. "Oh, Evan, let me bathe and bandage that!"

He clasped my wrist. "You can bathe me...any time you want but...later. We need information first."

I suppressed a smile and watched him walk away with a slight limp.

Back in my room, I hastily gathered up a change of clothes, cringing at the thought of those brutes pawing through my stuff. Using one of the washrooms to clean up and change, I returned to my quarters only long enough to scan my phone for emails and texts.

I hastily dispatched an *I'm fine* to Max, minus relevant details, and sent something similar to Peaches after reading that Rupert had been issued a Covid test by somebody in a hazmat suit. Rupert himself texted only to complain that he'd run out of his beloved tea bags so we had best return before he was forced to drink coffee. There was a message there that worried me. Connie emailed asking our location but I didn't respond.

Minutes later, I counted five doors down the hall and entered a barrel-ceilinged room where a table had been set with paper plates of food and drinks. Dr. Morales was already seated at the head of the table, her mask removed, talking with Ilda, everyone six feet apart. Don't ask me why it surprised me that she wore bright red lipstick.

"Señorita McCabe, I have just learned what a day you have had and heard that you encountered Don Santos," she said.

"You know of him? And please call me Phoebe. I am not used to such formalities."

"Phoebe, then, and you may call me Sofia. Yes, we know of Don Santos. He is one of the order of the Divinio brotherhood, one of at least twenty members spread across the world with an unknown number of followers."

"Are they all priests?"

"The ruling brotherhood, yes. 'The world is full of monsters wearing the faces of the angels'—an old Spanish saying. Please do not think that the Catholic church has been corrupted by this sect's beliefs. They do not represent the church today, though much has been done in the name of Catholicism in the past. There are many priests and sisters from various orders who work on our behalf. Please eat and then we will talk further. This is what you refer to as takeout, I'm afraid, from the restaurant nearby."

Evan stepped in behind me and held out a seat for me, which I took, catching the wry glint of humor in Sofia's eyes at this little display of gallantry. Ilda only beamed and passed us a plate of small ham sandwiches along with other platters of bite-size edibles like sausages and seafood. We all ate in silence while Sofia sat at the end of the table with her hands folded, her perfectly manicured red nails adding color to the otherwise austere room.

"Aren't you eating?" I asked.

"Thank you but I have already dined. Try the sangria. It is a local specialty."

"Not for me, thanks." Though I noted that Ilda had taken a tall glassful. "Do you live near here?"

"I live in Madrid with my husband and two daughters but I travel often for my work. I am in charge of the nation's historic properties. That is my official role."

"Are the museums funding this operation?" Evan asked as he carefully divided his tapas into even smaller pieces. He chewed carefully as if favoring one side of his mouth. "We'd appreciate an explanation of the resources you are able to command such as government helicopters and historic sites."

Sofia smiled again, a self-possessed glimmer of humor that seemed to flicker just below her otherwise severe exterior. I sensed that passions ran like an underground river beneath that surface. "My historic properties role is only a piece of my work for my employer. They are very powerful and generous. I have worked in their employ for many decades, since I was very young. They financed my education as a historian and I have devoted my career to Spanish history in order to stop this scourge that grows more powerful by the day."

"Do you work as a historian?" I asked.

"Yes, and my employer has provided me with all the resources necessary to assist you. Whatever you need, it is only necessary to ask."

"Is this room secure?" Evan asked. "Are all your devices masked against technological intrusion?"

"As much as possible, yes. My employer established a secure network solely for our use and Señor Barco is vigilant against hacking and technological intrusion. And what of you, Señor Barrows? I see your devices are active."

"I have them shielded through encryption, though I admit with the speed of technological change, I worry that our defenses could be compromised at any time."

Dr. Morales nodded. "We must remain vigilant. We understand the situation in Portugal grows dire and we have dispatched assistance. But the sect is far less disciplined there and we fear what they may do next. There is not much time."

"Our archaeologist, Dr. Collins, disappeared last night," I said. "As you probably know, he was hacked in Lisbon, which alerted the Divinios to the location of Prince Don Carlos's skull."

"Most unfortunate, yes. And now we must find the crown," she said. "Do you have an idea as to where to look? We hold great hope that you will provide a unique perspective."

I set down my fork and took out my phone, passing it to Evan to hand to Sofia. "These underpaintings were uncovered from a Titian portrait of Queen Isabella of Portugal. The first is of a watchtower behind her head. Do you recognize it?"

Her fine arched brows rose as she gazed at the paintings. "This was uncovered beside a portrait of Queen Isabella of Portugal, the Empress of the Carnation?"

"That one is by Titian and it was returned to the House of Aviz at the empress's request. It's hung there ever since. There is another, which is a copy of the Titian that hangs in the Prado, but this one interests me most."

"Those hills could be anywhere and that style of watch post is common throughout Spain. You will see it in many fortresses. There is one outside this very door."

"Can you tell me anything else?" I asked.

"I know of this painting, of course. There have been many efforts on the part of Spain to bring it back home but the flower...the empress's association with the carnation is legendary." Her dark eyes met mine. "Emperor Charles ordered seeds from a Persian flower to be planted for her, seeds which grew in abundance and pleased her enormously. The carnation became Spain's national flower as a result, but why would it be painted over?"

"That is the question," I said, tapping another photo and sliding my phone toward Sofia, "and why would this wilted carnation be painted on a Titian portrait by someone other than Titian?"

"Are you certain of that?" she asked, picking it up.

"Positive. The brushstrokes and style are very different. Though the flower is beautifully executed, it's not by Titian. No, it was deliberately painted and deliberately hidden. That means something."

Sofia sat back, her reserve temporarily disrupted. "But who would do such a thing and when?"

"The painting hung in the apartments of King Philip II for years, I understand, before it was shipped to the Aviz family in Portugal at the late empress's request. These clues have a feminine hand. What influential women were at court at the time of Prince Carlos's death besides his stepmother, Queen Elizabeth de Valois? I have gathered a few names but I'm not sure how they fit."

"Ana de Mendoza, Princess of Eboli, for certain."

"Yes, the woman featured in the Verdi opera."

"She was unique, completely revolutionary, and lived unapologetically for her time. Besides raising nine children, some of them rumored to be King Philip's, she remained a friend of the queen. If she did indeed sleep with Philip, he was probably exercising his Divine Right of Kings."

"Any woman he wanted he could have," I remarked.

"Indeed, and she was a beautiful woman despite the eye patch. After her husband's death, she became lover and ally to the king's friend, Antonio Pérez. He plotted against the crown and managed to get away with his crimes while the princess died imprisoned alone in 1592, suspected of treason. Pérez is who we believe to be behind the later manifestation of the Divinios."

"Could she have been working against Pérez all along and taken the blame for his crimes?" I asked.

Alma stood up. "As a spy, you mean?"

"A spy for the counter-Divinios."

"Nothing would surprise me about this rebel. She was intelligent, beautiful, and daring. Antonio Pérez, on the other hand, was known as a master manipulator who was responsible for assassinating the king's uncle at the royal request and now we think Prince Carlos, too."

I grew excited. "Meanwhile the princess takes the fall for his earlier crimes."

"Not so surprising, yes?" She opened a photo on her tablet, turning it around to reveal a handsome man in black velvet holding a scroll in one hand. "Pérez held great sway with King Philip. He advised him of policies that would eventually bankrupt Spain. His goal like many of the powerful men at the time was to increase his own clout using this breakaway cult to serve his needs."

I gazed at Sofia, transfixed. "And maybe Ana de Mendoza, Princess of Eboli, worked against him while pretending to be in his corner?" I was standing now, too, leaning over the table toward Sofia while Evan and Ilda watched.

"Perhaps," Sofia whispered. "But she could not have done so alone even if she was trusted by Pérez. By then, Don Carlos was locked away in 'strict confinement'—those were the king's words. Even the queen would not be allowed access."

"Did King Philip know how his son died?"

"We don't believe he knew the full details but there was evidence that Don Carlos had been plotting the death of his father so treason was already in Philip's mind. The king lost patience. He shut himself away and sat in an armchair the days before his son's death. We believe it likely that he had given the order for his son's agony to be brought to an end. By then Don Carlos had gone on hunger strikes and tried to jump from a window. To Philip, no doubt, Pérez had merely brought to an end a difficult and painful problem."

"But he didn't necessarily know how. Would he have seen his son after death?" Evan asked.

"That is not known. The matter was shrouded in mystery. Whether the crown was applied before or after the prince's death remains unclear. The moment Senhor Carvalho sent word that your archaeologist had located the skull and was able to identify it based on well-known abnormalities, the pieces fit at last."

"But supposedly the king retreated to a monastery to mourn?" Evan said.

"Yes, immediately following the funeral."

"And maybe during King Philip's absence, a woman managed to steal and hide the crown?" I asked, barely able to conceal my excitement.

"I do not see how she could have done so. This was men's work, dark deeds they were not likely to expose to women. Women were mostly shackled in the Spanish court, though these had more freedom than most and claimed far more than many dared. Still, I do not see how they could have gained entrance to the prince's prison especially after this horrible event." She retrieved the iPad, tapped it again, and slid the device toward me opened to a portrait of a strikingly beautiful woman in a starched ruff, black velvet gown, and an eyepatch.

"Yes, the princess with the eye patch rumored to be the result of a fencing match," I said, gazing down at Ana de Mendoza, Princess of Eboli, who had married the man who would later become the Prince of Eboli when she was only thirteen.

"More likely an eye disease but the more cavalier story suits her spirit," Sofia said with a decisive nod. "If any woman was deep enough into the court to counter the Divinios and work against Pérez, it would be Ana de Mendoza. She was supposedly involved with Pérez. Still, she could not have done this alone."

"Would Queen Elizabeth of Valios have helped?"

"The queen was not known for her strength of character but supposedly possessed a good heart and attempted to help Prince Carlos, to whom she was briefly betrothed. That was before she became his stepmother. She pitied him, as did Ana de Mendoza. Apparently, they were some of the few women he treated with respect."

"But there had to be others in this conspiracy." I nodded, gazing down at the portrait. "Whoever painted the empress's wilted carnation must have been in Philip's court at that time, too. It certainly wasn't Titian. I'm thinking Sofonisba."

Sofia snapped her fingers. "Sofonisba Anguissola! Slide to the right."

"She was a rare female artist of the Renaissance," I said, "talented and supported by the men in her life despite the prejudices against her gender. Though Italian, she had moved to the Spanish court at Philip's request." I had studied her in university and refreshed myself on the details in the last few days. "I believe she's part of this."

"I think you could be right. Her portrait of the princess is there, too."

Sliding through other portraits of the much-painted Ana de Mendoza, I stopped at one showing the princess wearing a dashing plumed hat. Here the princess was portrayed in a low-cut summer gown holding a tray of what looked to be roses. A pink bud was held delicately between two fingers.

The similarities to the style of painting between the flowers in this portrait and the empress's wilted carnation hit me immediately. Both had the same delicate application of paint, the same gray-green leaves, and though I couldn't be sure without viewing the actual portrait, I was willing to hazard a guess. "This is by the same artist. We have found the artist who dared hide a clue in a Titian—Sofonisba!"

"She was very much part of the court and even attended the infanta Isabella Clara Eugenia and served as a lady-in-waiting to Queen Elizabeth of Valois," Sofia exclaimed. "She gave art lessons!"

Our eyes locked. "We have found our allies in Philip's court; we have found the female counteroperatives to the Divinios."

Sofia smiled, a beam so dazzling that it transformed her face. "I believe we have!"

"However," Evan interrupted in sober tones, "and as much as I hate to disturb this euphoria, we are still no closer to discovering where the crown may be hidden."

20

Though it was true that we had yet to find the location of the crown, the story of the women in King Philip's court was a treasure of another kind. It was as though they were allies from another century trying to communicate with us using all the skills they had available—art, symbolism, and their very femininity.

For most of that evening we sat around the table with Sofia Morales combing through the research material accessed from her employer's private online archives. It seemed that most of the valuable tertiary documents existent from the court of Philip II had been transcribed into digital form for posterity's sake and that Sofia held the online keys.

"Your employer must be very powerful," Evan had commented, studying Sofia through his puffy eyes.

"Very," she acknowledged, "but not so powerful that we can see all things in all ways. A fresh perspective proves most invaluable. Consider your every wish my command."

I grinned at the illusion to the fairy tale. "You are our fairy señora, our godmother?"

"Not as old as that, I hope." She laughed and waved her hands. "My two daughters are still too young."

She ordered computers to be delivered to the room so that we could research more comfortably and even Ilda joined in with the help of the translation app left open on my phone. Anything spoken in either English or Spanish was automatically translated in Evan's mechanical voice.

"What shall we call them?" Ilda asked in Spanish, the app immediately translating. By now I knew our rescuer was twenty-three years old and had been volunteering in Don Santos's church since a teenager. In her own way, she was of the same ilk as the Princess of Eboli, bravely working to counter injustice in a world dominated by men.

The things she had seen behind the congregation's back, the many injustices Don Santos permitted in the name of his worldview, had hardened her. Now Sofia would be keeping her under her wing. Once things calmed down, Ilda would inform her grandparents that she would be moving to Madrid.

"What will we call our anti-Divinios?" I mused. "Does your employer's organization have a name?"

"No," Sofia said, "and we are not an organization but an—how do you say it?—a network. Yes, we are a network."

"What if we called them de Nuestras Damas or the Damas for short?" Ilda offered.

"'Our ladies'? I like it," I said, since all of the women we had now encountered in history were ladies of the noblest sort. We all agreed but that brought us no closer to the crown.

"The Damas must have had help," Sofia said while pondering a sixteenth-century court document she produced on her screen. "Three women: a queen, an artist, and a princess from one of Spain's ruling houses could not have stolen the crowned head from this poor prince after burial and hidden it somewhere by themselves."

"It is not a typically feminine act, for sure. Beheading is a guy thing," I said, half-jokingly.

Evan lifted his own battered head. Though the swellings had subsided, he now sported two black eyes along with those pulpy lips. It didn't make him less attractive. "What if Pérez and his men took the skull and the crown immediately following burial? The king was supposedly so grief-stricken—or guilt-stricken—that he retreated to his El Escorial monastery shortly after the funeral. That left a man with Pérez's power ample time to perform the distasteful deed."

"So you're thinking that Pérez stole away the head and the crown, maybe to Portugal?" I asked. "He would have had opportunity, especially if the priests of the Royal Monastery of El Escorial where the prince was buried were in league with the Divinios."

"Which they probably were." Evan sat back and tried to cross his arms, found the pressure on his chest too uncomfortable, and returned his hands to his lap. I had managed to convince him to take a couple of my painkillers but otherwise he soldiered on. "But I'm guessing that something happened en route. Perhaps Portugal was his ultimate destination and that Pérez planned to enact some kind of ritual at our altar in Sintra."

"But someone interceded, someone working for our Damas?" I asked.

"Exactly. They must have ambushed his party and stolen the crown somehow, possibly the skull, too. How else can we explain how the crown and the skull became separated?"

"But who would have the strength to ambush a troop of the king's guards under Pérez? Not Ana de Mendoza, not even the queen," Sofia countered. "That would have soon been communicated to the king with untold repercussions."

"Wait!" I had been skimming another biography of the Princess of Eboli. "After her husband's death, Ana retreated to the convent of the Pastrana monastery and stayed there for years before leaving and igniting the supposed affair with Pérez. Did she actually become a nun?"

"Of sorts, yes," Sofia said. "It was common for wealthy widows of the day to retire to a convent following a husband's death, especially to avoid another marriage and to grieve in peace. Ana's marriage to de Silva, her husband, was reportedly a happy one, or happy enough, and he was King Philip's chief councillor."

"So she may have formed a strong bond with the convent sisters?"

"Definitely. Both she and her husband had generously provided to the Pastrana convent and monastery."

My eyes fixed on hers. "What if the sisters of this convent were Damas' allies? What if Ana convinced them to help her retrieve this crown and skull?"

Ilda was on her feet. "The Carmen de Pastrana, founded by Saint Teresa of Jesus!" She was speaking so quickly that the translator app couldn't keep up. In fact, it garbled the last part.

"Yes, Ana de Mendoza and her husband were the duke and duchess of Pastrana in Guadalajara where Ana was born as well as great benefactors of the area," Sofia said, catching Ilda's excitement. "In 1569, the Princess of Eboli called upon Saint Teresa to found a Barefoot Carmelite convent, and Prince Carlos died in 1568—the timing is very close!"

"Saint Teresa?" I asked. Sometimes I felt like such a heathen.

"Saint Teresa!" Ilda said, quickly genuflecting. "Saint Teresa of Jesus!"

"She was a charismatic religious figure in Spain at the time and still revered today. She held that the Mother Mary must be worshipped as the Mother of God and not just as some holy receptacle," Sofia said.

"The sacred feminine again," Evan commented. "Men have long overlooked, underestimated, and undervalued the power of women."

I caught his eye and smiled. "Amen." Turning back to my comrades I said: "So are we now thinking that our Damas may have included an order of nuns?"

"Yes, it is possible! It makes sense!" Sofia was now pacing the room, her high heels abandoned for bare feet. "Saint Teresa was a powerful person in the church at the time, respected by many, including brethren, and eventual canonized. If she put her force behind the Damas to stop the Divinios, it would make a powerful obstacle."

"And nuns would have had sanctity to travel across the country dispensing assistance to the poor and needy. Travel for them would have been relatively safe in Catholic Spain and Portugal," Evan added. "They, too, would have had soldiers to guard them and reason to enter a chapel in Portugal to secretly deposit a skull, for instance. No one would question them."

"But what about the crown?" I asked. "If the sisters also took back the crown, where would they have hidden it—in Pastrana?" I scrolled through the photos on my tablet to land on the background behind Isabella's head. "That watchtower must be significant. Do they have them in Pastrana, too?"

Sofia threw up her hands. "They are everywhere. In Pastrana, yes, here, yes, everywhere, yes!"

"But with mountains behind?"

"Yes," she said, "mountains everywhere."

Sometimes history feeds you wisps of information enlivened by the shadows of those who lived long ago. At that moment, we all wanted to grab the past by the throat and demand that it give up its dead, tell us the full story, fill in all those missing pieces. But history, like time itself, speaks in code, leaving us to piece together the best picture we can with what little it offers. We had our Divinio counteroperatives and they had sent us clues but we still could not piece it together. Something was still missing.

"The hexagonal watchtower," Sofia mused, "the mountains behind. It is strange to see those arched windows below the roof."

I looked up. "Strange, how?"

She shook her head as if to clear it. "The Moorish influence is everywhere in Spain, either by the original Arabic builders or through their influence on our design, but when I first saw this, I thought maybe it was Guadalest. Still, it is too finished to be Guadalest. The Guadalest castle would have been in ruins even in the fifteenth century."

Evan summarized from his computer screen. "El Castell de Guadalest in Valencia province. It existed during the Muslim occupation until the Christian conquest of the thirteenth century when it passed through many hands until destroyed by multiple earthquakes. I see no direct link between that castle and our power women."

I gazed down at my own screen, flipping from the painting of Princess Elba by Sofonisba Anguissola to my picture of the hidden carnation. "We're allowing ourselves to be led down the wrong track," I said slowly, almost in a trance of concentration. "We're thinking like men, not women."

"How so?" Evan asked.

"Buildings, dates, rational, linear thought...that is traditionally male thinking. The princess is painted with flowers revealing her femininity at the hands of a female artist. Here she's vulnerable, unlike all the other formal black-clothed portraits of the princess encased in the armor of court fashion. Sofonisba painted a carnation on the Titian, a flower of great importance to Queen Isabella, who must have seemed like the ideal queen in their eyes—unblemished, a regent of the most powerful man of the then world who appeared to have loved her absolutely, the mother of the current king..."

"The carnation," Sofia mused, caught in the net of my thinking, "is a symbol of love, of Spain, the flower of God."

"And legend says that carnations grew at the Virgin Mary's feet when she cried at Jesus's death. And yet it is painted wilting," Ilda said, "as if it is dying, too."

I looked up. "Where would King Charles have planted carnations for his queen after her death—at their castle in Madrid?"

"The El Escorial palace complex was built by Philip, not Charles," Evan said. "I believe that a man who loved his queen and wanted to plant something meaningful in her memory would do so at a place special to them both. Charles and Isabella honeymooned in Granada, a honeymoon that lasted much longer than expected since the two were deeply attracted to one another."

"Alhambra," Sofia whispered, her face alight. "In Granada, where Charles initially buried her."

"Though Philip eventually had her body transferred to the Royal Monastery of San Lorenzo de El Escorial in 1574 to rest beside her husband after his monastery and palace compound was finished."

"The same place where Prince Carlos was buried," Evan said.

"They buried the crown at Alhambra," I whispered, turning to Evan.

Evan caught my eye. "When it comes to how a man loves a woman, it helps to think like a man."

21

It was settled: the next day we would travel to Granada, a two-hour drive. We decided it was best that we travel disguised and arrive after nightfall but that meant that Sofia had to find us wigs and a change of clothes by the next morning. She sent Salvi, one of our two guards, to start searching.

"Are you not staying here for the night?" I asked.

Señor Barco, who appeared to be in charge of security and had popped in and out throughout the evening, arrived to deliver bottles of water and a box of rolls and cheese that would serve as breakfast. The other guard, Luis, stood posted outside our building.

"I stay at a hotel nearby. We do not believe the Divinios yet know we are here, but just in case, I will follow my usual pattern. I frequently travel the country to visit our museum and national staff—or did before the pandemic. My presence here would not be unusual but my staying overnight would. Before I part, we must exchange mobile numbers." Holding her phone, she brought up her contacts. "This is my secure number. Few people have access. Why can I not do an electronic contact transfer?"

"It's Evan's blocking device. Here, let's exchange the old-fashioned way." We input our details before she gathered up her purse, stepped into her shoes, and smiled. "I hope you sleep well in Alcázar tonight. There are other guards posted around the complex and the necessary technology to assure your safety. It is best that you do not wander about the property without alerting Señor Barco. He remains on-site."

It was only a little after 9:00 p.m., too early to turn in even after the day we'd had. Besides, we were at a castle in Spain. Could I really be expected to ignore that? But my brain was filled with princesses and sisters and a knot of men intent to shore up their power using the bones of a poor, deranged prince.

Evan had already retreated to his room and I wanted to check on him. After biding good night to Sofia, I dashed down the hall to find him spread out across the bed.

"Evan," I whispered, sitting on the edge of the bed. "Let me see your chest."

"How I've longed to hear those words," he whispered with a quirk on his bruised lips, "but perhaps my manly abdomen is not currently...at its best."

"Oh, stop." I unbuttoned his shirt, spreading it open to see the manly chest in question, wincing at the sight of the livid bruising spreading down his torso and beneath his trousers. There were scars, too, signs of bullet wounds, maybe even a long-ago knife injury. It looked ghastly but I guessed his impressive musculature had protected his internal organs in the end. "Do you sense any internal bleeding?" I asked. It was all I could do to stifle my shock. "Any injuries I can't see?"

He gave me another lopsided smile. "All my parts are still working, I assure you."

"I meant *internal* parts. Did they kick you in the kidneys, for example?"

"They kicked me...everywhere, but I'll be fine. You've found our Damas, Phoebe."

"*We* found them. Let me ice that bruising at least. I see that Señor Barco has delivered a cooler." I left his side long enough to fill a zip bag with cubes, wrap it in a cloth, and apply it gently to his chest.

His hand caught mine as I rested the pack on the worst of the visible swelling. "I'll be fine. Bruises heal in time. When will yours?"

It took me a moment to grasp his meaning. I chose my words carefully. "Sometimes a wounded heart takes longer. Noel kicked me in the heart,

Evan. I really thought he loved me and I him, but he betrayed me again and again."

"Maybe he loved you but didn't have the fortitude to make you more important...than his cravings and greed," he whispered. "You need a man who will make you his queen, who will love you absolutely. Halloran was the wrong man, Phoebe. Can you recognize the right one even when he's been beaten...to a pulp?"

Oh, God. One hand flew to my mouth like a startled heroine, the other held fast in Evan's grip. I tugged my fingers away slowly. "It takes time, Evan. It's too soon for me to fall again." I couldn't yet admit the truth: that I had already fallen for him and had been fighting against it for a long time. I just was too cowardly to lower my defenses long enough to risk another shot. "I'm just not ready."

"When you are ready...to fall again, let me be the one to catch you," he whispered.

I left him to dash down the corridor, stopping halfway to sob into my hands. Suddenly my emotions were welling to the surface, carrying all my anguish and heartbreak with it. My feelings for Evan were in there somewhere stirring things up, tugging at me in powerful ways that I didn't have the courage to handle right then.

"¿Que pasa?"

I looked up to find Ilda gazing at me while the phone in my pocket said, "What's wrong?" in Evan's robot voice.

"Nothing and everything," I said, the phone translating as I pulled it out. "I'm worried about Evan, that's all, though I'm sure he'll be fine."

"You love him. I understand. He is a strong man who loves you also," she said with a little smile.

I was about to deny it but gave up. "It is more complicated than that. I am getting over my last boyfriend who was...a murderous, thieving bastard."

"I understand!" she exclaimed, throwing up her hands. "My boyfriend also. I told him about Dos Santos but he didn't believe! When the church was closed, the men would gather and then—" she shook her head "—he joined them."

"Your boyfriend joined the Divinios?" I couldn't believe that the translator app had got that right.

"Don Santos's guards, yes. Little men, big power."

"Was he one of the men I saw today?"

"Yes." She held my gaze, fierce and unwavering. "Juan hit me. I had broke up with him but still he hits me."

"And your parents and the church permit this?"

Her gaze lowered. "Both dead. I live with my grandparents. They are good people but believe the church can do no wrong. They knew that Juan hits. They complained and Don Santos visited and quoted them the Bible."

"The parts that imply that women must serve men?"

"Yes! Don Carlos said I was misbehaved. He urged me to marry Juan to be tamed. Marry the man who beats me? Never! I prayed to the Virgin Mary and she has brought me you and Señora Morales." And with that she genuflected and embraced me. I was so ready for a little personal contact that I hugged her back.

When we pulled away moments later, both our faces were wet. "I'm sorry you have suffered under men," I began.

"Many women suffer under men. Not all. Many friends are happy with good men but not me. I will join the sisters and serve God."

A statement both rebellious and traditional. I nodded and linked my arm in hers. "Let's take a walk."

We found Señor Barco working at one of the terminals back in our work room. He jumped up to accompany us on our stroll while speaking into his cell phone.

"Come, I show you the gardens," he said. "Much of the original destroyed but this they left."

He led us under arches and beside huge walls to a large square pool lined with marigolds and orange trees. Somewhere night jasmine bloomed and water tinkled from fountains running down the center of the pool.

"Very beautiful, yes?" Señor Barco asked.

"Gorgeous," I agreed, inhaling the scent of flowers under a balmy starred sky. Gazing around, I could see the deep crenellations and towers spotlit around the property. I thought I heard the faint sound of a flamenco guitar playing on a distant street beyond the walls. And this lovely place had once been the Court of the Holy Offices, the seat of the dreaded Inquisition?

Señor Barco strolled away to check his phone while Ilda and I stood arm in arm enjoying the warm night. "And here we are in the twenty-first century with a group of holy terrorists scheming to thrive again," I whispered.

"My church bears much shame, yes," Ilda said, "but it is the crime of men, not of God. God holds His hand out for the faithful to carry His word. I will work for the power of good, not evil."

"I know you will," I said.

"Why is that man on the wall?"

I followed her gaze to a figure in black dashing across the parapets. Scanning around I said: "Shit! Where is Señor Barco?"

22

A bullet pinged at our feet. We dashed under the trees, heading toward the portico while I speed-dialed Sofia. She picked up immediately. "There's a man on the walls shooting. Security has been breached!" I cried.

"Where is Barco?" she asked.

Ilda screamed, stopping to stare at Señor Barco facedown on the tiles. I didn't need to roll him over to see bullet hole blooming blood under his chest. I felt for a pulse at his neck.

"Dead," I said into the phone. "We are heading back." I grabbed Ilda's hand and ran.

Ilda was saying something to me in Spanish and my phone was offering a garbled translation. I thought it said that we couldn't just leave Barco.

"He is dead!" I told her. "Señor Barco is gone!"

Sofia told us to gather in the workroom and await instructions. I patted my pocket even knowing that I'd left my gun on the bed.

We burst into the hallway of our rooms scanning for infiltrators and security personal alike but how could we even tell the difference? They all work dark clothes. But then I saw one of our original drivers, Luis, running down the hall shouting while my app translated: "Gather your bags and follow me. Where is Señor Barrows?"

Where was Señor Barrows? I ran to his room and found it empty. Even his bags were gone. Damn. Dashing back to my room, I grabbed my gun and bag. He wouldn't have left without good reason and the moment I heard the first gunshot, I understood: Evan was at the far end of the hall firing at someone.

I poked my head out, saw Ilda standing in the workroom doorway, and waved her back. Luis was in the room opposite mine, firing down the hall. He caught sight of me and tried to beckon me to hide while he stepped out with his gun aimed. It was just a second, that moment when he turned toward me yelling, that at the same time I saw Evan struggling with a man while another ran down the hall. I spied a gun aimed straight for Luis and my hand cocked the trigger, aimed, and fired. Just seconds, burned into memory. I watched in shock as the man fell to his knees.

Luis cried, *"¡Buen tiro!"* and flashed me a smile before bolting down the hall to help Evan. By the time Ilda and I reached them, one man was trussed like a chicken while the other lay facedown, unmoving.

Our guard was speaking rapid Spanish, Evan responding in kind.

"Did I kill him?" I whispered, staring at the man splayed on the tiles.

Evan slowly stood up nursing his jaw. He glanced at the fallen man. "Looks that way. Luis says you saved his life and that you're a great shot."

"I killed someone!" I cried. "I don't kill people!"

But Evan wasn't listening. He'd taken my arm and was steering me down the hall behind Luis, who had Ilda by the hand. "We have to get out of here. Luis says that Sofia will get a car ready to take us to Granada. But first we have to destroy those computers. They know we're here."

I got his thinking. We entered our workroom only long enough to smash the computers with chairs.

"They could still access the hard drives, but not easily. Let's go. Put on your masks."

There was no time to talk. We wound through dark corridors and down long hallways decked with tapestries, scuttled along the sides of the old walls while keeping hidden beneath shrubbery. I thought we'd be heading for the carpark but instead Luis unlocked a small side door to the left of one tower and urged us out.

"To the street?" I whispered.

"They'd expect us to leave by car," Evan told me. "Walk slowly." He said something in Spanish and linked my arm in his. Ahead, Ilda did likewise with Luis, both of them slowing down to a stroll.

Couples passed us exclaiming at the beautiful fortress with its palm-treed fringe so glorious against the spotlit wall. One group were obviously British tourists. No one gave us a second glance as we strolled the evening like the leisure travelers we weren't.

Meanwhile, all I could think of was that I had now killed a man and blinded two others—*me*. I had crossed a line that day, something I could never undo. Somehow tasering Noel didn't seem half as bad, maybe because I knew that enemy well.

We crossed a broad boulevard with no sign of pursuers. At a street corner, Luis paused to look back at the fortress before talking into his phone.

"Salvi thinks we got away unseen," Evan said. "He's renting a car and says the coast is clear."

"But how does he know everything is safe?"

"Run," he ordered.

So we ran down cobblestone lanes and along narrow streets until we arrived by a bridge. A little red car sat double-parked on a curb with Salvi wearing a peaked cap and manning the steering wheel. We crammed in, Ilda, Evan, and me in the back, Luis with Salvi up front. Luis passed us a couple of hats.

I donned the baseball cap and Evan the broad-rimmed number. "Now I look like a battered matador," he mumbled.

"They breached security but how?" I asked as soon as we were zipping across the bridge.

"No idea. I'm afraid they either hacked those computers, we were tracked, or we have a mole."

"A mole?" I whispered.

"Perhaps. Luis and I heard gunshots," Evan said. "He tapped into the CTC system and learned the bastards had cut the wiring to the central alarm. We were too late to save Señor Barco but thank God you two are all right."

"He was a good man," I whispered. "Maybe my urge to take a walk led to his death?"

"Stop the self-recrimination, Phoebe." My name still sounded like

"Fweebe." If you hadn't gone out, they would have ambushed us in our rooms."

"But I killed a man, Evan."

"Tell Luis that. He believes you saved his life."

So take a life to save a life? Why did that make me feel so depleted? Noel would be laughing at me wherever he was. Maybe I'd killed him, too, and he had really been my first.

In so many ways I was ill-suited to be a warrior. At that moment, I just wanted to crawl away somewhere and paint pretty pictures and knit for the rest of my days.

The car drove on for at least twenty minutes with me staring straight ahead, oblivious to the darkened streets zipping away around me. We'd all been sobered by the recent events, heartsick. I gathered from the conversation up front, which Evan summarized, that Señor Barco was a loved and respected member of the team and that the younger men mourned him. They also expressed bitter anger over his senseless killing and cursed the Divinios.

We wound down into a little town with white stucco houses and blooming bougainvillea. The car pulled into a deserted parking lot and stopped behind a plain white rental van and Luis called for us to move. Out we tumbled, bags slung over our shoulders, and in seconds had transferred into a van. It took a few minutes for me to catch on that Sofia was behind the wheel.

"I cannot believe this!" she cried. "How did they know you were there?"

Dressed in leggings and a brown suede jacket with her hair all but hidden under a baseball cap, she was almost unrecognizable. Luis offered to drive but she waved him into the passenger seat while we climbed into the back seat and Salvi into the very back.

"Is your phone tracked?" Evan asked.

"Who knows? It is supposed to be secure but what is secure with these bastards?"

I leaned forward. "Maybe they listened in on our discussion about the possible crown's location or hacked those computers you thought were secure? Either way, they're on to us."

Sofia swore, my app kindly translating a garble of words. "Maybe yes, maybe no. How do we tell? We must arrive ahead of them!" She slapped the steering wheel with her gloved palm. "They should never have found us! Barco was so careful!"

She was furious—I got it. Her smooth exterior had cracked under the weight of fury. "We will stop these bastards, I swear we will!" she cried as the van peeled away from the lay-by onto a small paved road, the tires screeching beneath us.

After a few minutes, she regained her composure and began speaking rapid Spanish through her hands-free phone system.

"She's calling for reinforcements in Granada and issuing directives to somebody named Raul," Evan whispered while Ilda dozed on his shoulder.

"What kind of reinforcements?" I asked.

"Possibly police or army. I'm not grasping everything. It's clear that her employer has the cavalry at his fingertips."

"Good, because nothing less will help us get that crown," I remarked.

After that we drove into the evening without speaking. No one appeared to be on our tail and the night remained dry and clear. But that meant nothing.

After about an hour and a half, Sofia pulled into a roadside lay-by. Across the parking lot a truck stop convenience store washed a cold fluorescent light across the pavement. Eighteen-wheelers sat parked amid sedans.

"We stop here. I have brought clothes for changing and wigs—bad wigs. Such a hurry! Please use the back and be quick."

We took turns changing in the back of the van, me pulling on a frilly blouse under my jacket complete with an ankle-length skirt. Fearing I looked like a reject from a masquerade, I tossed off the skirt, figuring that with the blond wig and a face mask I'd be unrecognizable. Evan, on the other hand, emerged looking like an eccentric guy from hippie past in a long gray wig and limp linen jacket. Ilda took my full skirt and just looked lovely.

"Granada is ahead," Sofia said minutes later as we zoomed down a highway. I stared through the windshield as another illuminated castle complex rose from a forested hill far in the distance. I grabbed Evan's arm. "Alhambra amid the mountains!"

"Mountains everywhere in Spain," Sofia remarked.

We wove into town minutes later, a mix of old and new with white stucco buildings and terra-cotta-tiled roofs dominating the architecture and the palace complex rising like a golden beacon far above.

"I have called ahead the chief security officer for Alhambra to say you will spend the night but I have not told him the truth. I said that you are professors from Oxford who ask to sleep in the palace. Evan and Phoebe, you are doctors of history conducting research—married—who wish to capture—how do you say the environment of the place?"

"The ambience?" I offered.

"The ambience, yes. I said you are very well connected and pulled many strings. Ilda is your daughter studying Spanish and staying with me."

"My daughter? I'd have to have given birth at thirteen years old!"

"It happens." She shrugged.

"And my daughter doesn't speak English? And, I mean, two supposedly esteemed British professors of something or other suddenly dropping into a Spanish UNESCO World Heritage Site dressed like escapees from a costume party during a pandemic? How unlikely is that?"

She laughed. "Unlikely? What is more likely—that we hunt for an ancient artifact that a fanatical brotherhood will use to destroy the world?"

She had me there. I sat back and shut up.

"However, we hardly look dressed for the part," Evan pointed out.

Sofia lifted one hand. "This does not matter," she said. "In Spain we think the British very strange."

After that, he gave up, too. So we were eccentric professors of history who had pulled strings to stay overnight in a Spanish palace. Why not?

"So, Dr. Barrows, married at last. Are you ready for this?" Evan asked, turning to me. "We can have our honeymoon in Alhambra just like Charles and Isabella."

"Yes, with our adult daughter along for the ride. And I'm Dr. McCabe, understand? I refuse to sacrifice my independence," I told him.

"And I would never ask you to." He gave me his lopsided grin.

Sofia glanced at us in the rearview mirror and shook her head.

Soon we were driving upward, the lit fortress rising overhead—two round towers at one end, a square structure at the other, and myriad golden stone buildings with arched porticoed walkways and balconies in between, all revealed in spotlit splendor. Yet it was the hexagonal spired watchtower that caught my eye immediately.

"Look!" I touched Evan's arm.

"The same one as in the painting?"

"I'm sure of it. The crown is hidden in Alhambra!"

"And all we have to do is find it."

"I need to stand in the vantage point where Queen Isabella stood in the Titian painting. Does the interior have the same layout?"

"The Christian monarchs did not completely destroy the Arabic architecture but it fell into disrepair," Sofia said. "Much has been restored and still exists, this palace the Moorish poets described as 'a pearl set among emeralds.' The architecture was appreciated by the Spanish monarchs, if not the Moorish conquerors."

"But there must have been many renovations over the centuries?" Evan asked.

Sofia sighed. "Yes, of course—a Renaissance addition, parts altered to suit tastes, everything built outward in quadrangles. This is the same site where Christopher Columbus received his royal decree from the first Isabella and King Ferdinand in 1492 but in the Renaissance addition. There were changes, always changes, and Napoleon wrecked the site when he came through. Let us hope we will find this spot. Here we are. We will park and then walk up. This way is more protected. Come."

Sofia drove the van onto a grassy patch under tall cypress trees and we tumbled out, stiff from the drive. "Up," she said, "way up."

"Sofia," I said, touching her arm. "They know we're here. I can feel it. Someone or something has been spying on us."

She frowned. "I know. I have requested reinforcements. Let us pray that they arrive in time."

Leaning back my head, my gaze scoured the walls of the imposing fortress, surprised to see that the bricks had an almost reddish cast this close. When I dragged my eyes back down, Sofia was talking to a man who seemed to have appeared from nowhere.

"Señor Raul Saratoza, meet my good friends," she began, "Dr. McCabe and Dr. Barrows, professors of history at Oxford, England, and their daughter, Ilda. Ilda has been staying with me while studying Spanish. They will be our guests overnight."

The man, balding, about sixty years of age and surprisingly fit, probably from climbing stairs all day, had obviously been dragged into duty at the last minute. It was 11:15 and the complex should have been closed to visitors. He nodded, shrewd eyes glittering above his mask as he said: "Most welcome to Alhambra. We will make you as comfortable as we can."

I could just imagine what Saratoza must be thinking. Even as eccentric academics, our attire didn't cut it, and Evan's sunglasses couldn't quite hide the fact that he'd been in a fight. Still, Saratoza gamely played along. He opened an iron gate, deactivated a security system, and then unlocked another door while speaking into his cell phone. Soon Salvi and Luis were carrying our backpacks up a long narrow flight of concrete stairs.

"I say, but I understand that it was rebuilt over Roman remains in the thirteenth century by an Arab leader who constructed one of the most beautiful royal palaces in the historic world," Evan said in his most ponderous academic tone. Under ordinary circumstances, it might have been impressive but his lisp and inability to properly pronounce words ruined the effect. "When Ferdinand and Isabella assumed responsibility after the Christian conquest thus banishing the Muslims, it became one of their royal palaces."

"Yes, very true. A favorite royal palace, a pleasure palace, you might say, but it was still neglected for many years," Sofia explained. "It's since been restored."

"How thrilling," I exclaimed, "to spend a night here!" I felt rather than saw Saratoza rolling his eyes. I nudged Evan to keep him from trying to speak again. "Don't say my name, whatever you do," I whispered.

We climbed up the narrow stairway, through an iron gate, onto a plateau surrounded by the huge stone walls. Lighting picked out pathways and shone down on the mellowed stones and up on trees. Overhead, stars sparkled and somewhere water tinkled. My skin tinged with anticipation. And fear.

"Do I hear nightingales?" Evan asked, taking our bags from the men with a nod.

"Yes, nightingales," Sofia replied, turning to us. "Señor Saratoza has turned on the lights all over the property and will have a room where you sleep—nothing fancy, no bed. Just the floor and many blankets. It will not be comfortable but I know you wish to camp out like you do in Britain." Our eyes met.

"Oh, yes, we love to camp out in Britain," I remarked while watching

Saratoza march away, Salvi and Luis in tow. Had I ever camped out in Britain? There'd be no sleep for us that night, anyway.

"Is Saratoza trustworthy?" Evan whispered once the men had disappeared. He sounded like a bass-toned Bugs Bunny.

"We do not know who is trustworthy and who is not," Sofia said. "We have no choice but to trust. He is in charge of the complex and has called his men to guard the property while we wait for my employer's people. It is the best we can do until my employer sends help. Where do we begin to look? Do you need a shovel or another tool? We must hurry."

"I carry a portable shovel but something stronger may be needed—maybe even a pickax," Evan said. "Where would Queen Isabella have spent time?"

"Charles constructed his new palace over there in 1527." She was pointing to the left. "That part would have begun by then but not finished when the pair were first married."

"No," I said, gazing around at the walls, the trees, the spotlit ramparts. "We are looking for a garden where the king would have eventually planted his lady carnations. Our Damas were thinking of flowers."

"But there were many gardens in Alhambra!" Sofia threw up her hands. "One near the Puerta del Vino, another near the Square of the Cisterns, in the Generalife, in the Garden of the Ramparts, in the Court of the Sultana's Cypress Tree—everywhere gardens!"

"But which one would have been present during Charles and Isabella's time?" I asked.

"That we don't know. Many buildings have changed, and gardens, too. Gardens especially would alter according to the tastes of the time," she said.

"But surely he would have preserved some of this original beauty?"

"Yes, so I think. Charles appreciated the art of the Islamic conquerors if not their religion. He did not deface the inscriptions. There was respect."

I stood directly in front of her, fixing her dark eyes in mine. "Think, Sofia. It's 1526. The royal honeymooners are staying here. They stroll the gardens together, and Charles is eager to show his bride the most beautiful places. What would have impressed her most?"

She snapped her fingers. "Follow me."

We crossed the pavement, traversed a short hall, went down many stairs, and entered a porticoed courtyard carved of creamy filigreed stone so intricate it could have been lace. "Oh," I marveled.

"The Patio of the Lions, built during the rule of Muhammed V, 1362 to 1391," Sofia said, spreading her arms. "Emperor Charles thought this very beautiful. He would have brought his queen here."

I gazed around. But everything in this stunningly gorgeous place was tiled or of carved marble, including the round basin featuring the marble lions that gave the patio its name. All of it looked original. "But would there have been plants here?"

"Probably once but they are lost now. Come, we go to the Generalife where the rulers of Granada once took a rest from work in their gardens."

We dashed under deeply embossed ceilings with Arabic script carved into the stone and stepped through an arch into a long garden with a central water feature running its length and plumes of water tinkling into the channel every few feet.

Ilda exclaimed: "So beautiful!"

"Yes, the Patio of the Irrigation Ditch—not a very romantic name, I know. These fountains were in the Jardines Altos del Generalife here even in the fifteenth century. It is the brilliant engineering of the Arabs to feed water down from the hill to work the fountains and gardens at Alhambra. Once there would have been flowers and fruit trees but today our gardeners have planted mostly myrtle hedges to line the water."

I nodded and stepped forward, turning around until I caught sight of the hexagonal watchtower far in the distance. I positioned myself in the same manner as Isabella had stood and checked over my shoulder to see if it matched. It didn't—too far away.

Across the tiles, Evan stood near the myrtle hedge doing the same. "We can barely see the tower," he remarked.

"And no mountains," Ilda added.

"These buildings are eighteenth century in origin," Sofia said, indicating the comparatively plain white stucco buildings running on either side. "Only the arches at both ends are original."

Maybe I caught a flicker of movement in one of porticoed balconies at one of those ends but couldn't be certain. Every shadow moved in this place, a factor of the breeze and the spotlights casting patterns on the stone.

"Even if they weren't there, the angle still wouldn't have been right," Evan was saying. "The tower is shown behind her right shoulder."

"Come," Sofia beckoned, "we try another." We dashed back through the portico, up more stairs, along a walkway under trees with glimpses of the city far below, and through an arched door into another courtyard.

"Here we come to the Court of the Sultana's Cypress Tree, Patio del Ciphers de la Sultana. In Isabella's time there would be this central pond and inside that pond another. Charles marveled again at the engineering and there you see the Water Stairway at the end, the oldest stairway in these gardens. It existed in the Muslim period."

I stepped forward and stared. As enchanted as Isabella must have been to see those three flights of stone stairs rising up amid a tunnel of trees with water flowing down either side or the square pools with their treed islands, the tower was not visible in this section, either. I closed my eyes to hear the fountains tinkling, the nightingales calling.

"No," I whispered. "She is standing high up but not outside. On a balcony beneath an arch with the mountains and watchtower behind her." Spinning to face Sofia, I added: "She was pointing down to the garden with her right hand, not standing *in* the garden." I brought up my photo of the painting and showed it to her while looking back to the main courtyard where water ran in a rectangular pattern around two islands of trees and flowers.

Ilda, standing behind her, reached over and took my phone and posed exactly like Isabella. *"Alli arriba,"* she said, pointing behind her.

We all turned to gaze up at the covered porticoed walkways open on both sides, one of which overlooked the garden.

"Would that have been there in Isabella's time?" Evan asked.

"Yes, but not like that. It has been much restored," Sofia told us. "Follow me."

In minutes, we had climbed a stone staircase and stood in the open corridor scanning both sides. Opposite the garden, the illuminated guard post could be seen in the distance with the darkened mountains beyond.

Ilda, still holding my phone, posed again, her right hand pointing down toward the garden. *"¡Hir!"* she whispered.

Evan followed the direction her index finger pointed, using his phone to beam a red laser line down into the garden. It landed into a square planting of jasmine beside two cypress trees on an island surrounded by the running water. "There!" he whispered. "Perhaps once that part was filled with carnations."

Soon we were back down in the garden, kicking off our shoes to wade across the ankle-deep water to the square island. Evan waved us to stand on the marble edging while he scanned his detector app across the earth planted with trees and jasmine.

"It must be deep down," I whispered. "If it's here at all."

"This garden would be dug and dug many times," Sofia agreed.

"Still, if they wanted to preserve the original layout, they would only go deep enough to change the soil, maybe remove the roots of a dead tree," Evan pointed out. "The piping for the fountains is several feet to the left according to this, and yet..." He paused, staring at his screen.

"And yet?" Sofia prompted.

"And yet there is indication that something metal may sit much farther down...six feet down."

"But we have detected this earth many times," Sofia said.

"How long ago?" I asked.

She shook her head. "The last garden renovation was many years ago. We lined the flower beds with myrtle hedges."

"They would have run a surface detector looking for pipes and the ancient plumbing works. Look." He held up his phone, which marked out the grid in a blue light, something pale and pulsing from red to purple in the middle of the rectangle.

"What does that mean?" I asked, leaning forward.

"The blue lines are ferrous and trace the water pipes, which range between two to three feet below the surface, and the red to purple pulsing light indicates something lies much deeper between the two trees—maybe six feet down," he said. "Nonferrous," he added.

I caught his eye. "Nonferrous?" I asked.

"Not iron-based. Maybe gold or silver. The blue means something gold is encased in something ferrous—red and blue making purple," he said.

A momentary hush descended. I turned to Sofia. "Can you call the guys to help us dig?"

"Let's not risk it," Evan said as he pulled his periscopic shovel from his duffel and hung his jacket on a tree branch. "We don't know who to trust."

Sofia pulled out her phone. "But I must call my employer. Our backup should be here by now."

Sofia was talking rapidly into her phone while Evan climbed over the myrtle hedge into the center of the planting. He struck his spade into the earth and in seconds only the sound of digging broke the night.

"Evan, pass me your gun," I whispered.

He stopped long enough to pull it from his pocket. I leaned over the hedge and took it.

Sofia had put away her phone. "My contact does not answer. I left another message."

"Another?" I asked. "Do you mean that we don't know if help is coming?"

She shook her head.

"Can you fire a gun?" I asked.

"No!" she said. "That has never been my job. My job is research only."

Ilda stepped forward with her hand outstretched. *"Soy la hija de un granger,"* she said.

"She can shoot," Sofia translated. "Farm girl."

I gave Ilda Evan's gun and cocked my own and together we patrolled the edge of the courtyard, her going one direction, me the other, watching the parameters. Once Ilda thought she caught a shadow moving across the portico above but shook her head. False alarm. This continued for maybe twenty minutes while I kept thinking that I heard sounds over the walls, strange noises, cries. Were we surrounded?

Sofia paced the tiles, repeatedly leaving messages and calling her employer's agents. "Nothing!" she told me when I caught her eye. "I called Saratoza and the two boys but no answer!"

To say I didn't like the sound of that was an understatement.

Meanwhile Evan kept digging and digging. I was at the water stairs end of the courtyard the moment I heard metal hit metal. I quickly turned and splashed through the water to the island. Evan was lifting something from the earth.

We watched in rapt wonder as a rusted metal container roughly the size of an old breadbox with a peaked lid was lifted from the earth and deposited on the marble edging. I stared at it and swallowed. "It seems too big to be a crown."

"A casket," Sofia whispered, "a reliquary casket. The sisters may have placed it inside such a container or the monks transported it in one. We must open it."

"Not now," I said. "We have to get out of here."

Evan splashed into the water beside me and lifted the box. "Get my duffel."

Grabbing his bag, he laid the filthy box down on top of his clothes, shoving his spade in last as we pulled on our shoes.

"We're not going to get to just walk out of here," I said.

"I know. When they come for us, hope to God that Señor Anonymous brings the troops," Evan said.

I was about to respond when a deep voice called over a loudspeaker: "*Gracias.* Now set down the bag and step away."

23

But we ran.

We plunged into the fountain's rectangular canal system and waded toward the water stairs. Nobody spoke. Evan was up front, Sofia in the middle, Ilda and I bringing up the rear. We were shielded by the trees and hedges. Men were shouting from somewhere behind us. Over the wall to our left, more shouting and flashing lights.

"Do not be foolish!" bellowed the deep voice. "You are surrounded. Do not make us shoot!" He repeated everything in Spanish in case we missed anything.

We bolted up the stone steps, the trees bowing down over our heads, rivulets flowing down either side. If we just reached the top of the stairs, maybe we could head for the city below, Sofia had whispered. But the moment we reached the top, they were waiting. As we expected.

We were powerless to move.

At least twenty men stood facing us, all dressed in black, none of them wearing masks, all with guns pointed at our chests. Slowly they began to circle us like a pack of stalking lions.

"Drop your pistols and kick them toward us," the head honcho ordered. He was short, wiry, and appeared to wear a priest's collar under his shirt, though the epaulets were strangely out of sync.

We dropped the pistols, raising our hands while the men collected the weapons, every pair of eyes fixed on us. One man dragged Sofia from our group, holding a gun to her head, while another told Evan to lower his duffel and pass it over. Sofia, undaunted, spat rapid Spanish at Head Honcho until he slapped her across the face.

"If you move falsely, we shoot," Head Honcho said. "You follow now." He jerked his head toward his troops, three of whom rushed forward to bind our hands. We were told to walk so we walked, back down the water steps, across the sultan's courtyard, and along corridors we had yet to see.

The complex was huge, building after building passing while we kept our eyes peeled for help. Where the hell was the cavalry? Where was Saratoza and our two guys? Once, I glimpsed bodies sprawled on the floor while passing a doorway but couldn't identify anyone.

Soon we were back on the street, still in the Alhambra complex, heading toward a stone church. Don't ask me why it shocked me to see a church, but of course there would be at least a chapel in a complex this size. But this was no chapel and it looked to be more recent than most of the buildings, at least seventeenth century. We were marched up the steps of a plain exterior and shoved down the aisle of a stunning baroque basilica.

"The Church of Santa Mariá de la Alhambra," Sofia whispered. "Built over the site of the sultan's great mosque."

Once herded into the front pews and each assigned a guard to stand pointing rifles at us, we could do nothing but sit looking desperately for the escape we knew didn't exist. I wondered why they didn't demand our phones but figured they must have been afraid to touch them or thought we could set an explosive with the sound of our voices. Definitely they realized that as long as they remained in our pockets and with our hands bound, our devices were harmless, and they were right.

Six priests stepped into the nave from a side door, one of whom was Don Santos with a bandaged head. Nobody wore masks here, either. He caught sight of Ilda and frowned. How she must have disappointed him.

We watched in silence as the others cast us dismissive glances, if they looked in our direction at all. Their interest was fixed on the rusted iron box now sitting on the altar, which they gathered around while intoning Latin.

One of the brethren, the tallest with a head of thick silver hair and a beautifully embroidered mantle covered in a mix of pagan and Christian symbology, seemed to be the holy head honcho who could make his minions jump with a wave of his hand. He signaled for the army-type guard to lift the object from its crumbling iron case.

It was surprisingly easy since the metal practically disintegrated under his gloved hands. In moments, a glowing reliquary box was lifted from the rusted shards and laid on a red velvet cushion.

We gasped like spectators at a magic show. An intricate enameled and gold-peaked casket now reflected the candlelight on the altar, two embossed saints pointing toward the narrow crystal window through which we could just make out the contents. A hush descended over captors and captives alike. Holy Honcho prayed over the casket, his voice deep and resonant as he lifted his gaze upward amid his praying brethren. A gilded Jesus on the crucifix gazed on with an expression of profound pathos.

I felt sick. The piece was exquisitely beautiful and represented the faith of those who had hidden it. Still, I didn't want to see what lay inside, yet I couldn't tear my gaze away. My companions seemed equally rapt. Ilda was crying.

Now Holy Honcho had donned a pair of white gloves and awaited with a beatific expression as a second priest raised the casket lid. Holy Honcho lifted the contents, releasing the fastenings to raise the priceless object into the air.

Another collective gasp. A solid gold crown imbedded with twelve peaks each set with a ruby, diamond, emerald, or sapphire glittered in his hands. He rotated the coronet to reveal the central peak, which appeared to capture a shard of something in its rock crystal frame. His satisfied smile never waned.

Ilda was wailing, Sofia was praying, the priests were chanting, and all I could do was stare at this priceless wonder with loathing. It had been pounded into the head of a human being! Maybe all signs of that monstrous moment had worn away but the holes around the bottom filigreed edge were still visible.

For a sick instant I was afraid that one of the priests would manifest the skull right there but no skull arrived. A burst of hope hit: the skull wasn't here! It must be in Portugal awaiting the crown's delivery. There was still time.

At last the holy honcho lowered the crown back into its reliquary and snapped an order at a guard who stepped up to wrap the casket in velvet.

"What are you going to do with us?" I cried.

Holy Honcho turned as if he had forgotten we were there. In seconds, he was towering over me, his hair backlit in a silver halo. "You?" he spoke in his deep voice. "To you, Señorita McCabe, we owe a great debt." He brought his palms together and bowed his head. "You have found what centuries of our order could not. For you we reserve a great honor."

"I just bet," I whispered.

"You will accompany us to Portugal and to the altar where we will place the crown on our holy king on earth, King Carlos. To you we will accord the highest honor to witness this sacred moment before you join our king in heaven." The other priests began chanting.

Evan began speaking in Latin. The man turned and stared. Evan said something further and Holy Honcho answered tersely and soon the two men began conversing in that ancient language.

"What are they saying?" I asked Sofia.

"Evan asks if the order uses human sacrifices and the priest says yes, but only for special occasions and only for special sacrifices. He says you are very special and have been brought to them by God. Evan accuses the order of being more pagan than Christian and is quoting verses from the Scriptures. They are debating theology."

"Seriously?" I knew Evan was raised Catholic but his timing seemed a bit off.

Suddenly the army-type head honcho interrupted, pointing to his watch. The holy honcho nodded and folded his hands.

"They are taking us to the airport for a plane to Portugal," Evan whispered.

"That's not what he said. They are taking *Phoebe* to Portugal. Us they will kill," Sofia said.

We were ordered to our feet and separated, me dragged away into the circle of priests, the others marched down the aisle. I wanted to scream, to kick, to wail, but I forced myself into total stillness. Think, I needed to think.

I wondered if I could wait until on the plane and in the air and then order my phone to explode. Maybe it could do that. Maybe it would even be enough to down the plane and destroy the crown with it. But if it was a passenger plane, that would kill innocent people, too... However, they would all die, anyway, if this band of loonies had their way. Still, I couldn't be the one to kill the innocent.

Suddenly Evan slumped to his knees in the aisle; Sofia and Ilda quickly followed suit. As I was pushed from the nave, I realized that it was a delay tactic. One soldier moved to shoot but a command from Holy Honcho froze him to the spot. Evan took that moment to deliver a vicious kick and pandemonium followed.

I was rushed into the street by my priestly captors, Head Honcho joining us with four of his guards seconds later. A black limo sat parked by the curb, five similar cars behind it. Now I was sure I heard sirens. A helicopter was flying by overhead, someone was speaking Spanish from a loud speaker. Holy Honcho called commands in his booming voice as he and the priest holding the casket bolted for the limo. A guard tried to drag me behind. No hands, no gun, what could I do? I dropped to my knees.

One of the honcho guards tried to yank me to my feet but I kicked him away. He had his rifle aimed ready to shoot when someone slugged him on the head. As he fell to the ground, there stood a battered Luis.

"Luis!"

He grinned, helped me to my feet, and sliced off my bindings with the flick of a knife.

"Where's Salvi?" I asked.

He got the gist. In response, he ran a finger across his throat while making faces and then proceeded to air-throttle someone. Got it: Salvi had been our mole.

Meanwhile, everything was in chaos. Soldiers had appeared dressed in camo and a gun battle broke out between the two sides. Holy Honcho was now shouting from the limo as the car zoomed down the lane. More soldiers appeared from Humvees coming from the other direction.

"Don't let him get away!" I pointed to the car and held up my phone to transcribe my words into Spanish. "He has the crown!"

Luis translated, too, his voice traveling farther than mine. Next he was dashing up the stairs to the church when Evan, Sofia, and Ilda came down, along with a posse of soldiers, their hands now free.

"He's getting away with the crown! Catch the head honcho!" I cried.

Evan shouted to one of the soldiers, who in turn spoke into his head mike.

Sofia threw her arms around my shoulders. "I thought we were all going to die!"

"But your employer came through," I whispered.

The gunfire began to taper off as we watched an army helicopter land in the center of the parking area.

Evan turned to me. "They've caught them—ambushed the car and blown out their tires at the bottom of the hill."

My body nearly sagged with relief. I, in turn, threw my arm over Ilda's shoulders as the young woman stood shivering by my side. Sofia was walking toward the soldiers talking on her cell phone and Luis stood nearby with a soldier.

"Where's my backpack?" I asked no one in particular. Ilda translated and a soldier soon returned from the church with our bags. I took out a sweater and gave it to Ilda. We stood there like some kind of family unit still holding one another when we heard cars coming up the lane.

Moments later, a camo Humvee appeared with the holy honcho cuffed in the back seat. Once the vehicle braked, four soldiers piled out, nudging the priest toward us at gunpoint. One of the soldiers now carried the casket as if holding a ticking bomb.

"This is sacrilege!" Holy Honcho cried in two languages. "We are on God's mission!"

Sofia, who had been pacing in circles talking into her phone, stopped before me. "My employer, he thanks you for helping us find the crown. He commends you for your insight and bravery. We will go now someplace safe until he can take possession of it."

"Take possession of it? Sofia, that thing must be destroyed!" I cried.

She looked at me as if I had lost my mind. "Destroyed? A priceless artifact destroyed? Never! My employer will take possession of it, I said. It will go to the Prado Museum." Her eyes were alight with excitement as she returned her phone before nodding to me. "We will be transported by helicopter until a plane can take us to Madrid where my employer awaits. He will also ensure your transportation back to Portugal. Father Lorenzo and the other Divinios will go with the army to be dealt with through the law."

Father Lorenzo? The priest had never stopped praying since he'd been removed from the Humvee and dragged to the middle of the drive. Now he was lifting his bound hands toward the sky, no doubt invoking the angels to join his war. Occasionally he'd cast a particularly vicious glance in my direction.

Evan, with his arm around my shoulders, caught my eye as he stood tense beside me. "He says you're the scourge of the modern world."

"I feel the same way about him. Evan, we need to bring the holy honcho with us."

He almost managed to smile. "His name is Father Lorenzo—where's the respect?"

"Filed under serial killers in the ancient history department, subcategory religious orders," I said. "He gets no respect from me but we still need answers."

He called to Sofia. "Sofia, let's bring Father Lorenzo with us. This will be the last time we can question him about the Divinios before our efforts are absorbed by the Spanish legal system."

She considered this and nodded. "Yes, I would like to ask him many things." She turned to one of the army men and gave instructions and soon we were all being bundled into the waiting army helicopter. I had no doubt that Sofia was in command of this mission.

An expansive troop-carrying variety, the helicopter was impressive. That said, it wasn't big on amenities so all we could do was buckle up and wait.

I was in a window seat, Ilda next to me, with Evan and Luis opposite the aisle. Sofia sat in front of us with the casket in the seat next to her and the soldiers in the other seats surrounding a still-praying Father Lorenzo. Soon we were lifting off, affording me a brief view of a night-lit Granada as the chopper sped away.

I tried to relax but couldn't, not with that thing sitting only two rows in front. Pulling out my phone, I scanned my messages, zeroing in on a text from Peaches: *More smoothing lotion needed!* Followed by Rupert's demand for tea bags. I tried to catch Evan's eye but his attention remained fixed on the priest sitting one seat ahead.

Less than an hour later, we were crossing a dark expanse that could only be the ocean. I checked my GPS long enough to see that we were in the North Atlantic somewhere between Spain and Portugal. A long lighted rectangle came into view below. Ilda pointed and cried out, my phone translating, "Airline carrier!" Why not an airport?

When the helicopter landed on the illuminated bull's-eye minutes later, all I could think of was that casket. It could not go to a museum, no matter how right that sounded in theory. This was no ordinary priceless artifact.

Everyone followed Sofia's instructions including the upper ranks as the object was carried with great care down to the next deck, us following behind. I managed to catch Sofia's attention to ask about those reinforcements that had supposedly been sent to Sintra. "My friends are in trouble," I said.

"I was ensured that the Portuguese forces were on their way."

After that, everything passed in a blur of steely gray as we were ushered into a plain room centered by a long table.

Father Lorenzo sat at the head of the table until Sofia ordered the soldiers to move him one seat down. She then took the seat of command, catching my eye in what she saw as a shared moment of triumph. I was instructed to sit opposite her at the other end, which I did.

Evan, Luis, and Ilda sat around the table along with two soldiers as a man entered wearing a snappy white jacket designating a captain's rank. He was obviously so annoyed that his place was taken that he preferred to remain standing. Introductions were kept brief after which he gave us a curt nod and exited.

One of the soldiers positioned the casket in the center of the table, opened the receptacle, and set the crown on its velvet covering. Again that collective gasp.

I averted my eyes while Sofia began firing questions at Father Lorenzo. She asked him if he was the head Divinio, where was the sect based, and to give her names and locations. When no answer came, she moved on to the historical beginnings of the sect and demanded to know if he knew the identities of the order's opposition in King Philip's court. Though he gave no direct reply, I sensed that we knew more than he did in that regard.

Evan interrupted to ask where the skull resided—was it in Sintra as we supposed? To that, Holy Honcho only cast him a little sorrowful smile.

Sofia pulled out his phone. "We have now traced your calls to your allies and sent help to Sintra where your men are being rounded up as we speak. It is over, Father Lorenzo. Accept your defeat. Your order will now be crushed like so much dust between our fingers." To illustrate she rubbed her fingers together and wiped her hands on her pants legs.

"It is not for you to ask questions of me," he said finally, "and it is for me to pray for your souls as you plunge humanity into who knows how many years of further darkness." His gaze seldom left the crown.

Eventually Sofia gave up and turned to one of the soldiers. "Take him to your brig and ensure he is guarded. And bring us food and drink," she added.

"At least we have the crown in our possession," she said to me once they had taken him away. "This priceless sacred artifact will be treasured as it deserves."

"Sofia, have you forgotten what this crown represents, where it's been, what it's done?" I asked.

"Of course not," she said. "It represents a piece of history that has had a far-reaching impact on Spain. Never has such an item been recovered with so much brilliance and insight! And look at it, Phoebe—a work of art. The gold, the jewels! I am thinking that that sapphire may actually be the famed blue diamond stolen in the thirteenth century from the Ratnashastra mines in India, and—" she genuflected "—in the crystal, a piece of the True Cross!"

I stared at her, baffled. "But, Sofia, there must be enough pieces of the True Cross around Europe to reconstruct a forest. You know that. How likely is it that this is real?"

"You are not Catholic. You do not understand," she said.

"I understand this: Pérez designed this crown to fire up a group of fanatical monks who were already riled up by the Inquisition. He pounded that thing onto the head of a deranged man unfortunate enough to have royal blood." I leaned toward her. "It was designed as a political and religious weapon and in time took a life if its own. Think, Sofia: as long as it exists, it gives the Divinios the oxygen they need to rebuild and inflict more havoc in the future. It's a time bomb!"

"But we will round up and destroy the Divinios."

Evan shook his head. "More likely they will remain underground and rebuild in one form or another. Like a virus, we won't be able to catch them all, you said so yourself. They will mutate and proliferate. Phoebe's right: that crown is a global liability."

Sofia sat back, a brief flicker of panic crossing her face. She closed her eyes and crossed herself as a tear rolled down her cheeks. "It belongs to my employer; it belongs to Spain," she whispered. "I cannot be part of this. I could not live with myself."

Slowly she rose and walked around the table, taking pictures of the crown from all angles. Several minutes passed with her gazing at the thing without speaking. Finally, she whispered something in Spanish, crossed herself, and cast me a tremulous smile. "You, Phoebe, you are the brave one. You carry on the work of our las mujeres, our Damas. They were Catholic, too, and could never destroy something that had the possibility of being sacred. I must leave now and call my family. They will be worried."

Once she'd exited, Luis, Ilda, Evan, and I sat alone with the crown. I swallowed, my hands gripped together in my lap.

"Do you want me to do it, Phoebe?" Evan asked.

"Thank you but no. I have to do it—for the Damas." I gazed up at Ilda and Luis, surprised to see that they were holding hands. Ilda was crying, he was comforting her—how sweet. "You are all such good friends and I thank you. Forgive me if what I'm about to do causes you pain. It's not easy for me, either, but maybe for different reasons."

Evan translated while I photographed the object before he carefully packed the crown into his duffel. "I'll come with you," he said.

But they all came, the four of us leaving the room and heading for the upper deck. Sailors and soldiers asked us where we were going and Evan replied convincingly. "I said that we all needed air after our ordeal." One of the sailors was instructed to take us to an area of the deck believed safest for our promenade and then stood by around a corner out of sight, respecting our privacy.

I gazed around at the huge deck expanse, relieved that on this clear night the sea was calm and our progress measured in a relatively sedate level of knots. "Where are we again?"

"In the Atlantic approximately halfway between Spain and Portugal. I won't tag the coordinates just in case. Suffice to know that it's deep enough here to almost guarantee that no one will see the crown again."

"We need to video this, Evan."

"Yes—a social media moment. Just get it over with, Phoebe," Evan said. "Let's make sure the evidence of the crown's absence hits the news."

Luis and Ilda shielded us from view while Evan lowered the duffel and lifted out the crown to pass to me. He then raised his phone to video what came next.

This was no proud selfie moment for me but an act of total desperation. Here was Phoebe McCabe, the woman who had spent her life retrieving and preserving rare objects, about to throw a priceless artifact of historic and artistic importance into the sea.

The moment Evan passed me the crown it felt as if the cold metal seared my fingers. "This object is the crown of the Divinios," I said as Evan leaned forward to get a close-up. "It represents hundreds of years of pain and suffering. Now I consign this thing to the sea." A flash of pain and anguish shot through me moments before I tossed it over the railing, Evan filming every second.

Maybe I caught the glint of gold in the starlight seconds before the wash pulled the crown under or maybe that was my imagination under fire. Either way, my relief was bottomless and my anguish equally so.

In an instant, Evan had posted the clip worldwide.

24

It was a chilly mountain morning when Evan and I drove our rental car up to Sintra. The Portuguese police had proceeded us by days and most if not all of the known Divinios and sympathizers had been rounded up. But there had been no sign of the Carvalhos when the police swarmed the castle and we had been unable to contact Peaches or Rupert by phone.

"They must be there somewhere," Evan muttered as he drove through the forest. "They can't just disappear. I'm not even picking up Rupert's tracking device."

Neither of us would utter our deepest fear: that the Divinios had retaliated against the family and their supporters once the news of the crown's destruction hit. And it had hit—hard. The clip of me throwing the Divinios crown into the sea was all over the Internet.

After the deed was done, we had convinced Sofia to let us go directly to Lisbon rather than accompany her to Madrid. Apparently, her employer was dumbstruck once he'd seen the footage, but she had managed to convince him of the ultimate truth: that the crown could not be permitted to exist on this earth. Under water was bad enough. Had a forge been handy, I would have melted it down to bullion but, as it was, no one would find it any time soon, if ever.

Sofia had hugged me tightly before we left, the two of us crying at the loss of the crown and all the trials we had experienced these past two days. She had arranged for an army plane to deliver us from the aircraft carrier to Lisbon, leaving her to do the explaining to her employer. We had waved goodbye to our new friends, my hug for Ilda especially tight and long.

Now anxiety clawed my gut as the car drove up the drive, through the open gates, to the dark castle. Both Evan and I were exhausted and taut with worry.

"This makes no sense," he said. "That house was a community and communities don't just evaporate."

We climbed out of the car and gazed up at the castle. "I presume it will do no good to ring the bell?" I had my phone in hand and flipped through my photos until I found the one with Peaches's code. "Let's try this."

I tapped in the code, shocked when the door clicked open. Someone had to have been around to activate the security system in the first place. That gave me hope.

We stepped inside, the dark central hall that echoed with our footsteps, the place suffused with that heavy emptiness that occupies a deserted home.

"Let's try upstairs," Evan suggested, and together we bolted up the three flights to our bedroom wing, me to Peaches's room, Evan to Rupert's.

I looked around Peaches's space, shivering. Flicking on a light, I studied everything—the unmade bed, the towels on the floor, her missing bag. Peaches never left her room a mess and there's no way a kidnap victim gets to pack her bag, either. Plucking up an empty bottle of smoothing lotion left on her pillow, I smiled.

Immediately I was back in the hall, Evan striding toward me from the opposite end. "They have to be somewhere nearby!" he said, holding up a single unused tea bag. "His main Vuitton bag is gone but he left this."

I caught his eye and held up the smoothing lotion. "But where could they be?" Then I had a thought. "Follow me."

In seconds, I was back downstairs dashing into the library, making a straight line to the conservator's closet. "I'll call you from upstairs," I told Evan as I got down on my hands and knees to pull away the boxes blocking the hatch.

"Wait, I'll come with you," he said in that manly "I exist to protect you" way of his.

I paused to look up at him, taking in his poor bruised face, healing but still discolored. "Evan, you won't fit. Could you just wait and watch my back?"

"Against what—mice?"

I smiled. "I'll call the minute I get up there."

He didn't look happy but he left me to it. And so I crawled into the dark dusty passageway and up those narrow stairs, my phone lighting the path. Two little notes scribbled on pink paper had been dropped like bread crumbs along the way. One said *Follow me* and the other just said *Ana Marie*.

When I reached Senhor Carvalho's closet, I didn't know what I expected—to see the entire Carvalho family sitting around having breakfast, maybe—but the room was as empty as the house.

I spun around, scanning every inch. The same signs of a calm, seemingly organized exit greeted everything I saw right down to the made-up bed. Nothing seemed amiss except...the large photo of Queen Isabella now sitting on the dresser. I swear I would have noticed that before.

Picking up the ornate frame that encased it, I studied the photo—a paper photocopy, I realized. Turning it over in my hands, I noticed that one of the frame's ornate roundels centering each of the four corners seemed loose, and it fell off in my hand.

Seconds later I was on the phone to Evan: "Senhor left me sign—a signal of some sort. I just activated it. If my hunch is correct, the family is about to return."

And home they came nearly an hour later. By that time we had received calls from Rupert and Peaches, heard a rush of facts about hidden corridors and escape plans.

Senhor Carvalho and Rupert had cooked up a strategy to employ the property's secret passageways and tunnels to take the family safely from the castle to the village. There they had remained hidden in the homes of loyal employees until the police arrived to round up the Divinios and supporters. Senhor Carvalho and Rupert had only waited long enough for the infiltrators to reveal themselves before enacting their exit plan and had remained hidden until we returned to Portugal. Only then did they believe that it was safe to come home.

Evan and I were waiting on the walkway when the cars drove up the drive—five of them. In minutes, out came Senhor Carvalho, Adriana, Ana Marie, and Peaches, plus many of the staff. Rupert arrived in the last car looking pleased with himself with Senhors Abreu and Afonso.

Ana Marie burst out of a green sedan and dashed up the walk to hug me. "Phoebe, you came!"

"Of course I came," I said, hugging her back.

"They caught the evil ones! Mama, Senhorita Peaches, and I hid with Alma until the bad men went away! Grandpapa and Senhor Fox stayed with Senhor Abreu!"

Adriana, standing beside the child, nodded. "Please forgive me," she said quietly.

"There's nothing to forgive," I said over Ana Marie's head. "You were only trying to protect this little princess here."

"Indeed she was." Senhor Carvalho had arrived. "Phoebe, you are amazing. I could not believe it when I heard the details. You destroyed the crown? I swear I could never have done such a thing, though I admit that it had to end in such a manner. My Spanish friend was enraged at first but has come to see the light. We will talk more later. The staff is preparing a celebration feast for us tonight and I agree that it is time we celebrate. Until then." He raised his hand and shuffled away.

Peaches was standing by to deliver one of her enormous hugs. "So you went to Granada without me? You took on the Spanish army without me? That's going to take one pile of smoothing lotion to make better, woman. Better order up a year's supply."

I laughed and disentangled Ana Marie's little arms to ready myself for one of Peaches's mega-hugs. "I'll make it up to you somehow," I said, trying to breathe as she squeezed the breath out of me.

"Damn right you will. Are those Spanish soldier dudes as hot as I've heard?"

Ana Marie was looking up at us and asked: "What are hot dudes? Do they light up?"

"Kind of," Peaches said, finally releasing me. "They are like heating blankets for us ladies. You'll find out when you get older, honey."

Adriana took the child's hand and led her toward the house. The staff were bringing along bags and boxes of food as they wound their way into the castle, Ana Marie waving back to me. Turning, I caught Peaches's eye.

"Shit, woman, you had a hell of an adventure without me and that bodyguard of yours is looking pretty battered." She thumbed toward Evan, who was now embracing Rupert. For a moment we just stood together watching the two men hug one another. "What's up with those two?" she whispered. "Sometimes I swear that they're—"

"They're not," I assured her.

"They can't be. Evan's smitten by you."

"He asked me to let him catch me when I was ready to fall for a man again."

"And you said?"

"I said I wasn't ready and then ran away sniffling."

She slapped me on the arm. "Crap! When are you going to come to your senses?"

But luckily Rupert's arrival saved me from having to reply. "Well, Phoebe, you have done it again and with media-ready aplomb, too!" He was holding up his phone replaying the moment when I tossed the crown. "The daring triumphs of the Agency of the Ancient Lost and Found will now ring out across the globe and you will reach new levels of fame as the world watches art historian Phoebe McCabe—"

"Destroy a priceless piece of history—got it."

"But, Phoebe, you are a hero!"

"Let's go inside and have tea," I suggested before the moment became more painful. "I'm parched."

Because heroic was not how I felt—exhausted, maybe, definitely depleted, but not heroic. After a bath, a little breakfast, and a long nap, I awoke later that afternoon in much better spirits. By the time the big gala feast began, I was even ready to throw myself into the festivities, relieved that we'd all survived and that the Divinios had been bested if not eradicated. Actually, we had plenty to celebrate.

"Was Markus rounded up with all the others?" I asked Senhor Carvalho somewhere between the second course and the third, already stuffed with more food than I'd seen in days.

"We have not seen nor heard from him. I had expected the police to find him when they combed the property but there has been no sign."

"It's like the chap simply grabbed his bags and skedaddled," Rupert remarked. "He wasn't the bravest of sorts."

"It's still odd, even for him," I remarked, nabbing another piece of roast beef.

"The authorities will keep searching," Senhor Carvalho assured me.

"Phoebe!" Ana Marie interrupted. "Did you see the notes I left on the stairs?"

"I did," I laughed. "You are a princess. Maybe your mother will even let you have the turret room now?"

I caught Adriana's eye and she smiled. "Perhaps," she said.

But of all the matters I could not achieve amid my supposed successes, I could not bring the child's father back home. "You are not a miracle worker," Peaches told me later. "Ana Marie will survive and grow into the resilient, brave young woman we see in her now."

Still, it felt like a failure.

Much later, after our celebration in the main hall had wound down and most of the household had dragged themselves off to bed, Rupert, Evan, Peaches, and I withdrew to the library to sip port and regroup. Senhor Carvalho joined us briefly before heading to bed.

Pulling our chairs close to the hearth, we settled in to wind down for the evening. Though the night wasn't cold, dampness would have chilled our bones without the fire's warmth.

"Will you forgive me for mucking up your Titian?" I asked our host as I gazed across at him. Though he looked weary, a resurgence of energy had returned and his eyes were alight with youthful enthusiasm.

"Absolutely. There is nothing to forgive and, as always, I admire your audacity." Senhor Carvalho smiled and lifted his eyes to the portrait. "The empress herself remains unblemished and that is, indeed, the important thing. Besides, you were only carrying on a long line of female tampering."

"Titian tampering," Peaches murmured to no one in particular.

"Anyway, I doubt my rushed cover-up job will cause any damage. I used a very diluted wash to cover the carnation and the watchtower." In fact, the green foliage had already begun to run.

"Never mind. All will be duly restored and the portraits given to the Portuguese Museum of Ancient Art in Lisbon. It is time, as our Isabella has served her intended purpose. As much as my friends in Spain believe otherwise, Portugal is where she belongs since the empress herself had requested that her likeness be returned to her people. And what a story this painting tells. How incredible and inspiring! To think that three women in King Philip's court, along with an order of nuns, conspired to bury clues to thwart the Divinios—"

"And succeeded," I added.

"And succeeded," Carvalho acknowledged. "And you believe that Sofonisba Anguissola painted that carnation?"

"I believe it absolutely but I'm not certain about the watchtower. To me that looks much cruder. I'm guessing that one of Sofonisba's students at court may have painted that, perhaps even Queen Elizabeth of Valois herself."

"Amazing. Dear Phoebe, what would we have done without the Agency of the Ancient Lost and Found? Please do let me see those photos you took of the reliquary and crown one more time, if you please," Senhor Carvalho requested.

"I'll send you the photos." I passed him my phone, which he peered at for several minutes.

"Or you can download them from the Internet. They're everywhere, I believe," Evan commented, catching my eye with a smile. He sat with his long legs extended before the hearth, the picture of the adorable manspread. Every inch of him appeared to be healing nicely from what I could tell.

"Extraordinary," Senhor Carvalho announced after a moment. "The workmanship was truly exquisite. Whatever we may think of Antonio Pérez, he did not scrimp in the making of this piece."

Rupert, sitting to his left, the two men having become great friends in the past few days, agreed. "He required it to be a magnet for his diabolical brotherhood and to presumably trick the prince when Pérez and his henchmen arrived to perform the ungodly coronation," he mused. "Imagine how that would have played out."

Me, already a bit too relaxed after several sips of the rich liquor, kept my eyes fixed over the mantel on the portrait of Queen Isabella. "I can't—well, I can but it's too gruesome to dwell on for long," I said. "In many ways, I'm sorry that the crown is gone but not so much that I'd ever want to see it again. Hopefully, someday, somebody will find the skull since the Divinios aren't talking. Was it ever determined that Prince Carlos in his final resting place in Madrid is incomplete?"

"My friend has made inquiries. Unfortunately, the pandemic has delayed everything, including that investigation."

"Makes sense," I said.

"At least the reliquary still survives," Rupert remarked. "That much your Spanish friend will be able to place in one of his museums."

I took another sip of the port, not caring whether it would sail me into oblivion. Oblivion was what I craved just then.

"Indeed," our host said with a sigh.

"Senhor Carvalho," Evan began, placing his glass on a side table and leaning forward, "I realize now that your friend is a member of the Spanish royal family. I don't expect you to say who exactly, but it's clear to me that few people would have such a vested interest in the outcome of this case or the resources to commandeer the armed forces as the Spanish monarchy."

Peaches sputtered into her glass and sat up. "Seriously? The Spanish Señor Anonymous is really King Anonymous?"

"Or Queen Anonymous," I remarked.

"Did you know?" she asked me.

"I wondered," I admitted.

"I overheard Sofia speaking to her employers on the phone," Evan said. "The title 'your highness' was used at least once."

"You must tell no one," Senhor Carvalho cautioned. "We have been working with the House of Bourbon-Anjou for decades, striving to track down the Divinios to their source. The king is supportive of our efforts but it is not he who has emerged as the leader in this particular quest. I will say no more and I request that you do the same."

We all gazed at him and nodded.

"It has always been my theory that the queens lead the frontlines in this particular battle." Returning my gaze to Queen Isabella, I raised my glass. "To the Divine Right of Queens!"

"To the Divine Right of Queens!" everyone chorused.

And then the door flew open, pitching us all to our feet.

"Holy shit!" Peaches cried.

There stood Markus, looking as though he'd been dragged through the mud on his knees. His pants were embedded with grime, his face and beard filthy, and his jacket hung from his back in shreds. And yet a fever of triumph burned in his pale eyes.

Oblivious to the carpets, the tiles—anything—he tramped into our midst and dropped a moldy, lichen-covered sack to the floor. He glanced down at the bag and muttered, "Sorry, old chap," before facing us. "So, you thought I was in league with the devil, did you? Meantime, I've been working on the side of the good guys all along and it's been hell, I can tell you."

"Is that—?" Rupert began.

"The skull of Don Carlos? Yes. It's in a protective grille, don't worry."

"So you found a way to get the head, how exactly?" Peaches demanded.

"By pretending to be on the side of the brotherhood. That night in the morgue I said I'd act as their spy if they let me live. They needed an archaeologist with background knowledge of their quest with access to the Carvalhos and I needed to stay alive. Seemed like a good partnership at the time but never once did I waver in terms of whose side I was on. I did the double-agent thing."

"You bastard!" Evan stepped toward him.

Markus held up a grubby hand. "Never once did I give away anything that might cause you harm, either. In fact, I fed them lies, which they swallowed only too eagerly. If it weren't for me, they would have tracked down the Carvalhos to the village and killed them all. If it weren't for me, they would have shot that helicopter down sooner, too!"

"But where were you hiding?" Senhor Carvalho demanded.

"In the tunnels. They had a room set up there with an access route to the forest—quite undetectable unless you knew where to look. That's where they'd hidden the skull. Through them, I got to penetrate parts of the tunnels that even Ricardo didn't know about. Poor Ricardo. They really did do him in, by the way—my sympathies, senhor. I managed to find out where, but anyway, at least you can now reunite this poor bastard with the rest of his skeleton in Spain."

We all stared at the bag.

"Do you want to look at him?" Markus asked.

"No!" That was unanimous.

And then Senhor Abreu dashed into the room speaking rapid Portuguese, steering a blonde woman in head-to-toe camouflage by the arm.

"Connie?"

"What is going on?" Rupert erupted.

Connie shot us a little wave and stepped beside Markus. "Sorry I'm late but once I parked I couldn't find the entrance." She spread her hands. "Big place but luckily this nice chap helped me out. Right, so it's a bit of a long story but Markus got himself into a spot of trouble here and needed assistance. I tried to contact you but you refused to answer, Phoebe." She shot me a recriminating glance.

"I was a bit preoccupied," I countered.

"Yes, well, I took the next flight out, rented a car, and managed to pick him up before the Divinios caught up with him. Very exciting."

"Actually, they were about to toss me down a hole but I escaped," Markus explained.

"Yes, but I'm the one that picked you up on the road, Markus. Don't ruin my story." She slapped him playfully on the arm. "So I picked him up running away with part of Prince Carlos in his bag. We hid in the forest for a couple of days and now here we are. We saw that clip of you throwing the crown in the ocean—what a headline!"

"Yes, but let's wind back to the beginning for a moment, shall we? You got me into this business in the first place, sister dear," Markus accused. "Tell them."

"What do you mean by that?" Evan asked, hands on hips in full glower mode. "I thought that Markus approached you for help?"

"Mea culpa!" Connie threw up her hands. "So, I admit that I have been in league with a network of fellow historians to uncover this mystery for some time. I wanted to be more forthcoming, honestly."

"But?" I asked.

"But," she said, almost sounding a bit annoyed, "this was a *secret* initiative—we even took an oath, Phoebe. I asked my little brother to join our efforts a few years ago, which he did, and then his team discovered the skull. We couldn't disclose the whole truth, could we?" She turned her blue gaze on each of us in turn. "Sofia and others—all of us—were sworn to secrecy. But once we were certain that your reputation was well-deserved and that you truly were working on our behalf, we agreed to tell you everything. I sent you messages, Phoebe. I wanted to call but I was blocked. By then we were afraid our communication networks had been compromised, anyway. Forgive me?"

"So you were part of the counter-Divinios all along?" I asked.

"In a manner of speaking, yes, but you uncovered the originals! What a coup!" She clapped her hands together. "The art angle eluded us all, but you were just brilliant! What a story!"

"We were all brilliant," Rupert interjected. "Like any good team, we each played a part."

"Absolutely. We are a team," Peached added.

"You did! You are all simply brilliant!" Connie said. "And you'll feature on my show, won't you? This is already making international headlines!" I swear she was jumping up and down. Either that or the port had taken hold.

Of course, we forgave them both.

The moment Senhor Carvalho bid us good night, the drink began to flow in earnest. Someone brought in the wine. I have no memory of when that photo of us all standing in front of the fireplace toasting Queen Isabella was taken. Maybe Senhor Abreu snapped it, maybe not.

There we all were, me in the middle, Peaches and Evan with their arms over my shoulders, and Rupert embracing Connie on the other side. Markus stood apart—no one would touch him until he'd had a shower. Meanwhile the skull of our hapless prince sat in its bag at our feet. Someone wanted to remove him and let his skull grin away at the camera but I protested. He'd suffered enough indignities in his short life.

As it was, we were frozen in a group selfie moment of the worst kind and I admit that this was not our finest hour. As for which one of the team

JANE THORNLEY

had the gall to plaster the picture all over social media this time, I'll never know.

THE END

Coming next, *The Florentine's Secret, The Agency of the Ancient Lost & Found Book 3*

Book 3 transports you to Florence, Italy....

AFTERWORD

I always believed that history rhymes with mystery for a reason. How much do we really know for certain about the past? So much is a guessing game pieced together from the clues the dead have left behind. That means that all historical fiction is still fiction no matter how much research is involved.

Though most of the events described in this book are based on historical fact, I took many creative liberties. For instance, the unfolding mystery of what befell Prince Carlos on that fateful night in 1568 remains unknown. My version of events provides a role for women that is so often buried or overlooked.

However, just for the record, some of the strangest details in this story are actually true. Take for instance Prince Carlos sleeping with the mummy of a saint who had died a century before. Apparently that really happened. I can't "make that stuff up", as they say. Actually, I can and often do but in this case I didn't. Fact can be stranger than fiction.

As for the paintings described in this book, most of them exist and at least one was painted by Titian. However, even here I took liberties, my mission being to entertain you, dear reader, while allowing *herstory* to rule over history.

ABOUT THE AUTHOR

JANE THORNLEY has been writing for as long as she can remember and when not traveling, lives a very dull life—at least on the outside. Her inner world is something else again. With over twelve novels published and more on the way, she keeps up a lively dialogue with her characters and invites you to eavesdrop by reading all of her works.

To follow Jane and share her books' interesting background details, special offers, and more, please join her newsletter here:

NEWSLETTER SIGN-UP

ALSO BY JANE THORNLEY

SERIES: CRIME BY DESIGN

Crime by Design Boxed Set Books 1-3

Crime by Design Prequel: Rogue Wave e-book available free to newsletter subscribers.

Crime by Design Book 1: Warp in the Weave

Crime by Design Book 2: Beautiful Survivor

Crime by Design Book 3: The Greater of Two Evils

Crime by Design Book 4: The Plunge

Also featuring Phoebe McCabe:

SERIES: THE AGENCY OF THE ANCIENT LOST & FOUND

The Carpet Cipher Book 1

The Crown that Lost its Head Book 2

The Florentine's Secret (Pre-order) Book 3

SERIES: NONE OF THE ABOVE MYSTERY

None of the Above Series Book 1: Downside Up

None of the Above Series Book 2: DownPlay

SERIES: TIME SHADOWS Time Travel

Book 1: Consider me Gone